THAT
Darcy,
THAT
Dancer,
THAT
Gentleman

By the same author

NOVELS

Are You Listening Rabbi Löw
The Beastly Beatitudes of Balthazar B
The Destinies of Darcy Dancer, Gentleman
A Fairy Tale of New York
The Ginger Man
Leila
The Onion Eaters
Schultz
A Singular Man

NOVELLA

The Saddest Summer of Samuel S

PLAYS

The Plays of J. P. Donleavy

SHORT STORIES AND SKETCHES

Meet My Maker the Mad Molecule

OTHERS

De Alfonce Tennis
The Superlative Game of Eccentric Champions,
Its History, Accoutrements, Rules, Conduct and Regimen

J. P. Donleavy's Ireland
In All Her Sins and In Some of Her Graces

The Unexpurgated Code
A Complete Manual of Survival and Manners

A Singular Country

THAT
Darcy,
THAT
Dancer,
THAT
Gentleman

J. P. DONLEAVY

THE ATLANTIC MONTHLY PRESS
NEW YORK

First published in 1990 by Penguin Books Ltd., England, and by
  Viking Penguin, New York, NY

First Atlantic Monthly Press edition, May 1991
Published simultaneously in Canada
Printed in the United States of America

ISBN 0-87113-449-7
Library of Congress card number 91-9046

The Atlantic Monthly Press
19 Union Square West
New York, NY 10003

FIRST PRINTING

I

Sitting solitary in its lonely autumnal countryside, a full moon somewhere beaming behind the clouds illuminating the darkness settled over this great grey stone mournful edifice of Andromeda Park. Darcy Dancer tugging closed the heavy oak front door behind him, and standing to square his cap and pull on his driving gloves. Awaiting at the foot of the mansion's steps, the gleaming motor car. The ecclesiastic elegance of its black canvas roof sweeping back from the windscreen and the silver coachwork of its long bonnet polished to the end of the rippling fluted chromium atop the radiator grille.

Salutary. Is the word that comes most easily to mind at this very moment. Chill and moist. Look up at the sky. Sniff the air for rain. Fog lies over the low meadow land. But I better keep my bloody mouth shut. As per the past, appalling disasters always befall one at such beatific times. Which especially relates to the last twenty four hours and the recent plumbing and at least the vague hope of electricity again coursing through this house. And it was strange as I just now crossed the darkened front hall, a shiver shook me as if there were a presence and my hand paused on the latch. I turned and cast my eyes back at the fireplace and suddenly I had a vision of Leila kneeling there as she once did, her shoulders hunched and head bent sweeping up the ash of the previous night's fire from the hearthstone.

And whither goeth my life now, tonight. Down these wide and worn granite steps. To go and pause another moment to look out over one's parkland. Over breakfast this morning one did sit abed reading one's French irregular verbs. Which seemed to get more impossibly irregular by the moment. And then, under the slightly more pleasant subject of wine, studying at length the 1855 classification of Bordeaux growths, mindful that our own dear dirty Dublin had long enjoyed a reference as the claret city. A hole in my toast of course and my napkin, wouldn't you know, slipped beneath the eiderdown, so that bloody honey was dripping through onto my only last pair of nearly threadbare silk pyjamas. A Meissen side dish I picked up still so hot I dropped and chipped it. Not only prematurely breaking the yolks of my eggs but also smearing rasher grease all over. Then the rain without stint falling all afternoon. And instead of being able to concentrate, shooting a snipe or two as one trudged bog and oak forest, one had to also search for two cows and two calves gone missing. Getting lost myself, with one boot springing a leak and the other filling with slime and mud, as one leg descended up to mid thigh in a bog hole. And what else. O yes. Nothing, I suppose, too important. A rumoured pregnancy in an unmarried member of the staff. I shall no doubt know all too soon who the victim is. But as to the perpetrator, the guilt could be placed almost anywhere. At least it serves as a distraction of sorts in the battle against dilapidation and dereliction.

Darcy Dancer opening the door of this motor car. Crouching to climb in behind the steering wheel. And pressing the starter button of the great seven point one litre, twelve cylinder engine. The Daimler whined once, coughed twice, and then roared into throbbing life, shaking the panes of the east parlour window and bringing an unidentifiable face to another. O god what a bloody nosy staff one has got. Making sure I'm gone so that they may malinger unobserved in peace. And talking of noses, one can't blow one's own without sending a rumour of my impending death from pneumonia through the household.

2

The motor sweeping away down the long winding drive between the trembling oily leaves of the rhododendrons. The gleaming spokes of the wheels spinning and pebbles flying up behind the tyres. Past the shuttered and empty lodge at the front gates and out upon the wet road glistening now in moonlight. Across these gentle midland hills of Ireland. Giant beech trees forming a silver grey canopy in the motor car headlights. The winter branches over this stretch of shiny road. Leaves no question as to there being a Protestant still living beyond in these Andromeda parklands. But there are fewer and fewer of us being born in the midst of all these multiplying Catholics. And I suppose I must myself at some stage help contribute a Protestant needle or two to be then immediately lost disappearing in this enormous Catholic haystack.

Darcy Dancer stopping to read a road sign in the car headlamps. Bloody hell have never heard of the place and after all the turning and twisting lanes, now two roads in a fork that way and two more in a fork the other way. A veritable spider's web. And speaking of webs. This very morning not to incur bad luck one had taken two large spiders out of one's bath before filling it. And then, in the course of removal on a piece of toilet paper, one spider haplessly fell into another spider's web strung at the corner of the bath and floor, where an all too brief battle ensued. For, to my dismay and the erroneous assumption that any spider would know his way around another spider's network and that clearly the stronger one would anyway easily make his escape, I found myself entirely wrong. For in the fewest of seconds he was well and truly trussed up into a small tight bundle of future nourishment. O dear, in sometimes trying to avoid the present and take the broad outlook into the far distant future, one has suddenly to face up to the facts of life. Among them being caught in marriage.

3

And
It does
Much more than rather
Lower
One's spirits

2

Darcy Dancer's motor this rainy night slowing down to pass a tinker's piebald horse grazing the side of the road. Past a pub where the hunt has a fixture this coming season. Ah, and at last no longer lost. Just up this hill and down another. A vicinity said to be well drained limestone land and the very best for the grazing of cattle and horses.

The motor turning down an incline under a bridge over which a train thunders, sparks flying from the fire box of the steam engine. The Midland Great Western Railway. How nice it would be, as some lofty people in England enjoy, to have one's own private railway station on one's estate. The English seem to know how to do everything really well especially if it entails some privileged comfort. And one must suppose the Durrow-Mountmelltons have their share of theirs. As Sexton says they still do yet retain a decent sized property perhaps a bit overconfidently named Dreamstown Park. Of course one does know a lot more about the Durrow-Mountmelltons than Sexton realizes. Especially with regard to various sundry sauci-nesses.

The motor roaring along a stretch of straight road. Missing an unlit cyclist by only a whisker. Turn left now into slower but safer lanes along this high wall. Which could certainly do for a lunatic asylum. Which, apropos of asylums, more than rumours did abound of Felicity's father being a confirmed debauchee of sorts. Who, upon having a toilet installed in the bathroom, did sit there defecating while commanding his butler and two maids to be in attendance. And who were also required to be present upon his then taking his evening bath.

One young maid being required, so as not to soapily wet her uniform, to remove her own clothes in order to scrub the master's back. While the butler, suitably called Capability, served the master champagne. Of course through the confessional the local priest knows all that goes on among servants in the parish and it wasn't long before matters verged on scandal when the nude maid sampling the champagne fell drunk into the bath, banging her head and there remaining had to be attended by the local doctor. But that was nothing compared to his sticking a sheep's hind legs in his boot tops and rogering the nervous animal one night in front of some invited highly bohemian guests and describing it as an anatomical experiment in the furtherance of zoological knowledge. Although hardly anyone has caught sight of her recently, Durrow-Mountmellton the father had installed a quite beautiful and foreign titled housekeeper who, still relatively young after he died, was said to keep reclusively to her apartments issuing, as if to an army, bizarre orders to the dwindling staff.

Of course out in this god forsaken midland isolation one is apt to make up one's own rules. And too, as hard as one tries to keep up appearances and keep one's trousers from falling down, the accumulation of so much daily enforced familiarity rather leads to a breakdown in strict household protocol not to mention occasional insolence bordering on violence. And one's staff are likely to gradually assume airs of one sort or another which then conveniently prevent them doing their assigned chores as being beneath their station. And it's not any wonder one sees a member of one's own staff mincing along one's halls as a transvestite, sporting an earl's ceremonial robe. O dear, so many matters that one must avoid with all five senses to prevent finally reaching an hysterical dimension that inevitably ends one up more than half cuckoo oneself.

Darcy Dancer's motor pulling up and stopping at a crossroads. Just a tinker's sealed up little tent and not a house in sight to inquire at. More direction signs broken in half and

6

clearly twisted so as to be out of all recognition to the weary stranger. These lanes one might identify in daylight on horseback but at night from the low elevation of a motor car could be bloody anywhere. Now which way do I turn on this crossroads. Ah I remember that copse of fir where a fox went to ground and another was found. Turn left and it's the second gates on the right. But dear me, as the mansions, some more quickly than slowly, tumble down, one has the very distinct feeling that refined well bred people of our class are getting these days very thin on the ground indeed.

At an apron entrance, a chain and lock on the closed tall heavy barred front gates. Darcy Dancer reversing the motor round and returning back down the road to the open farm entry. Turning in and proceeding, bouncing along the deeply pot holed narrow winding drive as rain begins to fall. Cocks of hay still out in the weather. So haunted is Ireland at night that not a single peasant is to be seen. I suppose only we who have no guilty consciences about ghosts dare to venture out in the dark. And I can't say that my own superstitions recently haven't been giving me a thing or two to think about. My god the muddy ruts. No wonder there's a tractor minus a big back wheel tipped over in the downpour. Past these stone barns and hay sheds. Dogs barking and jumping up at the rungs of a closed gate and unfriendly enough. Sexton out in his pottingshed today, where I was attempting to rid myself of mud in front of his fire, had much to say regarding this evening.

'Ah your motor car sleek as a shark back from the hospital in England and roaring raring to go. The affluence, the affluence. It's on every lip all over the parish. And Master Darcy how could it be otherwise that the ladies would be tossing their caps at you. Or would I say bonnets.'

'One's circumstances Sexton, I do believe, have undergone such glowing exaggeration and been extended so far beyond the truth as to be plainly in the realm of the ridiculous. And it does make one more than somewhat nervous.'

7

'An invitation to dinner now should cause you no apprehension. But ah as to the husband hunting, sure a fox would have an easier time chased between high walls straight down a deserted road by the hounds.'

'Well that last remark has surely caused me apprehension. I hardly know of the Durrow-Mountmellton girl since we were at dancing school together.'

'And no more desirable reason than that is there as to why you shouldn't get to know further and better particulars of the lady. Just back from the fashionable goings on in London she is to get ready for a spot of hunting. And wasn't she at the ball your sisters Miss Lavinia and Christabel gave a while back.'

'It was a long while back Sexton.'

'Nevertheless well connected I hear said she is across the water. Been to one of them foreign finishing schools. Niece of a full blown earl. Sure the Durrow-Mountmelltons still have a decent bit of middling to good land. An heiress you might say. And the place here Master Darcy, if I were to speak out boldly now on the subject, could do with a mistress in the house. And that's a fact.'

'Well Sexton aside from treating me like some sort of mercenary fortune hunter, let me put it to you. Why is it that you yourself have never sought further and better particulars of some lady for the purposes of matrimony. You seem awfully good at sizing them up.'

'Now as to meself, there was someone, have no doubt about that. But it's an old and forgotten story now. Sunk below the waves. And I'm with only a small cottage to look after in these my maturing years. But Master Darcy you. Still a mere gossoon. With the gates of the great wide world open before you.'

'Well perhaps Sexton all the more reason that I should proceed out them in a singular fashion. For I am advised by some who have an acquaintanceship with the married state that it can give way to less than agreeable moments.'

8

'Ah now that would be cynical talk now. Abysmally cynical sine dubio.'

Moisture streaking down the windscreen, as the motor car passed under the branches of a tall grove of trees. Pulling up in front of this dour shadowy mansion. With its Doric porch and paired stone columns. Its windows staring blankly out over the surrounding fields and parklands, and the leaden grey darkness haunting the lonely landscape. Silhouettes of a horse and three solitary beasts grazing. And one did keep looking to see if some strange figure might be also lonely standing out there. Like the seemingly motionless apparition I've now twice spotted standing in the distance out on the boglands adjoining the lake at Andromeda Park.

Darcy Dancer mounting the steps up to the door of this mansion. Bits of moss clinging and green and yellow blots of lichen on the grey cut stone. Faint light showing in a window. Press the doorbell and knock as well. Ready oneself for one of those innumerable country occasions of stammering out a stream of excuses when one finds one was expected this same night only next or last week. And by the utter silence in there I'm already sure that must be the case, only it appears there's just one way one can find out and that is to push open the door and go in. And just hope I don't get a blazing shotgun blast in the face or have an iron bar flatten me as an intruder.

Darcy Dancer stepping into a great gloomy dark hall rising two storeys. A single candle up on the landing reflecting on the glass dome in the ceiling over the grand staircase. A musty damp smell and scent of woodsmoke. Armour on the walls. Bows, spears and arrows. Ah, I do believe I hear as I hope might be a friendly noise down that corridor to the right.

A man carrying a wood basket emerging in the firelight from a room and approaching along a narrow corridor out into the hall. And now stopping to lean forward to peer under his upraised hand.

9

'Ah with the dogs barking I didn't hear the knock and was on me way out to see if it was trespassers.'

'Would Miss Durrow-Mountmellton be at home.'

'She would sir. And you'd be sir, wouldn't you, the gentleman expected for dinner. Now don't tell me. I know the name famed enough. On the tip of me tongue. A moment now and I'll have it in total. Would it be Darcy Thormond Dancer Kildare of Andromeda Park over beyond. Ah but I am missing the first Christian name. Starts with an *r*. Am I right sir. Don't tell me. Richard. No. Raymond. No. Rory. Ah it's slipped me.'

'Reginald.'

'Ah yes. I knew I was getting close.'

'And Miss Durrow-Mountmellton.'

'Ah sir yes she do be in the kitchen. Now if you go that way down the hall and turn to your left and then to your right, and then straight on till you reach a landing. Do you follow me so far sir.'

'Yes I think so.'

'Take no notice of the stairs up or down in front of you and again turn left and you will be then by god's grace, standing in the hall on the way to the pantry. Go neither left nor right but take the direction dead in front of you. Now if you cross to the door you'll see ahead of you cupboards on either side. Take no notice of them either. For if you were to pull them open they'd only be full of crockery. Walk steadily between them and sure in less than seven paces you will then be in the kitchen and Miss Felicity, if I'm not mistaken, is cooking up the supper there. A grand great mess of cabbage and leeks. And a hind leg of lamb in the oven. But now I can give no further hint as to the other dinner matters sir.'

'Well I am quite sure they will be no less pleasing than the ones you've already mentioned. Thank you.'

Of course one did hope the other dinner matters weren't quite so unappetizing sounding as a boiled up mess of cabbage

10

and leeks. Delicious food does somehow always restore one's confidence in life if one's optimism is proceeding along in low gear. And my god in spite of odd miraculous bits of good luck I've endured no shortage of doubt and dismay these past many many months. One supposes that Sexton is right. One does need a mistress of the house. Perhaps not one as strict as old fussy boots Miss von B, but at least one whose culinary skills might be imparted to the kitchen staff so that they don't serve gravy instead of chocolate sauce for one's guests to put on their ice-cream.

Durrow-Mountmellton in a blue rumpled shift. A heavy leather military belt and big brass buckle around her waist. Her robust size and strong calf muscles flexing on her legs as she moved to turn off the sink tap, splashing water onto the floor.

'O my goodness Mr Kildare. Who let you in.'

'No one was answering the door and I let myself in.'

'O dear I'm not actually dressed. I wasn't expecting you for at least another half hour or so.'

'O I am sorry. Although I did get lost once I rather found my way here rather more easily than I had anticipated.'

'Cook of course suddenly chose today to have all her teeth pulled out up in the dental hospital in Dublin. Well now that you are here and well and truly in the kitchen, can I get you something to drink.'

A man, grey locks of hair hanging out from his cap and over his ears, seated at the kitchen table, munching some bread while making a note in a book. Pulls his forelock as he is introduced. His bit of supper steaming from the plate alongside stacks of winter vegetables in from the garden. His long worn farm soiled clothes stiff and greasy with wear. Grand as they still presented themselves to be, there was no question that the Durrow-Mountmelltons had long ago gone more than a bit native. Rubbing elbows quite closely in the kitchen with one's servants being the ultimate confirmation.

'O dear Mr Kildare but this won't do, you're simply standing there thinking your thoughts. Which, ha ha, could be unflattering. Let me please at least show you in the direction of the library. In fact I have some champagne chilling in there. O drat me. Or did I have it put in the drawing room. It's in the drawing room. Now that I think of it. It's not chilling of course. It's in an old vase of water from the well which is quite cold. Bottle's open, do help yourself. I suppose you're one of those people who like their champagne absolutely cold chill.'

'Well as a matter of fact I'm quite easy you know. But of course autumn room temperature in an Irish house is of course cold chill.'

'Yes quite. But I hope that's not criticism.'

'O no I'm perfectly warm.'

The smouldering drawing room fire letting more smoke than heat into the room and the wet logs hissing out steam. Statuary on the mantel with tiny cats' eyes. Something hauntingly evil about the way all the little eyes appear to be staring at one. Ah but this pair of mirrors look damn good and if genuine I venture a guess that they could be George III and Chippendale. It is too awful the way one starts to size up people's chattels. One wishes Sexton hadn't suggested concerning a mistress of the house. Merely having it upon one's mind makes me more susceptible to the husband hunters. And turning one suddenly into a fortune hunter like old Rashers Ronald, going round sizing up to the last minuscule the reward one might get if one got up the old splicing aisle as he would put it. But for a start there'd be a quid or two to be had from this cabinet display of snuff boxes. And one supposes these portraits are by decent painters. Two rather attractive ladies. Each of them sporting suitable jewels which could still be lurking in the family possession. O dear. And that portrait is definitely Felicity's mother. Rumoured she died in childbirth. But one can't help wondering if she didn't die of too

12

much of old Durrow-Mountmellton who, as he did his sheep, took her from the rear and of course tried to shove her feet down the side of his boots. Not a bloody exactly gentlemanly thing to do even driven to it at the most worst hard up of times. Also old Major Durrow-Mountmellton would have in his bathroom a gramophone thundering out military marches and he would strut the staff back and forth as he sang out troop commands from his bath.

Darcy Dancer pouring himself a glass of champagne, of a brand one has not heard of before and by its bouquet and first taste one might be glad not to exactly hear of again. But it will do I suppose to make believe one is living at the height of fashion out in the low bogs and, as one crosses this great grey green carpet of this candlelit drawing room to another wall, it is, but for a minor shabbiness here and there, all rather quite grand. And mellow aged by these puffs of smoke from the smouldering fire blowing out into the room. Which has darkened this painting of a little girl with her straw hat as she stands in a meadow's summer flowers. Rather sweet pretty little thing. But I doubt that it would fetch that much at a London auction room. Ah but on this side table, a doll's house inlaid with exotic woods and tiny carved bits of furniture. Fetch a damn decent price. Good lord must stop this as if I were actually thinking of hitching up with someone. And my god, a doll's house, there's a bloody cautionary reminder. One hasn't yet stopped to think of the consequences that descend from marriage. Children being foremost among them. And noisy little toys to slip and break one's arse upon. I suppose a nanny or two could take care of that possible nuisance. And then above all other things there are the standards one must keep up in such breeding.

A cattle moan coming from far out in the fields. Miss Felicity Durrow-Mountmellton appearing in the doorway. In, my goodness, a fairly tight silk skin clinging trouser job. Rust with gold trimmings. Showing off her figure. Heavens nipples evident no less. Of course she'll freeze to death. And my god she does look rather forward. I'm not sure I didn't prefer her prison dress in the kitchen. But I mustn't show dismay, as if one were a country bumpkin. This must be what they dare to be wearing in London. Post war influence. I mean it seems everyone is kicking up their heels. And I do believe such trousers are referred to in some awful American term as slacks. Quite clearly she's a mind to let me know of, and clue me into, the beau monde in which she moves.

'O drat this fire. It is awfully chilly in here. Let's go instead to the library, where the fire's been burning all day. Would you take and carry the champagne.'

Darcy Dancer with a glass in one hand and the vase of champagne clutched in an arm, following Miss Durrow-Mountmellton across the great front hall now lit with two more candles. A sudden shadow jumping back from the banister atop the landing overlooking the main staircase. I must confess that Durrow-Mountmellton's rear undulating quarters are nicely sloped and quite a delight to walk behind. And they even shimmer a bit in this dimmest of light. Terrible that one is already ready to grab a haunch of her. Especially now as her arse is further illuminated by the good hot fire in this library. Books in mahogany glass cabinets. The panelled oak walls gleaming. Stacks of *London Illustrated News*. Editions of times long gone past.

'Isn't this better.'

'Yes indeed. I do believe steam is already rising from my trousers.'

'I'll bet you're bookish.'

'As a matter of fact I'm not particularly, are you.'

'No. Not being brainy I seem only able to keep my nose glued between the pages of a book for only the very briefest of moments. Of course if the book's about hunting that's different. By the way, if you don't mind my prying, is there any truth in the rumour that you have been at the very last minute asked to be Master of Foxhounds.'

'O dear people do talk don't they.'

'O I do hope you shall take it up. But shall we go eat. Bring your drinkies.'

Out back into the front hall. The click of Durrow-Mountmellton's heels on the floorboards. And further down this hall under the stair landing. Dear me she is curvaceously tall and well bosomed and has rather a flash in her eye. But O my god this is a ruddy chill dining room. The only heat being from the four candles, and the steam rising from the food. Of course the candelabra are rather overly long stemmed and are sticking up too high. And before one's frozen hands drop off one will have to somehow heat up the conversation during the soup.

'I say might this be a much older house than it appears.'

'Do please. The name's Felicity. It was built in 1818 as a matter of fact. But it's architecturally confusing for its period. It's undergone many an alteration. Including many false walls, in which are hidden locked safes all over the house.'

'You don't say. Fancy that.'

'My father was awfully fond of partitions, making for a lot of old mouldy spaces with shelves full of chemicals and pottery. One almost felt he used them to spy on people. The cellars are chock a block with vases and ceramics. But even here upstairs father kept bits of old pipe and old tools, which I fear still lie in their place unmoved. You see he never trusted anyone with the plumbing after it was first put in, as when the water pump down the field was turned on, veritable fountains appeared sprinkling out of every wall and ceiling.'

'O dear. I'm just having my own plumbing seen to as a matter of fact. Sounds as if then I may need a damn umbrella doesn't it.'

'And well you may if this house is anything to go by. But you mustn't get too alarmed. The person Daddy employed was the village undertaker and only new to the trade of plumbing and he did get confused. You see we have three sets of back stairs going up to the endless attics and a pipe could end up going anywhere and that's where they mostly went. As a little girl I got lost amid the water tanks, horse tack, polo equipment, children's carts. And I was always wanting to see what was in all the ominous cupboards boarded over. And they're still that way. And O dear the pipes. No one has the faintest clue any more where they go.'

'Pipes do don't they seem to have such a habit. May I have another biscuit please. And that turnip was jolly delicious.'

'O yes sorry. And do please have more wine.'

Along with her generosity one felt Durrow-Mountmellton was attractive enough but somehow there seemed to be just that trace of her beginning to go off as a cheese might having reached its peak ripeness. And as a matter of fact exactly resembling the condition of the Brie from which one had just cut a sliver to pop on a biscuit and have with one's port. Of course she could be an entire three years senior to me, confirming perhaps that the husband hunting was indeed a serious matter. But in spite of going off, like a piece of cheese, she did seem to know how to conduct a household. My napkin beautifully folded at my place in the shape of a rose.

'When you finish your port I must show you about. And do please help yourself to more Brie. And apropos of nothing at all really, O dear, it's not a dinner subject and I don't mean to pry but I'm told Andromeda Park has a room where butlers have hung themselves.'

'I beg your pardon, are you suggesting one has an unhappy servantry.'

'O no, of course certainly not.'

'Well the fact of the matter is Miss Felicity Durrow-Mountmellton, I have, but for one member of it, both a dwindling and an absolutely unhappy servantry. Who do nothing but complain of low wages, long hours. All done of course while their bottoms and backs occupy and polish kitchen chairs and they strain their arms carving slabs off the butter to spread on slabs of bread thick as doorsteps which are then slathered in even deeper slabs of damson and strawberry preserve all of which is washed down by endless cups of thick tea. While of course the pasha of the manor is thoroughly derided.'

'You are pulling my leg of course.'

'Absolutely not. And we've had in the past I believe two successful danglings. More recent attempts have been bungled by not tying a good proper noose and not using a chair sufficiently high to jump off. And then our butlers employ the traditional expression, tally ho, when launching into their eternal oblivion.'

'Now you really are pulling my leg. O dear is that your hand.'

'Yes as a matter of fact. I was just reaching to feel where your leg was to give a tug. Ah but perhaps as the wine is making itself felt I might exaggerate a mite. But we did too have a scullery maid who tried to hang herself but the rope broke and she plummeted down a stairwell and straight through a rotted part of the servants' dining room ceiling and straight through into a huge hot cauldron of potatoes. By god if she didn't eat a pound of them on the spot.'

'Now I absolutely know you're having me on. You are awfully Irish aren't you. But one must say, at times one wishes certain servants would go hang themselves and do it successfully. Do you suppose butlers are much better at hanging themselves. I don't suppose it's really at all funny when O dear one wonders what is to happen to our sort of people. O dear it's all too too dire isn't it.'

'Yes it is rather. As we cower within our soggy damp drawing rooms, unable to replace the fallen roof slates, our houses will slowly topple down in the wind and rain. Then in order to at least replenish our wine cellars we piecemeal sell the local farmer the land for next to nothing, until finally his cattle are put sheltering in our front halls and munching hay on the parquet floors of our ballrooms. Under our by now tattered umbrellas we will be jeered at by the rejoicing locals. And then the burgeoning Catholic Romanish papish hordes, who are baptized the moment they pop like rabbits out of the female peasantry, and who have been indoctrinated into thinking we Protestants are doomed to hellfire, will simply squeeze us into a vanished infinity. That is what is to happen my dear. Indeed some of us may have no choice or vocation other than be servants ourselves to some rich gombeen man. That would be rather less than jolly wouldn't it.'

'O dear I feel faintly sick.'

'So do I Felicity.'

> So let's ruddy
> Bloody open another
> Bottle or two of
> Wine

3

Old Durrow-Mountmellton certainly fetched more bottles of wine. And each dustier and increasingly improved. A great grin on her face each time she stood in the dining room doorway holding aloft by the neck another vintage up from the cellars. Pushing back her oriental silk shirt sleeves and jangling bracelets on her wrist, and yanking out the cork and landing the heel of the bottle with a thump on a wine coaster. Then, leaning back in her chair, she took a deep breath.

'Well Darcy, my dear Dancer, with so much of the ominous looming let's have a right old good night of it if we're all bloody well going to be finished. Wiggle waggle our way through this old house like a pair of mad old snakes. Why not. Before the cattle come grazing in the front door. Just watch my hydrostatics.'

Felicity standing and suddenly shaking her hips, grinning and enlarging her eyes. And talk about reptilian insanity, O my, did the evening change dramatically. Of course I, once a runaway waif and lonely butler's boy, was at my very best painting a picture of the decline and fall of the landed gentry, being a featured player and knowing my lines well. But god forbid that our sort should ever cease to inhabit this land of ours. Of course Durrow-Mountmellton, her years in a finishing school, clearly had yet to get a taste of what it's like to be a servant before she suggests rope to choke them. But by ruddy jove did she ever have a strange sort of robust guts. One can be so wrong about people. In fact she turned out to be an uproarious and highly profane ruddy good skin.

Doubling me over with laughter. And did my mouth drop open as she took a poker to the several photographic portraits on the dining room sideboard.

'Bloody hell Darcy old chum, if we're in the descendancy, let's descend. And you, you stuffy old shirts, go first.'

I laughed like a drain. Admittedly we were finally as tight as newts, but I did think she was being a mite overdestructive in entertaining her guest. Wham. Crash. Sending glass flying. God, could she swing a poker. Wonderful the way she stepped into her backhand. And swiped away with such stunning elegance. I should have of course known that she was a brilliant lawn tennis player there being a grass court right in front of the house. And setting herself and lowering her shoulder into her backhand, she unbelievably, as I'd seen the Mental Marquis do, sabred a ruddy bottle of wine. Which I'm sure she didn't learn to do in finishing school. And of course, pouring out the contents and quaffing it down, we set off on a tour of the house and Felicity did not mince her four and seven letter words.

'Bugger this old ruddy rubbish of decline. We're going to debauch.'

She was positively wonderful to listen to in the midlands at midnight. And, as a total surprise in my life, one was taking a particular closer look at what was her surprisingly improving handsome profile. In fact if she were going off like a bit of cheese by god she was going off with a vengeance. She had, as she got tight, the rather attractive habit of sniffing up her nose and then tossing her head and throwing back a mane of hair. She put the gramophone playing in the hall. And out thundered her father's record of the massed bands of the Grenadier Guards drumming and blaring out the Slow March. God what an honestly ruddy inspiring night. Heaven knows what the spooks in the house leaping back into the shadows were thinking. Although I suppose, in this country mansion, most are not going to plunge through the rotten floors into a cauldron of hot potatoes. But old Felicity and I we were already quickly descending the Dreamstown cellar stairs to start the tour of her domain.

'Come this way darling and mind the footsteps.'

A cold damp air. Patches of wet on the great flagstone floor. Faint scent of Durrow-Mountmellton combined in the candle fume and musky smell of wood decay. And I must say her use of the word darling I found quite piquantly enticing. And quite marvellously distracting from my slightly down in the dumps condition.

One had earlier in the evening, driving to Dreamstown, got an awful crushing attack of terrible longing for Leila. Remembering her once in her sizes too big black uniform, and unable to shake off the vision of her on her knees cleaning out the grate in my own front hall. And especially now that I had heard a rumour of her taking up residence with the Mental Marquis in Paris for part of the year. But now, following Durrow-Mountmellton by the candlelight, I was certainly getting new visions. And was able to spy a few silver strands of hair on Felicity's head. And entirely becoming they were. For without even a decent wank recently, I was feeling distinct urges in the gonads, and, randily hard up as I was, was quite wanting to grab her. We were then in quite the most massive of servants' halls off which dungeon kitchens and sculleries seemed to radiate, and off which was her father's plumbing workshop. And into which like a pair of old snakes we tipsily slithered.

'I'm sure you must be inquisitive but I don't know why on earth Daddy got so interested in pipes. But he was always a one for drains and sewers.'

One did think it better not to too deeply inquire as to the nature and purpose of some of the plumbing matters or attempt to figure out the possible use of some other suspicious looking contraptions, especially as one was getting a rather clearer picture of old Major Durrow-Mountmellton as

21

an out and out pure sadist. But as we were in close proximity and I had put down the candlestick to examine a curiously serrated section of sewer pipe, one did suddenly grab her. Durrow-Mountmellton rather caught her breath. But did immediately turn her face towards me and open up her mouth to my mouth. Then during a kissing lull and while deeply digging in my fingers feeling her arse I was also taking one long look over her shoulder at the workshop walls covered with indescribable pieces of broken and twisted metal hanging on bits of string from little nails and stacked up on shelves and it was no wonder no one knew where the pipes went in this house. Up high on top of a cupboard a stuffed fox staring straight down at me. I was getting a slight case of the hee bee geebs. Plus in a dark corner were ancient man traps with jaws like great shark mouths and in and among which were handcuffs and something awfully resembling a chastity belt. And then by george just as I was leaning in close, placing a caressing kiss down the side of her neck, she let out a low animal groan. Which not only made me unhand her but jump backwards and also knock crashing into a shelf which then toppled over an old pot of paint, the cover coming off as it fell and hitting a work table. And as disaster would have it, pouring its oily, smelly contents right straight onto old Durrow-Mountmellton's oriental trouser job and dripping drops down on her black high heeled shoes and turning them into a rather awful bright orange.

'O god, O god, I am so sorry.'

'Ha ha, not to worry. See just take off shoes, wipe off. Then wipe the paint from one's feet, but leave a spot of colour on the toenails and presto it does for a pedicure.'

And now with dripping paint all over, one was feeling such a blundering idiot. Especially with the stuffed fox's glittering eye watching my every move. While old Durrow-Mountmellton in my eyes at least was becoming a most acceptable heroine, and one bloody sporting type by god.

Anyone could see she had plenty of the old feisty sheep rogering major in her. And one immediately decided that there should be more cheerful places to pursue hugging than down a dark and damp cellar amid bunkers full of mouldering wood, soggy turf and pulverized coal not to mention ruddy torture chambers which might have been behind further locked stout oak doors. But of course I should have known the night was only beginning. And it had to be out to the stables to saddle up two of her gigantic hunters already neighing and pawing the stable floor, all ready to ride to the moonlight. And my god in a trice could she saddle a horse as I'd never seen saddled before. Tightening the girth with an upward heave that actually tipped the big hunter over on his right sided paws.

'There you are Darcy climb aboard, let's go.'

'What about you.'

'I'm bareback. Makes me horny.'

God not only did she seem impervious to the cold but my, could she be bloody suggestively blunt in her language. I could hardly believe but then believed it when she said riding after midnight across country bareback actually gave her orgasms. While of course it gave me apoplexy made rigid with fear. Out this way from Dreamstown Park, I knew of one little hazard at least, a hundred foot sheer drop into a disused quarry which claimed twenty hounds killed year before last. Of course she could go flying off the cliff to her death's content in ecstasy. And all the while out in the stables I was really expecting and more than hoping old D.M., as I was now calling her, was simply going to chuck the hunters some hay and oats, fill their water buckets, give them a slap on the backside, and tell them go to sleep and then lead and let us both get back into the house for some further orifice inquiry. She said that's what the girls at finishing school called it, only they had nothing handy but each other's tongues. But a few seconds later we the ruddy bootless two of us were clattering out across the cobbled courtyard and under the arched entranceway beneath the Dreamstown clock tower. Past hay-barns, stacks of rusting old machinery and into this oblivion of night time countryside.

'Whoo who, Darcy, whoo who.'

Talk about riding a horse point to point. Old Durrow-Mountmellton could go up and down the Matterhorn at the gallop. Her blondish hair flying loose behind her in the moonlight. Of course the Mental Marquis was another who chose to ride cross country in the middle of the night and god knows what kind of perverted bloody orgasms he had. But we were flying at a good thirty knots and every second I was wanting and waiting to hear her suggest that we might simply repair back to a soft surface within the confines of Dreamstown house and there lie down mercifully in each other's arms generating body heat under an eiderdown.

'Whoo who Darcy, whoo who.'

And further to her galloping out there in front, all I could hear was old D.M.'s horse's hoofs which were busy flicking up sods clobbering me in the bloody head and she shouting back at me between her hoots, not to lag behind, or she would leave me lost.

'Be careful Darcy the quarry cliffs are ahead just a matter of a few yards to the left.'

Not only the risk of heading off a precipice but can you imagine flying through the unknown and also knowing that any second, as a nice little trick by the locals, a wire could be strung between the trees just at the right height to lop the heads off the gentry. But by bloody jove, coming back to husband hunting, imagine too a gung ho wife the likes of fearless old Durrow-Mountmellton. Whom by god one might even marry not only for the perversions she clearly has but also for these hunters she owned. Covering the ground racing like thoroughbreds, and jumping like giant grasshoppers. And I must say it was ruddy wonderful with the moist breeze and chill upon one's face blowing the wine out of one's head. The snortling of air from the horse's nostrils, giant lungs and heart pounding beneath one. Our moonlit shadows streaking across the meadows. Jumping walls, hoofs stretched over the ditches, leaping streams. With the foam flying from my horse's mouth. My own sweat soaking me. And good unbelievable god, not only did I have an unbelievable erection causing me extreme pain in my trousers but suddenly I realized old Durrow-Mountmellton was onto a fox.

'Tally ho. Tally ho.'

And by god weren't we following him like the wind. And I knew this was where further and better trial and tribulation were about to begin. Sure enough as any old wise fox would, he had already taken us nicely into a thickly enclosed field. On all four sides steep ditches with mountainous hedges as deep across as the nose to tail end length of a horse. And old fox got quickly the other side, promptly sitting on his haunches, laughing his head off. But not for long. For he didn't know he had old Durrow-Mountmellton after him. Who, retreating twenty paces back and crouching her head behind the neck of her steed, set off like a battering ram, collecting the great beast together at the point of impact to smash into the jungle of tangled briars, ash saplings and whitethorn, leaving a gaping hole through to the other side. Where let me tell you old laughing fox didn't wait long to be gone. Or to view old Durrow-Mountmellton with the shirt torn right off her back. Like an eel through a hoop I jumped to join her. And by god my mouth already dropping open all evening had now lost both jaw hinges and was sagging somewhere down around my Adam's apple. For there in the streaming moonlight, enveloped in a cloud of steam rising from her horse, streaks of blood seeping from scratches across her arms and shoulders, were her two nakedly gleaming breasts heaving in the chill night air. Something like my conscience said to me in quite a loud voice, now there's a little miracle of delight for you. Her nipples faint and soft like rosebuds, and bosoms only just that teeniest weeniest bit on the side of being large. O my god now eat my words. Or nipples. If this is a bit of cheese going off, then by god I am going to have a good damn bite of it. Mountmellton old girl I salute you. And your elegant finishing school. If it shaped you in any way at all, the way you are, it must be wonderful. And long may the landed gentry like us reign across these wild green windswept lands and if not reigning, long may they ride. And by jove tonight they ride and reign supreme. I can nearly hear the massed drums and pipes and bugles blaring God Save the King across these soft green meadows. Or rather I think I may have just ever so gently for a few seconds taken leave of my senses. And bloody ruddy hell, to use just a little of one's own profanity my nanny absolutely abhorred, I really at that moment fell for old Durrow-Mountmellton. Or at least tottered over a bit. It was just the ruddy sense of utter devilment in her deceptively quiet blue eyes and the way she dropped her lids and glanced at one sideways with a sort of sudden endearing shyness as if she dared not speak. And one wanted to whisper back, I say there Durrow-Mountmellton what entrancing catastrophe have you got next lined up. Well I did not speak too soon. Durrow-Mountmellton, with an enticing swing and bounce of her bosoms, turned and went ahead, galloping for home. And promptly disappeared from me into some enormous pasture's shadows. And of course I was speechless. One could understand her hurry to get home before she got and died of the new monia as it is familiarly referred to in the farmyard of Andromeda Park. And ruddy hell trying to catch her up alongside which I was trying desperately to do just to catch one more glance of the earth quaking sight of her two bosoms wonderfully bouncing, I was at full gallop and taking the jumps nicely enough in her wake, when wham. In the middle of a large field and nearly as we came abreast in what appeared to be an innocuous meadow it was as if my steed were poleaxed beneath me and I was flung flying face flat into the

26

ground. An eternity through the darkness before I landed. And then an agonizing stab of pain in the rib cage and my shoulder seemed surely dislocated. While the ruddy horse neatly somersaulted right back up again on all fours and ran off. Leaving me a seat on a cold stone shiveringly lost in the wilds of the midlands. I mean my god here I am fulfilling a dinner engagement and I'm tramping around for endless minutes soaked to the skin in the rain. Finally I found the creature by the sound of it munching up a late supper in a sheltered corner of the field. But trying to catch the wickedly wily animal as it dodged left and right was quite another matter. Chasing it as it tripped over its reins back and forth across the field from one end to the other. It must have been a quarter mile in one direction and half a mile in the other, and my breathing was agonizing. Even if I could catch the ball-less creature, I was now realizing both my wrists were sprained. While I was seated on the ruddy stone, I nearly bloody well cried only the raindrops just wouldn't give my tears a chance. It could have been fully an hour later that my plaintive shouts out into the night were finally heard by Durrow-Mountmellton in a sou'wester come back to look for me. She must have had sufficient orgasms because she was also on a saddle. And seeing me as a raincloud passed and moonlight shone down, she let out a peal of laughter you could hear all the way to Dublin.

'O poor you. Poor poor you.'

I finally managed with a goose or two from old Durrow-Mountmellton to get up and onto the quarters of her horse and was meanwhile trying to sniff in her perfume as a reminder that civilization still existed somewhere. Vaguely clutching old D.M. with my pained wrists and my arms unavoidably pressed against her wonderful bosoms, I most quickly had the most painful of erections pressing into Durrow-Mountmellton from behind in unison with our canter, adding to my discomfort riding the whole way back. Not the sneakily prodding sort of thing one does on a short acquaintance. Of course again she scalded me like a cat with her next remark.

'You mustn't think I mind that prodding into me. Feels rather nice as a matter of fact.'

Well as a matter of another bloody fact that was all one needed to hear, to create visions of a titanic body to body embroilment over which her breasts already had me salivating. Trying to give some semblance of appearing nonchalant, even through all my pain, I did feebly attempt to get in my motor but couldn't turn the steering. It was a full half hour by the time, agonizingly button by button, I was undressed with both wrists swollen up like soccer balls. Trying to tug on a pair of the old Major's silk pyjamas was like being in a potato bag race with your partner going the opposite way. Three a.m. by the clock tower bell when Durrow-Mountmellton knocked with a hot water bottle just as I had finally got exhausted into bed. Visible through her open dressing gown, she was wearing what one might refer to as an abbreviated négligé, revealing as she stepped forward a most wondrous pair of strong well shaped legs, adding further needless enticement.

'O dear, poor poor you.'

Of course she took the attitude one takes in hunting circles. That the more maimed you are the prouder one should be. And now I could hardly speak never mind move. So much for a casual supper engagement to which one motors in dazzling elegant comfort in one's pristine car. The worst thing about any horror while it's happening is that you don't think it's ever going to end. And now as crippled, maimed, scared, wet and chilled beyond my resources as I was, I was making every effort to be as abjectly thankful to my rescuer as possible. Who was now casually lifting up her own leg on the bed to remove a large rose thorn stuck in her knee. Which, with a squeeze of fingers, popped out. I don't know why she thought I should look at it, but she held the offending blood covered thorn under my nose.

28

'There, that's what Jesus Christ wore in their many around his head.'

'O dear that couldn't have been very nice.'

'Darcy do you ever think of Jesus.'

'Well not exactly.'

'What does not exactly mean.'

'It means I never think of Jesus.'

Of course I was to some degree quite well acquainted with religious mania, having for years been subjected to it by Sexton. But this was a little more disturbing because it was making me singularly horny. Dear me, one was now recalling nights down in the catacombs of Charnel Chambers in Dublin, and the sacrilegious black masses said there. And certainly thoroughly revolting were some of the litanies. O Lord for all thy faults I love thee still. Fruit of the juice of Joseph, spit of the horn most high. O holy tongue stuck up the arse most deep, treasure the pleasure there. I suppose you could say with a stretch of the imagination that such invocations did have a devotional quality.

'O then we are, aren't we Darcy, both pagans.'

'Well I don't profess to be entirely pagan, I am a member of the Church of Ireland.'

'Hello then. I'm glad to meet you Master.'

Durrow-Mountmellton standing back, lifting aside her dressing gown, raising her négligé and executing a curtsy. No wonder she can make her stallion go with such an exquisitely curving strong pair of thighs and calves. Captivatingly like her breasts and also just that teeniest weeniest bit tending on the side of large. If one were of a poetic disposition, I have no doubt that upon their utter long contoured muscular splendour one could write a sonnet. And if my jaw dropped open at the sight of her gleaming moonlit bosoms overhanging her slender waist, such mandible was now gritting my molars at my present incapacity and for being such a clot not to have steered her upstairs straight from the cellars where we'd already taken preliminary steps at orifice inquiry. For bloody hell when I think of it, it has been rather an awful long time since I put my old what for up something it is intended for. But here she was, smiling down at me by candle and firelight and considering her amusement at my injuries, rather surprisingly stroking my brow.

'They do, don't they, Master, call you Reginald. I like Darcy so much better. You're not a Reginald are you.'

'No I imagine not. And I'm not yet Master.'

I suppose despite a couple of dirty fingernails she indeed even had some of the qualities one so hoped to find in a wife. And if not outstanding beauty at least her features had a certain rugged elegance and her face a good deal of wholesome character. Obviously she was able to handle staff and horses. O god her fingers do feel nice through my hair. Clearly at a pinch she could also muck out a stable. Although in the matter of dependability, not to mention loyalty, she did leave me soaking and lost in the lurch a long enough time in the rain. So if one overlooked a few little things perhaps to be desired in the matter of beauty she would no doubt do as mistress of as grand a place as Andromeda Park. One could see to it that she was less familiar with staff such as happened down in her kitchen with her farm labourer seated eating with his cap on in her presence. Although such camaraderie might find itself conversationally useful at lonely times, it was at more times positively a god awful invitation to permanent insolence.

'And pray tell Darcy what are you ever thinking in this pretty head of yours.'

'I was thinking that handling horses is exactly the same as dealing with staff except that staff seem to require more to eat.'

'Dear me, but how mundane. And does one assume that you also think that a good thump once in a while is better understood if they step out of line. Or if they get too sour and

30

surly then you try a lump of sugar. But then make sure you don't stand in the way of their kicks and bites. But of course crafty staff, just like a horse, will vanish ungratefully to any new and better meadow whenever they can.'

Good god old Durrow-Mountmellton seems to have an answer for everything and is taking the words right out of my mouth. Or am I getting a little delirious and so daft that I am thinking of her for a wife. Or is the warm air of her breath on the edge of my ear positively making me so randy that I would marry anyone for the sake of putting my old what for in what it's intended for. O god. I am shaking. And am in this fevered state likely to do anything. Even before I've had chance to examine the marriage prospects in London or Paris. And maybe in the latter capital and closer to where Leila might be, I might come up with a lady who owns a château or two to which we could seasonally repair for wine tastings. Even find perhaps at least a minor member of the French aristocracy. Avoiding of course those who masquerade as papal countesses. My former housekeeper Miss von B certainly threw her weight about with her claims to Continental nobility. Although good god I suppose getting back to the matter of staff, if old D.M.'s taken after her father the Major, we could end up on portable toilets placed top of the grand staircase and sit overlooking the front hall while the whole of the household staff, spruce in their uniforms, parade to a gramophone rendering of the massed bands of the Grenadier Guards trooping the colour while the lord and lady of the manor are taking a shit. O my god, she is making an orifice inquiry just like Lois and putting her tongue in my ear. I thought it such a disgraceful habit until I got to like it. And O lord I completely forgot the matter of intellect and culture in a wife. Bloody hell, leaving aside books, and who needs to read a book anyway, and if you do, you're liable to forget out here in the midland bogs it's raining and a leak could be flooding the floor above, and escaping one's attention, has just billowed the ceiling so that the weight brings the entire bloody thing down and not only kills but drowns you as you sit. Ouch. Just my feeble reach with my hand to search in under her négligé to touch her breast is nothing but pain. When all that is there to touch should be sheer pleasure. Clearly old D.M., as well as her snuff boxes, must know her Meissen and her eighteenth century painters. But I imagine if we got tangled up as a couple, with so much hunting, shooting and fishing to do, culture would be the least of it. However, to keep us au courant we could motor up to Dublin occasionally, park the car and lunch at the Royal Automobile Club, take tea at the Hibernian, dine at the Kildare Street Club and then repair to the Gaiety to sit through an opera. Then staying overnight at the old Shelbourne we could next morning even buy a very occasional nice painting or damn it why not two. O lord, what on earth am I thinking of, certainly not matrimony.

'You know, don't you Darcy Dancer, you are so so pretty. I like your nose especially. You really could be Jewish you know.'

'I beg your pardon.'

'But I know you're not anything so exotic.'

'I once again I think, beg your pardon.'

'But one can't be exotic out here in the bogs anyway. Although let me rephrase that if I may. I think with a small effort and a little imagination, perhaps one can.'

One thing was more than amazingly and perfectly clear, if old D.M. were husband hunting by god did she know how to set a ruddy trap. And staring up from my lacy linen pillow at the strange canopy over my head of a star radiating out in all directions, I was at least already caught by a couple of toes. And she seemed to be absolutely sure I was about to be Master of Foxhounds. And then have to outfit hunt servants, replace their worn tack, compensate farmers across the countryside for all their broken fences and heart attacks their livestock seem suddenly to get in numerous numbers if the

32

hunt even comes within a mile. But I suppose at certain times, no matter what, certain things will happen. But god one did wish one weren't so presently ruddy well knackerdly indisposed. Even so I was getting more and more like that old fortune hunter Rashers Ronald, tabulating up the bedroom furnishings including the conversation seat upholstered with birds and flowers. And appropriately enough, it's all I am about left able to do is talk. When she did take my hand a moment to squeeze it, I stupidly cried ouch. I mean old Durrow-Mountmellton has got to be really ruddy randy. Not wise to be presumptuous but I could, one's pecker stiffening, sniff it in the air. Somehow she was giving every indication that she was ready to divest of her nightwear and climb in under the eiderdown and melt all over me in my arms, which of course were agony now to even budge or for me to even breathe. There was no doubt that I could feel two broken ribs rubbing their cracked blastedly painful ends together. O god. She is. She's taking off her dressing gown. And lifting up her négligé. She's stripping. And now more enticement her legs revealed. And one is lying here dying to suck gently upon those moist windswept and moonlit tits of hers which from just a fleeting glance now are forever emblazoned upon my memory. What a marvellous heraldic device they would make. Imagine having such a pair upon one's escutcheon. A warning motto. Do not suck upon our nipples. Or they will squirt milk at you. O god now look at them, they're glorious. God why do such things entice one so. And make one nearly ready to rush into anything. Short of course of matrimony and risking one's whole fortune. O but what an utterly splendid little bush of hair, which might perhaps be the teeny weeniest bit bushier. No no not perhaps, it's perfect just the way it is. Focusing like a bull's eye between the top of her legs. Delicious torture to the mind. But good god the ruddy woman's a mare as has the conformation of a ruddy thoroughbred. From her crest down over the withers, back over the buttocks, down again across

33

the flank and right straight down through her fetlock joint and pasterns. And she is leaning over, and she is. Reaching under the covers. And she is. Giving my prick a gentle squeeze. And her lips are. They are. Touching the edge of my ear. And she is. She is whispering.

Up
The Anglo
Irish

4

As the gales and rains roared outside Dreamstown Park, and within this north east bedroom fire embers
glowed brightly, there were little treasures of pleasures amidst
the penance of pain. Although one can't be positive that
it came of a monumental intelligence, old Durrow-
Mountmellton had the most thoughtfully magnificently adoring gaze. Propping her elbow into the pillow and her chin in
her hand, and with the slightest smile on her lips, and the
smooth satiny nipples of her breasts peeking at one as well
over the eiderdown, she stared into my eyes. One did feel as if
one were being held at the very centre of her attention. And
had ventured into her innermost world. Of perversion at least.
But of course in finally parting after three days and pausing
between the Doric columns before hobbling down the front
steps of Dreamstown Park to my car with Sexton at the wheel,
and with an enormous rainbow suddenly out over the fields,
old D.M.'s rather scalding tongue was at it again.

'Well Darcy my dear old crippled fellow, when one starts
forgetting the names of all the men who have fucked one, one
surely then has fucked too many.'

Talk about rumours, talk about gossip. And now that the
local doctor had to be in attendance, there was no stopping
conjecture. An almost overly genial soul the doctor, widely
noted for his gluing and nailing hunt members' bones back
together, kept chuckling at my indisposition. But I also could
not help feeling it was a little more than that. As he kept
glancing about the bedroom and spotted the lady's dressing
gown and négligé thrown over the conversation seat.

35

'Ah now I can see that there's been too much galloping. And you never know when to expect a fall out in open country.'

Amazing how much of one's life one ends up having to hide. And more being added to each day. Old D.M., like her father before her, turned out to be ready for perversions of the most absolutely highest order. At least the revelation was left till we had rather got on to advanced particulars and of course there wasn't a great deal I could manage in embraced body contact with the state of my wrists, ribs and shoulder. And old D.M. seemed most sportingly accommodating with her whispered suggestion as to anything special I would like her to do to me.

'Anything you like Darcy dear. Absolutely anything.'

Of course so hard up out in the bogs it did rather coax up a lot of wild fantasies. Although one did demur voicing same outright, I hinted. Especially as to some of those things one hears of the better bred people getting up to in places like Soho London.

'You're not are you Darcy suggesting I piss on you.'

'No. But of course not.'

But as one might have expected old D.M. was ready for anything. And, aside from not wanting to get her hair wet, was full of her own fantasies. One didn't mind standing there taking aim as she reclined back in the bath and having to direct the piss to parts she chose should be showered, but when she insisted I dress in ladies' lingerie for the purpose, I did demur. But that turned out to be the least of her requests. One of her Ascot hats was next, of which she had an enormous collection. Of course in my maimed state the least I could do was to agree to wear one but I thought for a moment I might be totally revolted and forever doomed to this saucy deviation. However, to my complete astonishment a minute later I was looking to a repeat pissing and trying a new hat. Bloody strange thing was that engaging in perversions with her increased our camaraderie and made her even more attractive. So raptly had I been glued to viewing her bosoms and the pee cascading down them that it was only when she stretched her arms and arched her back that I was aware of the rippling muscles over her belly, and that she was an extremely strong lady, and far from going off like cheese. And of course were the truth to be known, as bloody hell it might be soon all over the parish, one was really taking a fancy to old Durrow-Mountmellton. As well as already planning on our next assignation to make sure beforehand to quaff a pint or two of stout.

'That Darcy dear was far from being a downpour.'

Not that one would use the word exotic exactly but one was feeling now that more than a thing or two erotic was going on out here in the midlands redolent of that description. But my god the nosy cook back from Dublin with her teeth out put a damper on things. And one could see that she was the sort who would relish getting tongues wagging from one end of the parish to the other. And that Durrow-Mountmellton and I, if not betrothed, had by our indoor behaviour at least an understanding. However, the only thing that was recently true was that I had now taken up the Mastership of the hunt and had found that the hunt secretary was a positive and well nigh unbelievable pain up the arse and I should have been delighted with or without one of old D.M.'s Ascot hats to piss on him any time I could. He was, sidling up far too close to me in his conniving manner, clearly of the opinion in his exaggeratedly English accent that I was made of money.

'Sorry to bother you Master about this at what might be an inopportune time but there's this little shortfall in the accounts which I might venture to ask you at your earliest convenience to patch up. That would be wizard of you. What.'

Nearly needing a stepladder to get up on Petunia, I put in an appearance at the opening lawn meet held only a mile away from Dreamstown Park. Perhaps the only time the household work themselves up into a lather of activity is on the morning of a hunt and I was immaculately turned out. Petunia's mane braided, her hoofs polished gleamingly black. The mahogany of my boots burnished. And it did seem to provide an atmosphere of discipline up and down the halls of Andromeda Park as my boots clattered the floorboards and pavingstone. Although the pain of my ribs barely enabled me to climb up on a horse, it was rather nice to witness all the hunt servants cap doffing and to be called Master on every side and know that one in rank outranks a bishop. Of course one had to glare here and there at those incorrectly dressed. And discourage the bonhomie from those arrivistes whose second season this was. But by god what a plethora of old spinsterish hunt follower types and curmudgeonly curdled members of the hunt committee there were copiously quaffing back the port and asking me these inane leading questions.

'I say Master do you suppose apropos of nothing at all really, that too many are being allowed to hunt who are up from Dublin for the day.'

Of course as much as one did abhor the type, these nouveaux riches were saving me money by paying their caps and one did not particularly care where they came from. But god the effort of being polite on all sides had sweat dripping from my brow and into my pint of stout. Which, talking of stout, I was finding I could not now get the pissing off my mind. Nor the moment when poor old D.M. did say the urine rather burned into her scratches and wondered if my piss might poison her. But on the whole our little perversion had rather religious overtones and was, in a slightly terrifying manner, now becoming a most exciting anticipation. I was even practising peeing in my own tub.

'Darcy if only it didn't sting so much I do love the perfect temperature.'

But talk about not being fit for hunting and six solid weeks of ribs mending. Peeing was still about the only thing I could still do with perfection. With sprained wrists, merely attempting to get up out of a chair would give one such a shock of agony as to put one sitting straight back down again which also gave one a shock of agony. Also it wasn't of the best when my painter in residence had me at her conversational complaining mercy doing my portrait. O god could Lois go on. And on and on. Prattling like a Gatling gun. As I sat for her in my most pretentious chair in the ballroom, in my Master's pink coat still smelling fresh in from the tailor. But far less embarrassing than being done up in the unentitled earl's robe Lois had been previously insisting upon. Her voice echoing down on my head from the ceiling.

'You see dear boy philistine people who appear to have most of the money in this world take notice if you paint aristocrats and even more notice if you paint royalty. And you are merely county dear boy. Merely county. Although I shall admit, you are very very county. Now dear boy please don't sit there bored. Not at this exact moment when I am orgasmically worked up to my painting peak. There is nothing worse for the true artist than when he or she is prevented from capturing the true character behind a face at the split second requiring it.'

Lois had arrived with what appeared to be most of her worldly possessions and including her kitchen sink which must have been tipped off the back of the car coming up the drive. But my heart did quaver watching Crooks with his new butler boy we'd found living in the cellars who was sweating under the weight of a large easel and who was followed up the front steps by Norah and Dingbats lugging bags in his wake. But it was strange how one could in fact find Lois's constant complaints rather relaxing. I suppose artists do get so egotistically full of themselves that it's hardly believable and quite damn funny. And so I would not hesitate to be blunt.

'Truth of the matter is Lois I am absolutely bored. Nearly to sobbing tears. And I suppose I have quietly been this way for years, and so you are in fact really capturing my true

39

character. But I am also attempting to think animatedly of what Bordeaux to have fetched up from the cellars to delight you and Rashers over the snipe.'

'O how nice and thoughtful of you dear boy. I do love your wines. Not since my dear dear summer days in Montparnasse before the war do I recall drinking such marvellous vin ordinaire.'

'Bloody hell you've been drinking my very best superlative claret.'

'O dear, am I.'

'Yes you are.'

'Forgive me dear boy. Forgive me. You see how unaccustomed I am to finer things of life. Of course after my awful winters spent in Bloomsbury I did so like being in Montparnasse. Although don't misunderstand dear boy I was not then in Paris rolling in money. Far from it. I had awful bed bugs there. But it was the very cheapest place one could go for a holiday.'

'Lois, your days in Montparnasse and Bloomsbury with the bed bugs must have been very difficult times indeed.'

'I'll thank you not to if you please to be so sarcastic, it puts me off my brush strokes. I've just this second mixed the most perfect skin tint for the end of your nose. And I did not have bed bugs in Bloomsbury. I did though get those other deucedly dreadful things they call crabs and had to shave all my pubic hairs off.'

'Lois for god sakes when are you going to realize I'm your dedicated patron. Being absolutely and genuinely sympathetic. Of course I know you've had past hard times. With bed bugs in Montparnasse and your body lice in Bloomsbury.'

'Well I have. And you needn't repeat that information and overly pronounce Montparnasse and Bloomsbury in that more than slightly condescending manner of yours. Or I shall open up your flies and painfully tweak your penis. And don't think I don't deeply appreciate your being my patron. But I am a

40

divorced person with non existing maintenance and do have to contribute to public school fees for my son.'

'God Lois you really are the limit. And if I may gently suggest, you do totally ignore there are other people in the world besides you with troubles. Can we coax and have just a word from you on something that genuinely pleases you.'

'Well of course you can. You have absolutely no idea how wonderful it has been at least these last few days, that my body, out in this spacious freedom, hasn't known its usual pangs of hunger one suffers and endures for the pursuit of one's art in a lonely cold studio back in drearily dismal Dublin. I know at times I do make rather heavy weather of my difficulties. Of course it's taken you fully two years to invite me here.'

'Now Lois please I was in no position to, my life was very unsettled. Plus I knew you did not want to leave your cat.'

'Never mind the feeble excuses dear. I know I am not exactly what one's maiden aunt would welcome appearing on the doorstep. And of course you're sweating. And you will divest won't you so I can run off a few watercolour life studies as well.'

'Bloody hell Lois this ballroom is arctic and gets even more arctic with the fire pulling the cold damp air in from without. And the only reason I'm sweating is I've got a foot thick hunting coat on.'

'I do think you have the most attractive body. That American at Trinity College who collects me, bought all my previous washes I did of you. In your more rampant poses of course. Dear boy shall we then use your or my bedroom. But don't you dare think or entertain in the slightest that this is an invitation for anything else other than artistic endeavour.'

'Good god Lois I dare not think of doing anything these days with my still awfully infirm shoulder and cracked ribs.'

I was now lying abed at night, thinking of the drawbacks of marriage, having, as it were, a bit of a spiritual dilemma. Does

41

one piss upon one's wife. Or marry as a wife one upon whom one has pissed. Old Lois I knew was of a sort to whom one could address such questions and I knew she readily believed there was no such thing as perversion. And she had, after too much port, already made an overture one evening for me to visit her bedroom. I did honestly think now that wouldn't pissing on her be the most satisfactory way to temporarily shut her up. Sit her in the tub and as soon as she opened her mouth to complain send a showering jet all over her. It could of course put her off her erogenous brush strokes on my portrait for which I had already paid half of what I thought was an extremely overgenerous commission. Instead I suggested to Lois that she could in the pursuit of country habits go pull some ragwort but as the season was just almost over and it had already gone to seed she could instead go pick apples in the orchard. God she wasn't having any and what a rumpus she raised.

'You may think I do not know what ragwort is dear boy. It's a noxious weed and I'll be damned if I'll go and pull up any. As for the apples, if they are delicious, I'll pluck one for myself.'

But by god as a house guest did she have an appetite and could she ever be a nuisance. Bombarding the staff with requests. Boom boom boom went the floorboards, resounding all morning back and forth along the hall to her room. Sending Crooks up and down on the most trivial errands. Get me this, get me that. Of course if nothing else Lois did have the very haughtiest of haughty accents, and Crooks rather took her to be very grand.

'Did madam ring.'

'I would like Crooks, if you wouldn't mind, just the merest bit more soda in my whiskey.'

'But of course madam.'

Crooks on this occasion did trip and nearly break his arse on his way down to the wine cellar for the soda siphon. While the boy apprentice butler, to keep madam warm, was busy refuelling the turf fire with so much turf he set the chimney ablaze and sent sparks and flames flying out over the countryside. To get away from Lois's outside painting sessions during the day, one would proffer the excuse of urgent farm matters demanding my presence. She did of course try to follow me but by the time she got herself stuck in her wellies and bundled up as if for the North Pole, I would be already rapidly heading by the yard to escape up the farm tunnel and out through the orchards. And if smoke was showing from his potting shed chimney, I would double back through the beech grove and enter the gate in the walled garden to have a word or two with Sexton.

'Ah Master Darcy, Master Darcy. Welcome into the sanctum of horticultural endeavour. Here upon the woolsack sit down. Sit down.'

These days it never took very long to get Sexton back on to the same old bloody subject which was causing me quite an increasing amount of indecision. As there was distinctly something to be said about the advantages of spreading the daily responsibilities of Andromeda Park upon two sets of shoulders especially if half of one set was dislocated. But on this misty foggy day, you'd think it was Sexton who was looking for a wife, judging by the relish with which he again took up the matter. And he always did talk of such a subject as if he were buying a heifer at some country fair. Which I suppose really isn't that bad a method of sizing up a prospective wife.

'Ah we're back to the same old topic are we Sexton.'

'Well now Master Darcy it isn't as if I wasn't listening to the drover down in Clifden the other week trying to sell you his heifer. Ah now look at that now gentleman sir says he, she's got a nice young bag on her that will be swelling up like a volcano with milk to come pouring out of them dainty spigots like a stream in a storm down a Kerry mountainside.'

'Well he did sell us the heifer.'

'He did. But not until after I'd felt every inch of her from the end of her spigots to the tips of her ears. And if I do say so myself I was in my young days rather good at providing the necessary words to sell a heifer. But they'd better be true words you'd need said if you have a mind to find the long-lasting qualities of a wife.'

Of course too, old Sexton was as well as a botanical snob also a bit of an intellectual one. His diary, at which one occasionally peeked when it lay open on his bench, was not only full of laudatory references to the purity of the blessed virgin but also full of comments on the theory of existentialism and the freedom of the human personality it extolled. And he did take a particular fancy to Durrow-Mountmellton's educational background, who, he was able to now inform me, along with learning to iron shirts in Switzerland, also spent time at Oxford at the Ashmolean.

'Sure she'd have seen all them Leonardo do Vinci drawings. You must have had a grand three days of it, despite the injuries over there at Dreamstown. She'd know a thing or two about Tiepolo right down to them Pre-Raffelites.'

'Well we did Sexton get on to an art topic or two. And I do believe it is da Vinci and not do Vinci.'

'Well whether it's da or do, sure at the likes of them Swiss finishing schools not only would she know how to cook snipe or pigeon and see to the laying of a table but she'd have a little smattering of Homer and Cicero.'

'Well I don't know about Cicero but she did at least once allude to Homer and yes as a matter of fact she did lay rather a good table.'

'Ah Master Darcy sine dubio, sine dubio, there are possibilities there. Forgive me for referring and I do so with utmost gentlemanly respect, but a grander pair of thighs you'd only rarely ever see from one Spring Show to another. Can handle a horse like a puppet she can. Knows the meaning of the word cypripedium.'

44

'How do you know Sexton that she knows the meaning of the word cypripedium.'

'Well now I'll tell you, not only was I seeing her eyeing you in your pink coat when you made a showing yesterday at the meeting but wasn't I near by enough to help give her a leg up on that seventeen hand stallion of hers. And isn't she a smasher in her hunting habit. And even in a hair net you'd see that her bowler was capping a glorious head of hair. And I said to her while she was putting her fingers in the reins, Ma'am I said you're sitting as pretty as a cypripedium. And she said to me I do take that as a marvellous compliment, I do so adore orchids.'

'Well your English accent Sexton I must say is improving but I do wish the lot of you would let off in this attempt to get one married. And all this bloody gossip over my three days' indisposition at Dreamstown Park. Must I ad nauseam keep repeating that I just happened after dinner to want a breath of fresh air and out front of the house fell into an awful deep ditch, and the cracked ribs, dislocated shoulder and sprained wrists I got therefrom, which are all still most painful, prevented me from driving home.'

'Master Darcy a nod is as good as wink to a blind horse but nevertheless in three days a guest in the house you'd soon anyway know what was what about a lass.'

'You know Sexton I sometimes do wonder what it is that you yourself would want out of a wife or out of life for that matter.'

'Ah stop right there. A leading question. Or two leading questions.'

'Dear me Sexton you are in fact proposing nothing but leading questions to me.'

'Well now in answer to you then. Without writing a bible, I could give a few hints in a few words. From a wife there would be three things. Purity, loyalty and that she could feed the pigs, milk the cow and keep the clothes and the house neat and clean and mind the chickens.'

'Good lord Sexton that's at least eight things you require of a wife.'

'Nine. I forgot having the meals hot and ready on time. O and ten, keeping me socks darned. And I'd ask only from life the freedom to perform my religious duty and to save my immortal soul. To do no harm to any man other than he deserves it. And to be here in me potting shed and in the garden able to tend to my flowers and vegetables and be at peace with my thoughts.'

'Good bloody god Sexton, and pardon my French but that's asking for a bloody lot in this bloody modern world. Plus I'm sure you also want to extend the glass houses.'

'Ah and I do. Out there and along the wall for another sixty feet. But for me it's all I ask. And should it suddenly stop. Well I'm practical enough to accept the end. Sure isn't that the way the world goes. Like you'd dig my grave while I'm dying, to have it nice and ready.'

'Sexton we're not are we going to be lachrymose and mawkish.'

'Let me tell you Master Darcy. There's not a mite mawkish or lachrymose about the peace and joy I feel to be out there in the garden. Even in the rain and gales. And to be saying my stations of the cross. Only yesterday and it coming down in buckets I stood there. Contemplating that lovely compassionate woman. Veronica wipes the face of Jesus. Yes. You see tears in my eyes. And that's the depth of my wonderful, wonderful feeling. And Master Darcy if it ever be that you have bestowed upon you the blessing of a little daughter, please give consideration to that name. For out of such ancient sorrow she would be today's sunshine in life.'

A wind got up sudden and as Sexton spoke, out the window I could see the fog and mist clear away. My god he sometimes could go more than a little bit over the top. Just like his giant sunflowers that reached up fifteen feet tall to peek over the garden wall. But here he had hit upon something that made

46

me catch my breath. And were I to reveal that among Durrow-Mountmellton's Christian names was the name Veronica he would of course get absolutely ecstatically overwrought and urge me to rush up the aisle. Or were her middle name Mary Magdalen to run a mile. One must suppose Sexton in his celibate state tends to extol the desirability of matrimony. At least if he married he could get in bed with someone after saying his stations of the cross and after all the scourging and crucifixion, have a fuck. But poor man, he could end up with some nagging shrew. Despite that awful old Catholic codswallop connected with names, the name Veronica is better than being called Reginald as a boy. Amazing without the merest reference, what can be done to one. When so much of one's future lies ahead. You grow up innocently not knowing why you're ridiculed. And marriage I suspect, from what one already sees of it, is always going to be as if one has been sent out on a vast desert, confronting directional signs leading to oases and others pointing other ways out to nothing but sure slow death. And you know as you stand there that the signs might have been switched. And Sexton's life sine dubio is simply not going to be a happy one till we have conservatories and hothouses all along the garden walls chock full of cypripedium. And quite unbelievable come to think of it I can't recall after all these years, Sexton's middle Christian name.

'Ah now Master Darcy I'm not about to tell you that. Suffice it to say it's an unglamorous name enough. But now back to the business of marriage and weddings.'

'I'd rather not Sexton. One has had enough of that on the mind without its being further on one's lips as well. Indeed I'm sure ladies get equally bored with the subject.'

'Well I can tell you a little something on that. There's a young girl up in the town and she has no boyfriend at all. And she does on her afternoon off skivvying in the household of the dentist go on the train all the way up to Dublin. And there at a shop window she stations herself and stands for hours looking at the white bridal dresses.'

Again there were tears in Sexton's eyes. God he can be emotional. And once I recall seeing him by accident through a tiny hole in the garden wall at his last station of the cross, his head bent over, sobbing. It was one of those early summer long evenings when the leaves are first full green on the trees and the sky is clear and grown cold and it's as if the first night of winter is falling. It was also when something suddenly made me turn to look behind me. And there in the distance beyond where the hill slopes down to Andromeda Park's cemetery, and the bottom lands stretch in bogs to the edge of the lake, I saw the silhouette of a figure standing solitary and still in the fading light. And my heart began to thump, thump in my breast, a sudden panic overtaking me. Although far off the figure seemed so real. Standing motionless just as Leila often did with her aloof, dignified apartness. But then I thought that perhaps I was getting like Sexton and seeing the blessed virgin behind every tree. I had the urge to go towards the figure. But felt I would chase it away, as a hare frozen in alertness runs once one moves. I looked away and closed my eyes. Then opened and turned them back to where the figure had been and now the silhouette was gone. But my vision brought with it a strangely overwhelming sadness that brought tears into my eyes, realizing that I was seeing things only as one does from too long a time of living in the countryside. As often, when evening shadows fall, a tree, shrub or stump can look like a person, a ghost or monster. But I thought and hoped for more than a moment that who I had seen was Leila. And I know the direction on any desert I would have taken with that girl. Who still walks in my mind nearly every living moment of my day. See her dark eyes. Softly lurking beneath her pale brow. See her white teeth of her brilliant smile that radiated out all the sweet life within. It is with her that I could have lived here contented and happy at Andromeda Park. I so

48

miss her still. Purple ribbon in her soft dark flowing hair. She was my magic. Who without fakery vanished away. As do horses hoofs clattering at night on a distant country road. The faint clip clop growing fainter still. My miracle gone. And left me only her brave honesty. Under what part of the sky doth she be somewhere now. That I watch up at the wide spaces between the lonely stars at night. Where her spirit still dwells. And leaves me wondering.

Like
A magician
Fooled
By his own
Tricks

5

The autumn dawn mist slowly lifting from the sloping pastures and gardens surrounding Andromeda Park. An orange tint of sun flooding aslant on the lawns. A squeal of passing swans' wings in the sky. Darcy Dancer seated at one end of the long mahogany dining room table, the morning's opened letters on a salver and three newspapers folded to read at his elbow.

A click of heels outside along the hall and the door of the dining room swinging open. Rashers Ronald in an orange and brown checked tweed of hues squared off with a thin red line. The beige of his soft silk shirt, a large knot tied in his cerulean coloured tweed tie. A purple blue cornflower in his button hole. His eyebrows contracting seriously as he approaches the sideboard and sniffs his nose over each hot plate. The alcohol burners aflame under coffee and tureens of bacon and eggs, and racks of toast. Darcy Dancer clearing his throat. Rashers turning round. A broad grin breaking out across his ruddy complexioned face as he takes a sweeping bow and waves an arm with a glint of gold cuff links.

'Ah good morning Darcy my dear fellow. Didn't see you. And how good it is to see you. Along with this splash of sunshine over, dear me, is it an Axminster carpet. Or something more exotic. I do believe it might be. I was just reflecting upon what a most splendidly wonderful aroma it is to be greeted by as I am each and every morning. Bewley's coffee, breakfast blend I believe, is it not. Your dear Crooks didn't seem to be exactly certain of it.'

'Yes it is Rashers.'

'Ah I thought so. And then to such wonderful coffee to have added to it the immense pleasure of your dear presence. And what may I inquire brings you down from your apartments this pleasurable morning. We have rather got used to not seeing you till drinkies before lunch. Before you answer, do please excuse me just this moment. To bolster one's confidence in the mornings one likes to as soon as possible ladle out a plateful of poached eggs on soda bread toast and just here to spear a few butter balls to put on the edge of one's plate. Makes one recall our breakfasts together at the Shelbourne. O dear, isn't one an old sentimentalist. But now you may answer dear boy. And by the way I do think life here at Andromeda Park is simply idyllically adorable.'

'Well, I'm delighted it is idyllically adorable for someone. Since what brings me down early to breakfast are innumerable vexations various. One or two of which are contained in communications here at my elbow.'

'Dear boy turn eyes and thoughts immediately away. You must not make the awful mistake of allowing yourself to do anything more than to take a swift glance at such, only long enough to perceive they are unpleasant letters. Chuck them away dear boy. Into the nice blazing fire we have here this morning. That's what breakfast dining room fires are for my good fellow. To incinerate the disagreeable. Sending such in smoke up the chimney. My father always chucked his noxious letters in there. But I do believe once he also chucked in some very important army documents, from the War Office in fact. Could have been England's downfall. And except for his very senior rank he might have been court martialled. Of course I have long taken the precaution of not being at the address where such letters are sent in the first place. By jove there's a bit of frost this morning. Gets up the appetite a mite. And isn't it wonderful to look out these windows, and as far as the eye can see are your lawns, pleasure gardens and lands. But I do think. Just in that vista there. Out to the hill. You do need

51

an obelisk. An aesthetic erection so to speak. Not anything pretentious. Normal size would do. Now I'll just help myself here. My god what marmalade. Dark in colour, thick in texture. Pure nectar. Dear me I do approve of the way you live here Darcy. And please don't sit there so bloody silent. I should hate to think you're in the least bit sad. You're not are you.'

'Not particularly more so this morning than most mornings.'

'Your Crooks is such a darling fellow. Must be so useful with his crossed eyes to be able to keep one on the larder, the other on the kitchen, not to mention matters he must have to watch for in the pantry and wine cellars. But then that's what butlers' crossed eyes are for. And he knows to the exact degree of softness I prefer my eggs. Now dear boy to business. Namely the business of life. And the pursuit and preservation of comfortable habits. You are aren't you all mended up now from your fall in the ditch.'

'Yes I am Rashers. In body mended. However, in mind as usual I remain partially maimed.'

'Come, come my chap. Let us then get down to matters which really do matter over one's eggs. Talk to Doctor Happiness about it. Who is just breaking into this egg's cytoplasmic component and about to suck up from same this deeply golden and delicious yolk. And dear boy, are we perchance ready for the racing. I like the sound of the venue. Kilbeggan. To which I'm told one motors through a village called Horseleap. And how suitable. And I do have a few better than average tips. Understand there is to be a nag locally owned off whom, for the first time, the brakes are to be taken.'

'I'm not exactly sure I may attend Rashers.'

'What. Not go racing. Surely you must. Dear me you are serious these days. There's quite a troubled tone in your voice.'

'Well I can't say that facing my Friday weekly wages to be

paid plus an astronomical stack of bills for feedstuffs, fence-posts, tractor parts and repairs, blacksmith's and veterinary fees and legal threats concerning land puts me at my most cheerful. And even lengths of barbed wire being stolen off my fences. And as to the brakes being suddenly taken off any local horse I should be awfully damn suspicious.'

'Been studying the form since getting up dear boy. A mare bred by a quite famed name trusted in bloodstock circles across the length and breadth of Ireland.'

'And who on earth could that be locally pray tell.'

'Durrow-Mountmellton dear boy.'

'Good god, has she a horse running.'

'My dear boy you are, aren't you, out of it all and in rather a very bad way. Not to know of such matters under your very nose. Dreamstown Zephyr. By Golden Hero. Out of Cypripedium. A sprightly liver chestnut mare with nicely shaped ears. I mean the horse, the horse. But the lady too. Very stylish she is. Not only well shaped ears but well shaped. Rubbed elbows with her recently down the Hibernian's buttery. Dear me you did look up rather abruptly at that comment my dear Darcy. Rather as if you were jumpy about something. O my god, dear boy, I do not believe I have ever witnessed you blushing before.'

'I am not blushing.'

'O well must be the blaze of the fire on your face. But now as I see it you must seek out more leisure in your life and not be so bloody rural. Take your smart motor to go look over some likely stallions at stud to sire a couple of your own not unpromising mares I see in the stables. Be damned running high and low in your boots, waving a stick, chasing and counting bloody cattle.'

'Rashers these are half bred mares suitable only for hunting and as to those bloody cattle, they presently stand between me and a condition known as impoverishment and bankruptcy.'

'Well surely you have a herd to do such chores.'

'I had two herds. Both died within a minute of each other. One dropped dead while peeing on the rose garden. And the other one suffered a fatal heart attack while watching him out the window of a garden shed. And as to the stick I carry when counting cattle, it is in fact a gentleman's thistle cutter.'

'In nomine patris et filii et spiritus sancti, may those two souls rest in peace after their long lives of faithful toil to their benign master. O dear, but we are serious this morning. You see Darcy, it is only that I do so hate to see you demean yourself treading in cow pats and splashing about in farmyard muck. The whole point of country living is to disport in a manner which does not soil one's clothing or hands. Unless one is hunting, shooting or fishing of course. Indeed one should not allow too much bespattering even in the latter pursuits. And please, dear fellow cheer up. Especially with the birds chirping madly out under the clear skies. This point to point today is bound to attract at least a handful of people of poise, breeding and elegance. And racing circles are so wonderfully nice to rotate in. Look, a sunny day out there across the lawns.'

'Yes and I see two bloody damn horses loose.'

'O dear, but what can I say over my poached eggs. I suppose to my eyes all about here seems so agreeable. As I stood early dawn at my bedroom window I watched the jackdaws perched atop your trees, pecking holes in your apples. To you an unwelcome sight. But to me a pleasant scene in nature. And with the clouds pink in the sky and my prick perpendicularly quivering as hard as an American corn cob as it undroopingly saluted the birth of this beautiful morning, I did so in my heart rejoice. And dear boy, allowing yourself just to face troubles, one can go absolutely demented out of one's mind if one doesn't get light relief once in a while. Dear me, don't stare. Come now. Isn't that true.'

'I am listening Rashers.'

'Of course I do allow that your bohemian guest Lois is

rather a good laugh, among other things of course. She makes not a jot of effort to look beautiful but what a damn handsome figure of a woman she is. And making an absolutely marvellous job of your portrait. You look quite splendid in your Master's kit. She, I am sure, must help brighten the shadows. And that's precisely why Darcy I feel you ought to consider adding the other half to your life.'

'What. Good god. Hitch up with Lois.'

'Ah not that bad an idea dear boy. But inspired by certain rumours flying about, I do mean to present a different possibility. And ask you to consider for instance such a comely lady as Felicity Veronica Durrow-Mountmellton, only seven or eight miles away.'

'Ten miles and three quarters as a matter of fact.'

'Ah I see you already have it nicely measured. What a good start. Well just imagine. An heiress. You both sit down together to add up your cattle, pigs, chickens, damson and apple trees. And never mind all the blackberries gushing out of your miles of respective hedgerows. Then with the hefty sum totals staring you both optimistically in the face and with your better class of marriage broker called in to attend and advise, it might be construed that an understanding between you might be in order. With her mare Dreamstown Zephyr and your stallion Midnight was it Madness or Lightning, anyway Midnight something, the pair of you turn out foals fetching monstrous prices at Newmarket. You might even further barrel up the name of your heirs. I always feel the triple barrelled name is more socially piquant than the more common double barrelled variety. Think of it, two great country landowning families joined. Durrow-Mountmellton-Kildare. Rings with an awe inspiring profundity. And dear me, it could lead to another wonderful solution. Go reside at Dreamstown. Sell up Andromeda Park here. On the proceeds, winter in Monte Carlo. I'll come and be a guest or travel with you on the Orient Express any time you need me.'

55

'I will never sell.'

'Dear me dear boy, you're expressing that in what I feel is a rather unnecessarily emphatic fashion.'

'That may be Rashers but also let me emphatically add that this talk is as highly embarrassing as it is hypothetical. And the Orient Express does not as far as I know go to Monte Carlo.'

'But of course it does if you change at the right station. And I am sorry dear fellow if I've trod on what appears to be sensitive territory. Do please just tell me to shut up.'

'Shut up.'

'Ah of course I shall. And change the subject entirely. Do I by any chance perceive stuck under your elbow there a genuine copy of the *Daily Telegraph*.'

'Yes you do. And it is three days old.'

'Ah, no matter its age. Such a reassuring British newspaper is timeless. Might you when you're finished pass it up here. Just to read the In Memoriams, my dear boy. I gain so much confidence from them.'

'I thought your plateful of poached eggs gave you your confidence Rashers.'

'Ah a punch below the belt my friend, a low blow which I shall of course let pass over, since as your guest I can hardly do otherwise unless I want to see myself sent packing down your front steps and, enfeebled by my wretchedness, stumble a mile or more to your front gates and then find myself out again upon the harsh road of life. But you see, the poached eggs do really give me confidence. However, this morning as yet I see none of the usual delicious sausages stacked up on your sideboard and upon which I like to munch so they may go in culinary chorus, as it were, down the hatch with my poached eggs.'

Darcy folding the newspaper in a neat little square and, with a backhanded wave of his arm, flicking it flying up the dining room table over the candelabrum. Landing it with a thwack in the broken yolks of Rashers's poached eggs.

'O dear my dear Darcy that nearly leaves one, as the expression goes, with egg on one's face. And despite its finding its way into my breakfast I do so love this newspaper. It calls to book perpetrators against our way of life. Remaining a bright beacon in the dark depressing sea of socialism they say is creeping towards us across Europe. And I do know it may as a periodical occasionally tend to overly expose those who should not do what they do to choirboys in their charge. And others who may not uphold the dignity of their rank as we might wish. Ah but let me just read to you here. Listen to this very first of the In Memoriams. Darling Gwendoline, tread softly for you are treading on my heart. How sadly beautiful, don't you agree. Darcy, I should treasure the knowledge that when I am passed away someone would remember me thus.'

'I shall Rashers. In fact not only will I publish an In Memoriam in the *Daily Telegraph* but shall also provide for you, if you like, a grave here at Andromeda Park.'

'Would you dear boy. Would you really.'

'Consider it done. I'll have the site marked off this morning.'

'Good god Darcy don't do that.'

'Why not.'

'Tempting fate dear boy. Tempting fate. I'm too young, simply too tender yet of years, to even contemplate actually having a final resting place, which might indeed act as an encouragement to avail of it.'

'But surely Rashers you're finally going to need one.'

'I may not. I may drown myself in the sea at Monte Carlo as I've already once attempted.'

'Nevertheless Rashers I think it entirely appropriate that I provide you with a grave site. And you need not think of it again for fifty or sixty years. Stonemason in town will carve your title on a suitable monument. We might have, "Here lie the mortal remains of that crusty old aristocrat, Lord Ronald

Ronald, who throughout his life remained true to his own kind".'

'Just a moment dear boy. Just a moment, here please do take back your newspaper. And you Darcy soon seem to have damned well cheered up a mite on this subject haven't you.'

'Rashers I'm only trying to do you a good turn.'

'A good turn. You mean organizing a plan to clap me into the bloody ground. I think I might prefer at the moment to leave that discussion to a later date. And instead dip my sticky fingers into the finger bowl. And one does appreciate the flower petals. But back to you dear boy, one does hear rumours. Now while I'm chewing my bacon, why not come out with it all to your most anciently loyal friend. What's this about the little matter of your seriously considering the state of matrimony. Dare I think, aside from burying me, it one of your presently imponderable worries.'

'Rashers apart from my being far too young to marry I haven't even managed yet a second cup of coffee.'

'Here, do please allow me while I'm getting one for myself. I do believe, as one has heard from your most attractive sisters, that you are in the market for a lady of extensive property such as yourself. And as it should be of course.'

'Now Rashers for god's sake let's be quite clear on one thing. My sisters, who think this is some kind of watering place with free board and lodging between balls in London, and a house in which to entertain their friends at my expense, do concoct the most ridiculous stories which are designed to suit their own ends.'

'O dear. I am sorry. Forgive me. And please, would you mind if I rang for more of this marmalade which if I'm not mistaken has had its piquancy enhanced by a spot of whiskey. I do believe I just press twice with my foot this button under the rug.'

Darcy Dancer bending his head down over his coffee and toast. The pantry door opening. Crooks, a small towel over his arm. His fly buttons undone as he stands inclining towards Rashers Ronald. And had I rung I might be waiting a half an hour or so.

'You rang Lord Ronald.'

'Yes I did Crooks. Might one trouble you for some more of this delicious marmalade.'

'Immediately milord. And good morning Master Reginald, I didn't see you up there at that end of the table.'

Amazing how one's guests manage to extract such attention from one's staff. And one nearly feels as if I am intruding upon Rashers's privacy, which he has obviously been enjoying here in the dining room of a morning. And Rashers my god so insouciantly masquerading under his title. No wonder the whole bloody place is in turmoil with himself and Lois between them having everyone at their beck and call. O misery. How does one enjoy one's breakfast. Each several months, having sooner than one had planned, been forced, with the same speed that the slates are falling, to sell more of my lovely mother's jewels to keep this damn place going. I suppose I am really rather desperate. And in the sphere of fortune hunting there is no greater expert in this world than the man who sits down the table from me now. God knows how many pots of marmalade he has polished off. And I suppose at least one should perhaps get some advice in return.

'Well my dear Darcy. Since you in fact are nowhere near contemplating such a drastic step as matrimony perhaps I should not at this time proffer my advice.'

'Rashers please don't let me stop you making any comments I know you are absolutely dying to make on the subject.'

'First my dear boy let me just say I just simply can't get over your marmalade. Your Catherine the cook, a gem dear boy, a gem. Now then. Yes. Before we got sidetracked upon the matter of my final resting place. I was about to offer my feeble comments on the state of matrimony. Ah yes. Step one. There must be some written understanding straight off between the parties. Inheritance rights and all that sort of thing. Then a complete tabulation as to acreage, horses, cattle, pigs, chickens, damson and apple trees. And for god's sake don't overlook mineral rights under the land. And the furniture dear boy. Marvellous examples abound within this house. From the graceful rococo to pieces celebrating neo classical restraint. Plus an important library spanning fields of literature, science and travel. And precisely such things should not be overlooked in your betrothed's assets. Then with the particulars of same, all should be engrossed under seal on the usual vellum. Of course you want to make absolutely sure the lands are of mostly limestone underlay and well watered, but naturally, as one might expect, such lands perhaps will not be as well drained as might be hoped for.'

'Rashers I do think this is awfully mournfully mercenary talk this early in the day.'

'Ah dear boy you know I am the very last mortal in the world who would press upon you such a subject if I did not feel that you were not fully ready to tackle it. But marriage down through the ages has always been the method by which great fortunes are to be had, or in your case preserved. Please. Confide in me. Know that I above all other people have your most dearest interests at heart. Do let me counsel you. I think I may fairly regard myself as a bit of an authority on such matters. As heinous as it may be, times do come when it is mandatory to have to size up an individual's wherewithal. Somehow when the parting of the parties becomes an issue, land, assets, chattels and livestock, no matter how deep the previous love, always seem to surface and become a subject taken with the utmost seriousness. Not to mention hysterical violence in some cases. But I shall be quiet a moment while we both meditate and chew a bit.'

Upon a long elliptical slice of toasted soda bread, Rashers spreading three butter balls and spooning out on his side plate three heaped spoonfuls of marmalade placed in front of him by Crooks with a deep bow. The dark thick chunks of orange peel blanketed upon the butter. And all lifted up to this mouth so full of wisdom. But dear me Rashers does make an awful lot of noise in the enjoyment of breakfast. And is making even more noise pushing back his chair.

'Ah the moment has come. Just perhaps a little prematurely this morning with all our little talk about matrimony. If you'll excuse me dear boy, I must visit the water closet.'

'Do take some marmalade with you Rashers, and don't forget a spoon.'

Rashers making for the door and stopping midway. The boy butler entering from the pantry with a tureen of sizzling sausages. Rashers plucking one between his fingers, biting it in half and wiping his fingers in his blue polka dot handkerchief and seizing another. His footsteps hurrying away outside down the hall.

'Sir I am sorry for the delay with the sausages. The stove had to be got up hot again to get them cooked.'

'Bring them here please. And I do think perhaps Damian you could spruce up a little more. Especially while we are having guests. Your cuffs shouldn't have the threads hanging down and be in that green condition as I do believe that shirt is intended to be white.'

'They did be getting in the spinach soup I was serving sir.'

'But when was that.'

'It was sir the last Wednesday.'

'But that's a week ago. And that's still the same shirt you're wearing.'

'It is sir.'

'Well do change and have it washed.'

'It's me only shirt sir. Like the suit it was given me by Mr Crooks sir. When down the cellars I had only on me some rough old rags.'

'Surely Crooks has another shirt for you. And have Norah or Catherine see to putting the cuffs right. We must be smart.

And you must remember not to handle the plates with two hands and to serve guests from their left. And see a serving spoon is always in the bowl.'

'Lord Rashers sir said —'

'Lord Ronald.'

'Lord Ronald sir said he like to grab holt of his potato with his bare fingers.'

'Never mind what Lord Ronald said.'

'Yes sir. But sir I am not yet trained up. And her ladyship said she is requiring my attention sir. As I am busy keeping her ladyship warm. With the turf sir. It does be burning very fast and she would have me heap it up on the fire sir. I have only this minute put a basket up there.'

'Well now get more coffee please.'

Darcy Dancer frowning and grunting and spearing a sausage. Damian bowing his head and shuffling backwards towards the pantry door. The tongue of a shoe hanging out over its loose laces.

'Sir I would be delaying a bit with the coffee her ladyship is requiring me again upstairs.'

'Not when you are required to fetch more coffee. And what does her ladyship require you for.'

'She says sir, it is for the art's sake.'

'What's for art's sake.'

'She would ask me to pose.'

'Is that why the sausages are late. Speak up. Is that why the sausages Lord Ronald was waiting for are late. Bring more coffee here and I think you had better report to Crooks. And let's have no more fibs, do you understand.'

'Yes sir.'

Darcy Dancer spearing another sausage. Chewing the spicy meat and taking the last mouthful of his coffee. Yummy. In spite of staff behaviour bordering on insolence, the meaty content of the sausages tastes uncommonly good this morning. But my god. God knows what must go on when I'm not here.

62

The cheek, Lois commandeering the household. And bloody well painting pictures of them. And it will be a miracle if that's all that nymphomaniac is doing. One could see fifty lies formulating in the boy butler's crafty mind before he could choose one he thought was furthest from the truth. So many lies exchange in this household that it's a wonder that the place can keep going. Is it even possible to imagine Lois ever could have been a wife even for five minutes. Now I'm faced with the prospect that she may never be dislodged. Her apartments are already being kept like some attic atelier in Paris. But my god, although she is rather getting on a bit, she is, as Rashers says, an uncommonly handsome woman. With never a trace of rouge or make up on her face. And even in the most unfeminine long underwear she makes one's pecker perk up. But bloody hell I won't have it if she's corrupting my servants with her bohemian bloody habits. She was one awful coward the night we battled a rat in her studio back in Dublin. O god, such thoughts. I suppose it's time to look back at my newspaper even if it is the *Irish Times*. Perhaps put an ad in the matrimonial columns. Country gent desperate to combine elegance and fucking in one arrangement requires lady capable of administering large household where enormous useless staff are kept. Must speak French, knowledge of wine and Latin an asset. Must be able to look radiantly beautiful and to receive gentleman's guests and provide witty conversation when owner is suffering severe depressions. Plus able to diplomatically terminate the presence of guests who have overstayed their welcome. Dear me one may have to search the entire world for the perfect wife who knows her furniture, paintings and architecture. And I have not even been to Bangkok yet where the ladies know how to make love. Some sort of oriental princess might do if she could get her vowels and diphthongs correctly spoken and not all the time have to appear in a silk kimono.

'O there you are Darcy. I just knocked at your door to see if you were up.'

63

'Dear me. Good morning Lois. I was just thinking of you.'

'How nice. Well I need you dear boy at least an hour today. To touch up on your coat. And your lips are not yet quite right. They appear too pursed. Of course you do purse your lips. I hope that awful man is not here.'

'What awful man.'

'That awful impostor, Rashers. A philistine. May I sit here.'

'But of course. I thought you were breakfasting in your room.'

'Well I was, but I was also getting nervous waiting, very nervous. I do think the countryside makes me nervous and you country people.'

'Ah not like Montparnasse.'

'If I may say so, nothing could be further from being like Montparnasse. With a most bloodcurdling sound in the night. Unearthly.'

'A vixen barking.'

'Good god is that what that is. But don't misunderstand me I am very happy here. But that awful man. The nerve. He proposed I do a portrait of him, life sized, and offered me a fiver. Can you imagine, a fiver.'

'Well we know what your prices are Lois don't we.'

'Don't say it in that tone of voice dear boy. I highly resent any imputation that I am for sale in any guise whatsoever. If someone is intelligent enough to buy one of my pictures the price is merely a gesture.'

'Well perhaps Rashers is making a gesture in suggesting a fiver.'

'Well he may keep his bloody fiver.'

Outside a sudden wind rattling the window panes. Darcy Dancer glancing up from his plate. Lois bent over hers. And my god three poached eggs, two slices of bacon, four pieces of toast. And now she's plonking a dollop of whipped cream on top her eggs. Add Rashers's appetite to Lois's and by god it would take one cow alone to keep the pair of them in milk, cream and cheese. An entire twelve hundredweight bullock has been consumed by the denizens and guests at Andromeda Park in exactly ten days, with now another beast slaughtered hanging by the hind legs out in a shed. At this rate I am going to need all the Durrow-Mountmellton assets I can get. O god. What a slip of the mind that was. And presently randy as I am, I am also going to be glad to get her body. I must be severely panicked for such a thought to get into my head. Why must everything be so bloody materialistic. What of course could happen is, I could run entirely out of money before I get to Paris or London to find a young virgin heiress. And instead be doomed here selling off the carpets and the place falling down in ruin around one. But then, in spite of injuries that first fatal night upon my invitation to supper, one did at least see eye to eye with old Durrow-Mountmellton on a lot of things. We have in common our backgrounds. I mean you don't find rippling strong muscular bellies on every woman, and to go with it, a courageously exciting manner with which she and her horse burst holes in hedgerows. And when the fire flames were lighting the bedroom walls, she pulled back the eiderdown and opened apart old Major D.M.'s pyjamas and forthrightly grasped my private. And what a pleasurable sight to watch her totally absorbed, and so damn affectionately caressing the tip of my prick back and forth against the nipple tips of her bosoms. And just as the tiniest bit of blood was trickling out of one of her deeper scratches. O precious blood, as Sexton might say, saying his stations of the cross. I mean if one is drinking decent port and there's a sufficient stretch of roof intact over one's head and one is exploding in ecstasy like taking a snipe out of the sky with a shotgun blast. And milkily anointing such splendid bosoms. Why not simply accept such exaltation. Which provides something more and equally milky for one to add to one's escutcheon. And we lay back upon the bed, glued together with

65

sweat, side by side. And as my old nanny used to say, all between us was fair, firm and friendly. What more can one ask of life after a good supper. Except perhaps a pure bred beautiful slave who would soothe and caress one to sleep and work without remuneration in return for a little kindness and consideration.

'Dear boy you seem awfully absorbed with your thoughts up at that far end of the table.'

'Sorry Lois, I suppose I was for a moment.'

'Well would you pass me your salt cellar, this one of mine seems all out. And by the way that houseboy, Damian. An orphan I understand.'

'Yes. A bastard as a matter of fact. Parents unknown. They gave him the name O'Hanlon. Why do you ask.'

'O no reason really.'

The dining room door pushing slowly open. Rashers Ronald shuffling in, his head bent and a pair of glasses propped on the end of his nose as he looks down upon a red leather bound folder embossed with gold lettering open in his hands.

'Well Darcy I have just been viewing your racing calendar while having one awfully good, marvellously satisfying shit. O I do beg your pardon Lois I didn't see you. Please forgive me my inappropriate remark.'

'Well you might at least wait to find out before entering a room to whom your remarks might be addressed. No wonder one finds you insufferably rude at times.'

'Well of course my dear old tired tits, one does try to avoid being discourteous, but I'm also damn well trying to assess the bloody blood lines of today's runners. However, I do offer again my humblest abject apologies for announcing my having had a damn good shit.'

'Well as for the subject matter of your announcement, I hardly need to be apologized to as it is the first I've heard of something concerning you of which I'm sincerely envious. And as to being referred to as tired old tits. I'll have you know

66

my breasts have been painted by every major artist in Montparnasse. And in Parisian artistic circles they have achieved a reputation as possibly being the most beautiful pair of bosoms in Europe. And such paintings are on the walls in the Louvre as proof. And as I should not like to put you to the trouble of offering your apologies yet again, I accept those already proffered.'

'Thank you madam. I had no idea, absolutely, that your tits were hanging in the Louvre. And of course no one would dream of ever thinking that you were nothing but a dirty old sleazebag. On the contrary you are an extremely handsome woman. You see, with the door half opened and having just previously chosen a winner for today's point to point during a strategic moment of defecation, my enthusiasm couldn't be contained. Ah but I'm so glad that there might be something in which you envy me. I'm especially further delighted to know that rather than a pair of haggardly drooping tired old boobs, that you instead possess the most beautiful pair in Europe and that they can be feasted upon by the naked eye all over the what surely is considered one of the world's greatest museums. Ah but now, as for having a good shit. The secret is immensely simple. I take it you're a bit cemented up in that region are you. Well have no further worries. Cabbage leaves. Lois. Cabbage leaves. They'll blast a way through for you. And if not fresh cabbage leaves, then as sauerkraut. Kaboom. Plenty sauerkraut and kaboom, kaboom.'

'I do hope you're finished. I find this highly unappetizing talk at the breakfast table most thoroughly disagreeable.'

'Ah Darcy. I do love Lois here. And these artistic circles she moves in. And in which I must make a point of mixing more. Now Lois, my delightful dirty old sleazebag, and I use that purely as a term of affection of course. I understand that your wash studies of the male figure rampant are much in demand.'

'As a matter of fact they are. And as to the figure being

rampant that is simply a matter of accident. But of course the rigidity of the erect penis, especially those with a slight curvature, creates tension of line.'

'Ah we have unearthed here an artistic secret. Tension of line. By god now that's exactly what's needed Lois, I think, in my portrait. But Lois does that mean one may have to sustain an erection for hours on end. And also what about the foreskin. Mine is quite of an old leathery type. Should the penis be worn in its scabbard, as it were, or should that protective membrane be retracted.'

'In one second I shall throw this toast at you. And if I may call you Rashers, I would also have you know Rashers that I have no desire whatever to have your old leathery foreskin flapping or penis waving at me, never mind painting it.'

'Well now with my hopes dashed at least we have made our diplomatic peace here on this wonderful morning. And even, I venture to think, settled upon a few artistic principles which I shall in future apply to my discussions on art. And Darcy now that there is to be no more talk about my final resting place, I shall once again open your beautifully bound racing calendar, to which I have been referring while in the water closet. I do think we have before us in the next few weeks some of the most marvellous fixtures to attend. Phoenix Park, Fairyhouse, The Curragh. What. And Lois we must you know travel to France. Where the racing can be at its most elegant. Longchamps and Chantilly.'

'O well if I am invited I should of course go. One would so dearly like to return to and sit in one's favourite café in Montparnasse, where my arthritis simply vanishes.'

'Of course you're invited Lois. A good old bag of cabbage leaves will accompany us both. You see Lois the sigmoid flexure is the narrowest part of the colon. Forms a loop. Turds must navigate it. Mucho roughage. And presto. We shall the two of us have an awfully thoroughly good shitting time in those old squatting latrines where, if one is not

68

careful, the flushed water runs up over one's ankles. Ah viva la Paris. Not only rid of all arthritic aches and pains in the bones but of any concrete-like constipations up the backside. And imagine Lois. Just imagine. We may now also have the pleasure of popping into the Louvre to get a prolonged pleasant eyeful of your immortalized tits hanging there. Indeed might we expect to observe tension of line in an erected nipple or two. What.'

'In exactly one second from now I shall, if you dare continue and if I am forced to, get up from my chair, and I shall slap your face. I have had sufficiently enough shitty times in my life without your adding another shitty time to it with you in Paris.'

'O dear, O dear. Well then. If one must travel alone to Paris, and if we are to enjoy the splendour of your bosoms. But we must then know the name of the artist and the painter. Or do we presume to merely ask at the door of the Louvre for the Mona Lois instead of the Mona Lisa. And at this juncture I will I think have some sausages.'

'You my dear boy will also soon surely get yourself a bloody slap in the face.'

'Please. Lois. Do. You must slap me if you think I deserve it. And I assume your favourite café in Paris is La Coupole.'

Rashers putting aside the racing calendar. Damian entering with racks of fresh toast and another tureen heaped full of sausages. Good god as well as his green bloody cuffs, he's flushing crimson all over his face at the sight of Lois. Who in spite of her thick grey jersey and numerous underlays, hasn't entirely hidden the fact that she indeed has a pair of wonderful tits somewhere buried deep under all that wool. But if this bloody woman is corrupting my staff I shall bar my doors forever more to her. The infernal cheek. Here in a commissioned professional capacity. No wonder bloody hell that nuisance of a boy has been delayed up in her bloody room. An absolute inveterate prick painting nymphomaniac she is. And

69

now bloody hell, Rashers is baiting her. And would you believe it, also sucking up to her and inviting her bloody well to Paris. Good god and Crooks. He's been behaving strangely recently too. His fly constantly open. One must look at the world in the cold light of day. And if one does, one finds everyone scheming and up to crafty tricks. My god, how does one keep a moral standard up in this house. The way things are going if I do hire a housekeeper she is going to have to march the halls with eyes in the back of her head and carrying a whip to keep the bloody inmates of this mansion in line. Before it becomes a bourse for harlotry and the place takes on the proportions of the sort of thing going on down in the Catacombs in Dublin. Or reaches the heights of perversion such as the sheep rogering old Major Durrow-Mountmellton got up to at Dreamstown Park. But there is no doubt on one score. From my memory of them Lois does easily have the most beautiful tits in Europe. There may be just the teeniest weeniest fraction of pendulousness. But my god just recalling her in her g string at one of her parties doing a fandango back and forth, castanets clattering and wagging her tits in some poor sod's face, who was in fact deputy manager of a prominent drapery, who with his prick out suddenly ejaculated all over the floor. Lois then flying into a foot stamping rage over his having messed her red and gold fine old saddlecloth, which, with her Afghan rug, was her last remaining heirloom. And which, in spite of its small size, the draper managed to desecrate dead centre.

'Ah how nice Lois and Darcy, to be at breakfast with you two dear people. And on such a fine day. You see Lois we were only a moment ago discussing my final resting arrangements in Darcy's very attractive little cemetery and I wonder with your arthritis acting up, have you yourself yet made any plans.'

'For your insulting information my arthritis is not quite that bad. Dear me. And as for death. I dismiss it from my mind entirely.'

70

'Lois I had in fact early been saying to Lord Ronald here that I would provide him with a grave and suitable headstone. And the invitation goes, without saying, to you as well.'

'How very nice of you dear boy. And I'm sure it is entirely well meant. But I do expect to live long enough to at least once see the Prado and also to be walking down the Rue Pigalle and climbing the steps of the Sacre Cœur many times more before I contemplate arrangements for my final resting place. But if you don't mind, I think I'd very much like to change the subject. Racing might be more my cup of coffee this morning. Although I abhor the type who pursue such pastimes to the exclusion of all else.'

'Of course Lois you old sleazebag unlike Darcy and I, finally mouldering in the grave, you will always have your tits still pink and nipples sparkling there on the walls of the old bloody Louvre during opening hours with a constant little audience of heavy breathing gents foaming at the mouth, their flies open and wanking away.'

'I did warn you.'

Lois jumping up from her chair, barging past Damian at the sideboard, who winced backwards, thinking it was himself who was to be struck. Rashers a grin of disbelief on his face, rearing up in his chair and flopping back down again. Lois winding up. Leaning forward and her outstretched arm sweeping in a great arc. Kaboom. Someone must have just seen stars. The bloody woman has a right hand that could fell an ox.

'Ah Lois my dear dirty old sleazebag with the tired old tits, you have finally dared to strike me.'

'Yes I have and I shall strike you again if you don't shut up.'

'Well you are an old whore Lois. Who in Dublin hasn't already had his prick unlimited distances up you and his balls jangling in your own anciently leathery bifurcation.'

Another blow landing across Rashers's cheek. Rocking him

71

rearwards and nearly tipping him backwards over his chair. Lois's eyes blazing as she reaches for Rashers's plate. O lord she is. Picking it up. And my god. Pushing it. Poached eggs, sausages, butter balls and all. Right into Rashers's face.

'For god's sake Lois. You must control yourself, Rashers is only being conversationally convivial.'

'Well I'm only being lightheartedly jovial in return. And have simply plastered that lot into his insulting face.'

Rashers with his napkin, slowly wiping away the blinding egg yolk and licking grease from his lips and leaning forwards to grasp the pitcher of cream, which indeed, according to Rashers, an expert on such things, having swiped and pawned some, was made by Walker in 1732. And is among one of Andromeda Park's best pieces of silverware. Which, with a wave of arm, splatters the contents over Lois. And is putting white spots on the portrait of my dear old granny. And bloody hell they've now come to hair pulling grips. With the gap toothed boy butler Damian stupidly grinning all over his face while the coffee jug is hanging loose in his hand, spilling coffee down over his feet and all over one of my bloody best carpets.

'Damian stop spilling the coffee, and just don't stand there. Ring down to the kitchens.'

'Sir I wouldn't now be knowing how to be ringing down to the kitchens.'

'The knob there. Bloody right beside you by the chimney piece. For god's sake pull it.'

Tripping over a chair leg, Darcy Dancer coming down from his end of the table. A thump on the floor. Rashers, a sausage in his mouth, falling over backwards. Lois on top of him. A crash of dishes. Not only do my guests eat everything in the place but now with my help included they're breaking everything as well. And clearly no one gives a precious damn about my rugs or mahogany surfaces. Never mind my treasures of silverware.

72

'You old treacherous slut you. By jove how dare you assault a peer of the realm. Get off me. You daft thing.'

'I'll teach you, you bumptious philistine impostor not to be impudent to me.'

'Darcy damn girl is choking me.'

'You bet I am.'

Darcy Dancer tugging at the grey woollen thickness across Lois's shoulders. Good lord she really is really strong. Actually wrestling Rashers to the floor. Thank god I've never had to fight her. Or have I. Good god. Lois is throttling him. And like a foolish chivalrous gentleman Rashers is making no effort to protect himself. Dear me he's gasping. I just remembered. Lois in her sculpturing days developed the forearms of a blacksmith. Perhaps just let her turn Rashers blue first and then I shall try to prise her hands from his throat. At least with the pair of them like this on the floor no more furniture is being ruined. Or silverware dented. Ah she's let go. But dear me. Rashers is still and motionless on the carpet. I've left it too long. Only now my god Lois has got hold of the tureen of sausages. And she's going to. O no.

'Don't for god's sake Lois don't.'

'Well dear boy I won't for your sake. Dump this whole grease laden writhing lot on his poor old face as it so richly deserves.'

'And not to mention my carpet Lois. Plus I've hardly had a decent taste of them.'

'Sir should I run get the priest to himself his Lordship for the last rites.'

'No Damian. He's a pagan. Just bloody yank the bell again and give me the bellows.'

Darcy Dancer putting the bellows in Rashers's mouth and pumping the air in and out. Rashers's eyes opening. A flushing pink colour coming back into his face. Lois with a place mat, fanning him on the floor. The corners of Rashers's jaws beginning to chew again. Lois tugging at Darcy Dancer's arm.

73

'Is he all right. Dear me. I simply don't know my own strength. I did rather lose my temper. Of course it was in the midst of the most severe provocation.'

Rashers wiping his moustache with jacket sleeve. And opening and closing his mouth to test the continuing effectiveness of his jaw muscles and sitting upright to readjust the purple blue cornflower in his button hole.

'You did Lois, you awful old sleazebag, rather put my jaw sockets out of place. And your bloody fingers are like a pair of farrier's tongs.'

Faces at the dining room doorway. And more appearing at the pantry entrance. Catherine wiping a nervous hand back and forth on her apron. Crooks, his fly even wider open and his crossed eyes distinctly more crossed. Upstairs maids Norah and Sheila. Even Dingbats in hair curlers. This is like the monthly staff review which I've failed to have for the past five months. When one seemingly hopelessly suggests that a new era of efficiency and promptitude has dawned and one attempts to put a new fear of god up the staff. When instead I should be trying to put it up one's guests to stop them murdering each other. Only missing is poor old Edna Annie who no longer has the strength to climb the stairs out of her two steamy laundry rooms.

'Now everybody please may go about their business. Lord Ronald is quite all right now. Just a sudden fainting fit brought on by a spot of gristle in a sausage and an ensuing nervous palpitation resulting upon its catching in his throat.'

As the figures withdraw back into the hall and the others into the pantry, Crooks remaining to clap his hands to Damian, who jumps to attention and follows behind Crooks out the pantry door. Darcy Dancer watching Rashers lick the grease out of his moustache. Lois pushing back her sweater sleeves on her truly muscled forearms. A deer suddenly stopping midway out on the parkland. Looking this way. The sun catching upon its antlers. Of course it's wondering what on earth is going on in this dining room.

'And now Lois and Rashers, if you'll both excuse me, I think I must presently go deal with some rather indelicate farm chores and leave you two to your further animated conversation.'

'Dear boy, did I hear you say indelicate.'

'You did Lois.'

'Precisely what sort of indelicacy do you refer to, as I am rather at a loose end for subjects for my sketch book.'

'Well Lois, I can't really feel this is a matter for your sketch book.'

'Why ever not.'

'We are as a matter of fact dehorning and castrating.'

'O I should be most interested to watch.'

'Well I'm not sure how the men will take it.'

'You're certainly not castrating your men, so why should they mind.'

'God Lois you are sometimes really the limit. I should have thought you'd had quite enough imbroglio without now wanting to witness gore and a necessary cruelty to animals. It so happens that squeezing testicles on the cattle appears rather a private chore the men seem to take genuine pleasure from. Indeed it is the most festive of nearly all our farm occasions.'

And
Something you might
Try on Rashers
If you ever
Get to
Montparnasse
Together

6

I had just this morning in the mirror noticed two highly conspicuous grey hairs growing out of the side of my head. And seeking where silence might reign in order to take some quiet repose one did, following the dining room contretemps and one's own visit to the water closet, tip toe down the main stair and along the ballroom hallway to the library. With one's spirits in one awful slump, I turned the key and locked myself in. A positively strange sensation overcoming me. And bloody well not all that strange either. One realized suddenly one couldn't stand the sight of another guest or member of staff. It must be how one must feel in the jungle, at least from some films one has seen, covered in leeches. And one tries to hysterically tear them off. And yet finds them more attached to suck one's blood and bleed one white.

Darcy Dancer taking a match from a box of matches adorned with a picture of a little sailing ship. With masts and rigging but without any ocean waves. Whoever makes these must be getting rich, as allowed to get damp this is the seventh match I am about to strike. Ah success. But wouldn't you know whoever set this fire made sure one would die of cold before it ever radiated out some warmth from its flames. And who in bloody hell has burnt a hole in the side of the bellows which is blasting only ash now up into my face. O god just let me sit down. Splay out my hands on the shiny worn leather to stop me sinking further into utter abysmal despair. Amid all these ancient bindings of books the contents of which, except for Mr Arland's little tome on homoeopathy, can advise me of absolutely nothing. At the moment I need a cure for acute melancholia, chronic itch in the arse and nasal catarrh. Dear me I do so miss Mr Arland. His counsel was always so calm, elegant and wise. But at my age I suppose it is no longer appropriate to have a tutor in residence upon whose mental and moral advice one would have to depend. And perhaps I need remember only what Sexton said recently as I returned from finding another day old calf way out beyond the deer park, drowned in a pond. 'Ah now Master Darcy, as Homer said, "Singula de nobis anni praedantur eventes." Which not that loosely translated means, years as they pass plunder us of one thing after another.'

Of course it wasn't a year that had passed, it was only two bloody days previous that a yearling foal, standing out front of the house in the middle of the park sniffling from its nose, had keeled over dead from pneumonia. Yet as Sexton also said, if we had no bad news we'd be having no news at all. But I suppose I know what is and shall remain the greatest plundering of anything in my life. To have vanished from it the body and spirit and dark haired exquisite beauty of Leila. Taken from me. Her absence leaving a monstrous loneliness and a lingering pain. Simply to know she was somewhere under this roof. Where I would by any excuse try to have her near me. Her courage. Her wonderful anger, aiming poker swipes as she saved my life from attackers. It was in this very room that we had our first real conversation and as master and servant even took together a glass of port which she held in her trembling red chilblained hand. And whose body I had never caressed or even touched. Not even the tips of my fingers ever reached as they did once to rest on the back of her hand. And O god how I longed to enfold my arms around her straight slim, shy form. Which so independently walked the floors of this house and made everything tolerable from dawn till dusk and through my dreams at night. And then as the months passed and the hurt healed a little, there were still all those

77

terrible hours of agonizing jealousy spent knowing the lips of another were pressed on hers. So full of snobberies, I had not back then thrown myself at her feet and asked her to marry me. And she now a marchioness. Who has left my life a cemetery of dead dreams.

A creak of floorboards out in the hall. A rattling and click of the library doorknob. So much for reverie. In this room sacred to the memory of Leila. Where I should keep it entirely out of bounds by informing guests dry rot had recently made the floorboards treacherous and unseen under the rugs, they could tread through and could end up in the cobwebs and darkness of the cellar with splinters up their arse. But instead here comes an intrusion. And at such times one must be as insouciant as my melancholic condition allows.

'Who is it.'

'O begging your pardon Master Reginald it is me Crooks if I may have a moment of your time.'

Darcy Dancer unlocking and opening the library door. Crooks, a pair of white gloves on his hands. And good god a Trinity College tie hanging down his shirt front.

'We are awfully academic this morning Crooks.'

'What do you mean sir.'

'Your tie Crooks, your tie.'

'Ah it was what I grabbed hold of when I couldn't find to light me candle getting dressed this morning. But a serious word sir. That one Mollie has disappeared. And not a bed's been made in the east wing. And upon discovering the whereabouts of that one I respectfully request sir your authority to give her her notice.'

'O dear Crooks, is it as dire as that.'

'It is. Look at me fingertips. Black from testing for dust where that one should have wiped. Sure her royal highness Miss von B would have had a fit with the condition the east wing bedrooms are in.'

'Well when was Mollie seen last.'

'For breakfast where, when she left the table, you wouldn't find much remaining out of a pound of butter, half dozen sausages, pot of marmalade and two loaves of bread, never mind the kettles of tea that would make a spoon stand up in its cup.'

'Well Crooks we can at least leave it till after lunch and who knows she may turn up and have a very good reason for her absence.'

'As you wish Master Reginald but if you ask me that one's continued presence will lead to no good in this household. Now as you know holy days are off work but that one Mollie Dingbats said she'd rather another and different day off that wouldn't be so holy as the holy day to be having fun on.'

At least a decent fire glowing in the grate would have provided a bit of cheer in life amid hearing of more household difficulties with nowadays my having to get down on my hands and knees and blowing old ashes up into my face to get these bloody old damp sticks and turf alight. And that was another thing. Leila could build a fire which moments after a match was put to it was ablaze. O well. Bloody hell. I let her get stolen away. And nothing now I suppose will ever change things. But the fighting spirit she had seemed to soften somehow the farming mayhem. The slipped slates didn't crash on the terrace so loudly. And cattle dropping dead didn't seem to hit the ground so hard. But now all one has is a suitable out of date edition of the newspaper to peruse. I guess I could like other farmers read the matrimonial column looking for a wife.

'Will there be anything else Master Reginald.'

'O dear completely forgot you were there Crooks. No there won't be anything else. Except yes there is. I'd rather we didn't refer to Mollie as Dingbats. We mustn't get in the habit of nicknames.'

'Well sir, if she didn't get that name to go by, it would be far worse names we'd be calling her I can tell you.'

'Nevertheless put a stop to it Crooks.'

'I'll issue the order but I don't vouch for its being obeyed. Sure we're all slandered in this house.'

Crooks adjusting his Trinity tie and taking backward steps and turning, quietly closing the door. Heavens above. My reverie interrupted. And then Crooks asks me if there will be anything else. And I suppose he is hinting as to how I am referred to behind my back. Well I have a damn good idea. In a dream last night the peasants from the entire surrounding countryside came as a horde across the fields and went swarming up the entrance steps of Andromeda Park. Their muddy boots tramping in the front door, and wearing masks as they went tearing off the lace tablecloths and wrapping themselves in them. Then jeeringly dancing around the front hall, shouting kill Kildare till Kildare is dead. When suddenly Leila came storming down the main stairs, wielding a poker and screaming at them as she split open a few heads. And sent the peasants running. I barricaded myself in the Porcelain Room and when I came out I reached to kiss her in gratitude and then woke up. O god I must really be desperate if I'm seriously thinking as I am of shifting some female presence into this edifice. Who with a few well placed dirty looks and in shiny boots gaiting about the stables could put the fear of god in both the indoor and outdoor staff. And keep them off their backsides and stop their depredations of the biscuits, barmbrack, butter and bacon. But O dear me that could mean marriage and what if as a wife someone like old Durrow-Mountmellton suddenly changed her stripes, and became herself indolent, or even worse insolent. Or nearly as bad, started to let randy members of the hunt, or worse hunt servants, jump up on her for a quick gallop. Which is what the more uppity hunt servants seem to be attempting to do around here these days unless as Master I put my foot down. And of course some Masters do then put their own pricks up the better bifurcations. Of course as Master of Foxhounds one is regarded as having droit de seigneur. Which I believe means one not only can claim first privilege to plunge it into females of the household but also ladies of the hunt. But at least hunt servants do perform a needed service of sorts in giving the overly ripe old big arsed cows and sows on the hunt an old rollicking. After all it has become traditionally a ruddy part of the sport. And when the blood's up and horses are champing at the bit and flying over the fields, one is wont to consider pounding another's arse upon meadows soft and green. And, like a fox going to ground, cocks are bound just as frequently to be going into cunts. My goodness must pull myself together. Up and at them. It's time for champagne. Reach to pull the servants' bell and move my chair forward, closer to this feebly smouldering fire. Lean back one's head and reach up to cover one's eyes. Fingers go up into one's hair which heaven help me seems to have thinned somewhat since breakfast.

The squawk of a jackdaw coming down the chimney. A gust of wind rattling at the window panes. The library door opening. The boy butler peeking in.

'Sir did you be ringing.'

'Yes. But I want Crooks please.'

'He is away that minute ago upstairs in the house.'

'Then go find and tell him I want champagne. And perhaps you should attend upon him to learn how it's done.'

'I am busy sir attending as I am upstairs to her ladyship.'

'Bloody hell. Never mind her ladyship. Do as I say.'

'Yes sir.'

Darcy Dancer throwing his head back against his chair, putting a hand up to cover his brow. Pain still in the wrist from my midnight hunting accident. O god I must not lose my temper with servants. But imagine being told to one's face by a lowly member of one's staff that he is busy. Dear me trying to keep on top of things I am quickly losing my once boyishly joyous attitude towards life. I seem to retain only my desperate constant desire to put my prick in somewhere soft and nice. I suppose something similar in desire drove old Major Durrow-Mountmellton to putting it up sheep. A knock. Now who is it. With the library door opening slowly, coming ajar. A foot stepping forward shod in a shoe with the laces undone and a pink sock showing.

'Ah sir Master Reginald I was up changing me socks and tie. Were you after ringing for champagne.'

'Yes Crooks.'

'Well I had to check for sure, you wouldn't know now who would be making up a fib and be after taking an unauthorized bottle. With half a dozen whiskey bottles recently emptied down to the last half inch of their contents. And human piss filling the only full one left. Shocking. Some of those English aristocrats the ladies Lavinia and Christabel have invited here aren't of the best. But I'll be seeing to the cellar now, there's been awful inroads. But let me assure you Master Reginald I'll have the cellar book up to date. And interlopers will be prohibited.'

'Well I hope you poured the aristocratic piss beneficially on the rose garden. Even if it's of no discernible vintage it could lead to prize blooms. And Crooks I am appreciative for the lecture on the present state of matters. But as I am rather rushed at the moment, just please fetch me up a bottle and see to it that Damian is trained up to know how to serve champagne.'

'What sir. Let that little rascal be by himself attending to the wine cellar. Not on your nelly. Not if you value the continued contents I'm telling you. And excuse my expression Master Reginald.'

'Crooks for heaven's sake for the moment can we forget about who's stealing what. Pissing where. And making inroads. Just go get me a bottle that hasn't yet had its contents nine tenths drunk or hasn't yet been filled with someone's nouveau urine.'

'Very good sir but it is sad declining days we live in. With

82

people about now with no respect for standards. Vulgarity has hit this land like a hurricane.'

'Yes Crooks, yes. Sad and declining but there still sits here one bloody exception.'

'And to my mind sir, if you don't mind me saying, it's like now we were on a ship and you were the captain and I am the executive officer. I've been reading there in the encyclopedia before bedtime about the chain of command. And the ship-board discipline.'

'I assure you Crooks although we could use a ship now and again to navigate when being drenched in the rain, there is very little out here resembling a disciplined ship's company in these boggy midlands. And you can take that as gospel from the captain.'

'Aye aye sir. But when her royal highness von B sir was here, we may not have seen eye to eye but she took some of the awful load that do be now on my shoulders.'

'Yes Crooks I do realize how hard things have been for you but before it is time for me to have to go see to the balls and horns being knocked off the cattle can we now please have the champagne up before I expire with thirst.'

'Is it the Charles Heidsieck you'd want sir.'

'Yes. Provided its contents is champagne.'

Following Crooks departing in his pink socks, Darcy Dancer going to close and lock the library door. And holding the page of a newspaper open across the top of the fireplace. A draft creating and roaring the increasing flames up the chimney. Roast the squawking jackdaws away. And Crooks at least is on his toes this morning. Practically back in a flash. Ah he does at least know how to pour out my first glass. Which thank god is champagne. But of course that damn boy is nowhere to be seen.

'Now sir the bottle would be just that bit colder coming from the lowest in the rack. And I thought Catherine getting you up a little smoked salmon wouldn't come amiss.'

'Thank you so much Crooks. This has all come just in the nick of time.'

Darcy Dancer sticking out his feet towards the fire flames. Holding up his glass to watch the bubbles rise from this pale yellow liquid. Chew into the pink soft flesh of this gently smoked fish. Anointed with biting piquancy of lemon juice. The taste of bran in the bread. The sweet smoothness of the butter. I suppose as a first piece of detective work we can assume we know it would require a lady of aristocratic expert aim to fill a bottle with piss, squatting over it and by god a slip and she could get the neck up her what for. Heavens what are wine cellars coming to these days. God this really is the decline and fall of the once mighty estate of Andromeda Park. And at this very moment I am doing what so many of my ilk have done. Drink champagne and bash on regardless. One does long for to be back living in Celtic times when an insubordinate member of the household could be summarily executed. Or have his balls twisted so much he wished he were. Or even just ten years ago when the rebellious culprit would be trembling in his or her tracks, begging for mercy. Please master, please, don't do this to me. Shut up you damn impertinent, grossly idle numskull and bend your lazy backside immediately over. Take that. Wham. And take that you wretch. Of course there are some, especially ladies, who might ask to be whacked again. But at that point the arch disciplinarian Miss von B could march out in her hunting habit, boots gleaming and muscular thighs stretching the fabric of her breeches. Ah so, zees are zer culprits to whom I administer zee ten lashes upon the servant bottom. Little puffs of smoke rising as Miss von B warms up, snapping her whip and she only so very slightly foaming at the mouth. The smooth soft skin of her cheeks tinged with pink. The naked victim's face frozen in fear. Tied dangling helpless by the wrists. Her royal imperial Austro Hungarian and Polish highness bringing the eight foot long leather thong curling sizzling through the air

84

like a great reptile striking its fangs deep into its prey. Und take dis you indolent slacker, und dis, und dis. Yavol you scream in agony but it ist vas you lazy boots deserve. Of course I would be sitting up on a little dais with opera glasses surveying all and drinking as I am now, champagne, and nibbling my saumon fumé. The stable yard as an amphitheatre. The remaining staff lined up to witness Miss von B meting out discipline. Or if ever anybody at Andromeda Park were able to drive a nail straight and build a scaffold, even to put the malefactors to death. A miniature Tyburn. Hang draw and quarter the ruddy buggers. Hot pokers shoved up the arse. O dear I am beginning to sound like a certain Marquis de Sade. But as things are now, it would take more than red hot pokers up the arse or necks suffocating on scaffolds to scare anyone in this household into becoming a dutiful servant. Or even to make them think twice about chipping the Dresden, gouging the mahogany or scratching the silver. And speaking of chipping, I've just cut the tip of my tongue on a broken edge of this glass. A very unique way of having pink champagne. O dear I suppose I never fully appreciated the unstinting dedication previous persons gave who are now gone from my life. Especially Mr Arland. So far away now in his digs back in Dublin. In the bleak grime and gloom of Mount Street, still mourning the death of the woman he loved. One has left only the Trinity tie he wore which Crooks now seems to have taken to wearing. And I have a lower undergarment to remind me of Miss von B. Whose naked contours one would so much adore to see and caress again. How does one subdue this awful randiness constantly welling up in one. It does seem so prone to most impolitely fuck up my future. Which now I must face forever without Leila. But if her royal highness Miss von B were back here, I could kill, so to speak, about two or three birds with about forty or fifty stones. It would be no nonsense from the staff I can tell you. Plus I could perpetrate my lust upon her. No dirt swept under the carpet. As I kissed those tits. No greasy fingerprints left on the dishes and glassware. As I pushed my what for deep up her sweet hole. Or gobs of butter smearing the bottom of trays. As she would referring to it in French, so deliciously lick my arse. O dear. Between memories of Miss von B and this champagne I am becoming quite worked up. But look at this, here on the rug. A wood louse. Daring to nonchalantly march right out right in front of me. I have a good mind to throw it right in the fire. But simply have not got the heart. And like Sexton I can't be cruel even to this most primitive of creatures. Just chuck him up into one of the bookcases to let him eat and gnaw away to his heart's content in one of the learned tomes. Champagne does always mellow one. And I suppose one has taken serious things too seriously recently. When I should allow for pleasant interludes to intrude. And to luxuriate in them while one can. Especially at the crucial time of late morning when the disasters of the previous day begin to become known. And before one has yet to be concerning oneself about lunch. Or that the menu at the last minute has had to be changed. The day gets so bloody crowded. One hardly then has time for a long brisk walk which is often a case of just stumbling about in one's bogs, before one has to take off one's boots for tea time. Although I must say one is always glad to chomp jams, scones and cake. And by then darkness has fallen. And one does then finally feel that the day is well and truly over. And all that remains is to see if one can bear to go look at the accounts and of course one can't bear to do so and instead one peruses the newspaper before proceeding to bath and dress for dinner and hope not yet again to waste one of one's better clarets on an overcooked stew. But solemn peace seems to come only when I am alone evenings here in the library in my smoking jacket and am quietly sipping port and staring into the fire flames. Free of the outside world and indulging in melancholic memories. Perhaps it is for such brief moments and the lonely contentment of such times that

86

one lives. And as Rashers might say, there is nothing like utter peace and quiet for comforting an unrequited erection.

'Ahhhhhaaa. Ahhhhhaaa.'

Darcy Dancer sitting suddenly bolt upright, spilling champagne. Blood curdling screams and a pounding of floorboards upstairs somewhere in the house. As if someone were running for his life. And by the noise they must be. O god where is good news. Just after I'd locked it, unlock the library door again. Just when I was deeply thinking of ringing for some more of this festive wine. Murder is afoot. Someone at large with an axe, knife, or worse, a hedgerow hook. And the thumping is crossing east to west in the hall above or god rather I think north to south and heading for the rear servants' stairs beyond the ballroom. Must one unlock the library door again. And go out and risk the maelstrom. Or maybe one should wait till the oceans of dust settle. And the mayhem is done. Plenty of graves available at Andromeda Park if someone gets axed to kingdom come. A coffin can quickly be tacked together from all the slabs of timber which otherwise are just mouldering at the saw mill. And a little redundancy would not come amiss if one were made short a member or two of the staff. Plus the men enjoy telling stories of the deceased while digging their graves.

'Ahhhhhaaa. Ahhhhhaaa.'

The cry getting closer. O my god by the sound of the blood curdling timbre it's a younger member of the female staff. Upon whom perhaps some awful form of buggery is being attempted. Now what on earth put that imbecile thought in my mind. O yes. Old Major Durrow-Mountmellton, when he wasn't rogering the sheep, liked next best buggering the kitchen maids, who upon their all fours were held in place from behind by the Major, grasping tight hold of their ears and using pig grease as the lubricant. I suppose part of the midlands was once full of people like him without any regard for decent restraint. Having a damn good time in the privacy

87

of his country house and giving the gentry of this county a bad name. O bloody hell now I've just tripped over the bellows and dumped champagne on the rug and stained down my trousers. The cries are getting louder and closer. O god could it be Crooks upstairs with his prick out through his petticoats and after Norah or Sheila. And O god, occasional transvestite as he tends to be, I wouldn't put buggery past him and one doesn't relish pig grease all over the place.

Darcy Dancer turning left out the door. Past the ancient family portraits and double doors of the ballroom. Reaching the end of the hallway to the foot of the servants' stairs. Sound of slapping feet coming down the landing. Good god, I say. Mollie Dingbats dripping water and wrapped only in a towel. Her red frizzy hair flying out from her head as if struck by lightning. And wide eyed screaming down over the banister.

'He came after me.'

'Who came after you Mollie.'

'I am being hunted by a rat as big as a cat along the whole length of the upstairs east wing hall, afeared of my life.'

'For god's sakes Mollie be calm, there's no sign of the rat now.'

'Didn't he be just at me heels top of the corridor after chasing me and me without a stitch on. The teeth of him as big as knives. Jumped out at me from out of the bathroom clothes cupboard and the monster was trying to get up into the bath to take a bite of me. The rats will finally have us all in this house.'

'All right Mollie if you'll just calm a second I'll go fetch my shotgun and blast the damn bloody critter to kingdom come.'

Darcy Dancer raising his arms to demonstrate his aim. No harm in giving the girl confidence. And in referring to her adversary in American cowboy parlance one hears in the Hollywood movies. But at least things are improving. No recent vampires or bats flying around her bedroom. And the

88

last time a rat jumped at her it was as big as a fox and, as Crooks suggested, should have taken a bite out of her, as wasn't she like a tender boneless shoulder of pork.

'Don't leave me Master Reginald stranded here at the animal's mercy and kilt with the cold and terrified out of me wits. I am at this moment after saying the act of contrition and begging the protection of the guardian angel.'

'Well just say the act of contrition again and I'll be back with my gun.'

'O Jesus, Mary and Joseph, Master Darcy no please, please don't go leave me.'

'Well come down here.'

'Not with me costume abbreviated in this flimsy towel I won't. And with the icicles dropping off me, and frozen to the bone I am.'

'Well please, here take my jacket for heaven's sake.'

Of course transfixed. There was Dingbats as I had so often dreamed of seeing her. No wonder farmers across the county refer to her as a big agricultural girl and are slathering at the mouth. I am myself feeling I am going apoplectic cross eyed like Crooks with the sumptuous bulging bouncing sight of Dingbats's bosoms. Their pointed soft tumescence arching out upturned and billowing from her chest. Springing like a heifer a day before calving. Mouth watering nipples pink on their summit. And into which one wants to press one's face. Their fresh softness laden with sweet milk. Bury one's head, licking and sucking. My already rigid prick is trembling with a new rigidity at the bounce of these wet approaching breasts. Which one had to confess more than rivalled those of old Durrow-Mountmellton, whose were not so quite as exquisitely protruding as Dingbats's are in their emphatically pointed manner. And upon which my eyes may remain forever glued.

'O Jesus, Mary and Joseph, there he is looking at me there up on the stair. His ears be as big as jackdaw wings. Save me from the beast.'

'Well bloody hell for heaven's sake before he starts flying or bites your arse off, come down then Mollie.'

'O Master Darcy for the mother of saints he's after me again.'

One hand holding the banister and the other the towel around her, Dingbats coming round the landing and her bare feet pounding down the stairs, tripping at the bottom, the towel dropping off as she throws herself forward upon Darcy Dancer, flinging her arms around his neck. Who, with one arm still caught halfway in his jacket sleeve, tumbles backwards crashing to the floor, his head banging the anciently thick floorboards. Dingbats sprawled naked on top of him. Bright lights, stars, blackness. Dreams and nightmares flashing through the brain. Wet breasts pressing. On my shirt front. Dingbats's face is buried in the crook of my shoulder. And strands of her red frizzy hairs are caught in my mouth.

'My god Mollie are you all right.'

'Glory be to God I am. And you do be a grand gentleman.'

Of course as I was reaching trying to grab my jacket to drape over the freckled white skin of Dingbats's backside. Especially the now prominently displayed twin mounds of her rather marvellous arse. By god there is no doubt but that she's a big rangy filly. Against whose bifurcation my embarrassingly rapidly expanded private part now presses and is wont to go thrusting further. O god she's actually putting pressure on it. And if I send pressure back with an involuntary twitch as I've just done, I'll never get another ounce of work out of her to add to the meagre ounces one's got so far.

'Mollie I think you must get up before I can.'

'I will be looked upon by everybody without my clothes.'

One thing was for sure Dingbats Mollie was offering no explanation as to what she was doing taking a bath this hour of the morning and smelling of my mother's most exotic bath salts when she should have been making beds and tidying the bedrooms. By god whoever invented the remark, when the cat's away the mice will play, knew what they were talking about. And let me invent one too, when the rats are running all ruddy hell will break loose. Never mind the mice swarming all over the place. My goodness for a blacksmith's daughter she's amazingly soft. And she won't budge. My fingers sink into her arse like a feather pillow of swansdown. Why doesn't everyone go away. And let me luxuriate in the warmth of her pair of big tits overflowing on my shirt. O my god. Only fractions of a second passed and a glow is going through my gonads. Just as I caught a revealing glimpse of her nice rounded belly and marvellously large orange patch of bushy hair between her big strapping thighs. No doubt about it, Dingbats, if you could get any work out of her, certainly fits the bill, she'd be a great milker out of which to squirt milk and is exactly what every small farmer is licking his chops over in matrimonial columns all over the country. And my god she's coming to her senses. And I haven't yet come to mine. She's lifting up. And forcing me to discreetly disguise my trousers sticking out a mile. Move my arse and she moves hers, pressing against my rigid prick. O my god. She's rubbing her belly on me again. Which, talking of nicely rounded bellies, it could be that it's Dingbats the pregnant one among the staff.

'Master Darcy I'm staying right here like this till they are all gone.'

'Very well Mollie.'

'Master Reginald can I be of assistance.'

'No Crooks you heard what Mollie said. Get back all of you, I'm in control.'

'Ah it would seem you are well in control Master Reginald if you don't mind me saying so.'

'I do bloody well mind your saying so Crooks and if you don't mind please allow us some privacy.'

'Youse now heard what the master said. Now back the lot of you. Or there'll be sackings in this household I'm telling youse.'

Shuffling feet on the floorboards. Crooks's hands out-stretched, ushering the household members of Andromeda Park back down the hall. Crooks's accent of course slipping into Dublinese. My word, but Dingbats's buttock does feel rather familiar. O lord I did get absolutely squalidly drunk the night I heard that Leila had moved to a château in France somewhere near Paris. And which somehow made her seem a whole further world away. And then I sat intoxicating myself on port. So easy to do if it's damn good port which it was, laid down by my mother when I was born. And I mysteriously woke up in a servant's unused bedroom of which there are so many I have never counted them. Could I, inebriated one night beyond my senses, have got in bed with her. At least I suppose her present nakedness makes us even for the time she once surprised me in the bath with, as it happened, a similar rigidity except then my prick was sticking up like a periscope considerably above the water. And she deliberately paused to make conversation. And for nearly a couple of weeks after-wards she was unusually attentive to my comforts. Of course my crooked former agent Quinn was slavering at the mouth, paying her court and while I was away in Dublin, having her fetch and carry to him as he sat in the Rent Room, lording it over the whole household. O god just a handful of flesh can send such nightmares through one. How is it that some misery of some sort always seems to follow shortly after pleasure. Sexton said that Saturday nights, at the dancehall in the town, every teetotal non dancing bachelor farmer for miles around looking for a wife spent the week polishing up his dentures and practising smiling with them in some old cracked mirror and working up the nerve to ask her to dance or partake of a mineral water with them, while Mollie kept a list of how much land, cows, horses, bullocks and goats each had. Even Crooks was accused of goosing her and of interfering up under her skirts. And speaking of Crooks, ruddy hell, here he is back again with the mob behind him.

92

'Begging your pardon Master Reginald this is not a situation I find conducive to my usual household duties. Not in all the years here have I witnessed such a sight. And for the sake of decency shouldn't I be getting a covering for Mollie.'

'Yes Crooks yes. Do please go get something to cover her. She's distraught. And more so with the mob of you back here still watching.'

'With all due respect and again begging your pardon Master Reginald, what do you recommend as adequate covering.'

'I said Crooks go get something to cover Mollie and I don't give a damn what it is.'

'That one needs covering all right I can tell you, like a mare in season.'

'Bloody hell Crooks I am not to ask you again. And do mind to keep a civil tongue in your head.'

'Youse now, all back. Didn't you harken now to Master Reginald. Captain of this ship. Back, back. Don't be pretending you'd be of any help here. With the silver needing polishing, the fires laid, the beds made. Sure given half a chance youse all be upstairs with the bath salts wasting valuable hot water warming yourselves in the tub.'

Mollie glowering at Crooks, who is now standing in front of the giggling spellbound audience crowding the ballroom hallway, and who is tapping his fingers together in front of what appears to be one of my grandfather's deer skin gold buttoned waistcoats. And I suppose racking his brain for further military or navel words to delay him departing what must be this appetizing sight. With his crossed eyes recrossing in all directions, getting an eye full. Of what is for me this distinct mixture of pleasure and the most excruciatingly acute discomfiture one has had to confront in the increasingly chaotic history of Andromeda Park. And my god Mollie won't let go. Felled with a ton slate off the roof would at least be a straightforward event with one's head cleaved in two. But the way Mollie's got me gripped she is suffering a living case of

93

rigor mortis which has obviously deeply set into every one of her statuesque limbs. Of course now that the guests have got wind of it every hall from every direction will be pounding with approaching feet. As in fact, god help my ears, is happening. Then Crooks will take it as an excuse to give a conducted tour. Does one retreat with Dingbats up into the jaws of the rat or should both of us remain here, having committed what looks like a clear act of procreation and then bow to all pushing to get a closer look so they can witness the full frontal of Dingbats. Which the boy butler arriving clearly intends to do and whose sense of humour belies the few brain cells he normally demonstrates are in his head by grinning ear to ear. Crooks turning to him.

'Wipe that disrespectful grin off your face and youse be quick about it. And youse go get a curtain down out of the drawing room.'

'Never mind the curtain Crooks just get the bloody hell out of here the whole lot of you.'

'Very good sir. We are all in the process of retreating I respectfully assure you. All of youse now, the party and sightseeing is over.'

The wide eyed entirety of the staff of Andromeda Park collected in the ballroom hallway. Crooks ushering back Sheila, Norah and Catherine up from the kitchen, all their mouths miles agape. Luke in from the stables with a pitchfork. Henry the herdsman, clomping behind him in mud encrusted boots and who has let about thirteen cattle die this year. Thomas at least with his hat off but dropping wood shavings all over the floor, who should be at the saw mill. And behind him Lois and Rashers. My god nobody's leaving and everybody's arriving. And listen to bloody Crooks. He doesn't in that accommodatingly officious tone of his mean a bloody word he's saying.

'All youse please. Lords, ladies and gentlemen, please now back down the hall. It's all over. The incident is closed. The

94

master has everything well in hand I assure you. No need for panic. The rat's gone back up into his rafters now.'

Dingbats giving off an overpowering musky smell, turning and lifting her head to look at me with a Mona Lisa smile. From the expression on her freckled face it's clear she's a ruddy arrant exhibitionist and is delighted everyone has got a good look at her bare arse. And she is still deliberately pressing her thigh rubbing up against my prick. When I ought at this minute to be out seeing to the castration and dehorning of the cattle. And here I am, pasha of Andromeda Park, supine on my back, hungrily hankering just like any small farmer on his postage stamp of acres to plunge it to the hilt right up Dingbats. With my heart pounding, and lungs deep breathing while a naked servant is prostrate on top of me. Only my god I have. Just sent something inside my very best pair of cavalry twill trousers. With the distinctly unpleasant sensation of a wetness down my thigh. Which is what I do believe could be referred to as inadvertent lustful excretion.

> So much for
> My premature feeble attempt
> At a bit of
> Meditative privacy
> In the library

7

After such a nice active little beginning to one's morning one was glad to plan that following seeing that the men didn't cut their own balls off instead of the cattle's and having had a spot of lunch one would promptly depart for a somewhat more lighthearted life at the races. But, returning along the ballroom hallway to the library, one remained nearly doubled over as if ruptured with the pain of an erection which had been bent out of its usual shape under the weight of Mollie. And one was looking much forward to taking a much needed quaff of my champagne. And would you ruddy well believe it, someone had already polished off the remainder of my glass and finished to the last drop what was left in the bottle. My smoked salmon too was gone.

Climbing up the main stairs to one's chambers to remove one's clothes, somehow the weight of the world seemed to be on one's shoulders. And more than my usual mild paranoia was making itself felt. Never mind leeches, there clearly are lice abounding upon one as well. If a gentleman can't sit to his own champagne in his own library in his own house in his own parklands something extremely odious is ruddy well afoot. At least my prick, when finally reduced to flaccidness and examined in the mirror in a military manner with retracted foreskin, seemed to have no permanent harm done to it. In fact when I lay in my hot sudsy bath it went as usual up like a periscope, with Dingbats's tits dancing in front of my eyes through a gauze network of her carrot coloured pubic hair. But the terror of the thought assailing me. What would be my lot if indeed she were pregnant and I were to be branded father of Dingbats's child. Good god, she was already using my mother's bath salts. Next she could be in a ballgown waltzing through the drawing room, making free with the champagne, ordering servants about, and behaving in a familiar manner with guests. And now here I am, prick rigidly quivering to put it up between her contumely thighs, whatever the bloody hell the word contumely means. God I've got to travel to Constantinople or somewhere obscure in the Far East for a little distraction and relief. Or go see Lois's tits hanging in the Louvre.

Darcy Dancer stepping into clean underlinen and worn silk shirt and pulling on a pair of old cavalry twill trousers. From the walnut wardrobe selecting a jacket of hound's tooth, a strong thorn proof Manx tweed. Belonging once to, and bequeathed to me by, my Uncle Willie. As not one item of clothing ever has been by my niggardly stingy father, whom one recently hears is with his Dublin mistress hanging about in the flesh pots of Europe, racing and gambling.

Darcy Dancer descending back down the main stairs. Breath blowing steam out into the air. A chill breeze on the back of the neck. A disgruntled servant, not knowing which one to choose to jump out of, must have left a dozen windows open somewhere upstairs in the house. How does one hold together the moral fabric of one's life. Not to mention any continued shred of reverence for social standards. Even the mere vague entertainment of such a bizarre possibility as Dingbats as lady of the manor is most, most dangerous. And Mollie, dumb as she is, has been sufficiently around mares and stallions to know what happened in my trousers. From that it is easy enough for her to assume I am not above wanting to ram it into her to the hilt, which is the ruddy truth. And more ruddy truth is I ought to for my own bloody personal safety, quick as I can, plan to get hitched up. No reason why old Durrow-Mountmellton couldn't be in charge here, even though it could turn the place into a cesspool of perversion. With which of course, being constantly on the slippery slope of randiness, I'm finding myself more and more becoming obsessed. Old Rashers, waster, idler though he may be, certainly has the right ruddy idea to get to the races as frequently as one can. And bloody well put out of mind the aggravating and recently highly horny problems assaulting one at Andromeda Park. Where one does so sometimes feel as if one were an insect pinned to a board struggling to get free to fly again. At least the squalls of rain have cleared and for the moment the cold is not of the variety penetrating to, and lodging in, the bones. Although it makes not a wit of difference squeezing the future out of a young bull's balls, dry crisp weather at least helps congeal the blood oozing from the cattle's lopped off horns.

Darcy Dancer pushing feet into his wellington boots. Choosing a stout walking stick. A gnarled blackthorn. That won't break over the back of a beast. And speaking of breaking. A newly broken tile in the hall. Someone bloody hell must have dropped a sledgehammer having rushed in the door at the rumour of nudity. Skulduggery on every side. The bunch of them creeping around and, if not busting something, then looking to lay their hands on anything that can be lifted. O god. Can already hear distant moaning and groaning out in the farmyard. Now face the most terrible of embarrassments. The stories already circulating over the scene down the ballroom hall will by now have been repeated and embellished ad nauseam and have no doubt reached the main street of town and be on every bloody shopkeeper's lips. And then exaggerated some more will be promptly broadcast out into the distant parishes beyond. Stop off to see Sexton in his potting shed. Someone sympathetic to talk to. Which one seems to need more and more desperately as the minutes go by. One only wishes Sexton weren't such a religious maniac. But that dear man has, to put it mildly, more than once saved my bacon to fry another day.

Darcy Dancer treading down the front steps of Andromeda

98

Park. A mist hovering beyond the ancient pale winter green of the front parkland meadow. Down where my nanny pushed me once in my pram to see the little stream flowing. Go past the plantation of rhododendrons, their great roots curling like giant reptiles in the shadows. Where once too I played. Walk under the ancient towering grove of beech trees towards the high walls of the garden. I must find an heiress. And never give up. And become dispossessed of all this. And by god as I go through this squeaking gate, that's final. But how does one suppress one's lustful desires. Could be a cure in Mr Arland's book of homoeopathy. Anoint the affected area with a block of ice. One already has another erection just thinking of pushing one's nose deep into Dingbats's bush of orange curly hair. O god, one presently feels that whatever shreds of standards one previously possessed have now shattered. What a nightmare. Marry Dingbats. So bloody transparently a peasant that she is, it could ostracize me from every major manor house across the countryside. And right at the moment one is contemplating giving a grand dinner party and inviting only the very tip top elite of the county. If only the same thing could have happened while Leila was here. How grateful I would have been were it her chased into my arms by a rat. But she wasn't afraid of rats. She seemed in fact afraid of nothing. And could wear such a fierce look of determination on her face. I'd have more than given anything I could to have lain locked upon her body for even an instant. And that would be long enough then to remember the remainder of my life.

Darcy Dancer stopping in his tracks. A pheasant exploding up from the grass. And flying across the meadow to coast through the air down the gentle hill towards the cemetery. And coming in sight again, against the sky as it flew to land in the tall rushes of the bog near where the figure had stood whom I thought was Leila. What a hopeless imagining to have had. Upon which one must not dwell. And there's the turf shed roof. There presents another little matter assailing one.

The turf bogs of Andromeda Park, hardly a mile from the house, being systematically robbed. At least with a tree one can hear someone cutting it down and arrive with a shotgun to blow their ears off when they are trying to drag it away. But with someone silently and copiously helping themselves out on the deserted bog in the middle of the night to the stacks of our best dried sods and leaving not a trace or clue behind as to whom the culprit might be, they become impossible to apprehend. Sexton of course, announcing as I stepped into his potting shed, a nice new light on recent matters.

'Ah Master Darcy. Grand to see you still in one piece. By the stories you wouldn't know what to believe.'

'Believe what Sexton.'

'The unbelievable.'

'And what's the unbelievable, Sexton.'

'That one Mollie Dingbats. Raped.'

'Good god. There was no bloody such thing Sexton. I merely tried to calm the naked girl.'

'Ah not you Master Darcy. We all know you're as innocent as a new born babe not yet in its swaddling clothes. She has it the rat was raping her. But now she should have her hands full soon. Didn't I meet your erstwhile agent Quinn there in town coming out of the chemist. Rumour has it that he's employed a marriage broker to visit Mollie's father in Galway to ask for the hand of Dingbats in marriage. And that Master Darcy could take once and for all a domestic problem off your mind.'

'Well Sexton at least it would reduce the consumption of butter. However, one is just reminded of the ample amounts of turf which continue to go missing.'

'Ah now that's no inside job Master Darcy we're dealing with. But you trust me now to lay holt of the rascal. The time has come to employ an indelible method I have of catching the offender. He'll soon be purloining his last bit of turf I'm telling you.'

'Well Sexton as the Guards with their best sleuths have had no success, one hopes your method may produce results. Especially as one piece of turf is the same as another and particularly when one is helplessly viewing it as a heap of ash in the grate of the culprit next morning.'

'Ah that may be but you leave it to old Sexton. And as to sleuths. No sleuths are needed. I already know who it is. And before many more drops of rain fall the moment of detection will arrive and he'll get out of his fireside reverie and back into reality I'm telling you. And you won't be needing someone out there watching the night away.'

'Well I suppose Sexton, I suppose one shouldn't get too worked up about it, it is after all only an old little bit of turf.'

'Master Darcy there'd be a drop of somebody's sweat on every sod. And to him as dropped it, you'd have been paying wages. And if you let someone get away with it, next they'd be in stealing cows and calves out of the fields. Sure by slow piecemeal there would be over a couple of ton of turf gone already.'

'Well in that case Sexton I'm glad to hear of new and better methods of detection. It would be nice to cut down a little on the removal of implements, tools, buckets and other diverse articles from Andromeda Park. And I also do hear of these rumours of a property encroachment on the doorstep.'

'Master Darcy for a little cheer, here, let me put a nosegay in your button hole. And let me tell you too that that marauder lately come upon the scene, who's bought the parcel of land adjoining Thormondstown, you leave me to deal with him. We'll wipe the superior sneer off his face, trumped up little gobshite that he is. Sure he's about all over the parish, talking of rainbows and the idyllic wonderment of farming, while he's at the same time dropping hints threatening to build petrol stations every five yards along the approaches to Andromeda Park.'

'Good god Sexton there's no truth in that is there.'

'Well now it would be like this. There'd be truth in it and there wouldn't, if you follow me. He'd smile, pull his forelock at you, and stare down at the tips of his boots and lick your arse while he thought he could get something to his profit out of you. And thinking that your money grew on the trees, he'd want you to pay twice the price for the land he'd bought a fortnight ago. And he'd be by way of telling you what he'd do to you if you didn't buy it from him. Nothing but a gobshite land speculator. That's what he is.'

'God as if one doesn't have enough battles on one's hands already. Where's he from Sexton.'

'They say near and about the town of Limerick.'

'That's a long way off. And there's a ruddy good pack of hounds down there and I believe a distinguished family or two, and some damn decent hunting.'

'Ah now there'd be two kinds of people from Limerick, Master Darcy. There'd be your exemplary kind and there'd be your out and out dastardly kind. And by god this scoundrel would be from your latter category, born and bred to snatch the food out of your mouth if they could. But don't worry Master Darcy, we'll put manners on him and if he doesn't learn from that soon enough, we'll put the curse of bad luck on him.'

Of course leaving old Sexton's potting shed, one was far more troubled now than when one went in. Sexton could sometimes sound so insufferably sure of himself. But one had to admit, although he more than occasionally got his Latin tenses woefully mixed up, he could also sometimes be right. And except for the soot he mixed with his specially selected grease to smarm back and obliterate the grey of his hair, one could never question his genuineness.

Darcy Dancer scuffling through the drifts of rotting leaves covering the grass along the orchard wall. The rooster escaped from the hen run blocking the way, jumping up and attacking. No peace anywhere. Not at least until I give this bird a boot in

102

the breast and clout of my blackthorn across the neck. Which, even with the blows sending it flying, gives me only a second to escape. A squeal of rusty hinges closing the iron barred gate. And wondering when that will rust asunder. And when it does, then wondering when the wall will fall down. A flock of jackdaws screaming and flying from the top branches of the beech grove. And wondering when they will block up all the chimneys, cause a fire and burn the house to the ground. And now Quinn. Imagine my erstwhile bloody agent thinking he can come along and purloin a member of my staff for his own carnal purposes. I must take a walk. O dear the thought of this is suddenly awful. Can't get Dingbats's bloody body out of my mind. Even hear her voice in my ear. And you do be a grand gentleman. Even trying to remember which is her bedroom to go sneaking there for a mite more than a little hanky panky. But for the safety of my future, socially, maybe it's time to sally forth over to old Durrow-Mountmellton again. Quench the fires of desire for at least a bloody half hour or so. Or even try Lois near at hand. If she hasn't already got the boy butler on top of her. Or she on top of him. Lois was always a jolly good gallop. Even snorted occasionally and made a marvellous whinnying noise like a horse. Except that bloody hell one then had to listen to her moaning complaint of society's hostility to the artist and her moralizing over her artistic principles. But O god her tits too are pretty damn memorable. And my word if one includes Lois, there are three pairs now to remember. And one could commission some impecunious Montparnasse artist to paint Dingbats's and Durrow-Mountmellton's to be duly exhibited with Lois's in the Louvre. Dear me, I am obsessed. But as tits are one's original form of sustenance, I suppose to admire the shape of such things can't be counted as unusual. Dugs are always the first thing one looks at when buying a cow. And speaking of livestock, at least the sounds of roaring cattle coming from over beyond the farm roof tops is a distraction, making me think of the day when they can be sold.

Darcy Dancer making his way back through the shadows of the old oak trees bordering the front meadow lands of Andromeda Park. The drips of moisture falling from the lichen encrusted branches. The soft mossy turf under foot. The ancient secrecy of this land one does so love. The ruin there of a cottage. Starving peasants who fled to America. All the passing life and death rooted once in this soil before even my own ancestors were here. But where one now can commune with oneself. As Leila did. Be alone. Only the pale green grass under these trees to listen to one's thoughts. And now the threat to the precious grandeur of all this. Some awful gombeen bugger intruding. Interfering with my privacy. My god, petrol stations. One should have been warned. The marauder having already not only had the cheek to call without appointment to the front door of Andromeda Park and to suggest to see me but was also at the time tieless and wearing a sweater if you please. Then after leaving a message with Crooks that he had a proposition to make to me, he took the cigarette out of his surly mouth and stamped it out on my porch. Such things one normally ignores. But Crooks, easily given to a certain hysteria at such times, declaimed the scene as if it were a stage drama. And Rashers, having been a witness from the front window of the Porcelain Room, confirmed the incident.

'Ah Darcy one must give your Crooks full marks. Full marks dear boy for his most monumentally marvellous example of come uppance I've seen meted out in years. As your man was grinding out his cigarette under his heel, Crooks loftily removed a cloth from his pocket and with it and with the most splendidly orchestrated ceremony, he picked up the offending ditched butt and, holding it aloft, and as far from the tip of his nose as possible, made his casual way down the steps and slow marched across the gravel to deposit it in the ditch along the drive. The incomparably sullen, sneering look it brought to your man's face was a treat to behold I assure you.'

'And what pray tell were you doing Rashers in the Porcelain Room. Which I was under the impression was securely locked.'

'Dear boy your tone of voice cuts me to the quick. And I have long since returned the key I borrowed from Crooks. Some historically marvellous Dublin silverware in a case there you know and you keep it far too damp and cold. But I was in fact investigating to see if the rich rococo plasterwork of the ceiling was done by the noted Dublin stuccatore Richard Williams or by that greatest of Italian stuccatori, Artari, the latter who is responsible for your drawing room ceiling. You know how enthralled I am by your interior architecture. Nice if you had popped a plinth or two in there. A bust of Cicero or Homer would set it all off nicely as a matter of fact.'

Darcy Dancer cap set square on his head. Walking stick grasped in a pig skin gloved hand. Skirting the edge of the boggy pine grove. Boots sinking in the soft soil. Toppled trees rotting that could have made the best of fence posts. Amazing how just as one is in despair of carrying on, suddenly just a few encouraging words or pairs of memorable tits dancing in front of one's hungry eyes give one a new resolve to continue the battle. Or perhaps it's Rashers's shameless impudence. As I am sure his presence in the Porcelain Room was for no other reason than for his expert eye to size up the pawnability of my best silverware. And to maybe bloody well do as he once did before, disappear with a caseful.

The cattle roaring and mooing growing louder. And by the sound they're already squeezing balls and hacking off horns. Just beyond this stone wall here, my mother lies. Crooks never failing even with his arthritis to daily lay a flower there. What now could be left of her. As I still alive tread this ground where I was born. And near where I will one day too be laid to rest. One might even contemplate perhaps a modest memorial. Certainly I shall provide one for Rashers when he kicks the bucket. Which he gives no ruddy sign of yet doing as my guest and while fattening on the fare of Andromeda Park. But no wonder they say rest in peace. Even though there don't appear to be many nice ways of gracefully dying. Living life is no bowl of sweet ripe cherries immersed in whipped cream. And by the sound of the moaning and mooing in the mess I face ahead, nothing is going to rest in peace in the near future.

Darcy Dancer stopping in his tracks. A hen pheasant exploding up from the grass. And flying out across the meadow to glide down and disappear in the thick rushes the other side of the stream. Dear me. There flown right under my nose goes a good lunch or dinner which, bang, would have merited a good claret. And me without my gun. And caught day dreaming of Leila again. As if, were I to keep looking towards the stretch of mist over the bog, I might see her solitary figure standing there. Why must one person whom one has lost and whom one will never see again still lurk so deeply in one's life. I must resolve, here and now, never again to think of her. And avoid the pain of loneliness and dispossession the memory of her brings upon me. And now damn it, I do believe I'm feeling rather peckish. Not to mention somewhat horny. Strange how game birds do, even when seen foraging out in the fields, raise one's appetite as one envisions them nicely roasted and waiting on one's plate. And Uncle Willie, his blue eyes sparkling, often professed on such matters.

'Darcy nothing like a bird in the wild that, brought down and dined upon, does do for the constitution wonders.'

Darcy Dancer descending down the cobbled path towards the farmyard. Wellington boots make their hollow sound on the cobbles. Enter the gate into the cattle pen. A mist of steam rising from the backs of the beasts. Hoofs sinking and sliding in the mud. Horns pucking as they jump, climb up and crush down over one another. O dear one does wish one were instead back up in Dublin taking a leisurely morning over breakfast at the Shelbourne Hotel. But at least that's something done. Nothing worse than chasing and herding bloody cattle in from distant fields for dehorning and castration. They seem to know what's ahead. Attempting to escape and go breaking through fences and hedgerows. Some even leaping the walls. And one often ends up running a few miles just trying to drive the beasts a few hundred yards. The men ecstatically raining down blows with their pickaxe handles and stout sticks. The joy of cruelty to animals. Luke grinning as he holds up the great castration pliers and practising clamping them open and shut. Like a pair of shark's jaws one recently saw displayed in a book in the library concerning battles with giant fish of the ocean depths. White sharks and killer whales that could devour one in one bite. And Luke licking his chops just as he does over a heap of rotting mulch, which he is always fond of referring to in a singularly unappetizing manner.

'Master Reginald now that's what I call the best manure. You could cut a slab off that now and put it between two pieces of bread and eat it without butter or salt. And it would put you in the best of health. Better than a bar of chocolate any day.'

One found it always wise to indulge the men in agreeing on anything over which they showed the least enthusiasm. But I was not about to slice off a slab of worm riddled formerly fresh cow flop, straw and horse dung. Of course one knows that some of these old country remedies do have their merits. Sexton swearing by a cure for liver complaint with the juice of boiled up dock and nettle leaves. But one does not relish to be put in the best of health swilling sour old concoctions or chewing and chomping on slabs of compost. No matter how well rotted or recommended. One already knew that of an evening Luke would make his way over to the kennels to hack a steak or two for his dinner off a dead horse waiting to be fed to the hounds. And one thing was for sure now, Luke was raring to go to fasten the metal tongs on any young bull's testicles. Squeezing the scrotum as the beast slammed kicks

107

against the rungs of the crush, the animal roaring with agony and Luke smiling ear to ear. Giving a final satisfied nod of the head when, with the bullock now turned loose and still kicking the air, it was charging around in circles.

'Ah now that will calm him down now and shrivel his balls away. He won't be no more aiming his horns in my direction and be pawing the ground at me again.'

The hoarse mooing of more cattle approaching. Herdsman Henry and Thomas from the saw mill raining blows down on the haunches of heifers and bull calves driving them into paddocks. More belting and cursing in the piss and cow flop as the beasts are sent one by one into the cattle crush. Their backsides spewing and their swishing tails sending the chocolate coloured fluid flying. Come without my umbrella, and everything in range turning brown. The clatter of the gate locked around beasts' necks as they struggle to burst loose. The purple nosed Mad Vet in his green overalls with his little bag of tricks. Hypodermic in his cold red hands, slamming it down deep into the cattle rumps, and the shiny instrument bouncing off and falling into the mud every time he hits a bone. A wipe of the needle on a sleeve and the Mad Vet again pounding the now bent needle into the cow's hide. Of course the Mad Vet would always come when other more horsy vets wouldn't. But always not long after he arrived one would soon wish he remained away like the other vets. Dear me I suppose there is and one does certainly feel a certain distaste in this chore. The castration always giving one an unexplained strange pain in one's own testicles. Especially as one hears the men shouting.

'By god get that one trying to get away, we'll clip him good and proper.'

But one has always to make sure the men don't go splitting open and spilling out the brains of a beast trying to use an axe to hack off a horn which the cutter only mangled. Which bloody hell Thomas at this ruddy moment is doing. Henry

108

trying to hammer the poor beast's head. And O god has now broken the dehorning handle. Best thing is to keep one's mouth shut. And stay well back out of the chaos and mayhem. And follow to the letter old Sexton's advice.

'Master Darcy it's not your place to have to dirty your hands or soil your footwear in the muck. The men would think no better or less of you if you couldn't wield a spade properly and they'd think far worse of you if you could.'

Henry manoeuvring up on a rung of the cattle crush, sawing the remains of a horn off with an old rusty hack saw. Good lord, the blood. But if one complains, by god the panic things they then think of doing to remedy the situation are far worse. Head groom Slattery now wielding the hedgerow secateurs for lopping branches. The dents in his brow more obvious than usual, that Foxy his son put in his father's head with a hammer while he was sleeping in bed. Luke tying a hopeless tourniquet as the beast's pair of massive horns are sheared off. The blood gushing and splashing like a fountain. The bright crimson serum pouring out over the animal's eyes and down its nose and the hole where the horn once was oozing red gore. The Mad Vet shouting down the length of the cattle crush.

'Ah now I'm no member of the Royal Society for the Prevention of Cruelty to Animals but that's murderous, by god, you wouldn't want that done now to your own skulls would you.'

The Mad Vet shaking his head in disapproval. At least and at last someone has an ounce of compassion in all this conspicuous pain. But outspoken words spoken always lead to a smouldering discontentment in the men. And later inevitably lead to violence. If a fight doesn't erupt any second. Of course the Mad Vet can remove a cigarette from a man's mouth at six paces with his hunting whip. But Foxy's immensely strong father, who can lift five railway ties over his head in one hand, would attack anyone at the drop of even a remotely censorious syllable addressed to him. And has sent inmates running for their lives out of many a pub. And would stand in the middle of the road in the moonlight if there were any, shouting challenges to those escaped to come out of the hedgerows. No bloody wonder the jets of potential manure are spewing out from cattle backsides in fear and trembling. And faded yellow piss splashing down from heifers' rears and bullocks' bellies. Making a soup of the brown rapidly deepening mud. And the beasts' tails sending the spewing cow flop splattering in every direction. In the slippery mêlée the men as well as the cattle tripping all over themselves. Good god there are stones, rocks and boulders everywhere.

'Luke be careful someone's going to get killed. What on earth are all the stones doing in the paddock sticking up like treacherous icebergs.'

'Didn't we sir put them there. And they are for gaining a foot hold on.'

'Good grief. But you're stumbling all over them.'

'Ah that's a fact, it would seem.'

And O lord, what now is this. On the top rung of a stout timber fence overlooking the yard, Lois. Perched high, bundled up in her duffel coat and with a pencil sketching in her sketch book. This really is too bloody much. No wonder no battle blows have been struck yet. With Lois having a way of making it known that, with the recent exception of Rashers, she is open to all comers. And the men are too bloody busy showing off and putting on a spectacle to please her. Lois. Queen of the cattle crush. And good heavens Rashers too. Has just arrived, grinning ear to ear. Always a bad sign. Of something appalling about to happen which will be disastrous for me and highly amusing to him. But at least he is having the good sense to keep well out of horns way behind a wall. And I knew it. By god, now look what is happening. A beast has smashed a rung out of the fence and is loose. And Luke is making matters no better by battering the poor mad creature across the ears with a pickaxe handle. And wouldn't it have to be one of my best pure bred Herefords.

'Fucking get her, the eegit animal get her. I'll give her a fucking belt. She's going to fucking well get over the wall. Sorry for the language ma'am.'

The fear crazed wild heifer, eyes bulging and foam flying from its jaws, charging at the men dodging and tripping into the mud out of her way. The animal giving a blood curdling roar, leaping up against the farmyard wall. Its head and horns smashing again and again and hoofs scrabbling at the stone. Its tongue reddened with blood pouring out of its mouth. The heifer jumping. Landing bellowing, stuck straddling the top of the wall.

'Belt her one, belt her. Get round the other side and give her a bit of a tap of the pickaxe handle.'

The heifer instead hit between the eyes with a boulder and falling backwards down off the wall. The cattle in the paddock stampeding. The Mad Vet knocked over. The cattle hoofs trampling his instrument case. Luke in the middle of the paddock, yanked forward, holding onto a beast's tail. And catapulted face down into the sea of mud and pulled over the stones. Head groom Slattery butted from behind and sent skywards, flying over the back of the wild heifer and grabbing her horns. Never mind my best pedigree heifer, this could spell the end of one's ruddy outdoor staff. And O my goodness, also not to mention my guests and in ruddy particular the commissioned painter of my only half finished portrait, Lois. However, as heinous a thing as it may be to think, my prize heifer's safety is priority above all others.

The Mad Vet wiping the cow dung from his nose and lips and tottering to his feet. And, just as he adjusts his blue handkerchief in his breast pocket and flower in his button hole, is from behind knocked flat again on his face. Thomas trying to rescue the castration pliers from the trampling cattle hoofs, losing his cap as it is trod down out of sight into the slime. An hysterical cackle out of Lois as she quickly sketches, the cattle scrambling in all directions and crushing their weight up against the railings. The fence splintering, cracking and collapsing. And Lois with it. Dumped toppling backwards off the top rung. White sheets of paper floating down into the mud. Through one of which a beast's hoof has just been put.

'O my god. My sketches. My priceless sketches.'

Lois's wellington boots up ended, landing arse and wrists deep in the chocolate slime of cow flop and piss tinted mud. Her tweed skirt ballooning up under her duffel coat. Rashers safe on the other side of the wall at the bottom end of the paddock, bent over double, erupting with roars of laughter and beating his clenched fist on his knee. Lois still clutching her pencil, her back and bottom thick with mud as she struggles up, and falls back down again. Rashers twisting around backwards and falling helpless against the wall, holding his stomach as Lois's high pitched refined Bloomsbury accent penetrates the chill winter air.

'Please come someone and bloody well help me. I'm bloody stuck. And if you Rashers so much as dare to continue to laugh I shall, when I get up from here, kill you.'

The Mad Vet clawing his way back to his feet. Stumbling over the boulders and stones and dodging through cattle, attempting to gentlemanly rush to Lois's aid. Thomas finding his cap and throwing it back on his head, the cow dung leaking down over his ears. But wouldn't you know the Mad Vet is totally ignoring the welfare of my ruddy livestock to go dance attendance upon Lois. And has left his hypodermic stuck in the arse of one of my best pedigree Hereford cows. My god that's what one gets letting guests have the run of the place. And it is bloody evident that it is to them that hired help give their ruddy priority.

'Madam don't move I'm to your assistance this moment.

112

And before another two seconds of this cattle stampede becomes unforgettable local parish history.'

The Mad Vet in his formerly green and now brown blood bespattered apron still trying to make his way between the beasts and wade across the farmyard to Lois arse deep beyond the trampled fence. And whoops. He's bloody tripped yet again on a bloody projecting stone. And good grief is pitching flat faced sliding down the incline in the ankle deep muck. Lois half up, now falling full length backwards, laughing. Rashers shouting above the roars of the mêlée.

'By god. It's ruddy Vesuvius erupted again.'

The Mad Vet struggling slowly up to his feet, spitting the mud out of his mouth. Just as the big Hereford cow goes shaking the hypodermic out of her backside. And promptly crushes the glass instrument under her hoof into the slime. The white of the vet's eyes in his chocolate coloured face making him look like a golliwog. Henry and Thomas previously bent over double, roaring with mirth, now both picking the mud out of their own ears. The cattle all now safely escaped out into distant fields and bogs. Bringing the dehorning and castration to a halt with over a hundred more in the herd to do. Rashers, with an elegant bow, waving his cap down across his knee.

'Ah Lois not only do your white knickers have an entirely unnice but genuine farmyard brown colour, but also your sketches should now possess a suitable aged background reminiscent of the early Leonardo da Vinci. And, if I may say so, I do think your knickers, so marvellously authenticated as being involved in the struggle the true artist confronts in these tempestuous times, ought along with your tits go hang in the Louvre.'

'And I, you wretched philistine, shall bloody well promise when I get my hands on them to take those castration pliers and squeeze off your wretched balls and hang them somewhere.'

Till they resemble
Nothing more than
A couple of old
Dried up
Canapés

8

The wild heifer charging everyone out of the way and, with another leap, making it over the wall. Rashers briefly taking up the stance of a matador. And making a sweeping gesture with his cap as the heifer's horns sweep by him to tear the rusty spokes out of the wheel of a hay rake. Rashers suddenly deciding discretion better than valour and disappearing behind some old farm machinery. From which he emerged with rope fashioned into a lariat.

'This is heinous. Somebody please get me out of here.'

In the empty cattle pen Lois still stuck deep in mud. Rashers, over Lois's protestations, twirling the lasso over his head and landing it neatly around Lois's shoulders and, with an almighty tug, pulling her out. Luke looking like a golliwog, tottering over with laughter, and making a remark that one did not catch but Lois did, and, when upright and Rashers removing the lasso, slapping Luke across the face. By god one was furious. One doesn't mind one's guests making themselves feel at home but when they take to striking one's staff that's another matter entirely. Even admitting the cheeky buggers deserved it.

The heifer charging past the back of the barns and galloping up, tearing hoof deep holes across the side lawns of Andromeda Park. Chased now by Crooks who, hobbling out of the house in all his arthritic infirmity, is waving a poker. But as I rushed up the hill to the top to survey the pleasure gardens, the heifer disappeared from sight. Unceremoniously crashing splashing right into the lily pond. Its horns and white nosed head and big flapping ears finally emerging as it swims through the plants, and paws to get up out the other side. O god. What next. Yes, next. A mud encrusted Lois is now at the side of the lily pond. You'd think she already had enough to worry about getting her farmyard sketches safely retrieved from the cattle pen and on their way to the Louvre without now accusing us all of cruelty to animals.

'You must do something. That poor animal. Drowning. How awful. Its blood is in the water. It is absolutely the most disgustingly distressing display of heartlessness I think I have ever witnessed.'

'For god's sake Lois do please shut up. It fell in there. We didn't put her there. And I'm the one to whom the cruelty is being done. And it's financial cruelty. That's a prize heifer.'

The chug chug of the old tractor. Coming around the corner of the rhododendrons. The big wheels miring in deep across the lawn. With Thomas driving. At least for a moment someone has sense. Luke with buckets. And scooping water out of the lily pond onto the lawn. His brilliant idea to empty it which would only take until exactly this time next year. Plus leaving the heifer forever stranded deep down in a hole.

'Luke that's not going to help. Get ropes around the beast. Without fracturing or pulling off a leg. Tug her up over the edge of the pond.'

The tractor wheels reversing, cutting their way deeper into the lawn. Pulled by the neck, the heifer's strangled roars. Inch by inch, up and over the edge of the lily pond. Lois in her mud encrusted duffel coat, gesticulating and screaming. Her sheaf of mud splattered sketches in one hand and leaning forward, trying with the other hand to loosen the rope around the beast's neck.

'You brutes. You utterly callous brutes. You're choking her.'

'Lois please. Shut the bloody hell up and get out of the way of the rope before you get hurt.'

'O my god. I can't swim. Save me. My sketches.'

116

A piece of concrete along the edge of the pond crumbling under Lois's boot. Just as the heifer is on the verge of coming out. Lois falling in. All at the pond side straining to hold on to the heifer and not let go of the ropes. As Lois's mud encrusted face disappears down into the more than ten foot depths. My god. Which my grandfather ensured would give ample room to the carp. And into which Lois may now have eternally sunk, entangled in the roots of the water lily plants at the bottom if they grow that deep. I had thought of immediately letting go of the rope and making a grab for Lois but one has always firmly believed that non swimmers at least come up for a first or second if not a third and last time. Now one of the big carp may be nibbling at a nipple of one of her wonderful tits. While one racks one's brain to remember the amount one is insured for public liability. But at least, with a final heave and tractor tug, the heifer's out. And surely no court in Ireland would award much for the drowning of one genuinely impecunious protestantly pagan artist late of Bloomsbury and Montparnasse, who, when the mood suits her, professes free love. And paints the male nude with organ rampant.

'Please stand back everyone.'

Rashers on the lawn in his waistcoat and stockinged feet. Launching himself into the air and arching into a neat dive and disappearing down into the lily pond. Two house guests gone. Luckily one has two spare coffins. And Sexton need measure up only Rashers's grave. Although perhaps they would be furious to be buried together in one hole. My portrait left unfinished. Which, one must now admit, was coming on rather well and made one look extremely regal in one's Master's kit.

'Ah god now, you'll never see head nor tail of the two of them again. Sure no one's ever been to the bottom of that pond. It comes out somewhere in China.'

'Please shut up Luke and look to getting some straw to put around the heifer.'

Grey dark clouds gathering in from the west. Flurries of snow beginning to fall. Sexton arriving. Windows of Andromeda Park filled with onlookers. Norah, Sheila, Catherine and Dingbats. The heifer stretched out on its side on the lawn, catching its breath. Bubbles rising to the surface of the lily pond. Hold my own breath in horror as the seconds go by. In this present black cold eternity. Luke hanging over the water, peering into the depths.

'Ah now you'll never see the pair of them again.'

The shrunken brown faded shapes of the lily leaves just beneath the surface of the water. As one stares down and sees no sign of life. Until suddenly, up at the other end of the pool, Lois's head reappearing, shoved up out of the water by Rashers. A long plait of her hair floating on the surface. A pond plant across her quite patrician nose. And once again, but this time with some heartfelt relief, one heard that familiar voice of complaint ring out.

'I've nearly been drowned. My sketches. They're down there.'

Rashers treading water and holding Lois up and grinning with a goldfish in his mouth. A gang of escaped cattle arriving back to view proceedings from the edge of the lawn. Everyone fighting for the privilege of pulling Lois out. Including the Mad Vet ignoring my prize heifer unable to regain her feet and whose breathing has now become laboured. Rashers's lasso wrapped around Lois, nearly choking her. The Mad Vet a hold of one arm, Luke grabbing her by the other, and both tugging in opposite directions. Lois screaming.

'You utter idiots. Stop. You're pulling my arms out of their sockets.'

'By god now it's a fact, can't you hear the inhuman cries out of her ladyship. We're drawing and quartering her, the poor woman. Damn it man don't let her go she's sinking.'

Strings of long slimy pond weeds draped in Lois's hair and down the side of her face as she lies stretched prone on the

118

lawn, gasping for air. Strange how one notices strange things at the strangest of times. Looking up as I often did towards the roof to make sure a slate or two weren't loosening to plummet down upon us. And a face high up in a bedroom window of the servants' floor. A face I've never seen before, suddenly disappearing. And Rashers becoming a reassuring sight, dripping from his moustache and smiling happily now that I was clearly deeply indebted to him. Lois still seeming to expel water out of her mouth and looking like something the cat had dragged in. And I did gently comment.

'Good god Lois I did warn you not to come out to the castration.'

But before this drama was over another had begun. Hay was on fire in the barn. One really must finally bloody well play pop with everyone. A fire built under the tractor to warm the engine to start it, the flames setting alight the straw. Explaining why Luke was filling buckets and why the bell in the bell tower is ringing. And everybody everywhere running in all directions. Smoke billowing up from the farmyard. The heifer left laid out in exhaustion. And the ghost of Capability Brown will have to be resurrected to obliterate the landscape scars. The tractor tyres having dug ruts deep enough in the lawn to bury coffins in. Good god almighty, even though one has not soiled one's gloves or got splashed with water, there was no doubt one was entirely ready to abandon all forms of behaviour one supposes one attempts to retain as pasha of Andromeda Park's stately surrounds such as they are and to especially avoid agriculture forever and ever and ever. And simply make ready to go racing for the rest of one's life.

And absolutely every ounce of hot water was used in the house for baths. Of course everyone but me thought the morning was all a bit of a chuckle over lunch. No one giving a ruddy blessed damn that one was almost half burned to death and that the cattle would have to be rounded up again from all over the place. With about a third of one's hay destroyed before the fire was put out. Sexton saving the day and the barn with a hose from the rainwater troughs. However, having quaffed back three large sherries before lunch, I suppose the day's disasters could be looked upon much like the end of a day's hunting when one swears secretly to never risk life and limb again but then recounts with a certain relish how one dislocated a shoulder, broke a few fingers, sprained both wrists, but got only mild concussion bouncing off a stone with one's head. Of course, absent was all the damn tiresome refrain everyone seems to make concerning their unpremeditated dismounting, absolving their horse from all blame and ad nauseam repeating how it was entirely, completely and absolutely their own fault. But this clearly wasn't the summing up of a day's hunting by a table full of rural types. But rather the continuation of backhanded compliments uttered by Rashers just as the boy butler was rather smirkingly serving him the Brussels sprouts, and Rashers, unloading another six on his already heaped plate, was playing to the gallery as household faces peeked in the pantry door as it swung ajar. There was no doubt that he was enjoying to the full his celebrity for having recently saved a life.

'Ah Lois what an eventful appetite inciting morning we've had. And out of your muddy old duffel coat you do look quite marvellous in that silk dress. The cerulean blue colour goes with your eyes you know. And the silk fabric splendidly suits your figure.'

'Well that they may do. And flattery may get you somewhere, but silk is quite chilly compared to wool and without this shawl I should be absolutely freezing cold. Since my divorce from my parsimonious husband and in my present awfully impecunious circumstances in which he has deliberately and so wretchedly left me, one can't afford silk. It may be the very last time you shall see me so attired.'

'Lois I fervently hope not. Absolutely fervently hope not. And I know I speak here for my host as well who enthusiastically agrees with me. It damn well befits you my dear. Just as the slight muskiness of this noble claret does this sublime lamb. Damn suits you. But you must you know, with your quite marvellous legs we so rarely see, not wear those old passion quenching white long knickers of yours.'

'You may have saved my life dear boy but that does not now give you the right to assume you have an authority to advise me upon my lingerie. Which I choose solely to keep my arse warm if you must know.'

Mundane matters were tumbling through one's mind as one sat to this lunch facing out upon the back lawns of Andromeda Park across which already roamed stray cattle. While all kinds of sundry thoughts were passing through one's head. Montparnasse, the Louvre and the reputed to be exciting boulevards and cafés of Paris. Plus wondering had anyone yet cleaned up the mess of the front hall. Lois having left a nice trail of mud and slimy strands of pond weed across the tiles as she kept dancing up on one foot and then the other, attempting to shake the water out of her ear. Then when Lois presented herself to be outfitted from my mother's wardrobe, it did take some doing to convince Crooks who, in an apoplectic tizzy and with his fly conspicuously open, was beside himself and in obvious spiritual pain, unlocking and relocking the door and inviting me into the privacy of the Porcelain Room.

'Master Reginald I am not going to mince my words. It is sacrilege committed against the memory of your mother and my dear Antoinette Delia Darcy Darcy Thormond. To whom I am as devoted now as I was when her beauty strode through the halls of this very house. Don't I attend without fail each day her vault, to see there's always the fresh flower there where I kneel on the moss to pray, my arthritis permitting. Would you now have me beat my breast in contrition to her for allowing one of her dresses to be worn by another, who is after all, without casting aspersions, of Dublin's bohemian set and traipsing with her boots in the house.'

'Crooks I do understand. But I'm sure my mother would have wished that someone might have benefited, and certainly in an emergency, by being able to wear a garment of hers.'

'And Master Reginald, while we are on domestic subjects there is a further observation I should like to make. But since I see you are pushed for time perhaps it is better left for another moment.'

'Do please say what's on your mind Crooks.'

'Well I should not want you to think Master Reginald that I am getting above myself in venturing such a suggestion but to my way of thinking it is high time there was a mistress of this house. Having a mind to the dozen things an hour that need attention. Such as setting the menus and arranging seating at the dining table that your mother did. Now there'll never be another like her. But the presence of the Lady of the Manor would also keep some of the females of this household in their place and from getting their grand ideas, if you follow me.'

'I don't for the life of me now know what you're on about Crooks.'

'They'd be after thinking they could marry you Master Reginald.'

'Good heavens Crooks, that is rather a somewhat ridiculous assumption.'

'Well you mark now what I'm saying. And as you well know I have Master Reginald all these faithful years since kept everything in its place in her ladyship's apartments. Not even a speck of dust do I disturb if I can help it. She's there. I know she's there. She sees and hears me. I've answered her voice whenever she rings or calls.'

There was no question that it was damn true about the undisturbed specks of dust. But one doubted Crooks's wish for a new lady of the manor. As one did certainly continue to hear Crooks's imagined conservations with my mother. There were even moments when I shuddered, thinking I also had heard her soft lilting voice replying. Just as she used to say to me as she sat in the bath, please Darcy darling would you mind passing me my loofah. And when she used to say, don't Darcy darling, when I played as I sometimes did tweaking the nipple of her breast. One could not really blame old Crooks too much, approaching as he must be now half a century in age. Plus I suppose too getting a little more than somewhat slightly loony.

'Crooks my god we are getting to be snobs in this household.'

'Snobbery it may be but would you sir have an upstairs maid issuing me with orders.'

'I deign to suggest Crooks that we are, after all, all of us equal in the sight of God.'

Crooks leaving specks of dust was the least of it. And one had long ago accepted the progressively mouldering mildew which had already affected most of my mother's nearly one hundred pairs of shoes also left undisturbed by Crooks in her dressing room closet. A considerable amount of blue green mould having had to be wiped off the pair of inappropriately high heeled shoes Lois had chosen to wear to the races. But at least this was a chance to be able to banter a reference to god, equality and that there existed a flavour of democracy in the management of the household and also to inquire of Crooks as to the strange face one saw at the window.

'Ah sir Master Reginald I hope you won't mind now it's my niece, you'll remember is the daughter of my only elder sister, down from Dublin been visiting me these few days. I said she'd have to make herself useful and keep herself well out of the way. She'd like now to be an actress like that great Ria Mooney.'

'An actress. Good gracious me. Well Crooks clearly she's come to the right place. We've got enough stage performances going on left, right and centre here to inspire any intending thespian.'

'I take your meaning Master Darcy. Indeed I take it.'

Protracted by three bottles of one's best claret, and a decanter of port, lunch certainly delayed one taking one's ease on the gentle hills of Kilbeggan, and clearly we would miss the first race. But my goodness Lois's high heeled shoes really did show her considerably well shaped legs to advantage.

'Lois you really do don't you have well turned ankles.'

'Well yes, as a matter of fact I do, I rather think. As a little girl I did train for the ballet.'

Lois also without so much as a by your leave further chose to wear my mother's sable hat and coat. But indeed ending her up looking like some quite astonishing Russian imperial royal highness. In furs which did actually come from Russia's Siberian wastes. Crooks, as you might expect, bursting straight into tears and disappearing instead of going to look for an extra shooting stick for the races, having, as I had, given the one in the hall stand to Rashers. But as for Lois, one had never quite witnessed such a transformation in anyone. From an impecunious, woolly long underweared bohemian to becoming some frightfully regal looking empress. And the sudden haughtiness she had no hesitation in exhibiting took one quite aback as she postured about on the porch. To put it mildly she was quite totally unbelievable. Her very British voice up an octave. And I did find myself complimenting both of my guests.

'I must say Lois you do rather knock the eye out.'

'Thank you darling. Thank you.'

'And you Rashers are a wonderful, colourful sight of tweedy hues.'

Darcy Dancer pulling closed the great oak front door. Following behind Rashers Ronald stepping down the front steps. Rashers by the Daimler, wiping his monocle clean and sticking it in his eye. His tie blowing in the breeze and his long locks of reddish golden hair flowing from beneath his cap. The distant sound of a train whistle. Rashers opening up the seat of his shooting stick and propping it into the pebbles and leaning back to sit as he surveys around him.

'Ah Darcy I am just taking the precaution to see that my arse fits comfortably upon this. While I was just thinking that one must be coming up to one's hundredth anniversary of the number of times I have had sexual relations with my betrothed. And so nice that you have a roof that pulls back on your most handsome motor car. And one can look forward to our speeding along the roads of summertime. Good show dear boy, good show. However, for the moment with these few snowflakes and with a rather large amount of lunch under one's belt, a little chill breeze on one's face will rid one of that highly seductive lazy after lunch sleepiness when one's mind is wont to turn to saucy matters. But dear boy why do we delay.'

'We're just waiting for Crooks to fetch another shooting stick.'

'Well dear boy you won't mind then if I excuse myself to take a pee.'

Rashers sauntering off to disappear into the rhododendrons along the drive. A pair of horses go galloping over a hillside and disappear in the parkland. Crooks finally descending the steps with the shooting stick and a picnic basket for tea and halfway down nearly tumbling on his face. But one did feel a sudden lifting of the senses and a flicker of optimism. With two people whose acquaintanceship had now turned them into friends. And I suppose if I ever could find a suitable wife one's life could be complete. Yet can it ever be. Last night I was in a terrible dream. Haunted as I still am, I was shouting and chasing after Leila, who was being dragged off away from me in a huge railway station. And I awoke, my both hands clutching the bed post.

'Ah my dear Darcy, although hardly the moment for such reflections, I think that a good piss has settled my tumescence temporarily. And you know it has just struck me, emerging

125

from the darkness of your rhododendrons, that it is utterly unthinkable that you would ever deign consider abandoning all this. The quite splendid elevations of your mansion sitting in your glorious domain. Even the winterish meadows glow emerald. Of course perhaps you are a little short of well-drained level pastureland. And the house may indeed be in need of some modernization with electric wires, but it does marvellously proclaim your lofty station in the world. And your gleaming elegant motor here, ready to purr us off to the races, and into which will any moment climb great artists. Dear boy you must take heart, some families in England have remained put for twenty generations or more. And just every so often need only to put on a new roof. Out there beyond, scattered about your grounds, are damn fine stands of trees. From my premedical botanical studies I do believe I spy not only Norway spruce, oak, beech, larch, hornbeam, but ah too Spanish chestnut and a live oak. Provide a very nice bit of loose change, you know. Need only to apply to the Minister for Lands for a licence to fell trees. I could easily find you a buyer.'

'I'm not about to start cutting down my trees Rashers. And this Rashers is not England. Where ancient traditions and heritage are held in high esteem. Here it is the custom for everything to fall down. And if it doesn't, then the peasants which exist about one will knock or burn it down. The point always being to drive the squire out of his lair or his mind, to get his land. And to meanwhile keep giving him damn good kicks in his goolies.'

Crooks with the shooting stick and picnic and Lois waiting for him to open the car door for her. Tucking up her furs to squeeze in the cramped back seat of the Daimler. Holding her face askance under her sable hat as Rashers pushes his face in over the car door.

'Is that not right Lois, my old darling, best time for people to go bang, bang is after lunch.'

'Well for you Rashers I'm sure you do go bang, bang, bang

126

after lunch. But I simply as an artist definitely can't, having too much work to do to bang, bang after lunch.'

'Well bang, bang I suppose that settles that. And my old what for is decidedly detumescing. But Lois you do my old lovely, look so exotically magnificent.'

'Well as you've saved my life recently I shall take that as genuine compliment.'

Under darkening skies and more flurries of snow the motor car rolling its wheels over the drive, the rhododendron leaves shaking, pebbles beating up under the mud guards. Nearing the front gates, the great meadows flanking the roadway. Passing out by the gate lodge, Rashers pointing the end of his shooting stick.

'But your entrance lodge. Dear boy you absolutely must spruce it up a mite. And remove the tree growing through the roof. But of course it just occurs to me that back in the big house you have no Sculpture Hall. Ah but perhaps that hardly matters and I need hardly remind you that there is an artist in residence of some considerable rank and reputation, one of whose portraits shall not only soon adorn a proper place in your front hall but whose work shall be seen in the world's great museums. Is that not so Lois, my dear.'

'Darling as much as I enjoy to hear it, you do attribute entirely too much emphasis to my worldly recognition as a painter which sadly but as a matter of fact is practically non-existent beyond the limited confines of Montparnasse, Bloomsbury and Dublin.'

'Ah Lois, I'm sure our dear host here will agree when I solemnly predict that as your tits presently do, so shall your paintings hang splendidly, radiantly and triumphantly in the Louvre.'

'Darling Rashers I think I am going to rather regret the fact of your saving my life as it prevents me from saying, at least for the moment, something quite solemnly rude to you. Like fuck off. To Timbuktu.'

127

'Lois darling, you must believe me when old Lord Ronald says that immediately upon his return to Dublin he shall solicit sitters for you from the most elite of the non cheque-bouncing aristocracy, and at fees which will make your knees tremble with delight and which forever after shall allow you not only to adorn yourself in silks but also in such exotic furs as you are presently wearing. And my percentage as agent will be quite modest. Quite modest I assure you, you can count on that my dear. By jove one might oneself slash a few brush strokes on a canvas. And on this increasingly optimistic day, one is feeling damn chipper, and you Darcy must forget your old cattle worries and buck immediately up. Keep the old ligaments supple. The motto is. Endure, prevail, support life, cheat death. And by the way apropos of such motto, you couldn't my dear old chap could you, find your way clear to slipping me a fiver. And it matters not a damn if it's English or Irish.'

Darcy Dancer, a slow smile breaking across his face, removing a hand from the driving wheel, pulling off a driving glove and digging into a pocket. Rashers, who shifts the monocle in his eye, takes the roll of bills, doffs his cap, and peels off a large white English five pound note.

'Dear boy may I lessen the uncomfortable thickness this sheaf must be making in your pocket. Would you awfully mind if I took two instead of one.'

'Rashers I do believe that the number of previous fivers, whose removal from my pocket was presumably meant to make me more comfortable, is now considerable.'

'Point taken dear boy, point taken.'

'Well, since it is, you may meanwhile lessen my discomfort by another fiver.'

'Dear boy, multo, multo thanks. Not only shall I repatriate these after the third or is it perhaps the fourth race, in which the Durrow-Mountmellton steed is an absolute certainty or else I don't know my racing blood lines from a tinker's hole in a pot. But I shall also treat you to some bubbly and pop a codicil in my will which will more than mention something you will ultimately hear of to your advantage. Don't you agree Lois that our host is one divine gentleman.'

'Yes darling, I do, I do.'

The gleaming low slung motor car swiftly covering the miles across these boggy lowlands. Snow falling from the tumbling grey blue clouds. The glint of a lake through the trees. A farmer throwing hay from a cart to his cattle. Along the side of the road a cycle weaving left and right, a dark figure hunched over the handle bars. An inebriated man on two wheels.

'Good god Darcy you just missed the ruddy bugger. Shows you doesn't it, how people these days really don't give a damn how they inconvenience others who are having to hurry not to miss the second race.'

Lois, without a single recent complaint, luxuriating on the back seat in her furs. From the leaden sky ahead even the weather is deciding to respond to the swathe Lois is cutting, and one could ruddy well be out somewhere with her in the ruddy Ural mountains of Siberia. Her divorced husband's naval duffel coat left drying down in the kitchens. And of course one might have known that, throughout the carefully couched compliments and urgent great expectations delivered with his usual verve and ornate rhetoric, Rashers would have a non returnable loan up his old tweed sleeve. But his un-quenchable optimism does cheer one. And there is no doubt that to venture out socially does lighten the spirit and relieve the domestic burdens. If a roof top chimney now topples over or another rat big as a pig comes jumping out of somewhere and goes galloping down the halls sending the staff into rout, damn it all there's not a damn silly thing or damn all I can do about it. But my god how much longer can one hang on. Even if I further cut wages. Or discover the thieves of tools, trees and turf. Or sack the layabouts. Or ration bacon, eggs, butter, tea, cream and the barmbrack. Or even if I should find a Miss von B again to impose a military discipline. And march the staff back and forth, left right, left right, up and down the halls. Halt you buggers, now lick up all that dust.

'Rashers I know you won't mind my saying this in front of Lois and one does not want to raise matters which may be harmful to your future but I do believe your name appears rather heavily printed in the most recent edition of *Stubb's Gazette*.'

'Darcy this bantering about concerning my present very small indebtedness I take as a dreadful slur upon my character. The whole matter is de minimis. Damn unfeeling landlord. I have a little rent owing and a few miserable bills overlooked. Everything shall be put right in what is commonly referred to as a jiffy.'

The Daimler pulling off the road into a field to park. Through the flurries of snow the threesome crossing a whitening pasture to a hillside. Horses taking their last parade before the start of the second race. Everyone who is anyone from every parish for miles around. Rashers grinning optimistically ear to ear. The sky covered with dark clouds. The wind colder. Snow thickening on the ground. Lois with her coat collars raised and her hands dug deep inside my mother's big sable muff. Rashers leaning close to whisper.

'Lois my dear where is your sketch book. In your wonderful furs you seem not to be pursuing the muse as it were.'

'My sketch book has, for the time being, been left in the motor car, dear boy. This happens to be an occasion when my mind's eye records what I shall deem worthy of executing back in my studio.'

'Ah Darcy did you hear that. Isn't the artist's life wonderful. Just to gaze upon what is about them. And then when the moment should so inspire, to squiggle a few lines and splash a few colours on an old piece of paper. Tell me Lois do you ever give thanks to the gods for having blessed you with your genius which of course preserves you from ever becoming a seedy old boring hag. Even when you are at a considerably advanced age, fashionable Dubliners will still be flocking to gain entry to your studio.'

'O please shut up you. I'm here to enjoy the racing.'

Rashers watching Lois's departure as she saunters off towards the drinks tent. And followed immediately by various male members of the hunt, falling all over to introduce themselves. Both the First Whip and Amnesia Murphy the farmer foaming at the mouth. And the rear taken up by the Mad Major who, recent rumour has it, has got more than one of his housemaids up the pole, rogering them as he preferred to do, while he wore ladies' undergarments.

'Dear me Darcy the lady is in a huff. And the chaps rushing after her are clearly in rut. Makes one quite jealous. However, my dear friend, unartistic as I am, and when one has so recently escaped death, it is a rather wonderful feeling to be alive, isn't it. You do provide your guests with such marvellous country adventures and diversions. And so nice to get away from the sometimes blatantly resentful hostile hatred that some people cannot help revealing on their faces towards their betters up in the metropolis these days. You mustn't Darcy look so down in the mouth. Just sniff the air, wafting upon our nostrils from these rolling lovely emerald fields. Let the snowflakes melt gently upon the face. Ah. This is, if I may say so, a rather fashionable race meeting. Even the bookmakers, so hardened to the ways of the world, look quite decorously cheerful. And I see some of the bigger punters down from Dublin and a notable trainer or two. Yes, a splendid and wonderful feeling to be alive. And Darcy no need for you to continue your prolonged reflective silence.'

Rashers's repeated references to the present pleasures of being alive did not succeed in obliterating from one's consciousness the further imbroglio which promptly ensued following getting Lois out of the lily pond and who, as I was assisting

131

away towards the house, left Luke trying, as he said, to put manners upon the prostrate heifer. There he was, winding up, belting the poor creature with the thick end of his pickaxe handle to urge her to her feet from where she lay unable to get up from the lawn. The Mad Vet trying to grab the hickory bludgeon out of Luke's hand as he was aiming another blow down on the beast's head. And Luke turning instead to take a swipe at the Mad Vet, who, poor man, having just arisen from the slime of the farmyard, got poleaxed down again. With Rashers then intervening. And all three falling into the lily pond. Which at least had the good luck to frighten the heifer to her feet and she ambled off to join the loose herd. All distinctly adding to my further worry concerning public liability. But it did cross my mind, however, that one was possessed at Andromeda Park of a considerable fighting force which could be marshalled together against would be bill collectors, poachers, trespassers, marauders and like kind. But I really did deeply wonder when the surprises of this day would be over. And despite all the recent mayhem, the forlorn loneliness overtaking one these past many weeks seemed still to persist. One already toyed with the seemingly bizarre idea that instead of some débutantish immature flighty girl, that one should consider marrying a lady perhaps older and wiser than oneself. As appallingly shocking as it is, the truth of the matter is that one would not have to look further than an absolutely transformed Lois, appearing and behaving so splendidly statuesquely, not to say exotically royal and so totally full of her new regal self. Except, in my mother's shoes she chose, she is sinking in the turf with their rather too high heels and with each step has to yank them out. However, one was taking pleasure basking to be seen in her company. And in everyone's curiosity concerning her. What an astonishing change clothes can bring. With Lois's face framed in furs, her nose especially effected a certain haughty elegance reminiscent of Miss von B. One did feel an awfully sneaky snobbery overcoming one. Which to my astonishment was putting my penis into a state of painfully embarrassingly rigid tumescence. I mean good lord, could one suppose old bloody bohemian Lois, up whom everyone in Dublin is rumoured to have got, was of some aristocratic lineage. Even Rashers sporting his unentitled title and, arrant commoner though he is, is also clearly much impressed.

'By god Darcy old Lois has left us rather in the lurch. But you know I've rarely ever seen such a glamorously handsome figure of a woman as she presents this afternoon. And my, as the squire of Andromeda Park, your long county ancestry is earning many a tipped cap on every side. We do I think rather cut a swathe across the turf. And do look at that. Number four. In the mauve, brown and magenta racing colours. Now isn't that nice. Not the liver chestnut mare dear boy, I refer to the jockey rider on top. Who is she dear boy, you must know. What a robust well thighed young thing. Most nice. Perks up the old pecker. Very nice. Just plainly nice. Good god, number four. It's old Durrow-Mountmellton I see by my race card, on Dreamstown Zephyr.'

Durrow-Mountmellton adjusting a stirrup as her big mare nearly comes trodding over us as it turns to parade in the paddock. Old Durrow-Mountmellton's thigh muscles mouth-wateringly showing through the white tightness of her breeches. The gleaming mahogany of her boot tops. I almost thought for a moment, as she glanced in my direction, she was going to ignore me. And then by god she plainly did. One could even sniff the steam out of her mare's nostrils as she walked right by and never looked back. I did rather, I must confess, conspicuously wait to be noticed. And her eyes most certainly met mine. But then I suppose before a race one is rather with butterflies in the stomach. And also when mounted and another stands before you bootless and unhorsed one does assume a certain indifference to their presence.

'Darcy I had entirely forgotten what a nice well set up lass old Durrow-Mountmellton is. A very determined look upon her face. Worthy I do believe of placing a substantial bet. Shall I lay, perhaps, a little something on for you as well Darcy. And by the way before you blame it on someone else it was I who quaffed the remainder of your champagne and smoked salmon you left after you in the library.'

Rashers doing a pirouette and waltzing across the snowy grass to a bookie, a scarf flying from his neck and shouting and gesticulating up on his stand. Dreamstown Zephyr at six to one to win. And I must confess my reluctance in parting with a tenner on Rashers's insistence to place for me to risk adding more debit to one's debts. And one does so get a sinking feeling at every revelation which points in the direction of one being perhaps another's sole support.

'Here you go Darcy and now may I suggest a drink.'

Darcy Dancer handed his betting ticket and led by Rashers towards the refreshment tent. Entering into the din of voices, shouts of greetings, in the middle of which Lois's high pitched laughter can be heard. The smell of moist wool and fumes of cigarette smoke in the crowded warmth. Rashers proffering a glass of whiskey.

'A quick dram Darcy. Buck you up. Correct me if I am wrong dear boy but you do seem to me to be somewhat weighed down and preoccupied by what one might be tempted to think might be melancholia. The sort that should come only when one reaches an age when a fleshy pot appears upon one's belly. Jowls at the throat, accompanied by chronic penile flaccidity. And when out of one's luxuriously thick locks upon one's head, grey hairs begin to fall. But by god dear boy. You're a long way from that.'

'Rashers, from your medical knowledge, how easy is it for one to make another pregnant.'

'Good god. That is a serious question. Just let me tipple back my dram. Ah dat ist das besser as we say in the Deutsch. Now then, the sperm and the ovum. The phenomenon of

134

chemotaxis I believe comes in here. Which is indeed how life on this planet might have begun in a steamy old muddy puddle of water. The molecular mystery of why motile sperm seeks the ovum. Dear me, before one goes into further detail, you old sport you. You haven't have you prodded your flaming haired stunningly curvaceous upstairs housemaid.'

'Rashers please, this is not a joke. It just so happens there is the possibility of a person or persons at Andromeda Park rumoured to be pregnant.'

'Of course dear boy, females in your household could be in the grip of an outbreak of pseudocyesis.'

'Good god, what on earth is that.'

'Hysterical pregnancy dear boy. Phantom baby carried to term. Even the belly gets big but then labour produces no child. Just a lot of old ruddy pretence for a few months. Take no notice of it. Common among country households such as yours where daily proximity incites lustful carousal and where foals, piglets, calves and chicks are popping out all over the ruddy place. Now let's get to more damn serious matters. Upon her mount I would never have recognized old Felicity Durrow-Mountmellton of the old sheep rogering Mountmelltons. And of the enormous acreage of Durrow-Mountmellton Park. Or is it Paradise Park. Or some ruddy such, where sheep may not safely graze. Bang, bang goes the old Major, right up the rear. Take that you old woolly thing. Bang, bang. Confidentially, it's not easy to do you know Darcy. To roger the old quadruped. Tried it myself on my grandfather's farm. I was a mere mite then up on a stool, wanting to know further and better particulars concerning the wondrous mystery of sticking one's private perpendicular in somewhere soft. I'm sure it was such tendency which made me take up the reading of medicine. And the anatomical excitements one might encounter at anatomy demonstrations. And there I was, foolish little fellow, trying to put it up a rather mature Hereford heifer. The stool getting kicked out from right under me just as I was, with my dear little tool quivering with curiosity, ready to gung ho prang the damn thing. Then I got pissed on. The most god awful almighty shower of distastefully acrid bovine urine spouting all over my grey flannel suited innocent little person. Please Darcy please don't look at me in that reproachful priggish legion of decency manner. We're all mammals together you know.'

'Rashers I am merely concentrating my mind on the phenomenon of mammals pissing on each other. But I do feel there's no need to so loudly broadcast your attempts at bestiality all over the place. Some might think having it off with an innocent ruminant a highly ungentlemanly activity. It isn't as if one doesn't know people about.'

'Ah I fear the age of the gentleman, to which status I have never laid claim, is coming to a close dear boy. You, if I may timidly suggest, are one of the very last of that breed. Of course I suppose some gentlemanly remnants still must cling to one. Forgive me dear boy if I am remiss. But one does so easily slip back into the idyllic past to reminisce you know. Nostalgia from my early youth especially seems to overcome me at point to point race meetings. Drink back your dram dear boy and let's now see what one fancies in ladies among the numerous about here. And O I say, by my monocle, look at that. Lois has an ardent admirer in attendance, and also wearing a monocle no less. Do you know the gent Darcy.'

'Yes. He is a well known philanderer, a baronet and, as it happens, an enormous landowner.'

'Dear me Darcy, and isn't Lois clearly loving every minute of it. Meanwhile you couldn't could you dear boy, to save me collecting my winnings till later, see your way clear to advancing me another fiver. It's positively got to be Durrow-Mountmellton on her mare in this race dear boy. Strong boned but moves as delicately as an antelope. Bookmakers were rapidly lowering the odds. Luckily I had already popped a tenner on.'

136

Rashers with his monocle glinting, downing a second dram. And he was of course more than somewhat noticed. And did I suppose cut a very reliable looking county figure, and one might even mistake him for a local gentleman farmer. But meanwhile there is no mistaking that he has left me minus yet another fiver. Lois now totally ignoring us. In my mother's sables, throwing back her head, laughing her penetrating rather horsy laugh at what must be the baronet's joke. People do seem to get so bloody overanimated meeting each other for the first time. Then minutes later start looking over each other's shoulder for someone who might be in their better interests to know. And Rashers is right. One's heart these days does seem to have grown heavy. Melancholia could certainly be what I am suffering from. Even here amid these ladies' hats and faces I wait to look at each dark haired one thinking I might suddenly see Leila. If I gave some very grand ball, the talk of the county, the Mental Marquis would have to come. And she would come too. At least I would see her for a moment. It might relieve the terrible nagging longing. As one seems anyway to do nothing else but lay out money, and get poorer as the slates fall and cattle get maimed or die. Why not then be, for a brief night, extravagant. Then, if I must, go to Dublin or travel to London with another selection from my mother's remaining, but rapidly dwindling, jewels. I suppose I am hardly any different from old Johnny Gearoid, there by the bar with a pint of stout to his lips, who even as a small peasant farmer is a perfect object lesson. Selling his land field by field and drinking every blade of grass down in a pub till he had left just an old shed roof over his head. And as he said, sure that'll do me grand till there comes the day when there are nettles growing over me head instead. But now, somehow, not even racing puts one's burdens out of mind. One must look forward to rely on a day's hunting. When one may present an entirely new and different brand of difficulties, by managing to break an arm, leg or neck.

Upon a frosty and breeze swept knoll. Darcy Dancer viewing with binoculars a horse bolting, and the race's delayed starting on the distant landscape. Against the trees the bright colours of the jockeys blurred by the falling curtain of snow. Lois with her baronet admirer near by. And Rashers very close to one's elbow as he more frequently seems to be these days. Placing his arse on his shooting stick and clearing his throat. And with his handkerchief wiping snow flakes from his monocle.

'Dear boy don't want to distract you from the race about to start, but I have an additional and awfully big favour to ask of you. But I hasten to add as I see you flinch that it is not to do with negotiable instruments such as you have already so generously bestowed on me. This benignity I ask is rather more of a life saving nature. And is in fact in furtherance of my matrimonial plans. I do know it is not quite proper to push such a matter and one should in the full flower of correctness wait to be asked. But alas there is a certain life and death urgency afoot.'

'For heaven's sake Rashers, please what is it.'

'Would you dear boy in my present extraordinary circumstances make an exception as to how these things are usually done and possibly consider to put me up for membership of the Kildare Street Club. And before you say nae, I solemnly promise, should I ever be so fortunate as to be elected to membership, that I shall never once broach loudly to the other members in the bar, dining or morning room of the club my attempts at bestiality, even when one has had an awful amount of port and is waxing romantically lyrical and all within hearing are beside themselves anxious to know what it's like to roger a heifer, or as it happened upon the occasion previously mentioned, to be drenched in bovine piss. I know it's a lot to ask. But damn it all, truth of the matter is, my intended feels that it is a place where occasionally, upon a summer evening following watching cricket in College Park, the two of us might pop in for drinkies and dinner. I know I have spoken out of turn and perhaps deserve the reaction, but dear boy, as my very dearest friend, please speak, as your continued silence is deafening.'

'Rashers they're off and running. And I merely am turning this matter over in my mind. You would be obliged to dig up three members to second you for membership. But even if I did propose you, I do fear that your name published as a debtor in *Stubb's Gazette* would arouse discomfiture and possibly result in your being blackballed in a trice as several very prominent persons of the legal profession are indeed members.'

'O dear. However contrite I am, struck down again. What am I to tell my betrothed. Damn it dear, those stuffy old fogy fuckers in that awful old Victorian pile of brick wherein they release their port provoked after dinner farts, won't hear of my becoming a member. Wherein I might take succour, reclining back before their well known roaring fires, reading and whiling away the gentle hours in their midst, sipping one's Madeira and rustling one's newspaper. And not caring one iota of a fuck for the poor and starving masses who swarm without.'

'Of course that's precisely the kind of remark likely to put off the more conservative of the membership. Surely you can take her to Jammet's for a good dinner, also just a stone's throw across the street from the Provost's garden adjoining College Park.'

'Dear me you don't understand Darcy. You see I have already foolishly represented to my betrothed that I am already a member.'

'Good god Rashers you really are an old silly sod. They're all safely over the second jump. Mountmellton's in the lead by a length.'

'But Darcy I'm no interloper. And would not prevail upon you other than it is a dear wish of my betrothed to be able to enter the ladies' entrance of that revered club, whose stone pilasters are carved with nice little monkeys. I've been putting her off for weeks now. I mean the dear girl's got it into her head that shopkeepers and pub owners' daughters are expressly forbidden ever to be brought to enter the sacred confines of the Kildare Street Club. Terrible she should feel so, isn't it. And indeed as each week goes by I'm nearly driven to telling her that it is in fact the case.'

'Of course I shall propose you Rashers, but you must shush a moment. A ruddy horse over the third jump has gone way out in front. And it's not Durrow-Mountmellton. It's the favourite. O lordy sakes Dreamstown Zephyr has stumbled on the third fence. She's down. No. She's up. She's up.'

The cheers and shouts of the crowd swept away on the wind. As Rashers speaks, the snow now descending in great big flakes, whitening the peak of his cap and melting on his monocle. There are tears in his eyes. And one could now believe he is desperate. Not even being concerned with the progress of the race. By my binoculars old Durrow-Mountmellton next to last over the fourth hurdle. And one's ten pounds is in serious jeopardy. This morning, while dressing, I found myself not wanting to see the time on my watch. As if one had suddenly become conscious of the minutes ticking away in one's life. The increasingly haunting thought that perhaps one's destiny was totally meaningless. Merely to continue living and attempting to pursue the comfortable habits of shooting, hunting, fishing and racing. A squire without a wife, while all slowly dismantles down around one's ears. Never to be the father of little children. Whose arrival I suppose could make one feel even greater dismay. Kicking one in the shins. Placing bottles on the main staircase to tumble servants on their arses as one used to do oneself. And yet so many times I had imagined with some curious excitement a child of mine taking form in Leila's womb, where it was glowing red pink and warm. No wonder clocks and their ticking and chimes and even the usually wrong time they represented on their faces are recently so unnerving me. Even shivered once when the clock tower bell tolled two o'clock past noon with what seemed a mournful significance. And soon no matter what happens, I shall have to sell more of my mother's jewels. What is to become of poor old Rashers if he were to be blackballed from the Kildare Street Club and did not land his betrothed with her pubs and tobacconist shop and her ample acreage in County Dublin. Even he might have it in him to be a father. And were I not to ever marry I would have no heirs or wife to mourn my departure from this world. Or as could happen, who could dance and sing and make merry over my grave. A sad but I suppose not such a stupid thought, considering some of the stories one frequently hears. And how do I now dare to reveal to Rashers that even if proposed and seconded, it could take six months or a year or two or three years before he might ever be elected to the Kildare Street Club.

'Rashers she's made ground. She's second by two lengths. And briefly by the way can you tell me with regard to this chemotaxis business, can human sperm penetrate one's undergarments, trousers and gain entrance to the female reproductive organs.'

'This is a race dear boy, absolute thriller. And the answer is emphatically no to your question, unless of course you are both having a warm bath together which would then provide only a theoretical possibility. By god Darcy, she's ahead by a length. Isn't that mare a goer. I knew as she stepped by, her ears pricked, alert eye, well groomed, nostrils flared, that she had just that necessary touch of class.'

'You were Rashers, if you remember, also looking at Durrow-Mountmellton's thighs.'

'Ah same remarks apply dear boy to the marvellously turned out lady who clearly is possessed of a powerhouse in her own stunningly muscled quarters, who does too have that necessary touch of class. Just a fence to go dear boy. Around the turn. And up the hill. She's over. Like an angel. My god. Marvellous. Now down the finishing straight. The brakes are off. Look at the leg span of that stride. The last furlong. I told you, dear boy. A certainty. Knew the mare had a good jump in her, big strong quarters, tuned full of speed. And just sweating that correct amount as she came out of the paddock before the race. Here they come dear boy. Marvellous. Come on Dreamstown. Come on dear girl, you old whore. We are, both of us Darcy, ruddy richer by sixty bloody quid. O my god, my god. What's happened. O no. Ruddy bloody horse has crashed to the ground. Good grief. Ruddy mare's flung old Durrow-Mountmellton into a fence post.'

A groan from the crowd as Dreamstown Zephyr falls. Legs collapsed, nose ploughing into the turf. Less than a stone's throw from the finishing line. As the pounding hoofs of the rest of the field sweep by, whips lashing horses' arses. The favourite out in front across the finishing line with the shouts and screams of the crowd. And out there on the meadow, under the white flakes streaming down from the sky, the snow is beginning to drift up against the clumps of grass. And the liver chestnut mare. And the brown and mauve racing colours.

> As old
> Mountmellton lies
> Still
> And her horse
> Lies dead

9

Mountmellton's unconscious prostrate form on a stretcher surrounded by stewards. Covered by a bright red plaid blanket, she was carried through the crowd to the ambulance. As one got out on the course, all I could catch sight of were the tips of her boots sticking up and then, as she was lifted, I saw the side of her face and her elegant profile. There was a smudge of blood and mud high on her forehead and congealed in her hair. The ambulance, wheels skidding over the slimy grass and snow, had to be pushed by willing hands, including mine and Rashers's, all the way out to the main road.

'My god Darcy it's one awfully rum situation, damn decent girl and a damn decent horse downed like that. What.'

'Yes Rashers it is. Awfully rum. And I think perhaps one would like to call it a day.'

'Of course dear friend. Of course. I quite understand.'

As one walked back to one's car, a breathless Lois arrived to say she would stay for the rest of the racing and see us later and had a lift with her new admirer. One does so abhor people who so blatantly construe to advance themselves, and one was more than a little put out by Lois's rude behaviour. As there, in a matter of minutes, were two ladies already under threat to leave one's life. One was suffering too that moment's flash of nausea as one views someone maimed and bloody, as one so often confronts on the hunting field. And one tried to turn one's mind away from the tragic scene, and succeeded only too quickly having one's own difficulty, with Rashers pushing as we skidded all over, trying to get out of the field. Then, pulling at last over a little bridge onto the main road, an arriving light blue large motor car with a black canvas hood and plastic side windows was suddenly blocking the exit. One hooted one's klaxon at them as it appeared they refused to move. And they belligerently hooted back.

'By god Darcy there's some ruddy cheek, who the bloody hell do these chancers think they are, let me bloody well put them in their place.'

Just as Rashers was about to get back out of the car, a figure had already leaped from the vehicle blocking one's way. And one was suddenly confronted in the swirling snow by none other than my former dancing teacher, Count Brutus Blandus MacBuzuranti O'Biottus, whose lessons I took in the great castle and where I in fact had first met Durrow-Mountmellton as a little girl. There he unbelievably was, standing beside a great long chauffeured Delage limousine with three more similarly attired companions in camel haired polo coats alighting beside him. His eyes suddenly lighting up as he recognized me through my snowy windscreen, his smile so pleasantly welcoming as one got out of one's car. The Count, throwing his long scarf back over his shoulder and flinging hands upwards in the air, was shouting back to his companions.

'I know him. I know him. Ah my goodness me. Who should it be. I cannot believe. Ah but my dear Darcy, Darcy Dancer. Why do we not, my precious, see you in the Royal Hibernian any more. I am spending my inheritance on such a great spree. And you bury yourself out here from where I try so hard to escape. My god, Darcy my dear, don't you know it is nowhere out here. But absolutely nowhere my dear. Such pretty, pretty young boy who is now so much more the handsome man. Meet my friends I introduce you to. John John is from Paris. Prince Flip Flop from Florence. Count Ponce from Athens. But I joke. He is really a prince. But incognito. But the Count is not a ponce. Yet. But they are from the Mediterranean as you can see from their beautiful olive skin. They are frozen out of their wits poor dears. I tell them, you bring the sweaters. You wear the long long-underwear. They do not listen. But they are so happy. Happy to be in Ireland, where they come to see me. In my new wonderful big house I buy in Fitzwilliam Square. Très grand. Twenty five rooms I have now deliciously decorated. You come to my big party. Bring all your lovely friends my dear. I send you an invitation. But my god, have you seen Lois. I am how do you say strike dumb.'

'Yes I believe I have.'

'In her furs. My god. We pass on the road. I think when I see her I have gone out of my nut. I could not believe my senses. Can you imagine. Sable my dear, no less. And her hat. Did you ever see such a hat. My god. Even I should be outrageous in such a hat. What has happened to her. And to her old duffel coat. Maybe she has sold for a lot of money her portrait I commission of me in the altogether state of my nature with my big balls. But why should you have such an expression Darcy. Are things so bad you have to look so down in the dumps. Come smile. Yes. You smile for your former dancing master That is better. You come with Lord Ronald Ronald to my party. You do not forget. I shall expect you my dear former pupil. Darling boy. And how très bon it is to see you. Arrivederla. Goodbye.'

The snow packing down upon the windscreen of the Daimler back to Andromeda Park. The car having to stop every few hundred yards. Rashers getting out and with his sleeve wiping away the accumulated flakes jamming the wipers. And then grinning his marvellous gap toothed grin at me through the windscreen. The sky a pearly grey darkness. Cattle huddled along walls in the fields. Drifts building at the side of the road. All meaning one will be carting out tons more of hay to fodder hungry chilled beasts. And on this byway up and down its little hills we pass not far from Dreamstown Park.

Durrow-Mountmellton's wonderful haunches and her strong back. That night of our pleasantly kinky perversions gave us a strange camaraderie. Her soft skin. And flowing ample breasts. Her skull could be fractured, her body now bruised. As a little girl she wore a pink tutu once to dancing class. And I wrote her a misspelt note.

YOU ARE THE MOAST
PRETTIEIST GIRL
IN THE WORLD.

And then I watched her across the great hall in the great castle as she scribbled something on the back of my note in reply. She attempted a grand jeté recrossing the room and gracefully curtsied to me as the little piece of paper was handed back. And I was immediately chuffed and blushing all over my face as I thought something awfully nice was about to be written to me.

THANK YOU. BUT YOU ARE NOT
THE MOST HANSOMIST
BOY IN THE WORLD. NOR CAN YOU SPELL.

One always takes pleasure reaching at last the boundary of one's property and driving along knowing that nearly all in view is one's land all the way upwards to the sky. But at the front gates of Andromeda Park, just as one was turning in, the marauder stepping out of my gate lodge door. As one pulled to a halt, one could see his footsteps already in the snow which led in the gates and along the drive. My god the ruddy trespassing nerve. And there he stood, brazenly smirking at us as we drove by. A cigarette dangling out of his surly mouth. Bringing yet another pall to fall upon one's spirit this day. For now there was land encroaching upon Andromeda Park that I did no longer own up to the sky.

The snow continued to fall day and night for two days. The wind heaping it high to the eaves of the barns, and the men having to dig and shovel it away to get to the hay. Other than by horse or tractor one could not get out of the drive to the main road. Lois marooned with her monocled baronet in the next county. Rashers meanwhile had in the list of members found three, after much agonizing deliberation, to give as possible seconders to the Kildare Street Club. While I lay the night away awake, wondering if the attic beams would support the enormous weight of snow on the roof and how, without advertising in the *Farmer's Journal*, I would ever find a suitable wife.

I had flowers, Bewley's fudge and a book of Apollinaire's poems sent by horseback with Luke, who'd once been whipper in with the hunt, to Durrow-Mountmellton at the hospital. Where word had it now that she was conscious and comfortable but had badly sprained an ankle, broken two ribs, dislocated her shoulder and had a crack in her skull. Next afternoon, considerably chilled following going through the farm accounts stacked on the rent table, one retired to take tea in the drawing room. Where a message arrived back the eight miles on horseback from Mountmellton, the words of which left me entirely chuffed and remembering the pretty little girl in her tutu.

> You are the moast
> kindest man in
> the world

The drawing room windows were rattling with gusts of wind in what was now obviously a raging major Siberian winter. And the shutters were closed over as darkness fell. Damian reloading the turf baskets and Crooks serving tea. And as he often did, Crooks hovering about, pretending he was awaiting another instruction but in fact it always meant he had something on his mind to say.

'What is it now Crooks.'

'Now Master Reginald I don't want to be disturbing your tea.'

'Ah indeed. One welcomes your thoughtfulness Crooks.'

'But I thought sir before Lord Ronald joins your company I better mention it. I've given that one Mollie her final notice. And I'd like to confirm with you on it now.'

'I see. Well confirming it is rather a bit after the fact Crooks.'

'It was the final straw. She was up in her bed this morning pleading sickness with Kitty having to bring her her breakfast of rashers, two eggs, four sausages, fried tomatoes and enough tea to float a ship. And by the empty tray afterwards she had no trouble with her sickness polishing it off. And then didn't I not an hour later be hearing her humming and singing "It's a Long Way to Tipperary" inside her door and jigging on the floor. And the day when youse went off to the races and I was about me business in the house, where did I find herself but dressed up as for Sunday mass and sitting nice as you please in your favourite chair in the library with her big thick spectacles on and a big fire blazing she had the impudence to light for herself.'

'Crooks clearly that was taking a bit of a liberty perhaps but it's hardly a reason for a sudden sacking.'

'Well there's nothing sudden about the liberties she's been taking and to be in the library it was a diabolical liberty if you don't mind me saying sir. Wasn't she reading the *Burke's Landed Gentry of Ireland*. And wasn't the pages opened to four hundred and thirty six concerning your mother's ancestors the Darcy Thormonds. And there she sat. And went on sitting in front of me. Refusing to get up.'

'Well one could regard that of course as rather insubordinate Crooks.'

'But the final straw was her reply to me face when I stated for her to be changing back into her uniform and be about attending to her duties. I hate to use even the suggestion of the word in your presence sir, but she said to F off and that she was improving her mind for when the time came she might be giving me orders instead of the other way around.'

'I see Crooks. But I'm sure couldn't there be some little misunderstanding here.'

'I'll tell you the misunderstanding Master Reginald. It was that Leila in off the roads in service here gave her all these grand ideas. That it's only a hop skip and jump from scullery maid to marchioness.'

'I hardly think, Crooks, Mollie has any such ideas.'

'Sir, this one Mollie thinks that because those belonging to her have a bit of a farm with their blacksmithing down the west that she's but a few Georgian steps from genuine gentry herself. I have her wages tabulated up on a slip and will submit it to you in the Rent Room to await your attention.'

'Crooks I know you are trying to do your best during difficult times to keep the household in order, but Mollie you must remember had quite a fright that day the rat pursued her. And I'm not of course suggesting she has taken leave of her senses, but such would certainly leave her in a state of some discomfiture for a while.'

'Discomfiture is it. Comfort is the word you mean sir. That's what she's been enjoying in this household, going dancing of an evening in her tight frocks with boyos from the town panting at the mouth and coming out here to climb over the walls and stare up at her windows at night. Didn't Catherine get the fright of her life the other evening down the kitchens with one of them with his face between the bars of the windows with his tongue out looking in at her. And some I won't mention have something else hanging out. Sure I had your shotgun down from the Gun Room.'

'Crooks this I'm sure is all going to sort itself out.'

'Now you'll have been too young to remember the former girl we had who was later called slut at your school you attended Master Darcy. Now I don't want to go into detail, but wasn't she got in the family way. That's how it'll sort itself out. Ah now I'll say no more for the moment as I hear Lord Ronald's footsteps coming.'

Reverberating throughout the house, the incredible noise of Rashers's stout shoes, his heels landing resoundingly on floors, flagstone, wood and even penetrating rugs and carpets. God he does at times so exasperate one and then one finds one's spirits lifting in seeing him and one then nearly has to suppress the gladness one feels. Certainly he was now the life saving hero of the household, worthy of the Andromeda Park medal for bravery. With Crooks holding the drawing room door ajar. Indeed even imitating Rashers's military bearing, and bowing and clicking his heels.

'Good evening your lordship. Tea is quite ready.'

'Thank you so much Crooks. And I must say I am quite ready for tea. Ah but there you are my dear boy. Where on earth are you secreting yourself. Late for dinner last night and lunch today. Ah and what a jolly nice rip roaring fire. Well we are aren't we dear boy, marooned in all this stupendous silence on your big mysterious estate. It does make one ponder and do some extra thinking, what. Did it ever make you wonder how one can say quite reasonable things about people and they take offence. Of course I've had old Lois's tits on my mind. But how nice, tea. The smell of hot baked scones. Bowl of whipped cream. And Catherine's array of homemade jams. And my god Darcy, you don't know how tempted one is to throw dignity to the winds. And say to hell with one's spiritual standards and sentiments. And focus more on material things. Never having really been one of these big sexual activists, very little would satisfy my life. And as, anyway, I seem to have such a small circle of destinations left these days. If I came up with a few likely ponies, I could go back to playing polo but the damn game is being infiltrated by such a plethora of upstarts. My good Anglo Irish public school education at least has left one well scrubbed and the rigours there endured have made it possible for me to forbear these times of crisis. Mornings back in Dublin it at least gave me the resolve to get up and out from my awful flat to the Shelbourne or the Hibernian Buttery and the energetic expertise to avoid meeting someone on the way in whose deep debt I am. Ah, and having sat much of the day away reading, and having said so much to you without a word of your reply, it is good to sit down again and merely to say, wouldn't we be lost, lost and bereft, without dear, dear friends. My god one does seem to resort to darkly romantic rhetoric on a day like this. I say, but what was that. Sounded like a distant explosion. Sixty millimetre howitzer or something.'

'Rashers, I am not about to investigate. Would you like your tea weak or strong.'

'Strong dear boy. Strong. And do forgive me for rambling on.'

Panes of the drawing room windows misted with frost. And yesterday during the afternoon a crust of ice formed across the snow outside as a rain squall came, followed by another severe chill. And now the snow billowed up in great white ghostly gusts blowing across the front parkland. One did, just to bolster one's spirits, have Crooks bring out our most elaborate silver tea service. Which one could see Rashers was bursting with excitement to comment upon, but thought the better of it. However, it seemed instead to inspire another but not dissimilar subject.

'You know Darcy in finding three in the list of members who I hope won't throw a fit in having to recommend me, one does then contemplate how nice it will be to be able to leave the pavement throng along Nassau Street, turn smartly right and then smartly left and enter the exclusive sanctum of the Kildare Street Club.'

'And I shall, I assure you Rashers take much pleasure to see you there.'

151

'But Darcy is it true the members have open plan in the club latrine while taking a shit.'

'Yes it is quite.'

'Ah I see. By god shows you doesn't it camaraderie and how revered the members are of one another to bare their arses communally like that. Then I suppose too the whole point of a gentleman's club is to have an address where a gentleman's mistress can write him highly personal letters. And in an ancillary matter I have a further and most urgent request dear boy. May I please invite my betrothed to join me here for a day or two as I continue to so contentedly sojourn with you. Dear girl is dying to meet you again. You see I do have her highly impudent not to say insolent solicitors writing to my solicitors to elicit of my wherewithal and what it might amount to if blatantly expressed in pounds, shillings and pence that can be expected to be contributed to the marriage. And all I seem to have to offer as an asset is my replica Ardagh Chalice. All her deceased father's doing I may add according to a codicil in the old bugger's will. It has my dear girl dreadfully distressed. And time now dear boy is crucially of the essence. I must forestall and blind the buggers somehow. You see her solicitors are in such a lather as my betrothed is besieged by would be fortune hunters of the seedy question-able bred sort who lurk in and about suburban Dublin and who with their shops in town are hoping to expand their business outlets. One such gent being a well known homo-sexualist with a lisp and spectacles with lens an inch thick who is in the electrical appliance trade. And need it be said, he is not a wit interested in the dear girl's future sexual satisfactions. This same homosexualist dared to spread the story that I was heard to say aloud in the Hibernian Buttery bar that I found the dear girl's body repugnant. Can you imagine. That very word. Repugnant. Or my ever having resorted to using it. And let me make that point further clear.'

'Rashers you needn't get so hot under the collar, and shout.'

152

'Forgive me. I've just spilled my tea. But my betrothed dear boy, with her full upper and lower dentures taken out, provides a supremely erotic bliss. One might have to travel all the way to Bangkok to find similar. I mean she does have certain amplitudes of physique here and there which might not flatter. But in no way are her three Dublin pubs situated in squalid but good trading positions in north Dublin or her eighty acres, the full, complete and entire reason why I am so deeply attracted to her. But I damn well know this particular ruddy homosexualist is intent upon the freehold of her one particular tobacconist's shop which happens to be situated in one of the less fashionable but most strategically up and coming locations of the city, and smack in the centre of one of the capital's heavily trafficked thoroughfares. Has one of the best stocks of snuff. And the profits on packs of cigarettes alone dear boy, Sweet Afton, Passing Cloud and Woodbines in their tens and twenties that pass over that counter in an hour, not to mention matches at tuppence a box, would provide for an unstinting evening of duck and Beaujolais at Jammet's.'

'You seem to know more than just a little concerning this shop's turnover Rashers.'

'Dear boy please do understand that these are desperate times. Disguised in a rabbi's get up and false grey beard I did lurk a moment or two about the premises. I mean don't for a second think I'm avaricious or commercially minded dear boy, it's simply that I have got to know what my own equity prospects are in marriage. But this recent wretched libel upon me in this wretched debtors' gazette even though I've had my solicitors on to them giving them plenty of what for, is tantamount to impugning my pecuniary reputation. And they've again dared to currently list me in their wretched pages.'

'They have a perfect right to do so if you have a court judgment against you Rashers.'

'That may be technically so, of course. But it's altogether a highly false impression. My ruddy landlord who sued for rent arrears has bloody mushrooms growing out of the water logged walls and invading my bed.'

'What about your Ardagh Chalice, Rashers, might you not put it in to be auctioned at Adam's the Auctioneers.'

'My dearest possession Darcy. And to so suggest is most unthoughtful of you. I must say nae to ever parting with such. To quaff champagne from it is in itself the holiest of rites one attempts to preserve in my life. My the scones are utterly delicious crowned with cream and strawberry jam. But Darcy, may I prevail upon you for one last and final favour. You have no idea how painfully reluctant I am to suggest this. You see I do think I need at the moment a modest sum of a couple of thousand quid. Just to tide me over this rather presently bumpy pathway to matrimony. Might it be asking too much for you simply to act as guarantor in raising such a sum from my bank to whom I've already presented the proposition. Clears all my debts and leaves a little something for purchase of the ring, and of course the moment the marriage knot is tied not only shall you be released from such guarantorship, but I shall pay interest on the entire sum which I demand be part of our little arrangement. And then shall also follow a little champagne festiveness in the Shelbourne as of our days of yore. Nae. Speak not your answer just yet.'

A glint of gold from his cuff links as Rashers spreads the fingers of his hand out to regard his nails in the light of the gas lamp glow. His shirt laundered, ironed and collar starched by Edna Annie. And one had to give him credit, as he did call upon her to pay his compliments and descend to her steamy laundry rooms out of which she rarely ventured. Rendering the dear old creature delighted, who then, when I was bringing her some of Sexton's winter flowers, clutched me with her ancient wizened hands.

'Ah sir Master Reginald, his lordship, a true and grand gentleman he is like yourself. Brought me a bit of chocolate.'

154

Of course with a voraciously chocolate eating staff I had irritatingly wondered who had whipped my bloody chocolate away out of the dining room sideboard where one had carefully hidden it under some spare breakfast napkins kept there. And following dinner one would, when alone, take a piece with coffee and brandy and even sometimes secrete a chunk or two in one's bedside table to have with one's book one was reading in bed. A small stinginess indulged away from guests to which one felt as pasha of Andromeda Park one should be supremely entitled. The habit I suppose having been formed when my nanny Ruby occasionally as a treat gave me a bit of chocolate in bed before I went to sleep.

'This should assuage my little fellow Darcy's night starvation.'

Rashers emitting a great long sigh. A shutter rattling. The fire puffing out smoke from a chimney downdraft. Pour more Lapsang Souchong. Under the end of one's spoon, press the lemon slice down in the cup. Choose another scone. Tea time somehow always allows one to take a certain stock of matters in a sensibly calm manner. Which does mean that I dare not bankrupt myself by becoming Rashers's guarantor to his bank. But of course he will continue his beguiling chatter until I do.

'Darcy do forgive one if in the merest manner one's mood does rather blacken. My fame, such as it is from being listed in that debtors' gazette, is now even diminished. As the debts I seem now able to incur have shrunken woefully to such relatively minuscule amounts. One does so want things to return to normal. The common people like one's landlord back down where they belong, and such as ourselves left able in our loftiness to piss down when necessary upon them from a great height and in an awful great shower. What I do so love most about Andromeda Park are these moments one enjoys now between tea time and dinner. Where the utter perfection of the setting beneath the assembled eyes staring down from your family portraits seems to peacefully envelop one as one gazes into the fire flames and listens to the gently hissing and crackling logs, the deafening silence deepening one's thoughts. Selfishly at such times one tends not to give a tinker's damn about the rest of the world. And you know Darcy, I know I shan't ever be, but what I should like most to be is like you. Here on your estate. Winter afternoons comfortably sunk aseat on these so eminently comfortable swansdown cushions. That cake basket there by a famed Dublin silversmith whose name at this very precise moment happens to have slipped my mind, but that dish ring is by John Lloyd, 1770. Such little furnishings on display in one's life relieve of the need for phoney posturing. And in my presently sad case of having to constantly ingratiate to my dear one. You know the kind of thing. Jumping to light her cigarette. Opening the motor car door. Making sure waiters are attentive to her and all that sort of thing.'

'Rashers please. Do believe me when I say I shall take steps to see if it might be in order for me to consider this situation. But two thousand quid is a substantial amount. Requiring instead of my being guarantor for the bank to have me deposit my cattle in their vaults. Surely to tide you over what appears to be merely this little brief spot of interrogation asked by her solicitors, you hardly need that much.'

The boy butler entering to deposit a replenishment of hot water and nodding to Rashers as if he had just been given a tip on a horse at the races. And glancing at me as he left as if I were an ogre to be avoided and escaped from. And now a subdued contrite look overcoming the previous enthusiasm on Rashers's face. But then shooting his cuffs and sniffing the air in the horse inspired manner of all good Anglo Irishmen. Two cups of tea and three cream and blackberry slathered scones already down his hatch. And with his marvellously benign mouth, another look of weary sadness suddenly dawning on his face. As if he were awaking to find himself in a strange wilderness and not knowing in which direction to go.

156

'Dear me Darcy, I don't know, on this icy snowbound day you must forgive and I do deeply apologize for my variable mood. To be within swimming distance of shore and to know one may be swept back out to sea again. I suppose everything started to go wrong in my life in the army.'

'Good god Rashers, you've never said anything before about being in the army.'

'No indeed I haven't dear boy. And I suppose for a very good reason. For it may be the saddest tale of my life that I shall everlastingly have to hide from all others. Having wanted to be an admiral from boyhood, I was never exactly so to speak your long term military type, even though among my possessions I still have and cherish my bearskin head dress. But the Guards you must understand Darcy are like no other military force. Their elitism is unique. Just as their esprit de corps is supreme. There has never been a major conflict in which they have not bravely taken part. And once you have marched on parade with your men somehow it's as if one's very blood has forever been imbued with a certain heroic magnitude. Even as recently as now I can hear the beating of their drums. Like that distant rumble and sound of cannon we heard a while ago. At this very moment I suppose the very nicest way one might put it is that I am technically absent without leave, and subject to court martial and imprisonment.'

'Good god Rashers.'

'And the unnice way to put it Darcy is that I could be shot for desertion.'

'O no.'

'O yes dear boy, O yes. And well you might say good god. I've often said it too.'

'Honestly Rashers. You do sometimes totally astonish and amaze me.'

'Dear boy it might be the very reason I started to read medicine to discover what we poor mortals are all about. Also, that one day my regiment might be glad to take me back without too severe a punishment provided of course that I would see to the officer's latrine accommodations being well looked after on manoeuvres, in short lavatory attendant. But you see my career in the Guards went badly wrong from the very start. For alas due to some awful balls up, upon being commissioned I was seconded to my father's own regiment dear boy. That was an ignominy in itself. Immediately meaning that to avoid any sign of favouritism I would be the very last to rise above the lowly rank of second lieutenant.'

'Oh dear, how disheartening for you Rashers.'

'Well not entirely, the war being on I did finally add an extra pip in the field. Although I never made it to captain. Having committed one or two fatal faux pas which clung to me. Such as one embarrassing occasion in the regimental mess where it is the custom that at table should one choose to remain silent and not to be spoken to, one merely wore one's hat. A ritual I still resort to when I'm down in the buttery and you find me unsmilingly alone in a corner with my hat on. Well the regimental mess dear boy was quite a massive and grand dining room. Its long table laid with a wonderment of crystal and silver. Even at breakfast time very elegant and formal if you get my meaning. And so here as a newly commissioned officer I came to pop in quite hungrily from checking the guard and who should be sitting there alone in his solitary splendour but the Colonel with his hat on. You know Darcy when one's father is a full general you do somehow tend to lose slightly one's awe for superior rank. I mean one's father can haul you on the carpet where one is saying yes sir, no sir and then one can find oneself in a fit of pique and saying, please won't you shut up Papa. Well back in the mess with this particular colonel who anyway when he did speak always sounded as if his mouth were full of marbles, I did feel so conspicuous entering to find just the two of us there to take breakfast. And in what I thought was a gesture of regimental solidarity, as provocative as it risked being, I felt the decent thing to do was to sit directly opposite him. It was in fact a rather patriotic stirring moment, for as I entered the mess they had just begun playing God Save the King out on the parade ground. And I did rather slam my heels down to the rhythm as I marched to take my seat. I had only just around then dared to start wearing my monocle. And of course I already knew that ruddy well annoyed the piss out of him. Especially as he had chosen to remain silent and would have otherwise told me, take that damn glass out of your eye Lieutenant. I mean I must admit I was enjoying the moment. However, it wasn't long before I realized the Colonel also most certainly didn't like my seating choice one little bit. You see, having sat so directly close to him, it were as if in defiance of all regimental traditions I were threatening to speak to him. They were then playing a slow march on the parade ground. And, as the distinctly perceptible tension rose, I then got so damn nervous I suddenly uncontrollably found myself reaching for and taking my own cap and putting it on. And thank god it wasn't my bearskin head dress. I think that somehow I honestly did mean well. But I suppose, were the true truth to be known, it was that I was signalling to the Colonel if you're sitting there all the way through breakfast not speaking then you bastard I'm going to make it ruddy well clear that I'm not speaking either. Out on the parade ground it was as if the band were orchestrating our little drama of the hats and the band was playing quick march. The waiters witnessing the scene I knew had to vacate so contorted in laughter were they. Then as I got progressively more and more panicked and uncomfortable I then did the most stupid thing of all and took my hat back off. Well the Colonel went puce. I thought that even if it is the bloody Colonel sitting there not wanting to be spoken to then I damn well had a right to at least now make it known that I'd like it if I were spoken to. But such a simple little incident Darcy quite ruined my army career. The Colonel shortly afterwards made brigadier. But I within the week found myself shifted to special duties and freezingly soaked to the skin on the wilds of Dartmoor, taking recruits foot slogging through the bracken.'

'Good heavens Rashers, do have another little spot of tea. And how deucedly unfair of the Colonel.'

'Well perhaps I exaggerate a little. I did soon resort to a little military influence to get me back to civilization. But I fear my career wasn't helped by another incident befalling me not much later. Concerning a little social perk which came my way. My then duties to which I'd pleasurably been assigned happened to involve keeping the keys to Windsor Castle, which wasn't an altogether downward move in my career. But not quite as ceremonial as it sounds dear boy. One did bloody well actually have real keys for real locks. Now, because my father had certain distinctions I won't go into, I was in my present military capacity invited by the monarch to take dinner privately with him and the family on occasional evenings in the castle.'

'Rashers you do realize you're talking about the King of England.'

'Of course dear boy I'm talking about the King of England. Who else but the King and his family would be in residence in Windsor Castle. And an awfully nice damn castle it is too. I mean just to stride up the crimson carpeted front hall steps to its astonishing series of majestic state rooms transfused one with a certain sad concern for one's downright humble rank in life. But we were taking sup in the King's private apartments with his two wellbrought up princesses dear boy. Both with these extraordinary beautiful complexions that one could not occasionally between courses stop oneself staring at. God they were attractive delightfully charming creatures. The elder Lilibet especially.'

'You're not because of incarceratingly arctic weather conditions and with nothing better to do, pulling my leg Rashers, are you.'

160

'Ah dear Darcy nae and no. One wishes only that one were, as I now recall it all. I was always in such a lathered state, as was my batman dutifully on the job to make me look smart. Of course the King and Queen and his two lovely daughters appeared quite delighted with me and my occasionally amusing stories. Without boasting I do believe I had them, for a moment or two at least, laughing their heads off. The King perhaps not quite as heartily as the others. Indeed once I was indiscreetly relating the hat incident in the mess with the Colonel. In the course of which old Lilibet fashioned her napkin into a hat and with the most marvellous frown you ever saw, put the hat shaped napkin on her head.'

'Rashers, I do really feel you're painting with a full brush.'

'Ah perhaps in the glow of sweet recall for such moments I am a bit. But of course the Royal Family, were the truth to be known, are very simple down to earth people you know. Like nothing better than to hear a good story or to get out their little baskets blackberrying along the hedgerows to make their own jam. Or even repairing at times to a little old thatched cottage hidden out in the woods of Windsor to bake their rashers and fry up their own scrambled eggs. I mean basically Darcy, my kind of folk you know. Not like some of your lofty yobbos who, with their mightily puffed up presumptions, put on the dog. But of course it would strongly seem in retrospect that I went entirely off the deep end, conjuring up the impossible with two captivatingly unspoilt princesses I so innocently presumed were at my disposal to choose from. Both have such dazzlingly winning smiles and sparkling eyes. And both I had been worshipping from afar so to speak. Now of course Darcy I've not really ever gone into this too deeply but I am not without a certain eligibility you know. There are in fact among the usual sheriffships, baronies, knighthoods, etcetera, one or two not insignificant, not to say extremely ancient, titles on my mother's side of the family as well as a not too distant duke. And damn it all I did think when the

161

College of Heralds were done delving into my pedigree I might well be in with a very good chance in the marriage stakes.'

'For god's sake Rashers it's not that I don't believe you, but in marrying the eldest daughter of the King you would in fact upon his death be the Prince Consort and no doubt also at least a duke.'

'Well my dear boy what on earth's wrong with that. I'm really surprised at you. I should make an awfully nice duke. And ruddy hell actually everything was going along swimmingly, the princesses having invited me for a trot around Windsor Great Park to be followed by tea. The ride and the tea went off wonderfully and I don't believe I've ever had such an idyllic afternoon. And old Lilibet invited me to one of her madrigal singing parties. I was quite beside myself. Awfully nice you know imagining that one day there could be twenty one gun salutes wherever one's spouse and one would go. Naturally I overly celebrated my impending good fortune with a few of my fellow officers. And on the very ruddy eve of what was certainly to be for me a new and better life, I lost the keys to the castle. For the life of me I did not know what I had drunkenly done with them. Not only was I summarily sent as far away as possible from Windsor as news of this invariably spread through the regiment, but my career in the Guards took an immediate and everlastingly fatal downturn. Wherever I went whispers followed. There goes the chap who lost the keys to Windsor Castle. And I suppose too it contributed to my father disinheriting me. So no hope for my future in that quarter. Well of course the tears do finally dry upon one's eyes over such things. And long since have I sold off my Purdeys. And a man without his shotguns as you know my dear boy, is not much. But you know Darcy I was a good Guards officer, I really was. Even now nothing is more stirring and awe inspiring to me than to see a company on parade pass by on their horses, the band playing, the drums beating in their marvellous rhythm, their tack shining, the hardware tinkling, glinting and gleaming. And when they go away quick march, one always does at such times glow with esprit de corps. The whinnying of one's horse. O god Darcy I think my life may be descending in a downward spiral from the noble to the ignoble. But one must learn I suppose to say goodbye to things one wants most in life. Suffice to say I did, to save what was left of my bacon, pop off to this emerald island where I sit before you now Darcy, having revealed all. You do see now don't you that if I am to take my place in the better ranks of Dublin society how imperative it is for me to become a member of the Kildare Street Club and re establish my credibility and credentials in the world.'

'Rashers, I am sorry. I truly and honestly am. I had no idea.'

'O I guess it's only a lot of old pish and pother. And well behind one now.'

'But Rashers if one were to be in any way blunt about it, you remain at this very moment a deserter from the British Army. A fugitive.'

'Please don't use such words Darcy. And make one feel one is rather like a lightweight turd that refuses to flush away down the toilet bowl. I regard my absence without leave, in a rather prolonged manner I admit, as what some appallingly academic Americans call taking a sabbatical. I know you might be imagining dear fellow, that good god that old Rashers here could be taking a communal crap with the Kildare Street members in the club latrine and suddenly military police could come bursting in, truncheons drawn and the usual silver plated handcuffs reserved for Guards officers at the ready to arrest me. In Ireland you must remember one is safe from such apprehension or any ensuing extradition.'

'Do have another scone Rashers.'

'I've had three already but I suppose in this weather a fourth can do no harm to one's appetite for dinner.'

'I do believe you've actually already had four scones Rashers. This will be your fifth. But I assure you I am not in any way tabulating.'

'Tabulate dear boy, tabulate away. Black sheep that I presently am. I remain so willingly to be cleansed white again by the limited opportunities available in such socially impoverished a land as this. I must get my betrothed up the aisle. You do don't you Darcy see my dilemma. And I admit to being already much too deep in your debt. But I'm not all bad you know. There is good in me.'

'I know that Rashers. But dear me, the Kildare Street Club is full of colonels and some of whom are ex Guardsmen. And even boast of, I believe, a general or two. Your name connected to your father's is bound to elicit a certain notice when posted up to the board for membership.'

'Name. Who said anything about a name.'

'Well how else would you be posted.'

'By title dear boy. By title shall I be known and duly posted. Peers of the realm are always in any good club given priority as candidates for membership over any commoners in the waiting list.'

'Rashers you seem to know a damn sight more than I do about gaining a membership.'

'Well Darcy think of it, it makes sense. Who would you rather rub elbows with in your club, some wretched commoner of the professional mercantile class who might not know a snipe from a grouse or who has never been on the Spey or hunted with your better hunts. Or a gentleman whose cultural discernments are honed to a nicety and knowing his furniture, his ports and what the most fragrant perfumes should disclose to the olfactory nerves.'

'Perfumes Rashers.'

'Yes dear boy, you must always know the desired perfume to give a lady.'

'Well Rashers I shall bone up on my scents. And one must

admit to preferring persons about one, of a certain cultivation, but titles hardly are a guarantee Rashers, always of course excepting present company.'

'Don't you see dear boy it is incumbent upon one to live up to one's title and to behave like a lord if one is a lord.'

'Ah, as you do Rashers. Is that what you mean.'

'I think Darcy, if that's the way you want it, upon this subject I shall not say more.'

'O dear I'm not meaning to offend Rashers. Just want to get this matter in its proper perspective. I mean you could, remember, in using the club latrine be in quite close proximity to just a mere squire such as myself.'

Rashers wincing. An urgent rap on the drawing room door. And as the door cautiously opened, down the servants' hall could be heard echoing the distant cry of Crooks.

'Boots in the house. Boots in the house.'

And there in the drawing room light stood Sexton. Cap in his big hand, moisture seeping down under his eye patch. Snow clinging to his boots and beckoning me up from my chair. And then to follow him silently along the hall to the ballroom, where, entering and closing the doors, Sexton whispered behind his hand.

'Forgive me Master Darcy, forgive me for this unforgivable intrusion disturbing you. But I had to rush the news to you immediately before you heard of the event from any other lips. So you'd know the true and confidential facts of the matter. We got him. Sine dubio. We got him.'

'Got who, Sexton.'

'By gob the thief, that's who. Didn't you hear it go off not less than an hour ago.'

'Forgive me Sexton but I don't for the life of me know what on earth you're talking about.'

'I'm talking about the blast. Sent his own and his wife's dentures flying. It's your man over beyond. And in this case more accurately it's your woman. Caught red handed. Blew him right out of his own front door which the blast flattened and made a naked spectacle of her.'

'Sexton, forgive me but I still don't understand.'

'Well now, didn't I one evening hollow a hole in a nice big piece of turf and stuff in it a bit of the gelignite, and then put it back on top of the turf pile so it was like any other bit of turf as was ever dug out of our bog. And so whoever was stealing it would know all about it when he finally was using this particular sod to warm his toes by the fire.'

'Good god Sexton.'

'Sure it was the pair of them at it again as they were once before. Mick the blind man and his gossipy red haired bog trollop of a wife leading him and her donkey with the curled up hoofs over to our turf, filling her cart and helping themselves. She stole many a thing out of this house where she once worked in your mother's time while the husband Mick shovelled muck out in the yard. If they spotted two or more of a thing they made sure only one of it was left. Take jars of jam. Bricks of butter. Bottles of wine, whiskey, anything. He of course couldn't have known what hit him. Wasn't he closest to the fire at the blast, but didn't she get the clothes blown right off her as she was coming over to him with a cup of tea. The pair of them groaning, calling for the curate to administer the last rites. But Master Darcy we'll have to keep confidential about this, between ourselves as it were. But I dare say now you won't be finding any more turf gone missing in a hurry. They'd be thinking there'd be another blast coming from where the previous one came from. And that's a fact.'

Sexton departing down the hall as I followed his tall figure back to the drawing room, watching the snow melting off in his footsteps. A sudden strange feeling of relief overcoming one. That somehow, for all our setbacks, in the battle of Andromeda Park this could be the turning of the tide. And certainly deserved another cream and gooseberry slathered scone, ushered down one's throat with one's lemon anointed China tea. And maybe following one's finishing up doing the accounts in the Rent Room and a bath and dressing for dinner, one might in the library then indulge in just a smidgen of champagne.

Darcy Dancer returning to the drawing room. Pausing to listen at the open door. A muffled sob. The back of Rashers's head bent forward in his chair. His chin resting on his chest. His head lifting as he heard me come in, as if in an effort, as he usually did, to greet me with some merry quip. And then, with another heaving sob, his head falling to his breast again. One sat down again in one's chair, placed another log on the fire and felt the hot water jug which had grown too lukewarm to fill one's cup again. To hear a word of sudden unexpected justice and then just as suddenly to confront unexpected sadness. To find Rashers's ebullience shattered. His monocle hanging down from its black ribbon over his waistcoat. And tears dropping from his eyes upon his orange tweed tie.

'Rashers what on earth is the matter.'

'I love her Darcy. I truly honestly love her.'

'O dear. Sorry Rashers. But to whom are we now referring.'

'To my betrothed. I love the dear girl. She may only be a commoner and as peasant Irish as muck. And even rather useless around a farm. Nor is she, as the Princess Lilibet was, a crack shot. Nor can she change a motor car tyre in a thrice as Lilibet could. Or play the piano with the Princess's magical touch. Or so tolerantly speak fluent French as Lilibet did in answer to my pathetic schoolboy efforts. We sang duets together. Puccini. She has a lovely voice. And together we were most exquisite.'

'Rashers if I may suggest, it does awfully sound as if you were in love with the Princess as well.'

'I was dear boy. I was. Nor would that practical girl wince when one polished a saddle with a bit of spit. As does my betrothed. But you have no idea how, in royal circles, once

167

having blotted one's copy book, one can be so brutally shunned. With a dozen or so equerries giving one witheringly dirty looks. Even one of her dogs bit me. And now I am forever bleakly, along with my betrothed, to be shunned from the Kildare Street Club. Dear girl. I cannot bear to leave her so abandoned. While I might sink further in disgrace. Back in Dublin, rats run across my bedroom floor. Hardly can see my image in my splattered piece of mirror as I shave and brush my teeth over an old cracked bowl. Waste matters plummet to pollute outside my basement window. Sewerage backs up in the few pipes there are. The appalling smell assaulting my nostrils first thing of a morn and last thing at night. My bed linen is tattered and soiled. The outdoor water closet is missing its toilet seat. I must consort with newsboys who treat me as one of their equals and greet me with a dreadful familiarity as I pass on Grafton and Dawson streets. Even to using a mock British accent to accost me.'

'Rashers please. You mustn't fret like this. I will be guarantor of your loan from the bank. And shall also propose you for membership of the Kildare Street Club.'

'O dear boy. O dear boy. What wonderful words to hear.'

'And there are other words too Rashers which for the present I shall keep to myself.'

> They are
> Please for god's sake
> But mostly for mine
> Don't
> Blot your copy
> Book
>
> Or lose
> The keys
> To this house

10

Three consecutive hunting fixtures were cancelled and except for our after lunch forays out to ski on old warped skis and sledge down the front parkland hills with the creakingly ancient wolfhounds Kern and Olav, the snow confinement at Andromeda Park continued for eleven days before the rain came and the massive drifts blocking the drive and roads finally melted. And prolonged tea time discussions with Rashers concerning both our social and marital prospects became the norm.

'Ah London, Darcy, London. Of course although there exists a certain pinch and post war straightened circumstances, you would soon find there a suitable mare. I do so pine for it sometimes. Of course for one not to be found aseat abject, lonely in a bombed out ruin and infra bloody dignitatem and to matter in the contemporary world of Mayfair, Knightsbridge and Belgravia, one must make sure to be at the right parties and belong to the right clubs and hunts. Nor does it hurt to be a good dancer, skilled tennis player and a ruddy crack shot and to be seen to take tea occasionally at the Dorchester Hotel. You dear boy would simply thrive there.'

'Well sounds enough to do and be Rashers. And I'm not a particularly good dancer nor skilled tennis player.'

'I think merely being considered adequate would get you by Darcy. But of course you would have to rid yourself of a few, albeit very faint, vowels which sometimes do make you sound as if you might be suspected of being Irish dear boy.'

The scone one threw at Rashers was suitably adorned with whipped cream and gooseberry preserve and hit him smack in the monocle. Splotching his waistcoat which I then noticed was one of my very own.

'Sorry dear boy, I did truly rather deserve that. But let me make quite clear your accent is above reproach. It is merely an occasional coloration I was referring to.'

When the entire cake and cake dish went flying and nearly caught him in the side of the head as he ducked, Rashers did damn well finally shut up thereafter about any tendency I had of sounding Irish to possible English ears. However, one's attentions were quickly diverted from the glamours of London with Lois suddenly turning up in a spot of noonday sunshine and chauffeured in a limousine no less. Regally alighting in sables under a parasol and awaiting while Crooks was summoned to escort her up the front steps. And it was then that Crooks threw a nearly fatal fit, for she had somehow sacrilegiously ruined my mother's silk stockings she had borrowed. And it was everything one could do to calm Crooks and gently persuade Lois to replace my mother's clothes and revert to wearing her own bohemian garments. As she continued my portrait, she was sniffing up her nose more than usual and was at first strangely non committal about her new swain.

'Well darling, I'd much rather return to Dublin. I must say you people who live in your big country houses do seem to be totally enthralled by your own self importance.'

'I beg your pardon Lois.'

'O perhaps you not too much. You have a certain pleasantly youthful innocent charm dear boy. Plus I suppose I like you. But certainly you don't appreciate the hardships an impecunious artist must suffer these days in a crassly materialistic parvenu city like Dublin. Which leads me to ask if you might dear boy advance me a further amount on your portrait here so I may pay my next month's rent.'

'Of course Lois. Of course. But you're not suggesting I hope, that your man the Baronet is a philistine.'

'Dear boy he is much worse. One of those awful rural men

who keeps seven dogs in his bedroom. Can you imagine. Fleas. Peeing all over the carpet. And one of them actually jumping up on the bed trying to fuck me.'

'Good heavens Lois, that was rather rum. Surely your host wouldn't allow that.'

'Allow it dear boy. He was actively encouraging it so he could watch.'

'And what happened then Lois.'

'I'm most certainly not telling you dear boy.'

'Please, please Lois. We've been snowed in for days here without excitement.'

'Well, if you promise it will go no further than your ears.'

'I promise Lois. Promise.'

'Well firstly he did want me to live in, without even hinting at the courtesy of suggesting undertaking the responsibilities of a marriage contract, which I must confess wouldn't have been all that enticing anyway being that his first two wives are buried out under the front lawn. He simply wanted to enslave me in concubinage to entertain his friends and run his estate for him.'

'I say Lois what's so rum about that.'

'Well there may be nothing rum about it. But freezing around a massive old damp house, having to spy on his wretched servants, who, as it happens, are nowhere near as well behaved as yours dear boy, is highly disagreeable, while he of course goes up to Dublin to sit about playing cards in his club.'

'Ah Lois. I'm glad to hear that. I mean about my servants. But I'm damned sorry to learn that marriage and your becoming a titled lady of the manor is not in the offing.'

'Dear boy you at least ought to know me better than that, by now. My art will, has and shall always remain my sole and complete concern in life. Other woman may grovel about and part their legs for such things, but I shan't I assure you be so deflected. And do just turn your face a fraction left please.'

171

'Lois, both Rashers and I agree that we've rarely ever seen anyone so regally suited to life in a stately home.'

'Thank you dear boy. Kind of you to say. But your mother's furs had rather considerable to do with one's true colours becoming obvious. And of course if I weren't old enough to be your mother I'd marry you anyday, darling. And so long as you didn't start bringing your big wolfhounds into the bedroom.'

Clearly old Lois, despite her threatened little bout with canine bestiality, had a jot more integrity than one had given her credit for. And judging by hand delivered letters over a few days the Baronet, if not his dogs, continued to be in hot pursuit of her. And Rashers's prospects, it would appear, were somewhat brightened, as there seemed no problem to my guaranteeing Rashers's loan from his bank. Only requiring a display of deeds and word from one's bank to his bank and a flourish of my signature on a piece of paper. In fact, by my bank manager's welcoming manner and pleasantly obsequious behaviour I thought perhaps I must be better off than I had previously believed. But there appeared to be a damn sight more complications to joining the Kildare Street Club than one could have imagined. And, according to Rashers, owning at least twenty acres of land being one of them. And I could see from Rashers's big sorrowful eyes that he was again looking deeply in my direction.

'Surely that is not the case Rashers, but if it were then your gravesite at Andromeda Park, albeit minuscule, is at least a beginning in accumulating the necessary acreage. But do let me rush to suggest that such gravesite clearly is not to be put to use for deposit of your noble remains for at least another fifty or sixty more years or so.'

'Dear boy so kind of you to predict such longevity and that you should make available to me, a final resting place. But I fear I may never put it to use. I fancy when the time has come when one views continued life with jaundiced eye I shall not hang about. Once one's corpora cavernosa, or the better part of one's prick in lay man's language, begins to in the least droop, or testicles in the least shrivel, and thus blunt one's appetite for life, I shall then to Monte Carlo and after waging away at the tables my remaining funds if any, it's off the cliffs into the Mediterranean waves at midnight. After a damn decent dinner of course.'

'What if you should win at the tables Rashers.'

'Ah that would naturally indefinitely delay my final departure.'

'Well let me further delay you Rashers flinging yourself off the Monte Carlo cliffs. I am about to see my solicitors and put you in possession of your twenty acres. Not awfully good acres I fear but land suitable enough to portray you as a landowner in the eyes of the Kildare Street Club.'

Tears did then descend Rashers's cheeks and plopped on the shiny black lapels of his dinner jacket, sitting as we were over sherry in the library prior to proceeding to dine. And I motored into town to my mother's old long established firm of solicitors. Catching sight on the way of the marauder driving sheep up his tatty little lane where he had already erected a pair of lopsided piers for a gate. But in making the gentle climb up these carpeted stairs of this legal firm, one did sense a protective air about the place. The reception office guarded by an old but efficient battleaxe of a secretary. Safes along the wall, holding all the secrets of the town and of farms and farmers for miles around. Mr Questor's genial smile as he got up from behind his desk and offered his hand.

'Ah Mr Kildare. Pleased to see you on such a fine morning. So nice to have you call. And I trust all is going well at Andromeda Park, and if not I also trust we can be of immediate help in the matter. You know as I motor along on the road and come up the big hill overlooking Thormondstown and Andromeda Park, there's just that brief moment when one catches sight of the house through the trees. And it always rather pleases me to know as I see the distant lights and silhouette of the elevation that life still goes on there in that great house just as it did in your mother's time. One takes, you know, a comfort from the continuation so to speak. Ah but enough of my sentimentality. Pray tell me what can I do for you, ready as I always am to be at your service.'

'I want to convey to a friend a parcel of land as a present.'

'Ah. I should hope and I don't envision that there will be any serious problem with that. And I assure you that our services as they have always been in the past diligently await your instruction.'

Walking the main street of the town one was surprised by the odd presentable young lady. Indeed in front of the post office one such stopped to inquire the time on my watch. But of course even if she were not a shopgirl and of one's own class one already knew of the gossip which would ensue were one without proper introduction to make a social approach. Like come up and see the squire sometime. Basking in his self importance in his big manor house. Where most of the staff, inmates and certainly the impecunious guests are absolutely nonsensically silly out of their minds. And back next afternoon, sitting for Lois's finishing touches on my portrait, one did have distinct cause to wonder whether some very deep dementia or some perversity wasn't in fact already afoot. Having as I did somehow suspected by Lois's slight previous evasiveness that there was more to tell concerning her sojourn away during the snow storm.

'Lois you must as a long, trusted and dear friend tell me more now as to what happened with the old Baronet. Didn't you for a start find him a rather stingy old bastard.'

'Well darling except for his dogs, who are fed quite sumptuously on steak, he did have padlocks on everything I must admit.'

'And did the perverse old bugger do anything perverse.'

'Dear boy you are aren't you in one of those awful inquisitional Rashers Ronald moods.'

'O come on Lois, give this old boy here a few saucy illusions to alleviate his prolonged unrequited randiness. Spill the beans.'

'Beans. What beans dear boy.'

'Well for a start we do already know a dog jumped up on the bed and was trying to have it off with you.'

'Nonsense.'

'O come on Lois, you are a bloody old damn spoil sport at times.'

'Well darling if you must know I did let one of the dogs at me. Now having bullied it out of me, don't look so shocked dear boy, with your eyebrows hitting the ceiling. One has to try everything at least once. And as it happened I tried it twice.'

'My word, did you really Lois.'

'Yes I did. There was a little difficulty in the positioning but the dogs making love to me behaved quite well. It was the Baronet who turned into a veritable animal. Went nakedly barking around the bed on all fours. Of course he slammed his head into the bedside table. Knocked the candle over and set fire to the tapestries. Ha. Ha. It was rather funny.'

'What's the matter Lois. Do continue.'

'Is it this room that's echoing. I almost distinctly thought I heard someone else laugh. Anyway the dogs started fighting and with pillow feathers all over the place, it was pure bedlam darling. But don't you dare say a word of this to anybody. Ever. Understand. Ever.'

'Never Lois, never ever. Trust me. I mean, good god, to let news of a thing like this out you could have every large dog in Dublin dragging its owner after you.'

'Nor are you to ever make remarks like that again.'

'Sorry Lois. Mum's the word.'

'It better had be dear boy.'

'But Lois, please tell me what it was like.'

'Use your own imagination dear boy.'

175

'My mind's a blank, honestly.'

'Well then opportune darling boy for me to immediately remind, if you will but cast your eyes around these ballroom walls, that your ancestors were extremely fond of being painted with their dogs. But not for a moment am I suggesting anything rum or untoward.'

'I sincerely hope you're not Lois. But you do don't you Lois know how to make a rapier thrust. Whatever other diversions my ancestors may have engaged in, bestiality was never in evidence as one of them. But my word, in having it off with an old ruddy canine Lois, I can't honestly help not conjecturing that it must have been quite a feat of manoeuvring.'

'I've already warned you dear boy, if you don't want me to splatter your face with a blend of linseed oil and turpentine, not to remark further on the subject. Now please do sit still a moment while I get this highlight correct on the tip of your left nostril.'

'I can't Lois. I've got to adjust my private part. Which as it happens, having tumesced upon the recent subject discussed and which we have just dropped, is now painfully in a very wrong ruddy position in these tight breeches.'

'O god now don't be impossible please, do sit back. Must you always have sex on your mind darling. Now just lean a shade more to the left. I hope you don't mind but I should like to exhibit your portrait at the next Living Art Exhibition in Dublin.'

'Ah Lois you've been painting for at least twenty years now, may we assume then that you take into account posterity and are presently executing some of the most important brush strokes of your career.'

'I'll have you know dear boy, I always take into account posterity in executing the most important brush strokes of my career. For my art has afforded me precious little else. I continue to do as I do with the utmost humility and in homage to the great painters who have preceded one.'

176

'You must you know Lois have an exhibition, a one man show.'

'I am not ready yet my dear and you're not at this moment exactly being of any help. If you would only stop squirming.'

'I can't honestly. I'm in ruddy wretched discomfort.'

'O bloody hell. Take out your cock.'

'O my god Lois, shall I undo my breeches. Dare I assume that you are going to give the boy a treat.'

'No you may not so assume. Anyone could walk in that door. As they do in this house. I just want you to sit still so I may finish this protrait.'

'Honestly Lois, what about a treat. Shall I disrobe. My life as you've seen here is so utterly bereft of recent thrills and satisfactions.'

'Dear boy believe me my heart does bleed for you. But were I able to keep suitably warm I should not, despite my nearly drowning, at all mind living in the manner in which you do sans thrills and satisfactions. O god now you've moved out of the light.'

'I'm merely lowering my breeches.'

'O but my goodness, one does forget. But you are well endowed aren't you. But I'm certainly not painting that into the portrait.'

'Come on Lois, we're the oldest of friends. And I am your dedicated patron after all, heaping upon you as I have commissions. Please give the boy who needs it so badly a treat.'

'Well let me first lock the door. And I shall briefly kiss it for you.'

'O to be sure, what a wonderful treat.'

'Well I should like to get it over as soon as possible. To you it may be a treat but at this moment to me it is a damn nuisance. And my sucking your cock dear boy is purely in the interests of art and not because you have been my patron.'

'Of course Lois, of course. Fully understood. And O yes

Lois I have, haven't I, been your admirer, I mean in some ways we've been inseparable over these many months.'

'Do please shut up dear boy, although you may not realize it sucking cocks, although it may be devoid of ardour at times, is an artistic endeavour fully requiring just as much concentration as any other dedication in the fine arts.'

'Lois, mum's the word.'

> And please
> I do implore
> Get on
> With this present
> Masterpiece

II

On this morning of his portrait being painted Darcy Dancer, breeches down, eyes closed and standing on the dais in front of the throne chair. The faint chime ringing the half hour after eleven o'clock in the front hall. Long moaning howls outside from the wolfhounds Kern and Olav. The shutters on the ballroom windows rattling in a sudden wind. Lois in her thick Aran Island sweater bending forward. The light catching the grey strands in her mousy blonde hair as she stoops over my rigidly exposed private part.

'Do forgive me dear boy if, so soon after breakfast, I do not suck, lick and kiss with my customary gustatory zeal. But even so I'd appreciate if at the pertinent time, you wouldn't make too much noise groaning in ecstasy.'

'Aaaachoo.'

Lois jerking upright, a hand still held on Darcy's penis, her mouth open as she looks to the other end of the ballroom where another human sneeze explodes. Darcy closing his pink coat and tugging up his breeches.

'Darcy. There's someone there.'

'My word. Dear me where.'

'Down there. I think behind that tall backed sofa. I distinctly heard someone sneeze. Twice. Good god, there is someone there. There is. Come out at once, you, whomever you are. There Darcy.'

'I say. This is rather a rum situation. What are you doing in here.'

Slowly rising from her crouched position, Assumpta, Crooks's, niece, emerging. Her hands twisting in front of her apron of her maid's uniform. Her head bowed as she steps forward from behind the sofa, and approaches halfway up the ballroom. Her mouth opening and closing speechless. Darcy ripping buttons, struggling to return his stiffened organ to within his breeches. Turning his back on the advancing Assumpta.

'What is the meaning of this Assumpta.'

'Sir, I had come in to look at pictures, thinking you would not mind.'

Lois returning behind her easel and stamping her foot. Taking up her palette in one hand and sheaf of brushes in the other and suddenly putting them down again. Her eyebrows raised, sniffing up her nostrils and throwing her head back.

'But of course one must mind dear girl. Being spied on like this. Voyeurism. Simply outrageous.'

'Madam I am sorry.'

'And so you should be.'

'And I'll be going. I'll never breathe a word of a thing I've seen or heard.'

'Well I should hope not and you damn well had better not.'

'Lois please let me handle this. All right Assumpta you may go.'

'Thank you sir.'

The ballroom door quietly closing behind Assumpta. Darcy desperately manoeuvring to force return of his enlarged private to the privacy of his breeches. Lois watching and convulsing in laughter.

'Dear boy for god's sake leave it out, you'll never get that back in without, ha, ha, breaking it.'

'Do shut up Lois.'

Darcy back aseat on the dais, taking up again his pose on the throne chair. A beam of sunlight coming in the window, lighting the dust rising from the ballroom floor. Upon which footsteps can be seen. And even I used to hide behind that sofa, which is so large, long and old and upon which my sisters used to sit smugly poised to await invitations to dance from would be suitors.

'But what a damn bloody infernal cheek Darcy.'

'Lois no need now for you to get into such a tizzy.'

'Tizzy. My dear boy this has put me off my brush strokes. Imagine a servant witnessing my performing an intimate act.'

'Lois she is Crooks's niece, up from Dublin. Merely interested in pursuing a career in the theatre.'

'What. The theatre. Good heavens, the girl could be overnight famous if she but repeats stories of what she's just seen and heard in this ballroom. It so happens I nearly know everyone and nearly everyone knows me in the Dublin theatre world. And they dear boy would be only too pleased to besmirch my reputation further if they could.'

'O god Lois everyone is gossiped about in Dublin, don't be such a ruddy old paranoid.'

'Paranoid. How can you say I'm paranoid when bestiality is an unlawful imprisonable act in this repressed country.'

'Well again, it isn't as if a lot of people haven't tried it. Honestly I must say Lois, as a member of the artistic avantgarde and for a free thinking and behaving British bohemian you do get worked up over a little bit of innocent sauciness.'

'Innocent sauciness is hardly the term dear boy. And worked up. Of course I'm worked up. And for your immediate information I am not a free behaving bohemian. And I'd appreciate your leaving my being British out of it. But I could be taken into custody for having admitted having it off with a dog, not to mention fellating you dear boy.'

'But you hardly got going dear girl plus you said you were performing a work of art.'

'Don't please try to be funny dear boy.'

Next morning, claiming she needed the artistic solitude of her studio, it was ruddy amazing how quickly old bohemian Lois got up on her high horse to canter out of Andromeda Park, considering that she had only too recently been lolling

181

about on her all fours having it off with the Baronet's old canines. Crooks dancing quite surprising attendance, packing and wrapping her garments in my mother's green tissue paper. Then solemnly lugging down the main stairs her divorced husband's heavy leather suitcase which had the rank of Commander in the Royal Navy embossed upon it. But one could not long feel unamiable towards dear old Lois and, being that the day was decently fair, I had Luke bring the pony and trap to take her to the station. Of course following her signing the guest book with a quite blatantly large signature and in the royal manner commandeering an entire page, we were then elaborately kissing each other on the front porch, with my cock getting as stiff as a cast iron lamp post and being nearly choked as she stuck her tongue halfway down my throat.

'Dear boy how wonderfully thoughtful of you to provide such marvellous transport for me. And I do so hate to hurry away like this. But I shall be back to finish your portrait I promise. And do say goodbye to old leathery foreskin Rashers for me, won't you.'

There on the porch in that fair sunshine, the wolfhounds gambolling about us, the terrible thing was that I discovered, as I waved a last goodbye to Lois disappearing around the rhododendrons, that I was quite shattered at her departure. Since the first moment she ever stuck her tongue deep down in my ear hole and from the first few times I would furiously finish fucking her, or more accurately, her me, there were always glowing within me little glimmerings of fondness for her, especially as she would then gently stroke my brow and say are you tired now my dear. We did have some jolly good old times together. And I realized that the occasional gloom felt during the big snow meant that I was more than a little jealous when she went off with the Baronet. Damn it, even with her being nearly twice my age, one was more fond of her than one cared to admit. And god I was absolutely sorely pressed to have her take my mother's sables only one knew

182

one could not bear to undergo the wretched nervous break-down that would descend upon Crooks if I did so. But certainly I felt one thing was made clear in my life as to how one could so easily, by penetrating the wrong hole with one's prick, disintegrate one's future in a shambles. And one had a mind to take up the moral aspect of this conclusion with Rashers. As I soon did in the library, dressed for dinner and taking a second glass of sherry. I was reclining back in the big leather chair, reading a four day old copy of the *Daily Telegraph*. Damian, having brought logs and filled the turf baskets, furtively backing out the door. The tail of his shirt hanging down over his trousers.

'Is there to be anything else sir.'

'Yes I think we shall require another glass for Lord Ronald.'

'I'll be at that immediately sir. And sir sorry for disturbing you but I would be liking to ask you something.'

'What is it.'

'Could I be having a turn at exercising the horses, Mr Crooks said I could ask you.'

'I'd have to see how you handle a horse first.'

'I'd be gentle on the mouth sir. I have a mind to be a jockey.'

'Well for a start then tuck in your shirt.'

'Yes sir.'

'And be in the yard tomorrow.'

'Yes sir. Thank you.'

Returning to reading the newspaper, I gleaned snippets of gossip in high places. With headlines on page three. A wife taking her husband's revered cricket bat to bash her husband's mistress black and blue and then cutting up the entirety of her husband's wardrobe in elongated strips with a straight blade. Dear me the acrimony that can accrue in marriage makes one take another sip of sherry. Certainly these days one is not getting a pleasant view of what is oft referred to as wedded bliss. But then I suppose a wife keeping her keen eye on a household would immediately know why Damian, returning with Rashers's glass, is breathing heavily and licking what suspiciously looks like mashed potato from his lips. Then nearly tripping and falling with the tray and glass into the fire.

'Good heavens, Damian be careful what's wrong with you.'

'Sir, I do be a bit made nervous now from the commotion been going on down the kitchen.'

'What commotion.'

'Mollie took a heap of the mashed potato and crowned Assumpta on the head, and there's been a bit of a fight, and I be after shouting for Mr Crooks.'

Damian head bowing, backing away. Introducing an additional solemnity to retreating out of the presence. But with an unmistakable smirking smile from his lips. Seems that it's never long before some new botheration happens. Even in a household quietened by Lois's return to Dublin. Dear me from high exhilarating moments one can then sink so deeply into abject depression. I must I do believe take my body and soul soon away for a few days' respite. Hide out in the most remotest bedroom of the Kildare Street Club. With maybe a view of Trinity College, where dear Mr Arland once took me as a boy to watch a rugby match, with the players slogging about and tending to accidently kick each other's blood soaked teeth out into the churned up mud. Meanwhile, in spite of Crooks's niece having caught the pasha of Andromeda Park flagrante delicto in the ballroom, one must maintain a posture of regal rectitude. And be totally indifferent to her during her serving activities in the dining room as I take my soup. Which by that time I do hope she's managed to get the mashed potato out of her hair. Although no obvious great beauty, she does have rather delicate hands and surprisingly slim ankles. Indeed there is a certain matter of fact directness about her and a laughing sparkle in her eyes. At least when there is a plethora of dramatic household incidents coinciding with a change in the weather, next day one always seems to replenish one's strength of character. And one rehearses a whole new list of resolutions and what one might imagine were good intentions. Which immediately gets me in worse muddles but helps dispel the awful gloom such as today descended upon one learning of two cows out in the wood found poisoned dead at the foot of a yew tree. Following which another two cows and their month old calves missing. Then to be suddenly awakened by Luke to attend a midnight struggle to deliver a calf of a cow calving out in the wind swept wilds of a distant meadow. And being dragged along the field with the men hanging onto ropes tied to the calf's hoofs to pull it out as the mother towed us through the dark towards the river and promptly, along with Luke and Thomas, pulled them both down into the muddy depths, drowning the calf. And in the hours it took trying to get the mother out, she too died exhausted on the grass. If one had sold any of these animals, no matter for how little, they were at least sold. And there was money in receipt instead of wet frozen limbs and frustrated anger to show for it. Plus it would save hay and pay a fortnight's wages. And would help keep the bailiff from the door. But now the hunt servants come with their ropes to winch the carcasses up on their dray to bring to the kennels. To hack them apart with perhaps a choice cut reserved to put in a hunt servant's frying pan and the remainder thrown to the ravenous hounds, who not that long ago devoured the kennel keeper when he tripped and fell one morning in their midst. As Sexton said on the occasion, sure your man didn't have the chance of a fox. And one had no regrets having already sent off twenty two young bullocks to the town market to be auctioned at what seemed extremely depressed prices. Despite the auctioneer's elaborate entreaties that these were cattle straight in off some of the best pastures in the county.

'Come on now gentlemen here we are. Let's do business. Another golden opportunity is presented. A bid now for these prime cattle. Need you look any further than these hind quarters that would make your own mouth water. The best that the best of grass can provide. Can't you hear the roast and steaks sizzling away in the pan. And if you had a mind to keep them a while on your own good grass there'd be yet more than a good bit of weight left to be put on them profitably.'

The farmers and cattle dealers' elbows leaning on the barrier. Caps pulled shaded down over the many eyes. Cigarettes sending up clouds of smoke. The auctioneer's voice shouting over the moaning and mooing. Jets of manure spewing over the auction ring. The beasts sliding in the muck as the drover's stick comes hammering down on their haunches. Rashers at my side taking a deep interest in proceedings, surveying the enigmatic farmers' and dealers' faces and unable to discover who is bidding.

'Good god Darcy but I mean to say is someone bidding. Who on earth is buying.'

Of course with my pocket thick with my dung and urine stained hundred pound notes it was I who was buying when we repaired to a nearby pub. Bolstering one's spirits with a much needed large brandy in the smell of damp tweed and the low murmur of farmers' voices. And continuing as I did to remain comfortlessly randy after one's ballroom embarrassment of fellatio interruptus. Having erased from mind an awfully drunken attempt before the blizzard to visit Lois's bedroom one night. Losing my slippers and on the way stubbing my toes on some wretched hallway tallboy and then crashing unconscious over it till morn. And, hoping to look lovely to Lois, I was wearing my blue satin dressing gown which came half off, leaving me nearly freezing to death. Till awakened by Crooks, who at first took such a fright at my slumped over figure in the semi dark, that he fell backwards down the stairs on top of the recent cat let in to stroll the corridors for night time rats. Mucho squeals from the flattened poor old puss but mercifully it cushioned old Crooks from what could have grievously become for me a totally incapacitated, irreplaceable butler. But even with all the hullabaloo Lois deigned not to inquire outside her securely locked door. I may even have pathetically groaned a few times for her to come out and help me. Clearly too many swigs of brandy or port after dinner rather than calming my increasingly nervous disposition, seemed to insanely increase one's wretched need to shove one's poor private pole softly somewhere. Even to sending me stumbling venturing up the secret servants' stairs to the servants' floor. My excuses ready that although I was without the new house cat, I was in fact on the trail of a rat. Which I actually was. And, wanting to alert Dingbats to the imminent danger, I did knock on her locked bedroom door. But, on hearing Dingbats's heavy snoring inside, it was clear that not even an earthquake would waken her. Next late morning in bed, having had to several times yank the servants' bell as I awaited my long delayed breakfast, Norah finally appeared. Of course even though one had no appetite whatsoever one found it imperative to dramatize one's chagrin as much as possible.

'Norah to what does one owe such delay to one's breakfast being brought.'

'Ah now sir Mollie's been two nights running out to the dances that do be held in the town. And last night, god have mercy, wasn't she, she said, chased home across the fields. And she did come to my room in an upset state sir.'

'Good heavens above Norah. Chased. By whom.'

'Persons partially unknown. But Mollie led the pursuer into a bog hole where he drowned.'

'Well has anyone seen yet to recovering the partially unknown corpse.'

'They do be out their sir looking. Now I'm not making the accusation but there'd be talk now that it could be the fellow lately come bought the land and is occupying the new caravan he's put up the lane across from our front gates sir.'

One could never fully depend upon anyone telling the truth about nearly any event at Andromeda Park. But with Dingbats's curvaceous nudity forever emblazoned on my mind, I was not surprised at the flush of rage that went through me. This ruddy marauding upstart making free not only with my gate lodge but now coveting my staff as well as land. Of course each day passing now I seemed more and more to be drooling over Dingbats. The orange bush of hair there where her long fleshy thighs meet. Making one realize that the thoroughbred principles by which one stands as a gentleman were now on the verge of being fatally shatterted. No doubt the time had come to motor over laden with boxes of Bewley's chocolate and vanilla fudge, not to mention the hysterically randy item between my legs, to old Durrow-Mountmellton's and throw my body upon hers now that she was home from hospital. But O dear doesn't one ever learn lessons in one's life. It was so much wiser not to waste one's time with such thoughts. For one thing is certain. That whatever you plan to do to a woman, which is mostly to mount her while encountering the least resistance possible, she on her part invariably has plans that will require you to do something else. Which can, in high dudgeon, send you off to wank somewhere. Of course old Durrow-Mountmellton only required me to piss on her.

'Ah my dear boy here you are. Totally lost in thought. I've been waiting all this time for you to arrive in the drawing room. Thought I'd better look in the library.'

'Let me pour you a sherry Rashers.'

'Don't mind if I do. Life's damn quiet you know in the household with dear old sleazebag sag tits Lois gone, what.'

'Yes. It is rather. And it does make one speculate as to whether one should perhaps venture off somewhat indefinitely to the fleshpots of Europe such as old Lois's Bloomsbury or Montparnasse.'

'Dear boy it is not to say that London is not groaning with lust but you may I fear find that city and Paris priggish by comparison to dear old dirty Dublin. Ah but even considering such a plan my dear Darcy does make one assume that prior to dinner we are about to engage in a somewhat metaphysical discussion. What.'

'Well there is little metaphysical about the realization that simply soon one is not going to be able to carry on here.'

'Nae nae, dear boy. Here, let me top up your sherry. That is all ruddy bloody damn nonsense talk. Put such to rout immediately. What on earth has got into you to dare utter such pessimistic words.'

'Cattle prices.'

'But good god. Although I could not see anyone bidding, I could hardly help later not noticing dear boy your stuffing away your rather quite genuine looking if grubby hundred pound notes.'

'Rashers they are but a feeble representation of an occasional minuscule gain fighting its way upstream against a flood of widespread constant downstream losses and expenses. And at the moment affords very little comfort to one's fiscal spirit.'

'But dear boy, briefly setting aside mundane fiscal matters, look at the turf freely to be had out of your vast boglands. And so brilliantly glowing its warmth out upon us. Only a minute ago just coming across your front hall one had a brief chat with your good Crooks, who was trying to catch two wrens flying hither and thither. Poor birds kept flying into the candlelight in the mirrors. But it did remind one of other avian species and dinner and as one caught the aroma of cooking pheasant, one was further reminded that the latter is had gratis out of the sky which hangs over your one thousand six hundred and forty seven, or is it now, since you've so generously made me a landowner, twenty seven acres. Potatoes and Brussels sprouts from your kitchen gardens. And all being readied on table by the ministering footfalls one hears in the distance.'

'Those ministering footfalls in the distance Rashers do not

come free out of the sky but require weekly wages. As are shotgun shells required for the pheasant and labouring hands for the vegetables.'

'I know I've said it all quite vehemently before. But you must join up with other forces. A substantial heiress dear boy. With lots and lots of lolly. You must seriously speedily look to it. And an American heiress to be precise. One out of those big palaces which I believe populate the shoreline of Newport, Rhode Island.'

'That's all very well Rashers except that America is three thousand miles away. And if I remotely knew how to get to Newport, Rhode Island.'

'Bring them here dear boy, bring them here. Invite them over to loll about on your estate. Chuck them a few suits of long underwear, boots and a sou'wester and install them in your mother's quite splendid apartments. They are all such avid social climbers. Aeroplanes now span the Atlantic. From Gander to Shannon. All very convenient. I mean to say, even I have had, because of one's humble entitlement in the peerage, an odd brush with one of these immensely well heeled Americans. But she seemed to dislike the constant smell of garlic and onions on my breath. And for my part I could not abide her whiny voice. Nevertheless I have a spare *Social Register* with telephone numbers and addresses.'

'What on earth is a social register Rashers.'

'Like *Debrett* dear boy, like *Debrett* but without the breeding. They have little pictures next to their names of yachts with smoke coming out the smoke stack to indicate that's where they are. On board.'

'How quaint.'

'You mean how bloody ruddy rich. Some of these yachts would stretch across the front elevation of Andromeda Park, dear boy.'

'Rashers, forgetting me entirely for a moment, I should dearly love to know what it is that you want most out of life.'

190

'I knew it. Metaphysics. Dear me. What a question. But dear boy, as I cross my legs and pull up my socks a wee bit and admire that rather splendid purple or is it mauve smoking jacket you are wearing, and if you really mean to force an answer from me, I can tell you in less than a small nutshell. But I'm sure you're looking for an answer far more profound than I can give. Ah, very nutty this sherry. Well the answer may seem to you rather trivial but it does sum up the general picture. I want most out of life not to have to remove myself out of my pyjamas or bed until it is time to go racing of an afternoon. But I rather expect my betrothed of a morning is going to want me out overseeing the livery matters in her stables once we are wed.'

'Well Rashers I believe you did one night, to the Philosophical Society of Trinity College, put the motion that this house moves to find the greater truth in the statements, that deep in every woman's heart is a whore, or deep in every whore's heart is a woman. Certainly affirming such a belief lays an adequate intellectual foundation for pimping. Which staying in late in bed may require. So do we take it that you are to engage in some occasional poncing again. And by the way my smoking jacket is blue.'

'How very unparliamentary of you, dear boy. Low blow. But by jove you do have a memory. However, I do hope too you don't think me some kind of poncy fake while admitting that in one of my more dire impecunious periods one briefly touted and negotiated the sale of sultry Sheena. Who of course drinks too much and disgraced me in polite, if socially sham company, by pissing down between her legs in a rather revered Fitzwilliam Square, Dublin, drawing room just as I was at the point of consummating an agreement for her services at top prices. Bathed, brushed, up, coiffed and perfumed, she is as you know quite strikingly attractive. But poor girl soaked the carpet and got me a totally unwarranted punch on the nose. Of course I kicked the chap firstly and immediately in the balls and then as he was convulsed in pain I neatly knocked out his front teeth. Poor bastard was not to know he was messing with an expert in unarmed combat. Then as I was exiting out his front hallway I also tore one of the paintings of a phoney ancestor off the wall and was about to put my foot through it when his butler up from the cellar rushed us. I thought it a much better idea to simply perforate the painting over the butler's head and let him wear it like a necklace. Well you never heard such screams coming down from the landing. My Rembrandt, my Rembrandt. And poor Sheena. Girl's kidneys just act up on her like that out of the stress of her previously poverty stricken life. She also gets the giggles while she's pissing, which is why people take it as deliberate. But one would absolutely not, despite her leaving a pool of pee on some old damn Dublin carpet, see her spurned in such manner.'

'Rashers you do sometimes just dumbfound me.'

'Why dear boy. Why.'

'Your life, if I may delicately suggest, does seem to be a morass of moral inconsistencies and a series of débâcles. Not that one does not have one's own share of both.'

'Well I suppose I have had to, on some occasions while under a certain duress, take what might be described tactically as a little ethical manoeuvring. While always of course defending, if one can't entirely redeem, the honour of a woman. Ah but my proposal to the Philosophical Society, however, in the cloistered confines of Trinity College Dublin did not go unnoticed or unchallenged. In fact it rather met with strong exception and objection. From the University Elizabethan Society, a society exclusively meant for women. They were waiting next day for me as I crossed front square and the whole lot of them poured out of number six college. Even to bearing flags and banners. They proceeded in their little march across the uneven cobblestones. At first I had no idea what they were about and stood there foolishly clapping and cheering. There were even assembled the vice presidents, of which there are eleven, its six officers and five general committees. Even a lady called to come over from Paris. All led by the society's titled patron. Then they started jeering me. Mortifying it was. Fingers pointed. And for the remainder of Michaelmas term one got these sidelong disapproving glances from college ladies almost all of whom were members of the society. To be publicly ridiculed like that is not awfully nice. And I was, in the furtherance of mental and moral science, absolutely sincere in proposing my premise to the members of the college Philosophical Society.'

'Well Rashers that could be the very reason they marched against you.'

'Do you know Darcy. I think you are absolutely right. No one wants to find the real truth. And I take the point your smoking jacket is in fact blue. But you see Darcy don't you why chaps like us must find ladies of property to marry. Who have no need to make whores of themselves. That's why dowries have been so popular down through the ages. We must both be damn sensible. That's why, should you not be able to fish out of the American *Social Register* a suitable heiress, you should as soon as possible consider proposing to, say, the likes of old Durrow-Mountmellton. About whom, by the way, a rumour circulates that she owns several streets of freeholds in Edingburgh. Lolly isn't of course everything as we know dear boy, it's simply that hardly anything else really matters if you don't have it. Yes now, take this sherry, and the joyful pleasure we take in drinking it, very nutty, very special. And there all this time in your cellars awaiting us. I did take a little peek down there. And you mustn't be alarmed that I took such a liberty. Crooks required me to translate a label for him. Quite an astonishing labyrinthine series of vaulted crypts. And quite generously populated with bottles. In fact, a veritable library of oenology. I mean for you to say you are not going to be able to carry on here is sheer apostasy dear boy and treason to your forbears who laid down your cellar. Plethora of Louis Roëderer champagne 1927. Or was it '26. Dusty old ports, vintage 1924, '27. Rums, brandies, Armagnacs. Dozen upon dozens of Romanée Conti 1929. You see such things matter dear boy in the ongoing momentum and purpose of living. And to dispossess yourself of the proper circumstances in which to tipple would be a nasty jolt to the senses. We could not have had this conversation in your drawing room or your Porcelain Room, or other of your reception rooms. Only in this library of accumulated erudition, which utterly perfectly fits the occasion. I mean to say imagine what your existence would be without having this chamber in which to down your sherry. So here's to Newport, Rhode Island, and to your taking upon yourself a rich wife to ensure this tradition.'

'And if one does find a rich wife, what about love and affection Rashers, and well, just simply love.'

'Ah dear boy yes. Yes indeed. Now I don't want to put myself in a morally indefensible position. Nor do I mean for a second to overlook such things. Now with these ruddy rich American heiresses, they're not easy to like on a daily basis of course. Especially, as it were, having to sing for your supper. They have these awfully fussy habits wanting to be seen everywhere that is regarded as highly socially acceptable. But, depending upon the extent of her wherewithal, such a thing as love does have a tendency to grow out of necessity. I mean if the lady has what you need you do somehow become quite fond of her. As one does finally become of the potato, as it were, when one is awfully hungry.'

'Surely Rashers one can regret quite considerably marrying simply for mere mammon. Or a potato as you put it. As I'm sure in the end my impecunious gambling father did in marrying my mother.'

'Darcy the world is so full of pain that we do it a sincere service to pursue comfortable habits while we live and then

194

one must go down to death without tears. As I earnestly intend to do. Just slip away under the waves. Food for the fish. One's spirit dissolved in the sea. To ebb and flow with the tides. But meanwhile dear boy, stay put on your acres. Grasp the ruddy tried and true potato. Roast it in its skin. Anoint it with butter. Devour it. And as it says in the book of common prayer, and forgive me if I shout such words out awfully loud. Put to rout our persecutors and our slanderers. And bugger all else and all others who dare in our lifetime to fuck us about.'

Rashers smiling, shooting his cuffs and readjusting his monocle as he sniffs the air in the manner of Lois and raises an eyebrow. Reaching for the sherry bottle, he pours toppings up into the glasses. The moan of a beast and a bark of a hound out in the night. A gentle knock. The library door slowly coming ajar, and the straighter of Crooks's crossed eyes peering in.

'Is there something amiss Master Reginald.'

'No Crooks. Merely Lord Ronald giving us a recitation.'

'Ah well, I just thought it better to check with the goings on recently. And if it be to your present convenience sir, whenever you are ready, dinner is served. And I have the bottle of that wine his lordship read the label of chilling ready for you for the dessert.'

Crooks suddenly ducking. Two wrens flying in the door over his head. And fluttering back and forth across the room from bookshelf to bookshelf. A small white deposit landing on the left shoulder of Darcy Dancer's smoking jacket. Crooks waving his hands at the ceiling.

'Ah be jabbers now Master Reginald I've been doing my best to catch the little buggers. All over the front hall. Wait now till I get you a towel.'

'Ah now there Darcy, shat so neatly like a major's crown upon your shoulder is a piece of certain ruddy good luck. Don't whatever you do touch it.'

195

'Yes I do believe you're quite right Rashers. And not to worry Crooks as Lord Ronald says I think this little sudden decoration on my shoulder does, provided we leave it there, represent good fortune.'

'Fair enough now Master Reginald. Fair enough. I'll leave the birds so. And I'll be getting back now to the pantry. And praise god, maybe the other little fellow will drop a little something on the other shoulder to double the good fortune.'

Crooks's eyes suddenly becoming uncrossed and then crossing again as he bows and withdraws, gently closing the door. One wren letting out a little cheerful chirp from a bookshelf on high. Rashers putting a piece of turf on the fire. Wiping his hands and smiling.

'Darcy expect something absolutely quite wonderful to befall you soon.'

'Well Rashers although I am not quite optimistic these days, I am ready to take absolutely anything as a good omen.'

Rashers reaching and picking up the *Daily Telegraph*, staring at the page and putting the paper down. Then taking his sherry and draining the glass and placing it softly back on the side table. His hands placed out on the armrests of his chair, and his head slumping forward upon his chest as he stares into the glowing turf flames.

'What's wrong Rashers.'

'Nothing really. At least I suppose not unpleasantly wrong. The King's eldest daughter is betrothed.'

'O dear. Poor you. Rather puts you fatally out of the running. What an heiress she would have been to wed.'

'Please don't treat it lightly Darcy. I know I had little chance in such august circles.'

'But you don't do you any more Rashers really give a damn about England.'

'Darcy I do. I do. And I more and more now inexplicably imagine sounds in my ear. Horses neigh. And I suddenly realize I'm hearing the Guards on parade. My regiment coming to attention with a great woosh and resounding clatter. The Colonel calling shoulder arms. Right face. And then the announcement to the King that His Majesty's Guards are ready to march on. The base drums boom. The bagpipes skirl. And the footfalls moving away fade into the distance. Echoes of commands coming over the parade ground. And Darcy I do grieve. I solemnly grieve. You see in this world there is nothing quite like being English. I dare say something else might matter a bit, like being Anglo Irish, but never as much as truly being British and English.'

'Good god Rashers, honestly, you do, you do really dumbfound me. Not that there's anything particularly wrong but I mean what's so particularly ultra important about being English.'

'Ah dear boy, up on that exact ultra specific you do have me somewhat at a disadvantage, being that you are my host and that I am your eternally grateful guest. Nevertheless my good chap I do you the courtesy of recognizing your courage in facing such matters. And know one can be explicitly honest to you as you sit there. But can you really say the same thing about being Irish. That it really matters. I mean good lord with everyone Irish around you. I mean it might matter more to deny one's Irishness. Imagine. This wretched little country. Neutral through the war. Ruddy little nation which has never conquered abroad and only been a colony of its powerful strong resolute neighbour across the water. Its tenant peasants wretchedly subsisting in their thatched little huts, scheming and plotting their treacheries upon their noble landlords such as yourself. Perhaps from what I've just said you will not be enjoying my savouring the Romanée Conti at dinner.'

'By god Rashers, you are verging very close to being nearly damn right. I think I rather resent what you've just said.'

'Dear boy you mustn't take what I've said personally.'

'Well I am Irish. Born and bred. And although you've adequately made it known that you have dined with the King of England I would remind you where you are now and we are ruddy hell not exactly on our knees eating off the floor here with our hands. Or cowering in a thatched cottage. Let's please proceed to dinner.'

'O my dear boy. Dear boy. Nae. Nae. Some of my own blood is Gael. More than I care to readily admit. I am behind the Free State in all that she endeavours. But we must not blind ourselves to the loutish scheming treachery of the general Irish. O but I grieve if I have offended you. I grieve. I honestly do. I grieve.'

Tears falling from Rashers's eyes, as he removed and wiped his monocle. Sadness etched upon his face. The wrens flying overhead once more. And one watched Rashers with his soldierly stride, shoulders so resolutely back, as he strode out the library door. The heavy fall of his heels on the floor. The wavering light of the wall sconces as we turned right to proceed to the front hall, and then left in the gloomy darkness down to the dining room. Wherein the bright candlelight sparkled in the crystal candelabra. The fire blazing. The soup steaming on the sideboard. And there at the table somehow Rashers's sadness made itself felt upon one. One secretly wants so much to be truly English. And Ireland made me Irish. My ancestors staying in this land as others fled. Here in this house where I once knew love. And it were as if it were back one day when I opened a farm gate to a field and stood there not wanting to go either forward or back. Just stood there. Unable to move in the mild autumn stillness. The sun gently on the fluttering golden leaves of the trees. My mind in a strange sweet perfumed pain as I thought of Leila. Her face, her smile, her hair. Her aloof dignity. And my heiress I would marry. Who had all the riches I could ever want from this world. Her soft dark beauty my dowry. Her sweet body next to mine as my love. Grey green her eyes. Into which I could look. Her gentle melodious voice so softly saying things I would listen to and hardly know what she was saying. One was not to know how long one stood at that open gate, my elbows leaning on the rungs. My eyes staring out across the boggy meadows to the lake. The white of two swans floating there. The soft blue and tumbling clouds in the sky as night began to fall. The light of the late afternoon slowly disappearing. The air growing chill. To leave me colder still in the great great loneliness I feel. And like Rashers I too am grieved. Left in my own sadness as I was that day. And since have so oft whispered a little prayer. Praying for you, my Leila, to come back to me. And yet you were never mine, for me to miss you so. And still within me I weep as I did once as a little boy. Going to my sister for comfort. To put my arms around her. So she would put her arms around me. And she said. Get away. Get away.

> You're
> Wetting me
> With
> Your tears

12

The night outside silenced with shutters closed and drapes drawn over the dining room windows. The candle light sparkling and flashing orange, purple and green in the crystal pendants hanging from the candelabra. The mirrors over the sideboard misted with steam rising from the vegetable tureens. The clank of spoons and dishes and clatter of plates in the pantry as soup was served. Rashers aseat the other end of the dining room table, his mouth going like a great maw as he spoke.

'Dear boy apropos of nothing at all. But you know how pretentious and assuming people get who are merely from the higher ranks of the bourgeoisie. There's a constant lingering impertinence about them, which, if one can't tear oneself away from their presence, becomes intolerably tiresome.'

Dingbats dutifully serving instead of being off to another dance in the town. And Crooks's niece Assumpta standing at the sideboard by the tureen of sautéed potatoes, her hair from which the mashed variety had been removed still damp. And as she was refilling Rashers's bowl with seconds of soup, her face flushing crimson as our eyes met. Rashers again referring back to the incident in Fitzwilliam Square. As usual he had little or no awareness as to who might be overhearing our conversation. And through a crack in the pantry door I could see Crooks, dishing out the pheasant, didn't want to miss a syllable.

'O my god, O my god. Upon my word.'

'What is the difficulty Rashers.'

'No difficulty dear boy, none whatsoever. It's this wine

200

which is so utterly superlative. A miracle of man and nature with its strength of character emerging from its exquisite velvety smoothness. Of course I do believe 1929 was one of the best vintage years so far this century.'

'Yes, it is rather superlative indeed.'

'O Darcy, Darcy, pray the gods on high will let this life continue. In ducas in tentatsionem.'

'Your Latin Rashers escapes me.'

'It escapes me too. Just a little mixture I put together to express when one is feeling particularly on top and when one fears the world not. And when too I know and verily believe something awfully good is to befall you Darcy.'

'Crooks do decant us another bottle if you will.'

'I already have sir. Lord Ronald having anticipated the wine's excellence.'

'O.'

'You see Darcy. Told you. Did I not. Something awfully good would befall you. But of course getting back to dear old Sheena when she was unable to hold back her bladder. Sheena as you know had those wondrous eyes of hers glowing like coals in a fire. Which can dramatically escalate the price of her services. I did suggest to the owner that a carpet of such dubious quality as he had on his floor could be improved only by a good soaking of piss. I mean to say chap called me a rogue, imagine rogue. Chancer or cad perhaps one might tolerate. But rogue. Nae. I wasn't having it of course. When I popped him one on the old proboscis. I rather put the weight of my entire shoulder into it.'

'Rashers, I thought you knocked out his front teeth.'

'I did dear boy. I did. And with a neat sweep of my left elbow I extracted one of his right bicuspids. But also I fear I flattened his nose, and fractured four of his fingers. Purely as an afterthought of course. I mean I wasn't about to have highly defamatory comments heaped upon one in that fashion. Now he has a dozen unseemly solicitors wanting ruddy satisfaction for my occasioning their client actual bodily harm and for the permanent disfigurement of this pretentious chap's face. Which was already regrettably objectionable. Sometimes one wishes one weren't constrained by having to behave as a gentleman. You see Darcy deep down I am not a ponce but I was desperate at the time, having been that morning evicted from my flat and having already run up enormous unpaid bills at the Hibernian, the Shelbourne, Buswell's, the Russell and even some lesser hostelries beyond Dublin's social pale. And so had with my pathetic possessions to repair north of the Liffey to a bed and breakfast kip. Indeed not far from Amien Street Station where, in that grim dark cold bereft vicinity of Dublin, one had in the faded lamplight to find shabby diggings which in a thrice corrode the soul. My god through an open door one sees the bleak light inside a hallway that seems to lead into oblivion up a staircase and there at the top of the stairs, like a sentence of death, a sign, bed and breakfast. Overcharging at seven and sixpence for a narrow lumpy horsehair bed behind grimy curtained windows above some shopfront. Also as it was on a cold bitter winter's night and a Sunday, nothing quite in this world is as lonely and abysmal. And a far far cry from this present pheasant and wine. But getting back to your marriage prospects dear boy. You must think of finding a lass sophisticated in the domestic disillusionments which inevitably follow espousement. You know how it is in bed after a big dinner, too much sherry trifle, many cigars, brandy, chocolates and what have you, and you lie there on the recently ironed linen sheets next to one's newlywed, having rogered the dear lady to a standstill, and one decides it is time to take the diabolical liberty of relieving oneself of the discomfort of singularly bottled up flatuosity. Of course when one was betrothed one dare not release an explosive fart bomb which would blow the covers off one and in permeating the air would peel the paper back from the bedroom walls. Then too as dawn breaks one wants the dear girl to be tolerant of one's hocking and spitting and roaring to clear the throat. So that one does not remain in tense discomfort. Darcy I dare say, it would seem that in life one is never finished worrying.'

'Rashers do have another little bit of pheasant. Do have that leg. And I am beginning to think that worrying is life. And that when one stops worrying, one stops living.'

'Darcy dear boy, dearest friend. You have spoken truly and wisely. And it gives me courage. And I shall indeed try that leg. I should really you know return to Dublin. Been here a fortnight or more.'

'More actually.'

'Well, then, it's time I got the train. And arrive to descend the granite steps of Amien Street Station, and into the North Star Hotel. I have always liked that name you know. Inspirational. And I shall stand at the bar and have a tall ball of malt before I stride back onto the hard wet cold grey pavements of Dublin and face the begrudgers. I would of course from my dingy bed and breakfast quarters often proceed there to the North Star to quaff a few rosiners in its dignified confines. A way of retaining one's sedateness, having to reside nightly in that part of town.'

'O dear you mustn't think I want you to go Rashers.'

'So kind. So awfully kind of you to say that my dear Darcy. So awfully kind. But I must. My betrothed awaits.'

'But what about her visit here Rashers.'

'Do you know Darcy I think that should be left till we are wed. I shouldn't like the girl to get too familiar with the privilege of meeting my nearest and dearest friends. Because one did not want to tempt fate I have not told you this. But I've been offered a job.'

'Good god Rashers, I don't think I believe my ears.'

'It is still a little up in the air. You see it's also why I need some little financial help to look the part. Before money comes rolling in. I merely lie upon my back in the Shelbourne of a morning and make phone calls up and down the country to various selected shops to put in their eager orders. You see it's my voice, not my singing but my speaking voice, that's regarded as so suitable for the work.'

'Orders for what Rashers.'

'Ah I'm so glad you asked that question. Sanitary towels of course. It's a very important business you know. Not to be sneezed at. Potentially a big market, dear boy. O I know it doesn't sound like the sort of thing that goes down well in polo and racing circles. But do remember that nearly every post puberty girl in the country who has a notion to be of a modern hygienic disposition needs a little absorbent something unless she's intending to be a downright disgraceful nuisance at a certain time of the month. Sorry, I know this isn't exactly appropriate dinner conversation, but the fact of this matter could be the changing of my life.'

'Rashers I find it quite hard to believe you will be able to conduct your business from a bed in the Shelbourne.'

'You mustn't look so absolutely amazed my dear boy. I have it all already satisfactorily worked out. You see Darcy at the end of the day I am no idler you know. I don't want to belabour the fact, and I do count my blessings, but dear boy being without fixed permanent abode, without furniture, crockery, silverware, linens, crystal, fine paintings and excepting my replica of the Ardagh Chalice, and with hardly a pot to piss in, does play severe havoc with one's optimism. My past use of the minuscule kitchen sink in my flat and with the present basin in my bed and breakfast chamber notwithstanding.'

Darcy Dancer pulling the table bell. The pantry opening. Damian entering to pour the wine. Assumpta with sprouts, Dingbats with sautéed potatoes and Crooks coming to carve more pheasant for Lord Ronald's heaped plate. Upon which the second leg of this bird has already left only the trace of its bones. In spite of the astonishing upheavals in Rashers's life, at least dinner is going smoothly without a hitch. And one may as well toast the future.

'Sköl Rashers.'

'Sköl Darcy.'

'Well Rashers, the advent of your new profession does rather sound as if it is providential intervention. I look forward to calling upon you in the Shelbourne to find you viewing the purple spires of the Wicklow mountains while lying the morning away in your pyjamas and then I presume dressing just in time for at least the second race somewhere.'

'Well I dare say, to be more specific, it's not actually what the chaps who rule their sanitary domain have in mind dear boy. Especially having provided a highly unnoteworthy vehicle in which yours truly is expected to motor to various towns and villages soliciting for business. Can you imagine anything so disagreeable. Well of course I had to appear to give it a try. So just before I came to visit I chose upon my first investigatory mission to head south to the Golden Vale and to the richer farming communities. As you know it's quite wonderful the plethora of chemist's shops all over this country, for which we have the chronic constipation of the natives to thank.'

'Rashers do you mean to tell me you've already taken up being a travelling salesman.'

'Good god. You must not get the impression that I am a broker for fancy toiletries and ladies' requisites. Nae. Nae. You see I'm afraid you entirely misconstrue. The chaps and powers that be regard me in another capacity entirely, having served years as a medical student, I am in fact a Vice-Presidential Surgical Representative. At large as it were. In addition of course I have a rather profitable card up my sleeve as well. Thought it quite appropriate. I also dabble a little in the old forbidden under the counter contraceptive trade. Best quality French letters. Condoms fresh in from America, all that kind of thing. Spanish Ticklers, Australian Quiverers, Black Jumbos. You name 'em, dear boy I've got 'em.'

'Rashers good heavens despite your awe inspiring title one

can hardly imagine you entering a chemist's shop and illegally putting it to the proprietor if he is all right for Australian Quiverers or stock in the other varieties you mention.'

'Well if you must know Darcy it did rather all turn out rather inappropriately and go badly wrong on my first attempt. When I did in fact do that very thing. One was somewhat overenthused thinking I might bring some sexual solace to the farming population. At any rate I had to see how the old ruddy drill might work in order that I then be able to assign it to a subaltern. I deliberately chose a more than usually Protestantly populated town. But it was a very quiet and peaceful sunny afternoon when one's voice seemed to carry inordinately. And of course I did make the mistake of being overheard by a clearly post menopausal lady customer with a bloody pug dog on a lead. And upon my offering the proprietor this unbeatable offer of four gross of the best quality condoms with the American tips the chemist threw the most astonishing fit I've ever witnessed, knocking over an entire display cabinet of toiletries and then in trying to throw a toilet roll at me he slipped on a small canister of lozenges and smashed his coccyx. And I had already invited his young lady assistant with a wonderful pair of tits to dinner. Of course in trying to help pick him up he fought me off. With the lady now raining blows down upon my back with her parasol and her wretched pug dog biting me in the ankles. I picked up the beastly creature by the collar and flung it howling towards the dispensing counter, not realizing of course that the dog's lead had wrapped around the lady's legs, which were promptly yanked from under her and she too was thrown on her arse. However, the chemist was a singularly sinister little fucker who kept staring at my monocle even as he lay among his lozenges. And Darcy I don't think the membership committee of the old Kildare Street Club need know much about any of this.'

'Good god Rashers the Kildare Street Club may prove to be the only place you'll be safe. You're certainly never going to be able to show your face or monocle again in the Golden Vale and most likely not elsewhere either.'

'True dear boy. True. Ah. But there had already been long laid contingency plans. One now has a little card upon which in the very smallest sized engraving indicates who one is. The title dear boy does help you know. I don't use the Right Honourable Lord so and so or anything like that. Just your plain simple old common or garden Lord Ronald Ronald. And I have in places with telephone communication arranged with the various hotel porters in the various hotels in the various towns to weekly just slip in to the various halls of apothecary and in solemn whispers to take the proprietor's order. Of course slip them a few bob to make it worth the porter's while. It's all going to work quite nicely now from the Edwardian mellow red brick sanctum of the Shelbourne. You know dear boy that hotel was among the first places in Dublin ever to use gas light. And the entire population would of an evening come patrolling Stephen's Green just to look upon all the gloriously glowing windows golden within.'

Rashers's most winning smile appearing, illuminating his whole face. The space between his two protruding front teeth looking larger than usual. And suddenly raising an arm. The cuff of his sleeve showing. And even at the distance from me down the table, I could see instead of his own gold ones he was wearing my mother's father's cuff links. A diamond set centre in mother of pearl. And unmistakable even across the crystal reflections of the candelabra. And as one bites through the skin of one's roasted pheasant and quaffs back this superlative wine with its softly enveloping bliss, one simply does not have the heart to call this charmer and chancer cad into question.

'Darcy you must get out and be more about. You do seem to have adopted a recent reclusive tendency, a standoffish aloofness, unlike those wonderful partying days of yore in Dublin. As if you were enduring some deep disappointment.

O but I mustn't preach dear boy, like some sort of smug poseur.'

'I should like to, Rashers. But the moment my back is turned worse things seem to happen than when my back isn't turned.'

'Of course one does admire that there still is about you a cloistered innocence.'

'I hope you don't by that mean I'm a potato digging bog trotter Rashers.'

'Nae, nae dear fellow. It's your continued kindly concern for those less endowed with the world's riches that one considers you may too overly indulge. Such as the gurrier ruffians and the crawling up the arse opportunists. But I'll tell you exactly what one must avoid above all other things in life.'

'I await with baited breath to hear Rashers. What.'

'O but I mustn't preach. But we must rid of this desolation. And I have the immediate solution. Be my representative here in your local town where there are five thriving chemist's shops. I mean the porter of the local hotel isn't quite the type suitable.'

'As a pedlar of prohibited condoms.'

'Now. Now. Darcy. No need to put it quite like that in that tone of voice. The French letters are merely a commercial embellishment in the marketing of sanitary requisites for women. And then you see we expand of course to other towns of the county.'

A crash of dishes and a scream from the pantry. The boy butler with the wine basket at Rashers's elbow, looking up from his task of pouring and the wine promptly soaking Rashers's dinner jacket sleeve and silk shirt cuffs. Damian then rearing back at the sight of the soaking of his lordship and spilling wine instead onto the surrounding table. Crooks's voice from the pantry up a distinct octave shouting above the mêlée.

'In the name of the almighty unmerciful god, stop this

208

immediately. Stop while the master and his lordship are at their dinner. Youse Mollie you trollop get off me niece.'

'Fuck off you old bugger.'

'Don't use that language to me, youse.'

'Let go, let go of my hair, you fucking bitch.'

'I'll teach you to try kick me in the stomach you whore from Dublin.'

'Let go of her Mollie. You've had drink taken youse have had. By god I'll summon the law I will.'

'Help she's tearing my hair out.'

'There'll be lumps more torn out than this if you're not gone from this house in a hurry.'

The crash of glass. A scream and screech. A heavy thump shaking the floor and rattling window panes. Sound of fabric ripping. Another thump. A groan. Crooks's jacket half off, trembling at the pantry door, blood trickling from his nose. His torn rugby jersey showing under his butler's coat. As Rashers licks wine from his wrist and two handedly picks up his pheasant's leg and sinks his teeth in for a big bite. Crooks shaking, leaning forward, his hands on the table supporting him. His crossed eyes looking around him and for a moment glancing in supplication to my mother's portrait up on the wall. The dining room floor vibrating with more thuds and thumps.

'O merciful lord, merciful lord Master Reginald surely this will go down in history as the worst yet ever to hit Andromeda Park. A disgrace to your dear mother's memory. That one Mollie sir has got to go. Or I go. One or the other of us. She is a source of both physical and moral danger to the household.'

The pantry door flung open and banging back against the wall. Another crash of a dish. Another door slamming. Assumpta entering the dining room, her apron wrapped around her neck, and holding up to her chest the torn fabric of her clothes.

'O please save me, save me from that one.'

Rashers rising from his chair and making towards the open pantry door, pheasant leg still in his mouth. And to be stopped in his tracks. Met there with the remaining contents of the bowl of cabbage, the soggy buttery leaves splattering him full across the face.

And at long
Last
A smile appearing
On
Darcy Dancer's
Countenance

13

A fortnight of sleet and rain. And the last little piles of snow melted into the moss in the sheltery shadows of the woods. Fog out on the land this morning. Drizzle falling. The air chill and damp inside the front hall. Smell of turf smoke from the fire. Looking appreciably rotund, Rashers in his checked tweed. Returned from the servants' dining room and dispensing his appreciation to the household. As now we awaited Luke to repair three flat tyres to motor him to the train station.

'Dear boy sorry for my swift change of plans. I do so hate to go. But must. To prepare to take these important steps in my life. I do have so much to thank you for that I shall not confine myself to saying merely thank you. But saying it twice. Thank you.'

A look of pleased satisfaction upon Rashers's face. And in Andromeda Park's visitors' book on the hall table, minutely scrawling his tiny signature and the word 'raconteur' following his name. He squares back his shoulders and grins. His silk shirt, yellow tie. A gold watch chain hanging across the silver buttoned bright crimson waistcoat. The tips of his leather laced stout shoes gleaming.

'I do so hate to go Darcy. But O dear. Commercial matters beckon.'

Crooks grunting at the bottom of the stairs, holes in the heels of the socks, having just brought Lord Ronald's bags down to place the two portmanteaus in readiness inside the front hall door. And who knows they could again be full of silverwear as once before disappeared from Andromeda Park in Rashers's clutches. Dear me. The frailty of one's trust. And such ruddy ceremony Crooks gets up to as he appends to Rashers's lapel a bog flower button hole left by Sexton.

'Thank you Crooks.'

'It has been my privilege your lordship to be of service to you.'

Crooks standing back a pace and giving Rashers a little salute which, having somewhat music hall overtones to it, could hardly be considered military. However, it will not harm to attempt to turn Andromeda Park into an army outpost if possible. Have steel shuttered gun emplacements at each window. Drill the staff in marching and hold target practice. Ready to put a load of shot into the backside of the likes of the marauder next time he trespasses my land or lurks anywhere in and around this house.

'Dear boy you are so very reclusively silent this morning. Of course you will won't you be popping up to Dublin to attend upon the entertainment to be provided by the good Count MacBuzuranti in his town house. I suppose it's sure to be the usual sort of masked ball at which his invited homosexualists wear nothing else. They are, some of these Italians, such arrant exhibitionists. Especially when Lois is, with her exquisite tits wagging and castanets clacking, providing them with a rhythm to nakedly cavort to as she does in her Salome dance. Of course if you have a mind to miss it, all that kind of thing comes later on in the evening. But by god what on earth was that awful extra loud thump I heard last night.'

'The extra loud thump heard last night Rashers was in fact a sizeable chunk from the masonry gable that bestrides the roof over the front door of this house and which plummeted to the front steps. And which has just been removed in several wheelbarrow loads. And why Rashers do you find that so damn funny, grinning at me like that.'

'Ah because dear boy, as you but follow a plan I have laid for you, all such dilapidation of that kind will be ere long

212

something completely of the past. Soon, instead of the likes of MacBuzuranti's poofters, you will be enabled to import a gang of ultra masculine Italian and Florentine stuccatori, and together with stonemasons and painters and decorators, put this whole house right in a trice.'

'What on earth are you talking about Rashers.'

'Your future of course. And our previous little natter on this matter. You see I have not been idle. After making certain discreet inquiries I took the liberty of communicating on your behalf so that you might have a look see as it were.'

'A look see at what.'

'Ah dear boy, although I do now understand why you should be ill humoured this morning, none the less you mustn't take what I am about to tell you like that. And before you know what auspiciousness it proffers.'

'Of course I take it like that, knowing exactly the sort of perverse thing you are wont to get up to.'

'But dear boy, here you see tucked under my arm my trusty copy of the *Social Register*, the existence of which I have previously brought to your somewhat surprised attention.'

'What in heaven's name has that got to do with anything.'

'Ah well you might ask dear boy. Well you might ask. Indeed I should take a poor view of you if you did not ask such questions. Let me elaborate further. Now then. As you know in this volume, to which people who feel they are so entitled apply, are listed alphabetically the names, addresses and telephone numbers of its subscribers, right down to the folk they have married, the children they have parented, the schools they have attended and the clubs to which they belong. I know such as we may regard that as being, if not plebeian, rather blatantly public.'

'Well yes, isn't it rather a bit.'

'Ah but. To me. Pisser without a pot. To me. I adore each and every name and entry. And so regard it as I might *Debrett*. Or *Burke's Peerage*. In which latter volume you are all embracingly treated as one of Ireland's landed gentry. To which Darcy you so rightly and deeply belong. But we must be open minded dear boy about Americans. They did rather help us win the war.'

'You're forgetting I happen to be Irish Rashers. And we were not in the war.'

'Of course, how remiss of me dear boy. But the point I should like to make is, I have from a selected list chosen a few of the pertinent names and addresses of the suitable eligible ladies therein to whom I have taken the liberty of issuing an invitation to your grand Andromeda Park ball.'

'You what.'

'O dear I do so hope you're not discriminating against me since one's launching into the commercial field of supplying feminine artifacts of hygiene.'

'Most certainly not.'

'Then you are taking all the wrong way.'

'Wrong way. Of course I'm taking it the wrong way. Whatever way would you expect me to take it. Inviting people I don't know and have never even heard of. You must revoke and cancel them immediately.'

'But I have in fact already done it. They've accepted by cable. They could even be on their way. And the whole point of the *Social Register* dear boy is that you have a list of socially vetted, acceptable people at your fingertips. Not that one holds being socially acceptable as any guarantee against bad behaviour which anyone might get up to.'

'Or what they may look like. Good grief. As if I didn't already have enough bloody unpredictable trouble in my life.'

'But I've already explained dear boy. They behave and look like money. Mucho mucho money. Rich beyond even the most inebriated dreams of avarice. Americans are today's financial giants bestriding the world. Surely even out here in these deserted boglands, you've heard of dollar bills dear boy. Green backs, spondulicks. And something I believe the American Indian refers to as wampum. And Newport. Which I've already mentioned. Is the utter zenith of sumptuosity. And by the way I've left an older edition of the *Social Register* behind in my room should that interest. Dear me I think I still do denote an expression of disbelieving puzzlement upon your countenance.'

'That's absolutely right, you do.'

'Well dear boy. Newport is simply a financial bona fide. The two young ladies I've invited both reside during the summer upon an avenue with houses or rather palaces which adorn a stretch of coastline demarking the American state of Rhode Island. Whopping great big palaces some of them are too. Thirty room jobs, that kind of thing. With your actual pantries and sculleries. Of course this time of year they are in their Park or Fifth Avenue apartments. Or care of their banks in Rome, Paris or Geneva. And it is from these heiresses that acceptances have been received to the invitation you have sent.'

'I have sent. You mean Rashers invitations you have sent. God, you can be a bloody chancer.'

'O dear. Of course. Yes. But I mean to say I admit that they may not be possessed of the social profundity we take for granted. But with their homespun qualities they do manage decently enough. I hope you're not asking to look this gift horse too deeply in the mouth.'

'Yes I am. You don't know what they bloody well might look like, do you.'

'It's the names that matter dear boy. I beseech you, believe me. And with whom, should things go right, will provide, on the basis of a little prenuptial, matrimonial pact, pecuniary resources. Deposit in your distinct favour a certain nonreturnable sum in the bank. You'll have in these two particular cases not only a substantial house in Newport and a ranch in Texas. But also in one case, a schloss in Austria, repatriated to this august family from its occupation by the Germans. That sort of thing.'

'Good god. Sing for my supper. Do you think I've come to that.'

'Dear boy, without wanting to trample optimism entirely, we can all come to that. I've been singing hysterically in high C for not only my supper but for my afternoon tea, my lunch, my elevenses, and for my breakfast. But when one is already possessed so marvellously and extensively of a plethora of assets such as yourself, to ensure keeping those assets, the getting of more assets should not be eschewed. Ah but do not for a moment think I do not sympathize here with your most commendable high moral tone.'

'It is not a matter of my commendable high moral tone. I am simply not about to be somebody's lackey or dogsbody.'

'But of course you won't be someone's lackey or dogsbody. And I take your reluctance to be well meaning. But we are here dear boy dealing with substantiality. And for the sake of the long term financial security nothing requires you to put aside or impugn your principles which I know are of the very highest moral purpose. Of course I did have to take rather a further tiny liberty with a little embellishment of your already adequately renowned name. By the attachment to it of a modest title.'

'You what.'

'Now Darcy my dear boy, please don't this early hour of the morning for god's sake spiral into a tizzy and do your nut. Rather do as Yanks are wont to suggest in their parlance. Stay cool kiddo. You see Americans like to meet someone not of their commonness, mediocrity and plainness. Although there are of course fifty two not very different flavours of mass produced Americans to choose from dear boy. But those I've chosen might be construed as being of your first three top drawer flavours. That's the good thing about Americans. They all want to desperately be your ordinary homespun sort of folk. Saves everybody so much trouble. And being as they nearly all are one and the same, you can without much surprise be quite sure of what you're getting.'

216

'What makes you Rashers assume that in getting anything, I want one of them.'

'Please dear boy I do know I have taken a diabolical and sacrilegious liberty. But you must believe me that here we are dealing with limitless lolly. And these American girls absolutely go gaga over titles. Gee wiz, gosh can I touch you, are you really a lord. Then they pat you on the arm. Just to see if you are real. And of course, up to a point, I am real. I simply thought it appropriate to style you a baronet. And nothing as conspicuously lofty as a lord. But whose Hibernian patent of knighthood was especially distinguished.'

'Lofty as a lord. I'll be damned. My ancestors and their kin are bloody well as lofty as any lofty lord.'

'Of course they are dear boy. Of course they are. No one denies that one little bit. And as I'm sure you know there are baronets dear boy who can make many a lord look common indeed. Even including yours truly.'

'Damn it Rashers. What have you actually done.'

'O dear in flourishing an innocent minuscule of enticement I can see perhaps I have rather overextended in my efforts to save my dearest and nearest friend.'

'Yes I think you have quite.'

Luke arrived in front with the motor car. Smoke pouring out into the morning air from the exhaust of mother's old Voisin, much in need of paint. Crooks loading on Rashers's bags as one stepped down the steps marked where the lumps of stone from the gable had fallen. I did think I might be being a little harsh and hasty with Rashers especially as I could use oodles of limitless lolly. But one could tell that Rashers felt he might have overstepped the mark in one's friendship. A sad seriousness on his face but as we stood on the bottom step of the porch, it wasn't long before he was proffering his usual plausible explanation for his behaviour. The worst thing of all being that one found oneself having dreamt in an otherwise sleepless night of actually walking up the aisle to wed to a fortune, my bride an awfully plain looking sort and carrying an armful of ragwort as a bouquet. And the vicar announcing wilt thou take this homely woman in order to forever relieve the daily attrition of holding Andromeda Park together. But what also occurred to me was that it was more than entirely possible that old Rashers was also entertaining similar thoughts and of discarding his present beloved for one of these bloody financially giant striding, affluent Americans, and that it was for himself that he planned to ensnare an awfully rich heiress. Especially as one had to listen at length when he launched into a long announcement concerning the trappings and appurtenances he considered essential to his daily life.

'Dear boy you must see and understand that one does not want forever in the future to be without one's proper kit.'

'Kit.'

'Yes kit.'

'What kit.'

'Well good heavens isn't it absolutely clear. You are amply possessed of your kit dear boy. And I have distinctly not got mine. Having for a start no mansion situated in its proper curtilage and surrounding extensive parklands. Take for instance a racing day, and assuming I did have a country place, from which one might intend to go stay overnight at one's club in Dublin, say in order to pop next day to the Phoenix Park Races. I would have no cook to make breakfast. No maid to ferry it up to my bed. No butler to assess and to anticipate the immediate weather and to announce suggestions for and to instruct one's valet accordingly to lay out one's wardrobe. And then summon one's motor from one's garage or chaise and horse from one's stables. Then I would have no footman to fetch bags from one's apartments. Having no apartments in the first place. Then as one descends the main stairs, no gardener to rush just in time into the front hall with a nosegay for one's button hole. Nor would I be followed by one's valet as my shoulders were brushed free of dust and dandruff. Imagine by god to have to summon a local taxi instead of being chauffeured by one's own chauffeur to be let off at the train station. And be distinctly without a man loading one's bags into one's compartment prior to ascending into its first class confines where the morning papers are to hand in order that one might cross examine form as one sits back to enjoy a first cigar of the day as suitably pleasant rural countryside passes by one's train windows. And then Darcy with fancied runners in mind, arriving in the city to be able to step up the steps of one's club. But perhaps first having a look see down the buttery of the Hibernian for a spot of companionship with one's peers but avoiding your ne'er do well hung-over lay-abouts. And then if there is someone worth exchanging a word or two with, I might have another cigar and a restorative snipe of decent champagne. But should the buttery be full of a damn lot of silly old trumped up fools one would take oneself off to the Kildare Street Club, in which, were I a member, one would pop into the lavatory for a relieving pee and would then back to the morning room to plonk down to peruse more papers prior to lunch, and reassess the winning prospects of the nags. And there reclined in a sofa chair and if no other members are close about, to be able to relaxedly let off a few good wholesome farts. That dear boy, in a nutshell or perhaps coconut shell, is having one's kit.'

'Good god. Having your kit Rashers could end you up a fat old useless farting bastard. What a damn lot of palaver and procedure. As if anyone should have the time to go through such a routine. Next you'll be telling me one should require someone at their elbow to keep alight one's cigars for one.'

'Well at least to light them dear boy. You see one's life can never be deemed to be financially all right until all one's battles concern the fighting against one's overindulgence in good food and good wine and the various adherence to the exactitudes required in the pursuit of one's comfortable habits.'

'Well Rashers, as one is apparently attempting to provide you with temporary substitute kit, please do get in the car or else you'll miss the train.'

'I shall. I shall. But meanwhile dear boy do forgive me for what I have innocently done. You see before you a sad and utterly contrite man. I shall discreetly retreat from your presence and die without trace.'

> Sinking
> Beneath the waves
> Off Newport
> Rhode Island
> Totally
> Unsocially registered
> And kitless
> As well

14

Aside from anything else one could not wait for winter to be over. However, from that Monday, in spite of being possessed of what Rashers referred to as my kit, one spent the remainder of the week in a cocoon of lonely leprous despair. Recoiling at every opportunity from all in the household. But at least one did have a somewhat spiritually uplifting seance or two with Sexton in his potting shed which did help one from becoming more desperate. Then tramping the bogs and knocking down a few snipe did also help break the evil hold that gloom held one in. And I was, I suppose, even regretting that one had insisted Rashers put off his invited guests. But of course I needn't have worried, as an expensively long cable, charged to me, finally arrived from Dublin.

MY ESTEEMED DARCY

EVERY EFFORT MADE BUT TOO LATE   STOP
HEIRESSES ALREADY AIRBORNE   STOP   MIGHT
CATCH THEM AT GANDER NEWFOUNDLAND   STOP
IN THAT RESPECT REQUIRE A FEW QUID TO DEFRAY
CABLES AND EXPENSE OF SENDING MAN OUT TO
AIRCRAFT TO ANNOUNCE GET OFF YOU DAFT
SOCIALLY REGISTERED SILLY SOCIALITES YOU'RE
NOT WANTED WHERE YOU ARE GOING   STOP
GANDER AWFULLY COLD   STOP   GROUNDED
PASSENGERS JUMP AROUND FIRES BUILT BY RUNWAY
TO KEEP WARM   STOP   BUT YOU KNOW WHAT'S
GOOD FOR THE GOOSE IS GOOD FOR THE GANDER

RASHERS

Grey heavy clouds. A damp chill wind blowing. Spots of rain falling. Darcy Dancer crossing through the beech grove. Treading the soft layer of leaves. The chattering crows up in the tops of the trees. The sweet scent of turf smoke in the air coming from the chimney of Sexton's potting shed. Rashers is right. Protect this. Even the dried winter stems of the thistles, nettles and docks in the grass. Of the land I love which has always been my life. And all that I have ever known. And I must. As I once resolved. To continue to fight. Never give up. Put to rout those who would oppose me. Stop the tumbling stone from falling. Cherish the gleam of mahogany. And silverware shining. Someone must defend. Preserve. And keep the jewels of life.

Darcy Dancer stopping, taking the cable from his pocket and rereading it. A moisture drop landing appropriately, mottling the paper over Rashers's words. That he requires a few quid. And now he has me thinking of a colossus of a female giant strewing dollar bills all over Andromeda Park. Then some mousy haired bossy fat creature, chewing gum and munching chocolates who has come to Europe imagining she is mixing with the aristocracy. And then discovers she is rubbing kneecaps with fortune hunting bog trotting potato diggers. Poor girl waking up, if she were able to get to sleep in the first place, and finding bats flying around her room, mice running all over the bed and rats scrabbling above in the ceiling and underneath the floorboards. In addition to flakes of plaster decorating her face. And by evening dining, wine dumped over her dress by a cross eyed butler and past midnight seeing him transposed into a ghostly transvestite promenading in the corridors. O god. Then discovering that one was not even a baronet, modest as such ilk might be. But worse. Much worse, bloody hell imagine in one's own house having to lend aristocratic credence to one's ancestry while, to use one of Rashers's expressions suitable to his own behaviour, freeloading visitors are waltzing about in one's life. Whose arse one is supposed to kiss. So that we can walk up the aisle together. To seal a pre nuptial agreement. And of course one does now recall Rashers waxing lyrical on the subject while rather drinking too much port late one night in the library.

'By god Darcy in marrying one of those American heiresses you could make a dashing couple. Brush up her accent to get rid of her atrocious whine. Teach her to shoot. Bang, bang. And to ride. Even to be a judge of claret and cigars. And dear boy when you come to think of it, what is more meritorious than money, except more of it.'

'And what about erotic affection.'

'Ah dear boy, as far as fucking is concerned, as a sophisticated European you are expected to keep a little bit of fluff for yourself on the side. For your more passionate pranging.'

If only old Durrow-Mountmellton's limbs were mended and in form, I could go and place something constantly stiff in her bifurcation and escape from Americans. And why must nature seemingly always drive one to prang as Rashers would have it. And also to risk the very dire consequences of putting it up a member of one's staff and creating insubordination and insolence that appears to have already been created and spread in every direction.

Darcy Dancer closing the creaking gate through the wall. Approaching along the worn path in the grass. And raising a black gloved fist to knock on the potting shed door. Mid air hesitating at the sound of Sexton's voice inside speaking.

'Hail Mary full of grace, the lord is with thee. Blessed art thou among women. And blessed is the fruit of thy womb, Jesus.'

The whine of the wings of two swans flying over the tops of the trees. On their way to land in the lake. And dear me it must be the angelus and twelve o'clock. Sexton does get so flustered and embarrassed to be interrupted at his prayers.

223

And there are times one must admit when one does wish he would do more potting than praying. And by the sound of it, being a Catholic must leave one with such a seethingly wretched conscience.

Darcy Dancer waiting. Silence inside. Raising a fist again to knock. The shed door suddenly opening. Sexton holding up an arm and rearing back.

'Begob Master Darcy you gave me a fright there. Your fist raised. To give me a box. Sure I thought it was himself, the turf stealing eegit over beyond thinking about revenge for the shock we gave him and his missus with the recent blast. As soon of course as he recovers from his other concussions.'

'What other concussions Sexton.'

'The one he got last night. For while your man was drunk asleep in front of the fire he was, as reports have it, groaning out the erotic name of our own Mollie. He was moaning. Will you give me a little bit Mollie. Will you give me a little bit. And the wife announced. I will. And sure didn't she herself give him a belt over the left ear hole with a tractor clutch. Well enough said, I was about to do me stations of the cross around the garden before I go to me lunch.'

'Sexton please don't interrupt your religious duty on my account. I'll come back.'

'Come in. Come in. Sure with god's limitless patience can't the stations of the cross keep till three o'clock when the sun starts to sink. Come sit down and get warm by the fire.'

'Ah, I must say, you do have it agreeably comfortable in here Sexton.'

'Mind you it's not for meself Master Darcy but for me germinating orchids, there on their beds of cotton wool in the test tubes. And I'll tell you about orchids in a nutshell. It would apparently be that the word comes from the Greek for testicle. And as Nicholas Culpeper observed in 1653, the perfume of an orchid provokes, if you'll pardon the expression Master Darcy, lust exceedingly.'

'I say Sexton, things are getting more than somewhat risqué in the potting shed these days.'

'Ah master Darcy sure I'm nothing but a lonely old man with a few biological fantasies to brighten his life every now and again. Sit down. Master Darcy, sit down. You're a stranger. Long time no see. You'd of course been having your hands full with the visitors.'

'Well they're all gone now Sexton.'

'Ah next will be the ball. It's all over the town and far beyond the parish. As to whom is to be invited. And as to whom isn't. The who isn'ts will be kicking up a fuss I'm telling you. And I can tell you also they're in there waiting to catch sight of the plane load of débutantes I've heard tell is coming from America.'

'Good god, Sexton, what.'

'Sure the post office counter has been wiped clean with the cables going back and forth with the news. Ah now faded may be the rest of us. But indelible is Lord Ronald Ronald. Master personified he is of ceremonies. Now by god if ever there was a man of the most steady friendship, unblemished integrity, extensive charity and universal benevolence.'

'Sexton one would imagine you were quoting such words off a gravestone in some old churchyard.'

'Ah you have me there fair enough. Off a gravestone they are. But appropriate to his lordship, a fine upstanding figure and worthy of every word. Ah it will be great to see the ballroom done up in all its magnificence as it would have been in your mother's time. And there'll be suitable corsages for the ladies.'

'Sexton I rather think from the sound of these rumours that things are getting rather out of hand.'

'And why wouldn't they get out of hand. Sure I remember when there were two orchestras either end of the ballroom playing different tunes and there would one partner be dancing to the melody of one of them and the other partner hoofing it to the other. You were but a gossoon then. And a man halfway up the ballroom playing the spoons. The drink flowing freely. Potted palms along the walls. Isn't it time now you made a splash. And let it be known you're on the international social map. Ladies from London. And now ladies from Newport. And there will be too I fancy a local lady as well. And speaking now of local ladies, ah god now wasn't that an awful fall her ladyship Felicity Durrow-Mountmellton took. What news do you have of her mending. In time for her to be dancing at the ball.'

'Well if like other hunt members who will be limping in on their crutches, and crawling up the front steps mouths open in thirst, she too should be there Sexton. Not for a moment to suggest of course a low opinion of people's motives.'

'Sometimes Master Darcy and no disrespect meant, low opinions are more often not low enough. But there's the likes of some of them in this parish would bleed you white. And drain every bottle in the wine cellar they could get their lips to. But isn't it great news now of the heiresses Lord Ronald will be supplying for the festivity.'

'Good god Sexton, you make one squirm with embarrassment. No need to make it sound as if this is some kind of house of ill repute.'

'Now I meant no meaning of that kind. But the ladies from Newport would be like visitors from another planet. Sure as millionairesses they'll be coming here with no need to brave the Atlantic waves in their own ocean liners.'

'They're flying actually Sexton.'

'Ah flying is it.'

'Via a place called Gander. Now don't you tell me Sexton by your startled look of recognition that you've heard of Gander.'

'Why wouldn't I now hear of Gander. Of course I've heard of Gander. I could reel off to you half a dozen places in Newfoundland. Sure isn't it a refuelling stop for the transatlantic flight to Shannon.'

'Well in this case it so happens it was the last opportunity for these American ladies to be discouraged in making the trip.'

'Now why would you want to be discouraging to an excitement the like of the introduction of beauty from the new world. Ah sure now you could do worse than hitching up with one of them Master Darcy.'

'Not you again too Sexton. Seems the suggestion of marriage these days is being made to one ad nauseam. The fact of the matter is that I am distinctly not, at this moment at least, and for many moons to come, looking for a wife. But I do hear rumours Sexton about you.'

'Ah god confidentiality, sine dubio, is a lost cause in this country.'

'O dear I don't mean to pry Sexton.'

'Ah pry away. Sure now I'm guilty. Guilty as accused. And I admit openly to you but for your ears only that I advertised for a wife in the *Farmer's Journal*. And less than nothing has come of it. Altogether a sad enough tale. But I'm not going to remain numb with grief over it.'

'O dear I honestly don't mean to meddle Sexton. I was in fact merely pulling your leg.'

'Well pull away. While I as a poor old gardener shake my head in shame.'

Sexton reaching his enormous hands behind the old tail coat he wore to lean back against his bench. Sweat stains around the band of the crumpled brown fedora on his head as he bowed forward. Grey locks curling up on the back of his neck where his concoction of chimney soot and vaseline had not reached to blacken the hair. The rooster crowing out beyond in the hen run. A spattering of rain hitting the window pane. The lonely sadness of this man in his lonely shed.

'Dear me Sexton I do hope I haven't put you into a gloom.'

'Well wasn't I in a bit of a one already. No one will have me. And that's a fact.'

'Of course someone will have you Sexton.'

'Well let me tell you, at the same time as I put in me own ad in the *Farmer's Journal*, didn't I answer one. Sincere widow it said, who is still game for a laugh. And who also might cheer someone up. Tearing up one draft after another, it took me two days and two late nights to write the letter. In which I listed all the usual. Gardener living alone. Although not considered handsome is of a tall, dark and reasonably good appearance. That I was a broad minded Roman Catholic with some intellectual pretensions in Latin, Gaelic and Greek. A non dancing, non drinking, non smoker who, young in spirit, would occasionally lapse in all three categories. That also I had a good to middling sense of humour depending on the circumstances. Hobby, growing exotics and Ireland's tallest sunflowers. That I considered myself without artifice, refined, honest and sincere. And was a lover of all living things save fleas and bedbugs. Sure I didn't want to put a foot wrong. Well as luck would have it didn't she answer straight back and suggest a visit.'

'And did she cheer you up Sexton.'

'Well she came sure enough cycling to me old cottage, the thatch still looking newly enough. Cheer me up she didn't. Sure wasn't I inside having fainting fits of anticipation, with me old jam jars all over the place stuffed full of flowers and already with the kettle boiling over for a cup of tea. Tried my hand I did at a batch of scones that went all black in the oven. And she still outside I could see was already annoyed at the sight of me. I didn't like the tone of her voice one little bit. It was as if being accused of being alive. Ah god, as a social occasion it was a shambles. Sure you don't Master Darcy want to hear any more of the likes of that unpleasantly memorable afternoon.'

'But of course I do, Sexton. If you're in the mood to tell me.'

'Well with my moods as black as the patch over me lost eye,

228

I'd be the first to admit I'm no Hollywood star. But the brazen nerve of her as I offered her the hospitality of my humble abode to be remarking that I'd be as tall as might be long in the tooth. And to that insult came more than painful injury, I'm telling you. Says she, you're missing something are you. Now stout as she was, she wasn't that bad a looker. And I was doing my best to keep my temper. And says I, I am. I am missing an eye. Doesn't she turn on her heel then to go back out the door and says she, she was expecting to find somebody who was in one piece. One piece is it, says I. And begob it was not quite underneath my breath that she heard me say that I've still got something in one piece I'm not missing. Well Master Darcy doesn't she stop in her tracks, spin round, come back and take a swipe at me, with the flat of her hand landing across my face. Sure the breeze of the blow left the stems of me flowers swaying outside along the garden path. Well let me tell you I saw a few stars. She must have had an arm on her the size of a full grown bull's hind leg. And then in an almighty fuming huff she went back to her cycle parked at the gate, shouts back. Youse, says she, should put your own ad in the *Farmer's Journal* and you would be better off describing yourself as an old goat with what's left of your grey hair greased down.'

'I say Sexton that was awfully rum of her.'

'Well I says back to her, begob, I said, if I do put an ad in the *Farmer's Journal*, I won't be advertising for the cruel, cranky, battle axe likes of you. But Master Darcy I was cut to the quick. Ah that's what I get for my smartology announcing myself as a broad minded Catholic with intellectual pretentions. Here I am just here with my plants and flowers. And there's nobody out there in the world now will ever be shouting bravo for me Master Darcy.'

'Nonsense Sexton.'

'It would be no nonsense now Master Darcy. Ah sometimes life would be as contrary as trying to chop through a slab of our best seasoned oak with an axe as blunt as a pig's arse.'

'Well at least you haven't lost your aptitude for being graphic Sexton.'

'Well I suppose an account of the matter would make good reading in my memoirs. Sure is it any wonder that news of the ball would put a bit of enthusiasm back into me ould life. When all the tell tale signs are that I'm not long for this world.'

'Now Sexton. Really you must stop promulgating such foolishness.'

'Ah there's no use pretending. These days I'm no skylark rising singing into the sky. Sure the end comes in so many tiny little ways you'd hardly be noticing it coming. Now I'm not saying my days are numbered and you should be digging a hole for me, but the likes of an incident like that let me tell you didn't add to me longevity any. Old Tom Hennessy beyond had the right idea. Sure he sold up his big farm, and bought another cheap and mortgaged it to the hilt and launched himself on a skite, drinking every last penny. And then didn't he on the very day he had not a farthing left, and at the very second that he placed back his glass of whiskey on the bar after emptying it, didn't he then drop dead in the pub, two of his comrades catching him by the elbows either side before he hit the floor. Then didn't they bring him in his own ass and cart outside to old Joyce the Victualler in town and help put him into his coffin. Dressed as he already was to meet his maker. Sure he left all belonging to him to starve. But wasn't that a fine well calculated way to end your life, without a surplus penny remaining.'

Darcy Dancer stepping out of the potting shed, Sexton slowly closing the door behind him. Across the stretch of gardens Sexton's neat rows of winter vegetables. His piles of manure ready to be shovelled over the soil. The blackcurrant and raspberry bushes pruned back against the wall. Go walk the lawn paths along his herbaceous borders. Where he grows his parsley, mint, tarragon and thyme. Rosemary, basil and

230

sage. His neatly kept compost heap. High on the wall, his stations of the cross every few yards. The worn patches in the grass and indentations of his knees where he has knelt on the cold ground. How sad for him. He who was so unfailingly kind to all living things. Whose large hands brought forth from this ancient ground such bountiful abundance.

Darcy Dancer venturing further between the rows of fruit trees. Their lichen laden branches, cold and grey against the sky. Returning now again. Past Sexton's potting shed door. Stop a moment on the crescent of flagstone he's laid here. His voice inside. Praying

'O most holy and revered spirit I doth beseech thee. You who show me the way to reach my ideals and have given me the divine gift to forgive and forget all the dreadful evil that has been done to me. You who in your perpetual glory and wisdom have given me at least some small solace that I may take from being an intellectual sophisticate. I beg you virgin mother have pity on this humble gardener. Who offers to thee all he grows. I am not mad. I am not. Pray lift from me this present awful burden of discouragement. And please, please spare me from more suffering.'

> And that I may
> One day join thee
> In the joy of eternity
> With thee and thy son
> On high
> In heaven

15

Darcy Dancer aseat in the library. Storm force winds roaring outside. Rumbles of thunder in the distance. The shutters banging. Smoke puffing back down the chimney and out into the room. Wednesday. The middle of another week in one's increasingly precarious life. And the reminders come in the moments before lunch in one's day. Damp envelopes arrive with dry bills inside. My subscription overdue to the Royal Automobile Club. And, as its notepaper would have it, founded in 1901. With the object of furthering the interests of motorists and motoring in Ireland. Good god what happens when one no longer can afford these useful accommodations in Dublin. Leaving one with nowhere to privately park, dine or sleep. Be ruddy well slung out barefaced into the world like Rashers cheek by jowl with the hoi polloi.

The gusts outside splattering rain against the library window panes. Darcy Dancer tossing crumpled up envelopes into the fire. Pouring another sherry. The golden tones rise up the glass. One does seem to more need a drink earlier and earlier with each passing day. And here in my hand an exam in Latin and Greek which Mr Arland my dear old tutor devised for me. And which I miserably failed. Perhaps a warning of dire things to come. And piercing one's dreams as one lay last night asleep was the blood curdling screeching of a vixen out somewhere in the frosty moonlight. Till one woke to the sound of someone discharging a shotgun. But from that day forward of hearing Sexton at prayer one realized yet again for the umpteenth time that to temporarily avoid inevitable fate and for a small amount of optimism to remain in one's life, one had to keep in front of one matters of purpose and plan. And to bloody well kick the arse off marauders and intruders. As one now descends to the very last of the last jewels of my mother's to be sold. One's heart did so take to sinking in the chill of the Rent Room, as one looked down the long columns of figures so ornately scripted in ledgers and on statements from the bank in which the deeds of Andromeda Park were deposited as collateral against the monumental debt. It did seem to one that only the cattle dealers, with their big hands gripped around glasses of whiskey, appeared to have money. And their drovers to have joy. As they delighted with nails in their sticks to belt hell out of livestock. And often in their efforts at cruelty, falling on their faces in the spew of cattle dung. And now with calves wandering where they can't be found until they're dead, cattle numbers are dwindling. Mr Arland, counselling me on the way of the world, once said, Master Darcy there is no euphemistically kind word to apply to fiscal erosion and debt. And even Sexton, who had served only on big estates, was conscious of the slow demise affecting all Ireland's land and all who attempted to survive on it.

'Ah Master Darcy may god bless and save from ruin and have mercy on the small farmer of this country.'

But at least one did notice some recent consistency. Everything seemed to happen just before lunch these days. For having repaired to the library to read the paper and pop down a sherry, total and suspicious silence seemed to lurk over the household. No sound of a brush or a broom or someone coming or going. Not even the usual dish or vase crashing. Breakfast an hour late and nearly minus anything to eat and the tray left anonymously outside my door. Of course one should ruddy well bloody reduce wages instead of going on tolerating the ineptitude of all one employed. The departures of Miss von B as housekeeper and Mr Arland as my trusted mentor and teacher did so make me conscious of one's servantry's rapidly increasing shortcomings. The whorls of dust collected now along the skirting boards. Finger marks on the walls. Smears on mirrors. Silverware tarnishing. Beds in the bedrooms left unmade. One had already tripped over a lump of debris swept away under the carpet. But I suppose it's retaining one's own personal principles that matters. One attempts to hold to rules for good habits, especially the sensible ones written in my grandfather's tiny scrawl in his small pocket notebook. Which I have so many times reeled off in a litany to myself. Always propose a course of action beforehand for every day. Acquire the habit of untiring industry. Cultivate perseverance. Be an early riser. Remain a master of your temper. Learn something from every man whom you meet. Of course in this latter little bit of advice one had already well learned that you learn nothing but a pack of lies from a bunch of crafty shirking layabout chancers that you would find, if not on every highway, then certainly lurking down every laneway and boreen.

Darcy Dancer putting down his newspaper, listening. The hall clock chimes striking one o'clock. Footsteps approaching out in the hall. A knock on the library door. Crooks entering with a tray of food. And nearly himself pitching forward on his face over the lump of debris under the carpet and spilling a glass of water flooding the tray.

'Forgive me sir. I have a bite to eat here. I had been wanting to request a private confidential meeting with you about the matter.'

'Well what is it Crooks. And what are you doing with that tray. I am just about to tipple the last of my sherry prior to lunch.'

'Sir, Master Reginald it is with great sorrow that I am forced to announce that there will be no lunch, as service has been suspended in the dining room.'

'I beg your pardon Crooks.'

'And concerning which, if you will but now permit me to broach. There's a strike.'

234

'A what. Am I to believe my ears Crooks and what I do believe you may be actually saying.'

'A strike sir, throughout the household. There is no one coming nor going. And my position is difficult. It is a general laying down of tools and refusal to work. It was against opposition sir that I brought you this little bit of sustenance to be having on a tray.'

'Who exactly is on strike Crooks.'

'Everyone Master Reginald, save for Edna Annie and Sexton. They're all there now down in the kitchen and in from the stables sir, at this very moment.'

'Good god, this is more than a little bit of nonsensical nuisance. What on earth is the difficulty Crooks.'

'Now it's not what you would term Master Reginald the Bolshevik revolution. Or an armed insurrection.'

'And I should bloody well hope not too Crooks.'

'It's merely that little bit of an increment and rise in wages they are after sir.'

'Good lord, I can't afford the wages that are already being paid.'

'Well sir it would mostly be a matter as regards too much working unpaid past and over and above the regular normal hours Master Reginald.'

'What regular and normal hours Crooks. It would be hard to find anybody in this house working regular and normal hours. When it's mostly tea drinking and gossip. And the same goes for those lurking around on their arses and home-made seats in the tack room.'

'Sir it would be the extra work in the care and looking after of guests. And to do now also with the unexpected visitors and the ball coming up. And I've been reluctantly elected as a neutral spokesman for the aggrieved to put the matter before you sir.'

'Well damn me, it is rather your job to keep people in line Crooks, don't you think.'

'Well sir I did do me bit I could, to try to quieten them down. Then soon as I thought I had them settled, up one particular one of them again would pop voicing subversivism, till now it's got out of hand.'

'Well I do hope Crooks that during the present protest no one is going without, and that they are all having their usual normal and regular tea, slabs of butter, shovelfuls of sugar, and lorry loads of barmbrack.'

'Put your mind at rest sir. They are indeed sir.'

'Not to mention as well the normal and regular sausages, bacon and eggs, the quantity alone of which consumed last week would feed an army. And I am being sarcastic Crooks.'

'Now sir I told them you would take the matter amiss. I told them. And as for that one Mollie Dingbats. I've been here going on thirty years Master Reginald and I'm not going to be told now by some blow in to fuck off, if you'll please pardon me repeating the same expression. Sure she's the ringleader. And my niece is ready and willing to assume immediately that one Mollie's duties.'

'Well Crooks. As no one at the moment is assuming any duties at all, shouldn't we take a little time to think all this through. We don't want to incite Mollie or anyone else to do something even more extreme.'

'Sir I know what you're suggesting. Suicide. Isn't it. That she'd throw herself out the window or down the stairwell. Isn't that what you're suggesting. Let me tell you now that one, she'll not harm a hair of her own head. You can be certain of that. With every boyo for miles around panting after her, a shotgun going off last night from one of them. The people who won't commit suicide are the people who a lot of other people want to see dead.'

'Good heavens Crooks. Put the tray down. And you mustn't cry.'

'O merciful god sir, forgive me. Never in my service has such a terrible matter as this ever been before. I would not

236

want such a thing to be a testimonial against me. To be at my age fired out of me job. Where would I go. Without references. What would I do, an old broken down butler like me.'

'Buck up Crooks. Do please pull yourself together. Here take my handkerchief.'

'I'll dry the tray now sir.'

'Good god Crooks, use the serviette, not my handkerchief.'

'Sorry sir, with the troubles, I just haven't got my wits about me a'tall. I have a roast beef sandwich for you. Rare and extra thick as is your preference. Together with a bit of cheese and an apple. Sure they even tried to stop me bringing up this little bit of a bite to eat to you.'

'Thank you Crooks. I do appreciate your remaining loyal at a time like this.'

The library door clicking shut. Another rumble of thunder. The branches of the spruce out on the lawn bending in the wind. The sound of a nose being blown out in the hall. Surely the fatal soiling of one's few remaining silk hankies. In spite of being outraged by even the mere suggestion of a strike, one must pretend to be utterly unruffled. Imagine. I, who pop their pay in their pay packets in the Rent Room and feed them with the milk squirts into a pail from my cows, and from which the cream is whipped and the butter churned, am about to be starved. Appropriate enough, I suppose, in this, reputedly the most devious, the most forgotten of counties. From which few want it to be known that they originate. Full of primitive damn peasants. Of course Mollie's from Galway. And I don't suppose people from there are much better. Line them all up against the wall of the servants' hallway. Find the instigator. Or better still sack the lot. O dear one is really getting upset. Pour another sherry. But imagine. The infernal ruddy ungrateful cheek. Here they are surrounded by fine paintings, marvellous stucco and some exuberant plasterwork. Wandering at their own bloody behest through spacious stately rooms. And no one wants to do a decent damn day's work any more. Of course as captain of this ruddy ship sailing these parklands, one is tempted in the brazen face of this mutiny to fetch my shotgun. Throw open the servants' dining room door in the middle of their lunch. Command the buggers to lay down their cutlery. To stay out of the kitchen. Lock up the larders. As if I didn't have enough woe. With Rashers with his Americans in tow on the way. Perhaps best one attempts to bluster it out. With a few flourishes of discipline. Give Crooks my hunting whip. Have him crack it up and down the servants' hallway with a few remonstrations. Pull up your ruddy socks you idle lot. Take your ruddy fingers out that you've got stuck several indolent miles up your arses. Then, when their sobs of fear have reached a crescendo, they can be told that the pasha of course will next Christmas reconsider the matter of a rise in wages. It's on the pasha's agenda. But ruddy meanwhile for penance each one of you is summonsed to come kneel before the pasha as he sits upon his throne chair in the ballroom. And each bloody one of you ungrateful shirkers will beg his forgiveness or else be sent packing out the farmyard door with a good boot up the arse to hasten your way out over the cobblestones. But O dear sometimes one does contemplate, without of course being unnecessarily too depluming about it, a more modest country house. Say with a dozen or even less bedrooms, and maybe five or even four reception rooms, provided at least the drawing and dining rooms were of certain significance. And smaller demesne. I mean three or four hundred acres would be enough to be going on with, provided one had the necessary formal gardens to walk in. Containing a certain amount of statuary, small chapel and tea house which still might uphold the dignity due one's rank.

Darcy Dancer chewing down the last slice of Cheddar cheese. Footsteps approaching along the hall. A knock. Crooks entering the library with another tray. My handkerchief tucked up his sleeve in the French, or is it the Italian manner. And a

238

reminder of Father Damian who would on occasion call to have tea with my mother. I suppose he was, in spite of being very Catholic, an elegant priest. And who, in contrast to the mumbo jumbo of his religion, was possessed of a great knowledge of the paintings which hang in Andromeda Park.

'I have a bit of hot apple pie here for you Master Reginald. And a good dollop of whipped cream, the way you like it. Let me take this other tray away now. And don't worry about dinner. There'll be a bit of the duck you brought down out of the sky the other evening and I'll have decanted for you a nice drop of claret.'

While Sexton saw to the horses, cattle, milking and cows, counted sheep, fed the pigs and chickens, doves, geese and turkeys and generally kept his one eye on the farm, one's initial shock and outrage did subside a mite. And one only turned and tossed away a couple of sleepless nights. Although it was rather a damn nuisance eating in my rooms or the library and not knowing the exact time and from where my next meal was coming from, I was astonished to enjoy the peace, quiet and solitude above stairs. And enjoyed immensely to conspicuously be seen striding along the lawn above the servants' basement windows. The bunch of them down in there behind the bars, which I must confess seemed entirely appropriate. Of course too, when it was suitably dark, I did clank like hell up and down the far end of the east hall above the servants' dining room below. And especially on a thin patch of floor just outside the school room where Mr Arland held our tutorings. And upon which I jumped. Just to let them know umbrage was on the bloody rampage above. Which of course was not lessened when I crashed through a rotten section of floorboard. However, at least a good reaction was reported at breakfast next morning by Crooks.

'Now you should have seen the expression on their faces Master Reginald as the thumping came. And then the crash. And the flakes of plaster snowed down on their heads and landed sprinkled on their bread and butter. You put the fear of god into them and no mistake.'

'I beg your pardon Crooks. That wasn't me.'

'Was it not.'

'No. But I must say Crooks, these nights about the house, I've been hearing the strangest of strange unexplained sounds and thumpings myself.'

'Jannie mack, Master Reginald, sure I thought the footsteps were yourself. Would we not then get the priest out here to hold an exorcism.'

One did take considerable satisfaction having scared the shit out of them as well as now establishing that a ghost was at large after dark at Andromeda Park. And instead of, in their usual manner, skulking and sneaking about up and down on the servants' stairs, they were now with the smell of many candles ascending at night in convoy to their bedrooms, to which I now had all the keys, in order to keep them open and let the ghost in to scare further shit out of them as they lay awake throughout the night. And I did in fact past midnight let out a few disembodied wails and groans from atop the main stairs which even had Crooks deeply shaken. And the rat population mystified.

'Master Reginald there's something wrong right enough. The staff, they'd like now for there to be some kind of investigations as to the ectoplasm or a walking dead man abroad in the house heard giving out last night.'

'Well Crooks I do think it would be jolly appropriate that before one deigns protect one's employees from any ghoul, vampire, banshee or monster, whom I agree is clearly at large, that they first abandon their strike.'

'They are sir beyond listening to me. Sure I lectured them in loyalty and I couldn't repeat to you the language they gave back to me sir. I'm blacklegged now, bringing you your sup of food.'

Although freezing cold without any fires, it was also

suddenly quite distinctly wonderful to go strolling along empty halls and corridors not having to worry whose footsteps were retreating before one, and trying to go and hide. Or as one opened a door to enter a room, not to wonder who was cowering behind a sofa, and upon the verge of being discovered, ready to pop out at one from behind a pilaster. Forcing one to speak and having to play the disciplinarian. Which, if one had nothing better to do, could be on occasion amusingly satisfying.

'I say there, whomever you are, come out at once. Chop, chop.'

I don't know why on earth one chose to say chop, chop twice. As a guillotine needed to do it only once. But somehow it seemed to get the strength of one's disapproval across. Naturally the culprit would be found munching my scarce chocolates, smoking cigarettes from my mother's platinum box or, as those who inhabited the tack room were wont to do, consuming one's whiskey from the bottle itself. And one recalls the incident of the young pear tree in the orchard. With the miracle of its very first singular six pears on its branches. And where no pears had been in evidence on any tree for three years. Each day one went to peruse and admire them as they matured. With one's anticipation increasing, looking forward to the moment when they were finally at their zenith of ripeness. And when that balmy, sunny autumnal day at long last came, I ventured out, already licking my chops to sink my teeth into what I knew would be for certain the nectar sweet flesh of this fruit. And I stood there in the long grass in disbelief. There was not a single pear left on that tree or the remotest trace of one. I nearly wept with frustration. Indeed tears did actually come to my eyes a few minutes later as I walked utterly bereft amid the overgrown cascades of yew and the now neglected ragged box and holly hedges and along by the once so lush herbaceous borders. Feeling that everything and nearly everyone I had ever loved were now gone

from my life. Leila especially. And damn servants anyway.
Here they are in the midst of one's own private world,
scheming to get the best of what you have for themselves.
God when one thinks of the unprecedented tranquillity, one
could happily be shut off from the whole damn bloody lot. I
mean it's not impossible for me to descend from my apartments, less than half a mile there and back, to the bloody
kitchens to get my own bloody breakfast. And have just
myself and Sexton, who I am sure would not mind for lunch
and dinner, one eyed waiting on table. Or perhaps do with an
all round sporting butler. Such as the type known who goes
hunting, shooting and fishing and keeps his own horse in the
stables. And except for perhaps cleaning the lavatory drains, is
willing and able to turn his hand to anything. And such types
need not necessarily be descended from the Ascendancy. But
of course one has to be a bit of a snob and keep such chaps
from borrowing one's underwear, cravats and boots. Albeit
such individuals do tend to leave their flies constantly unbut-
toned. Then try to have it off with the mistress of the house or
with any of the female guests who might flash them an
inviting glance through the steam rising off the bowl of
potatoes they are serving. I mean, my god, even I have
managed to be a servant. Admittedly a very bad one and of
the very lowest outdoor rank. Although come to think of and
remember it, I did manage occasionally to carry a bit of turf
indoors for the Kellys but then of course immediately flopped
down to read their copy of *Tatler* and the *Horse and Hound*
and to help myself to a drink. And did while doing all this
damn all, rather enjoy to desecrate my employer's upholstery
by propping up my stable begrimed feet on their feather
cushions. Not chop, chop but how dare you. Is what Mrs
Kelly, the mistress of the house, said upon accosting me. How
dare you. Get your muddy filthy boots off those cushions at
once and get outdoors out of this house. It was the reference
to the outdoors which so irritated me. As if one were not

242

entirely at home in far grander rooms than those the Kellys
lived in. I did, I must confess, out of one's sense of superiority,
piss on these nouveaux riches' turf in the barn which I had as a
chore to fetch into the house for them. Which, when it resided
in their drawing room turf basket, would give their fuel a
piquancy and just that added little bit of objectionable fume
such urine created upon burning. Of course I did not wait
around in their employ to sample the aroma. But certainly I
was the Kellys' social superior and certainly I was ten times
the trouble of not having a servant at all.

All in all the strike seemed to be causing more boredom for
the staff than it was causing me inconvenience. The usual
singular footfalls continued to echo as they slowly approached
along the halls. Crooks looking more crossed eyed than ever,
bringing my tray of a sandwich for lunch again to the library,
along with a decanter of claret. And a cable arrived in its small
faded green envelope. One did lift it from the salver with a
certain nervous trepidation. However, outside the weather
brightening. And my absolute intention now, despite Sexton
admonishing that I shouldn't, to go and mend some of the
more serious motor car axle breaking pot holes along the
front drive.

'How are they all managing down there Crooks.'

'With everything locked up, vituperative they are sir.
Having to fetch for themselves and climb over the wall when
Sexton's gone home from the garden.'

'Well Crooks don't give them any of my damn duck.'

'Well sir, they did try to get at it. And that one Mollie
nearly had the remaining wing and leg left gone off it the very
second my back was turned as I was reaching to stoke the
stove. Using every name at me under the sun as I called her to
book. Saying I am in cahoots. But I'd say they'd be beginning
to know which side their bread is buttered on. And it wouldn't
surprise me one bit if they be on the verge of a truce. With
talk that they would not want to let you down over the ball.'

With the exception of Crooks and Edna Annie the whole staff were keeping to their beds till nearly noon. And with Crooks trying his hand at a spot of cooking, one did notice the standards of lunch improving. Although the decanter of claret which one had nearly emptied was a bit past its prime, but decent enough. But with no one washing dishes, one's somewhat charred cheese omelette which ancient Edna Annie attempted, was presented on a greasy plate with tarnished silverware upon a greasy tray. Of course one could sum up that I was giving as good as I got and was quite prepared to last out indefinitely and although poverty had me by the ears, my balls still swung free. Even though at the moment they might not ring musically. Plus there was a certain degree of optimism as I opened the cablegram and downed the last of my claret, and felt an unaccountable growing randiness with a painfully contained hard on.

MY DEAR DARCY AND OLD REVERED DEAR
FRIEND   STOP   AT THE SHELBOURNE   STOP
GIRLS SAFELY IN TOW   STOP   YOU WILL NOT BE
DISPLEASED   STOP   HAVING A FINE OLD TIME NON
STOP AS IT WERE   STOP   ARRIVING TO YOU MID
AFTERNOON MONDAY PROVIDED YOU WIRE
IMMEDIATELY ONE HUNDRED AND SEVENTY SIX
QUID EIGHTEEN SHILLINGS TO DEFRAY
SHELBOURNE BILL   STOP   SO NICE TO BE BACK
ABOVE WATER IN THE SWIM AGAIN   STOP   YOUR
EVER FAITHFUL AND OBEDIENT SERVANT

        RASHERS

Of course one was ruddy well tempted to send in reply to his monstrously exorbitant request the singular word STOP with the added words GO GET STUFFED. But of course what are good friends for but to go fuck up one's life. Which in turn saves theirs. Thank god one was relievedly

244

distracted by a hunting fixture which made at least a welcome if brief change from a strikebound house. Crooks laying out my kit. Sexton making a most marvellous night time job of saddle soaping tack and braiding and grooming Thunder and Lightning. Even to polishing each hoof to immaculately gleam. Petunia in the adjoining box, neighing in jealousy that she had not been chosen to hunt. While Luke, eschewing his duties, sourly and resentfully watching and teasing the horse as Sexton worked but nearly got kicked out of the stall for his trouble and skulked away at the sound of my approach.

'Ah you look great Master. You look great.'

'Thank you Sexton. And Thunder and Lightning looks spiffing.'

I rather immediately regretted using the word 'spiffing'. As it so nearly resembled the word 'spiv' applied to black marketeers during the war and which Rashers was so fond of applying to all and sundry of whom he disapproved. Never mind. It was nice to be addressed as Master as was customary on a hunting day. Sexton giving my pink coated figure a leg up and, snapping and cracking my whip, I felt spiffing enough, as, with a red ribbon warning upon Thunder and Lightning's tail, I roared clattering over the cobbles, out of the stable yard, aloft on the mighty eighteen and a half hands of the most intrepid mount in the country. Nearly lost my cap, knocked off by a chestnut tree branch as I jumped the ha ha, and like a storm force wind galloped out and down across the front parkland. I reached the meet and we moved off from the crossroads. We didn't find for several hours, but then in quick succession we killed two foxes. And, based on the ruddy number of humans near dead and injured, it was already an eventful day out. Two broken wrists, one broken arm, a suspected collar bone fracture and a couple of ribs cracked. One hunt member, concussed when his mount threw him on his head on the road, was later found in a cottage, explaining to the bemused inmates that he was the King of Wales. Of course the general ruddy horsemanship, with so many visitors, was appalling. And a damn nuisance, forcing one to resort to profanity to keep them in line and from heading the fox. One of this ilk, on finding our third fox, was knocked out of the saddle by a tree branch which slapped several of his teeth back in his throat, then, with a foot caught in the stirrup, was dragged through a boggy field of rushes and then into the bog itself. Which, save for one leg, turned him completely brown from head to toe. Serves him bloody right as the impertinent bloody bugger, an ex service type fresh from the war, was in the process of attempting to overtake me. And also had the damn cheek to pointedly refuse to address me as Master.

Amid the hunt Darcy Dancer atop a hill conspicuous on Thunder and Lightning. In the stillness of the chill air steam rising from horses and riders. The huntsman and whipper in ahead and below in the furze with the hounds hooting and howling investigating a covert. As one availed of the opportunity to aquaint with a newcomer or two. And especially a very blonde lady with a most ingratiating smile and a big sparkling diamond pinned to her stock. And who also was possessed of thighs rivalling those of old Durrow-Mountmellton. And there she was, teeth blazing, regarding me. Of course with the appearance of new ladies on the hunt one had to act fast. For one had all about one the randiest bunch of hunt servants fox hunting has ever known. And at the kennels were busy using the horse boxes to jump upon any and every girl groom or female hunt member who deigned stoop that low who ventured near. However, almostly instantly arrived up the hill to join us from among the stragglers is another choice item indeed. Albeit slender thighed. But with marvellous brown tresses coiffed up under her bowler. Almost like a little toy Dresden doll one could play with. Her two splendid brown eyes in her delicate doll like face. And my god, the look one got from her. Of instantaneous smouldering communication. Master you can put it up me and go bang bang whenever such opportunity shall to both you and me present, and in which we may then delight. And bloody hell. As you might expect, here one is for half an hour and now, before one can engage in further and better particulars of this darling creature, fox is found. And tally ruddy ho. And just as I chose to lag a little and be nearer our Dresden doll, who the hell is that taking up the lead. Good heavens. That worst of all offenders who thinks as a once British brigadier he's mounting a cavalry charge. Afflicted as he remains with his previous military exploits. But is in reality now an old bachelor codger, a widower and retired. A wiry little bugger who speaks with marbles in his mouth and in recent times has, in spite of his diminutive stature, and in a secluded turret of his castle, either attempted or succeeded in putting his old what for up every dairy and scullery maid who has had the temerity to come work for him. And there he is, up with the huntsman and whipper in, usurping me.

Hoofs thundering, sods flying, hounds baying, the hunt down into a boggy valley, along a stream and clambering up a hill. Crossing two meadows at the gallop, a wall twenty lengths ahead. Collect old Thunder and Lightning to jump in front of the field. And good god. Down there in the ditch. As I fly over. The Brigadier. His face puce with indignation, shaking his fist up at me, sailing through the air as he lays half submerged and otherwise ignored in the mud of a deep drain obscured by a crumbling stone wall. It was impossible to know the Brigadier was there until it was too late and you saw him beneath you. Dear me, this scarlet coated figure looking up in terror as you passed above. He must at least have a broken leg. As no one else has had one yet. Of course, as is always the case in such unpredictable hunting encounters, every speedy horseman up front with the hounds leaves it to those stragglers lagging behind to close gates and assist the injured, and always the better riders detesting and regarding

247

these two tasks as ruining their sport. And admittedly me signally among them. At least that's my excuse. But pity it would inconveniently happen for the old Brigadier on this the most exciting of our runs. Hunt members shouting 'tally ho' as they swept over him. Must be a rather rum situation dawning on the Brigadier that no one is soon going to his assistance. And I must say, considering his considerable war record, it was quite surprising that I heard him voice a reference to man's inhumanity to man. Rather a dampener when one starts to bloody well moralize on the hunting field. But there was no way I could prevent landing on him. Although Thunder and Lightning could make up ground with an acceleration you would not believe, at the same time, over half a ton of horseflesh did tend to lose altitude rather rapidly. I had also, in the absence of old Felicity Durrow-Mountmellton, been rather actually further looking to size up the female talent in the thigh department for perhaps a quick romp in a copse. And at the moment of approaching the wall above the hidden drain where the Brigadier lay, I had just spotted again the most wonderful pair of the thicker thighs. But as ill luck would have it for the Brigadier, and my whip laid across Thunder and Lightning's quarters, half the wall collapsed under his take off.

'I'm here, I'm here. Don't bloody well land on me.'

As one was already airborne, it was also too late when I saw the Brigadier below, spreadeagled in the ditch and his face contorted in justifiable fear as I plunged down upon him. But miraculously Thunder and Lightning's extended legs easily spanned the supine figure and stepped on only a couple of his stray outstretched fingers. God did he yelp.

'Ouch, damn you Kildare.'

However, thundering on my way, I was not to know that it might not have been his arm or something more serious I'd crushed. But the incident was enough to make me lose sight of Miss Succulent Thighs, as I had now named her. It was not

248

that one was harsh and cruel or that I callously neglected to go back and look at the Brigadier. But it was at the precise moment I was above him that he also had chosen to shout something referring to the battle of Gallipoli. And although I don't have the vaguest notion about this presumably historic clash, I naturally, along with a dozen others, took it to be a shout of encouragement to bloody well leave him be and go on and get this damn particularly cleverly elusive fox. Anyway he was already busy again bracing himself as more riders sailed over, with not one of them taking any damn notice of this stricken terrified arm waving former warrior. And that was another point on this hunting day. Many of those lagging behind, being visitors, were beside themselves not to lose the leaders and to make up ground to be in on the kill, as this made them far more socially acceptable. And that in confronting the fallen and maimed, the ruddy thing to do was to instantly take more notice of the fastest way to get away from the unhorsed and wounded. But now the time had come with night fallen to sound the horn for home.

And we are soon on this particular evening back at the crossroads, getting sozzled at the pub. And you won't know who's been left dying until some poor sod's horse, looking for a bucket of hot mash, arrives outside without its rider. But then, as the day's horror stories resume, the poor missing sod is again forgotten. And exactly that happened concerning the Brigadier. His horse trotted up to the pub without him. And as it was now raining cats and dogs and a wintry cold wind sweeping the night, not a ruddy soul in the pub offered to accompany me to go groping back in the miles of sodden darkness to find him.

'I say, you are, all of you rather a rum lot. You would be far better off going back to where you came from.'

Before proceeding outside to remount a tired Thunder and Lightning and, riding off, I shook my fist at the inmates who were maintaining in the fire blazing whiskey swilling comfort of the pub, that it would be no trouble for the Brigadier, who'd survived loads of battles, and even with a broken limb or two, to hobble and crawl across the countryside back to civilization. There was no question but that one was surrounded by a regrettable group of socially and morally spineless self centred pipsqueaks who were entirely beyond the ethical pale. And one sincerely sometimes did wonder why I should yearly bequeath money to the hunt, clothe hunt servants, contribute hay and grazing and generally bloody well provide sport for these blatant arse kissing smug poseurs. And to whom I did not hesitate to more than loudly answer.

'However, if such were the Brigadier's atrocious luck to have both legs broken, the drain would be by now full enough to drown him. With thanks to you, you wretched bunch of spivs.'

Darcy Dancer with a thwack, slamming his whip against the side of his boot and spurs clanking and heels resounding and sending up dust from the floorboards, marching out past the grocery counter end of the pub, and slamming the pub's front door, which limped another distinct inch lower on its hinges. Unhitching Thunder and Lightning, mounting a wet saddle and clip clopping down the dark road. Off into the oblivion of grey, black and purple shadows looming. The rain beating down in fury. Wind slashing across the face, whooshing high in the trees and then suddenly hushed in the lee of the thick high hedgerows. Past the Protestant cemetery and church. Brigadier at least doesn't have far to go to get buried. Indeed he lives with his young scullery maids and handful of ancient retainers who stumble about his castle not more than a few miles from here. And as I go wandering in the blackness, he could have already crawled home. Damn it what am I doing out here on the advent of the American ladies. Mouse holes in bedrooms to be blocked up. Give myself a chance to steel myself for the new blows and unwelcome surprises Rashers is certain to have in store for me. Clean linen to be put on beds. Thank god dear old Edna Annie has not laid down on the job. I'm sure that soon as the guests arrive Crooks will pop on his monocle he ceased wearing some time ago. Which amusingly had, when Crooks wore his, stopped every squire and lord within knowledge distance wearing theirs.

'Whoopsie, dear me. Steady on.'

Thunder and Lightning lurching sidewards. Darcy Dancer in the darkness thrown down into the drain where the bank of the ditch had been eroded away by horses' hoofs and where the Brigadier was downed. And of whom there was now no trace. And damn me just as I was further thinking, or rather forgetting, that I must now be near the fateful place. My god. I even think I hear the fox we chased and lost laughing with his high pitched bark there on the opposite bank. Hugely enjoying watching me splash around in the darkness. Some people don't believe this phenomenon about foxes, which I know now for the second time is true. As true as I know bloody ice cold water is soaking into my chest and the pain is awaking in my previous injuries got in the company of old Durrow-Mountmellton. My boots are filling. Spit the mud out of my mouth. God how true it is. One should rejoice and count oneself bloody lucky to be even alive each day. Thunder and Lightning has disappeared up the bank. And, despite whistles, shouts and the worst of profanity, is gone.

The rain ceasing. The clouds breaking. A three quarter moon out. The wind chillier. I think surely two hours have elapsed. And there at last he is. Thunder and Lightning. Totally and bloody well unconcerned for my welfare and chewing the twig ends of a chestnut tree. And on what is quickly becoming the longest day of my life, I drag my shivering self up on his back and canter another hour away back to the pub from which most of the hunt members have departed. Save for Johnny Gearoid, the horse holder. Always ready to cadge a drink. Making it known that for a few pints of stout he will impart recent news of the hunt. And as my teeth were chattering like Lois's castanets, I offered him a drink and myself a triple whiskey.

'I'll have another pint. Now do you know Master, sir. Sure I have a lot of information for you. Believe it or not the Brigadier's been found. Wasn't he with the drain filling up and his head barely above water, on the verge of drowning. The poor half frozen military gentleman was discovered by Murphy the farmer. He heard this singing of words "Abide with me", and wasn't he chasing his heifer, out of whom he was pulling a calf. Didn't he while tugging hear more singing and then groaning. And more groaning than his heifer was making till she had the calf delivered and up on its feet. And then Murphy, while the calf was having a suck of the beastings, investigated beyond down in the ditch. And then didn't Murphy find the Brigadier, his ears submerged and his nose just able to breathe. And then up he lifts him to carry on his back half a mile away to his cottage where wrapped up having a cup of tea didn't the randy old fellow in spite of a fracture make an indecent suggestion to Murphy's wife. And lucky only the wife understood them big words the Brigadier was using to make the overture. Sure she was next to me elbow in this pub only an hour ago repeating it to the post mistress. While Murphy in his pony and trap and in the pouring rain was bringing the Brigadier to the bone setter. But didn't the Brigadier as they stopped have Murphy hammer a message to the pub door. Which now Master I have here in my pocket for you to see. And considering the embarrassment I thought it should not remain up.

TO ALL WHOM IT DOES CONCERN

I SHALL NEVER FORGET NOR FORGIVE THOSE OF
YOU WHO SO CALLOUSLY LEFT ME
INJURED IN THE DRAIN TO DIE. NEVER. REPEAT

NEVER. NOR SHOULD ANY OF YOU EVER DARE AGAIN
TO COME AND PRESUME UPON MY HOSPITALITY. AND
ESPECIALLY THE MASTER OF SUCH HUNT.

Darcy Dancer ordering another round of drinks. A pint for
Gearoid. Triple brandy for the Master of Foxhounds. Who
has to ride yet six miles back to Andromeda Park. And dear
me. Imagine. Me. The alleged culprit. Bloody faced from
briar scratches. Soaked to the skin. Caked in mud. Trying to
find the silly old bugger. And, also quickly forgotten, no one
thought to go look for old Kildare, Master of Foxhounds.
Ranking in the county above the bishop. And certainly way
above any lot of Catholic clergy you want to mention. And
damn the old reprobate Brigadier. Stingy old bugger as are
most of his ilk. Bloody miserly mean and British to the core.
Who, upon one visiting their houses, welcome one waving a
fez and expecting one to eat a sample of last month's roast
beef, served with stale biscuits and bottles of their vintage
fizzy soda lemonade with rusty bottle caps. But I suppose one
could say that's what the hunting field is all about. People
who get themselves up all adorned to voice and do horrid,
unpleasant things to each other. And reserve to do the very
worst things. To poor old puss the fox.

Hacking back through the black bleak night along the
winding lanes, clinging to the warmth of Thunder and Lightning. Then up and down the hills of the straight stretch of
road that finally leads to where one turns off to Andromeda
Park. And tempts one to jump the six foot wall to shortcut
across the fields and come home by the lake shore. Then be
without Thunder and Lightning's clip clop sound echoing to
guide one. Not tonight. Enough bloody chaos has already
happened. And what's that. Something or someone ducking
out of sight behind the wall where a fallen tree has demolished
the top of it. God I'm so cold I'm having apparitions.

Darcy Dancer reigning up Thunder and Lightning. Staring

out across the dark under the branches of a great oak tree. Whatever it is one has already put them to rout. A damn poacher. In on my lands. Or the marauder hearing me coming has gone to hide with his measuring tape from across the road where he intends trying to open up his bloody petrol station. And skulk around trying to fuck and perhaps use as a spy a member of my servantry. And by this same way one's own dear mother returned, as she did at night from hunts. Upon this very road she came. Clip clop, clip clop. Past these very trees, so ghostly looming with their great ivy leaves in the shadowy dark. Like great gods who might suddenly reach to snatch one away as death must do when it comes in the flower of life. And as it came to my mother. When my world stopped being carefree. There would then have been no strike by the household. When Andromeda Park teemed with servants with yet other servants whose stern authority made them keep their obedient place. And who were banished from sight below stairs and who, if they heard one's foot falls approaching, would unless summoned retreat out of one's presence. Menials not to be seen at all. Going to and fro below ground to work in the fields. And one then could at a window daydreamingly cast one's eyes out across the parklands, without one's contentment being interrupted by some lazy figure leaning on a scythe or shovel or just being there reminding one that they would soon be leaning on a scythe or shovel the moment they were out of sight. But where now in the tunnel, to be out of the wind or rain, they hide and skulk and smoke their cigarettes. Although nothing changes in the clip clop and thump thump as one turns in the gates of Andromeda Park, it so seems now that the world has grown old and tarnished and in tatters. When back then all who worked here at least seemed to do all that was best. And so worshipped and adored my mother. How even when she went blackberrying in her white gloves in September the men would go out to her favourite hedgerows and copses and cut away the thistles and nettles so that her fair delicate wrist could avoid any stings or pricks and need contend with only the worst of the briar thorns. Tonight no lantern lights ahead. Nothing to guide one through the blackness of these rhododendrons. No sign of life. And my mother back from hunting would have awaiting her a retinue. Dismounting at the front steps instead of on the cobbles of the stable yard. Crooks ready to hold open the door for her. Bowing as he said, it is good to see you back safe and sound madam and I trust the day out was to your enjoyment. Her horse then led away down the road to the yard and immediately surrounded by the grooms rushing to unsaddle and take her mount to its box, where the mud would be wiped down with handfuls of straw and dug out of its hoofs. Cuts cleaned and anointed with poultices. And its nibbling equine nose stuck in a warm bucket of bran. Oats crushed and ready to be put in the trough. Her tack wiped, saddle soaped and hung in readiness in the tack room for the next day's hunting. Her escutcheoned brandy flask polished regleaming and refilled. Slices of rare roast beef put between Catherine's nourishing soda bread to be packed in her silver sandwich box. And upon that still and chill evening. When the clip clop of a horse's hoofs on the road is heard for miles. Just before the mist settled and fog thickened across the lower land around Andromeda Park. Just before then. And just as the mist did settle. There was the commotion of feet shuffling up the front steps. Crooks at the door. She had returned. But now had been gently taken from where she'd lain across her horse. Brought along this drive, upon which the heavy hoofs of Thunder and Lightning go thump, thump, thump. And upon which she came back dead. On that day I can never forget. I stood just above the first landing of the main stairs and saw from the balustrade down into the front hall. The men hunched and silent, carrying her. All of them in their boots in the house. And wearing their caps to then remove them later, held behind their backs. And although I was at first not close enough to see, I knew Sexton in from the garden was weeping. And Crooks had already broken with a sob echoing in the hall. The clumps of mud from their boots left scattered on the tiles. And how that evening there seemed more darkness and fewer candles burning. An unearthly silence all throughout the household. While tears were falling upon my tiny hands as I wrung them in anguish. Coming step by quickening step down the stairs that day. Knowing something dreadful and awful had happened. From which they had tried to hold me back. Big strong hands. I twisted away and ran into the north east parlour where she'd been taken. And those first moments when I stood over her. Tresses of her hair hanging down across the gilt arm of the chaise longue. The blood dried on her brown riding clothes. What is dead. Why does she lie so still in here on the chaise longue in the chill north east parlour, the flickering candlelight throwing shadows across her face. Why do her eyes not open and turn to look at me. The one that is green and the one that is blue. And in disbelief. And then in belief. She is just tired from hunting. She just needs to sleep tonight. She will be awake and kissing me in the morning. As I come running in to jump up on her bed. In the bright sunshine over her breakfast. The flower from Sexton on her tray. Which she would always reach to put to my nose to smell for its scent. Shall I then feel her petal soft hand, that is now so rigidly cold, warmly caressing my face. My mother's husband back that morning from London. Master of this house then. Until the lawyers read the will. And I was master. He saw me minutes later, standing on the stair. He called me a bastard. Entered his study where he drank dry bottle after bottle of whiskey. My whiskey. And played again and again solemn music on the gramophone. My gramophone. And upon the day she was taken in her elm box to her grave. On the cart covered in black velvet upon which her coffin lay. No more miserable collection of household ever existed who wended their way down the steep hill to the dell.

256

Enclosed by walnut trees. She was buried by the ruins of the ancient chapel with its ivy clad lancet windows. Near by Sybilla my sister who one knew had gently gone to sleep one day closing her eyes, holding close her little bear with its own brown glass eyes. As my tears stream again. As I now go down over this cobbled road clip clop to the stable yard.

Darcy Dancer in the dark, feeling for buckets, clutching an armful of hay. Petunia neighing in her stall. A rat scrabbling away under the straw. No one would say to me my mother was dead. It is not a lie to sometimes prudently withhold the truth, I heard Mr Arland remark. Dear Mr Arland. His dark hair hung always so sombrely over his smile. And he knew more than anyone that by my mother's death all the gaiety in my life had ended. Left with a father who only favoured me with resentment and dislike. And made me wonder whose child am I. Who was to mind and love me now. Or give me a cuddle. My sister Lavinia, when I came to her crushed and from whom I sought comfort, had said get away from me, you are wetting me with your tears. And then both Lavinia and Christabel stepped back. As if I were an enemy. As if never again to be in my life. I was not to know that in my tiny innocence that Andromeda Park had become mine. And that away at boarding school my sisters would henceforth come to me only for money. And never in fondness. They would come for what they regarded as acceptable social occasions. To débutantely flaunt themselves around Andromeda Park. But then Mr Arland later had said, Kildare the betrayers and people who do not love and who are dishonest people, they are ipso facto unsuccessful at life. For it is the conjoining of kindred spirits that matters. I did so love the way he might ramble on. And then he would say in his Italian, I pazzi per lettera sono i maggiori pazzi. And of course now I can these words so memorably translate. Learned fools are the biggest fools. Ah and since Kildare you are so wonderfully unlearned, you may be sure never to be a fool and to be unsuccessful at life. And by merely remaining safely here at Andromeda Park, conducting your comfortable habits, little that is untoward can befall you. Ah but dear me, Kildare since the beginning of the war you know things have rather sadly changed and certain things have come far more into prominence. The Land League. Socialism. It was once a matter recognized of the duties of inferiors to their landlord. Of course he doth not scorn them for their low birth nor doth he vaunt his own high birth but rather holds the dictum, every man in his place and a place for every man. In the case of inferiors proving remiss one bloody well gives them a ruddy talking to, reminding them of penalties of the past. The birch over the backside. And Kildare, I dare say, given your nice little headstart at Andromeda Park, you'll remain an all round squire of the old school.

Darcy Dancer, boots resounding across the front hall faintly illuminated by a single candle. And the light from another high up on the landing making one just able to see the stairs. The beech grove out there. The big old trees in the moonlight. Yes I am here. Still attempting to conduct my comfortable habits. And where is Mr Arland now. Could he still be in his unkempt squalid digs across from the gentleman's convenience in Mount Street, Dublin. And I did heed his words. I tried then so hard to be honest and to love. Even when I heard Protestant words uttered to fuck all Catholics and kick the Pope. And who now since my mother have I loved. Petunia my horse. Kern and Olav my dogs. My nanny for moments when she wasn't bossy and mean to me, I did. And Miss von B for somewhat longer moments. When Foxy Slattery and I saw her marvellous body in the candlelight while drying after taking her bath. Which still so many years past makes me tingle in the groin. And who else. Who else can I name. Who else has notched a fondness or torn a claw across my heart. Just one. Just one. Who was ripped away from me. And left terrible longing. And unhealed scars. I did but touch her hand. Slender small and white. Now she doth another touch. Away under some part of the sky somewhere. And will never any more ever be mine. Not that long ago I woke in the middle of the night from a dream in which I heard her screaming. And in a long flowing frock as if it were centuries ago, she was running away. Escaping it seemed from a great ballroom that then turned into a vast crowded train station. That seemed somewhere distant on the continent of Europe. Her cries echoing above the loud throb of great steam locomotives pulling out of the station. And I had never heard her scream. And she screamed. And all went silent in my dream. Could she. Could she now be dead. Like my mother. Leila. Her purple ribbon tied in her lovely long black hair. When it was as my mother's was. In death.

> When
> Her tresses were
> Still so shiny
> With life

16

As the rumour circulated throughout the household that the pasha himself was going to apply his own lily white limbs to lift a pick and shovel, faces were hiding at the top floor windows of Andromeda Park to peek out to witness. Following lunch in the library, Darcy Dancer, changing to his worst worn old clothes, and under a sky bright and blue, led the stubborn old donkey and its creaking cart the mile trip down the drive to the front gates. Starting to fill the deeper pot holes, red weals appearing and turning into blisters on the palms of the hands. The bloody old pick is heavy. Trying to cut and dig into the hard surface stone of this road. Scraping together the pebbles and gravel to push them into these deep ruts and holes. And I'll be damned if I'll ever make a menial.

Darcy Dancer leaning on his pick. To look up at the low squawk of a raven flying over. A man walking in the gate. Approaching Darcy Dancer from behind, stopping to watch and then to speak as Darcy Dancer turns around.

'Ah god them old pot holes would drown you. But sure you look in an awful hurry there. What's the rush. Them holes will come again soon enough. But sure better still why not leave them. They would be grand for giving the gentry a bounce coming in and out. Tell me now. Would there be anything to be got out of them from up there beyond in the big house. Would they give you a bit of fire wood. There'd be a power of trees I'd see down. Or a sup to eat. A hen.'

Darcy Dancer facing this shabby figure, his fingers pulling tight a piece of twine tied around his coat. Oily skinned weathered face. Dark rheumy eyes. From which one could tell he was a tinker. Who must be from up where they are camped at the crossroads. Saw their fire and around it their faces as I rode by on Thunder and Lightning. Probably just been in on the land of Andromeda Park to poach. And good god, he thinks I'm a workman on the estate. So much to be said for one's aristocratic features that it could be thought that I am bending my back as a drudge for them up in the big house. And if he thinks that. Perhaps why not add to the authenticity of my lower caste and give him a bit of my brogue.

'Ah god now, you'd be getting little next to less than nothing from them up there in the big house. You'd hard find a more miserly bunch of mean old stingy buggers than the lot of them up there.'

'Is that a fact now. I heard tell once they were easy going. That you'd easy get a bit of straw or hay and a turnip or two.'

'Not since the mother now. There'd be a new terror of a boss man out patrolling around with his shotgun. Shoot the leg off you if he caught you with a rabbit for the pot.'

'Is that a fact.'

'Sure they wouldn't throw you the carrot tops out of the garden. They'd catch you poaching in a trap before they'd fling you an old dead hen.'

'Is that a fact.'

'It is.'

'There was a time now except for an old bastard of a gardener up there when they'd give you a bit of fire wood that you'd be later selling in the town. Or bargain a piglet for a price now and again.'

'Ah there'd be a new bunch without mercy or kindness in power now. Sure they'd shoot you down out of an apple tree and you be starving.'

'Would they now.'

'They would. And set the big hounds on you as you hit the ground. You'd be afeared of your life to go up there.'

'How would they be treating you.'

'Ah not well. Not well. Sure the squire himself would in his rages up and down the halls be with his shotgun blowing the heads off the innocent portraits on the walls. The whole place up there is on strike. And I haven't been paid now this fortnight.'

'Is that a fact. Well so it sounds you couldn't get something out of them then. Sure you yourself look as if you could do with a decent meal.'

'Ah I could. But meanness is all you'll get in plenty up there I'm telling you.'

'I heard a rumour the last butler hung himself, after putting every female in the house in the family way. And that now it's himself the boss squire has them the female staff pregnant. So I'll be on my way then. Good luck now.'

Darcy Dancer, as night fell, abandoning brogue and road mending and once more repairing as squire to bathe in the copper tub. Drying in warmed towels from the hot press. The strike over. The kitchen range roaring out its heat once more. A household meeting was called soon after they saw me with donkey and cart heading down the front drive. This evening one took an added pleasure dressing for dinner having learnt that outward appearances are all. Crooks in his old boiled detachable shirt and his Trinity College rugby jersey beneath, serving dinner in the dining room. And sporting his monocle flashing in the candlelight.

'With your permission sir I have put the bath salts created for your mother by André the perfume maker of Paris in the ablution rooms to be used by the American ladies we are expecting.'

Crooks, as he poured the wine, was bowing deeper than usual at table. Damian casting side glances at me as he took plates away. Only bustling instead of busting heads to be heard in the scullery. But my god rather shivery cold in the library. And one seems to be so fraught with memories tonight.

262

As if one were on the brink of some great change I do not seek that shall befall me soon. And at least something else as well as the staff was working. New batteries put in the wireless. A choir singing behind such a clear woman's voice. Broadcasting from Britain. That war song they sing. Or is it now a peace song. Keep the home fires burning. And then their tune about the white cliffs of Dover. A pity one had not served in a Guards regiment or the naval service. As Rashers and Mr Arland had done, and not be thought a lowly serf at my own front gate. The way they both carried themselves with a certain commanding confidence. Although I must say Mr Arland did occasionally rather slouch about a bit. The civilization of England so far away and yet brought to me so near by both of them. And yet here I am in my daily trepidation. Debts mounting from every side faster than I can sell cattle or cut down trees. Having still to steer Thunder and Lightning to side step the pot holes in the drive with only the handful I got filled. Surely break a horse's leg yet, or the axle of my dear old Daimler.

'Excuse me sir but will there be anything else this evening.'

'No thank you Crooks. But you're limping Crooks.'

'Ah sir the old gout just lately is giving me an awful wallop in me left big toe. But just let me put another log here for you on the fire Master Reginald if you'll be staying up with your bit of wine. That would be nearly next to the last of the bottles now that was laid down of the half a pipe of port.'

'Good god Crooks, that would be then the last of twenty eight dozen bottles. Are you sure.'

'I am sir. I'm after checking. I can show you the cellar book.'

'Well that's the veritable end Crooks. The veritable end.'

'I knew you would be upset by the news sir.'

'Disastrous. And in its present venerable age, it is so magnificently improved.'

'That would be a fact sir. Not to be denied by anybody. And including myself.'

263

Tonight as one reached the gloom of the front hall and went past the great portrait of my mother's grand aunt upon which Leila would gaze and of which she said she thought it was so beautiful, is it any wonder that out of one's accumulated loneliness one felt an overwhelming desire to be gone up to Dublin. To stay at the Shelbourne. Instead of having guests once more descend. Good god, half a pipe of port. Dozens of bottles have clearly gone missing. Just as my precious pears did off the tree in the orchard. Unless I soon have installed a large safe in my apartments in which to keep honey, butter, bacon and eggs, I will be stripped of everything. And even of things I don't even know I own. It would do my spirits some good too, if instead of trying to hide from, that I be temporarily shut of the crafty half arsed sheepish household. One member of which it appears the whole parish wants to fuck. Be away too from the constant cold wet chill of the countryside. Sit upon the enveloping softness of the Shelbourne's flowered sofas. With coal fires burning, be all warm and cosy under the gleaming chandeliers. And as Rashers says, pop off into top hole. Which of course meant giving orders to the familiar waiters. And to the one whose thick wads of grey hair are slicked back on his head. Whose stature and dignity and extreme nonchalance would better suit being an ambassador to a backward nation. As he was an irritatingly eccentric waiter. Who always first time so politely forgets to bring what one orders. And especially to chill the champagne which one wants to quaff to further rouse one's appetite before crossing the lobby to enter upon the stately elegance of the dining room and be among what one imagines are worthy citizens among whom no spivs abound. Sniff at the onion soup brought to one's table. To be followed by duck à l'orange. Life still awake on the street, with the odd passing pedestrian as the last tram to Dalkey rumbles by. The cold hungry groups of barefoot children in their tatters still wandering on the pavements. The sound of them still selling their newspapers.

Wailing out *Herald* and *Mail* far into the night to the empty streets. How often, high up in the Shelbourne and wakened from sleep, I would listen from my bed. I suppose one did take comfort that one was not as I once had been, like an animal. Grateful to find a handful of blackberries to eat. And then to see these ragged little urchins again next day as they crowded round Rashers and I as we were heading out to the races and asking, give us a penny mister. Rashers creating fights as he would step up on the step under the glass canopy of the Shelbourne's entrance and flanked by the torch holding female statues, fling coins, of which one was usually the source, out on the pavement. Announcing as he would.

'My dear boy, although one tolerates the scruffiness of bohemianism one does so detest and abhor filthy disgusting poverty.'

Then of course back in the Shelbourne one would again hear Rashers's phoney title paged by the bell boys as they solemnly paraded with their ringing tones through the public rooms. Lord Ronald Ronald, please. And he would sit there. Sometimes totally ignoring the summons. And one did think it was his compassionate concern for squalor and hand to mouth existence that brought tears to his eyes. But then as he often did he would unexpectedly remind of the realities of the world.

'Betrayal my dear boy Darcy, for all its usual sudden abruptness, is also usually and best preceded by a long period of loyalty, during which, as it were, one ethically builds up an equity of trust in the relationship which is then discharged in one awful surprise to the usually awfully disappointed victim.'

Of course sentimentality has rather overtaken one in the wake of a bottle of agreeable claret at dinner tonight and in my present pleasant obsequies one observes in the drinking of the near last of my port. But damn me if one is not now randy and entirely hard up. Even to the point of wanting to pay a call upon dear old whorish Lois. To roger her. Pose around naked in her freezing bloody studio as her cat goes meowing about. God she did so carry on about her artistic principles. One wonders if I could even bear suffering them in order to sow more than an accumulated few stray wild oats. And good god one must not forget old Lois has had damn unsanitary dogs recently up her. Dear me drinking too much port. I must stop thinking of the past. And O my god. I've just remembered Count MacBuzuranti's party. Of course it would be jammed packed with a plethora of queers. Sitting in each other's lap, pulling each other's pricks. Dear me, in the dark, my imagination and randiness is getting the better of me. But for the Brigadier one would have made overtures in the sincere interests of plunging it goodo into one of the new ladies lagging behind the hounds. Especially the Dresden china version. God what a memorable look she gave me. She might even be an heiress or a princess or something equally inviting in my present circumstances. Of course readily available were the usual hunt sluts. And usually at least numbering three. Who if not already surrounded by impregnators and hunt servants rogering the arses off them in a copse would have sufficed to at least reduced and lessened one's present licentiousness. Although after one piece of crumpet one finds one wants soon after another bite. Masters of Foxhounds have droit de seigneur and the first right to fuck the most desirable of hunt members. Put old Lois upon a horse. Could be a hunt fuck. Instead of wasting her time flaunting her tits doing her samba in front of the smiling queers. And here I am wasting time when I should instead be planning to wield the whip over tomorrow's chores. Chop, chop. The hen house stinking like an abattoir full of hen shit and needing to be cleaned. The calves weaned. Broken fences. Walls tumbled. The edges of lawns to be trimmed. Roses pruned. Lost cows are somewhere mooing unmilked. I don't know, at times one feels it would be so much easier to die. To go off quietly somewhere with a flask of one's best port. Bang. Who would know it wasn't simply an accident. Safety off, poor chap tripped over his cocked shotgun. Must not slip under the waves of gloom. Rebound upwards as a new calf tries to do as it jumps up at the sky. God now what is that. A rat behind the books on the bookshelves. Or does one hear a floorboard creaking out in the hall. The latter indeed. Because that is the sound of the door handle turning. And a hinge squealing slowly opening the door. Good heavens. I do believe I am about to witness an invasion of my privacy. Or is someone gaspingly fainting.

'Oh, oh. Excuse me sir, I didn't know there was someone in here. You gave me a fright.'

'Dear me you're after giving me one Mollie.'

'Crooks himself a while ago I heard go up. And I thought everyone was in bed. I was just coming in to find a book to be having a read to put me asleep.'

'Come in Mollie. But shut the door. There's an arctic breeze.'

'I did, I thought you'd long gone to your bed sir.'

'Well apparently I haven't. Well do please light the candles, and get a book.'

'It will do another time. I'll be going on my way now to my own bed sir. I'm sorry sir to disturb you.'

'Well as a matter of astonishing fact you're not disturbing me.'

'Am I not.'

'On the contrary Mollie I do believe I'm sitting here not quite bored out of my wits but nearly. Can't you see I'm bored out of my wits.'

'No I can't sir.'

'Well then. Here I'll light a candle. Now. How's that. And you Mollie even in this faint light are not looking bored out of your wits. In fact you look in bloody fine fettle.'

'Thank you sir.'

'Don't thank me, you should in fact thank your scones and jam. Now you mustn't get a long face. Come. Have a glass of port.'

'I am after taking the pledge against drinking.'

'Ah. Very commendable. Like to see more in this household taking the pledge. Well then. So as not to be inhospitable perhaps I can offer you a mineral water. While I'll have my glass of port.'

'I won't be needing a mineral water sir.'

'O well. But I shall be needing more port.'

'Shall I go fetch it for you sir.'

'Ah thank you. But I think I may be able to manage Mollie. Now then. We've rather been having a lot of damn silly nonsense in this house recently haven't we.'

'I'm only after wanting to get a book sir. And not to disturb you.'

'Well get a bloody book. Look at all of them. From the bloody floor to the ceiling. Travel, astronomy, fly fishing, tap dancing, philosophy. There's even one there at the end of the shelf. On the morality of marriage.'

'Oh I wouldn't be interested in that.'

'Well then. Whatever the bloody hell subject it may be you're interested in. Most of these bloody tomes of course could jolly well be got rid of. Nearly a hundred ruddy bound volumes of *Punch* full of jokes supposed to be funny.'

'Sir I am, I am disturbing you.'

'Well you'll bloody well disturb me more just standing there in bloody fine fettle. You are in bloody fine fettle aren't you.'

'Well I could be in better fettle.'

'Now that's where port comes in Mollie and is a hell of a lot better for you than mineral water. That's why I'm in fine fettle. Indeed so much port has obviously been drunk in this house as would put and keep permanently an army in fine fettle. Ah but you are clearly Mollie, helluo librorum.'

'Sir I do not know what that is.'

'Ah well, helluo librorum means in Latin a devourer of books, a bookworm. Now just don't stand there, what the bloody hell book do you want to read. Come. Come. No dilly dally. Now what book is it.'

'It's the *Burke's Peerage* sir. And the *Landed Gentry*.'

'What. Good god. I say.'

'They are over there on that shelf. Above to the left of the little statue.'

'Bloody *Burke's Peerage*. Ruddy *Landed Gentry*. Heavens above. Put you to sleep. I'm not surprised. But they'd bloody well keep me awake. Full of some of the most blatant bloody inflated previous bombasts, pederasts, rogues, land stealers and impostors.'

'The Darcys, Thormonds and Kildares sir are therein listed.'

'Well of course they're listed.'

'And were they not and meaning to disrespect sir, land stealers back in the times long ago.'

'Of course they were. How do you think land is got. But the Darcy Thormonds were high minded indulgent landlords who conspicuously distributed largess during the famine. We occasionally too married for a bit of land or a fortune. All right Mollie, enough of this ruddy old awfully ancient gossip. You can read *Burke's Landed Gentry*. Why bloody not. Can't say it improves the mind. But at least it shows a very commendable curiosity. But first we must pop off into top hole. Dear me don't look at me like that. Don't you know what top hole is.'

'No sir.'

'Top hole is nirvana.'

'I don't know what this near vaner is.'

'It is the Buddhist attainment of the perfect beatitude.'

'What sir is that.'

'Ah never mind. Go fetch another glass. Chop, chop. Yes we must have another bloody glass. And when you do go fetch another bloody glass, don't forget to come chop, chop back. In short, don't bloody well disappear. And while at it bring whatever is left in the dining room. As you can see this decanter is getting rather empty. And a few slivers of cheese might not come amiss. Must have a bit of cheese.'

'It's long after me hours of duty sir.'

'O ruddy bloody blessed hell, this isn't to be more shirtiness is it. Damn strike's over isn't it.'

'It is sir.'

'Well then chop, chop. Go fetch the port. Like a good decent girl. Pop. Pop. Chop. Chop. And let's bloody well then pop off into top hole.'

'Very good sir. If you are insisting.'

'Ah now Mollie I am not insisting. You might go straight on ruddy strike again. But you know what I might just bloody well go and do.'

'No sir.'

'Get my hunting whip and lay on a few lashes of discipline. What about that now.'

'Well I would be giving you a few lashes back of it sir. And where it would hurt.'

'What. Good god. Ah there's a power of terror in you Mollie. Ah but I see you are smiling Mollie. That's a little better. You'd not lay on the lash heavily would you.'

'Ah now I wouldn't be telling what I'd do.'

'Ouch. Ouch. Please don't hurt me. O no. Ouch. Not that. Ouch. You see Mollie, I am terrified. Ah and that's much much better. You're laughing Mollie. Now you see there is much kindness and consideration in this house. Don't you think Mollie. Ah so you don't think. Well then let's say before it all tumbles down on both our heads that we should have some blessed semblance of fun first and pretend there is much kindness and consideration in this house. Meanwhile bloody well both of us can sit down and check up on the Irish landed gentry. Bloody damn sight less preposterous than the American *Social Register*.'

'Shall I be fetching the port for you now sir.'

270

'Ah yes Mollie very very good Mollie. Pop. That's what we must do. Pop. Pop off into ruddy bloody top hole.'

'I will only be a little time now returning chop, chop with the port and cheese sir.'

Darcy Dancer draining and refilling his glass. Putting another log and sods of turf on the fire. Lighting a rod of incense and placing it up on the mantel. Winding up the gramophone and putting on a record. The Glasgow Orpheus Choir singing Ellan Vannin. Which Rashers tells me is the Manx national anthem. O god I'm drunk. My word, absolutely inebriated. Dressing for dinner and dining alone. Perhaps one is making a bloody show of oneself. Letting it be known and she must know I want to fuck her. Better not be here when Mollie chop, chop returns. Or I may try. And go the evil way downwards like many of my ilk who deigned do the deed of poking it up their servantry. Like the chimney sweep putting a brush up the chimney. And whose poor arse once got singed right out of his trousers. Crooks setting and lighting the fire while the poor bugger was still up there cleaning. Or else practising for Christmas to be Santa Claus. Only he came down plummeting in a black cloud of soot. And Crooks's monocle fell off his face. Damned funny. Except that soot went all over the library. And one still gets black fingers opening up a book. But where I am now sitting, looking a rather lonely if not a most stupid all dressed up sight, one thinks not of soot. But of Mollie's body. And of a previous night I got so awfully drunk. In this same room. Her Mona Lisa smile. Then falling all over on stairs. My feet clanking on bare boards. I was blotto. Something I was saying. There you are at last. Waited all this time to get you. You fatty bats. You dingbats. You pink freckled big soft cushion. The memory of kisses. Musky smells. Of soft swelling breasts. Her hair. Were they my lips kissing her neck under her ears. Was it she on top of me. Smothering me with kisses. My hand caressing her buttocks. Thinking if I could think anything, that I must have more of this. It will be served whenever I want it. There was an explosion in the gonads. And then I woke in a servant's unused bedroom in the freezing frosty morning. On a bare mattress. My mouth dry from too much port. Staring at an old dresser and broken vase. And shelves on a wall full of dusty crockery. A pile of rusting fireguards. No gloom was ever greater. Then the days went by avoiding Mollie's gaze, with nothing ever said or mentioned. Then her slowly growing near hostility, calling me coldly, sir. Insubordination. Attacking Crooks's niece in the scullery. Hearing words shouted one did not want to hear. Which was something about someone sucking a prick. Dear me I feel as if I've already committed suicide. But I must preserve protocol. My god what is protocol. A sense of command. Exactly why one dresses for dinner. To demonstrate toploftiness and to thereby please other toploftinesses who dress for dinner to please in return. Me an old toploftiness and pleasing myself. Nothing wrong with that. Poor bloody world if a toplofty chap can't dress to please himself. And maintain his rank. But dear me. Familiarity can breed a hell of a lot more than contempt. Especially in making desperate blatantly obvious overtures and excuses to get a little companionship. And not to feel that a household lurks and awaits to vent their malevolent spleen and do me evil mischief. Good god. She says past her hours. Thinks I'm taking advantage of her. Bloody hell dear girl count up how many bloody hours you have spent on your arse during your hours. But my word, no wonder everyone is randy after that one. With her crafty eyes fearlessly staring at me as if she were daring me to do something. Knowing as she must, that one's trousers are expanded out like a tent. Her inspired cunning making her even more enticing. Even bundled up as she is, in at least three thick sweaters. Must be why all the rats in the house randily chase her. Even one's erstwhile agent's beetle brows quivered, his hands trembled and he nearly licked the lips off his face in

Mollie's presence until I fired the insolent bastard still trying to sue me. The marauder who is going to build his petrol stations and monuments to gombeenism, out there panting after her as well. I must not make a fool of myself like these lowly types. Maybe too she could scream rape and slap my face. Waking the household. To announce up and down the halls that the inebriated pasha had reached to put his ruddy dirty filthy hands all over her. And Rashers did comment. Dear boy, the lust in her, smoulders, positively smoulders and emanates out on the ether. And one did always think that the freckles on her face would all fall off when she broke into a laugh. Tonight I could put my hands all over her. Up under sweater after sweater. Where she wears that awful Catholic scapular. Take her up to my bedroom. That would only be just a little more difficult than sending her there like an obedient servant. But O god just to already know what smooth soft pink white flesh is underneath her bundled up clothing. And does she know. She must know what I'm thinking when I look at her. Aroused even by the veins on her hands. And know that I want to pop off into her top hole. Chop. Chop.

The toe of a foot pushing the library door open. Mollie returning. Crossing past the book stacked library table. Imagine kicking her indifferent way back in if you please. The neck of the decanter disrespectfully grasped in one hand and a glass in the other. As if to throw them at me. No tray. No napkins. Good god. No cheese. Not a sign of proper service in this house. As if she'd never been taught or trained up. And as if I were some sort of casual person or some left footed bog trotter. And not gentry with a distinguished lineage. Bloody hell what point is there in her reading Burke's ruddy Peerage. If she doesn't bloody well observe the proper solemnity, punctiliousness and propriety in performance of her duty and service to one who is listed in its pages. Exactly as one might expect from a shirty ungrateful lot who would be hair pulling and fighting in the pantry and would deign go on strike and for whom one must mortgage one's mansion and lands to pay their wages. I would bloody well like to dispense with effrontery. Dispose of the impertinent. Have done with the bumptious and insolent. Who trespass and immediately jump to take advantage the instant one is kindly, understanding and humane. Which one in the tradition of one's mother always aspires to be. Albeit there are distinctly occasions calling for and demanding upon one to be lordly and imperious. Not that one means to be in the least assuming, overbearing or domineering. But one must have chop, chop. Plenty of that. Plenty of more port. Empty the last of the bloody pipe. In this room where erudition remains silently packed between the pages. Imagine Burke's genealogical and heraldic dictionary. Which is hardly much of a who's who in these midlands. Although one may boast of there not being many spivs out here. Good god is she thinking thoughts of getting above her station as Leila did. To become a marchioness. And if Rashers ever reaches Andromeda Park we're soon to find out who's ruddy bloody who in the ruddy bloody American *Social Register*. Bring on the bloody rich Americans. Ending our penuriousness. As we all together pop off into ruddy top hole.

'I say Mollie, no cheese.'

'No sir. I searched all over. Every last bit there was at lunch is gone. There was a rat who got a bit of it too.'

'Good god. There was a mountain of it. And I say Mollie, sit down.'

'It's gone way past me bedtime sir.'

'It's bloody well past mine too and I'm bloody well sitting down. Come. Come. Chop, chop. The incense is fragrantly burning.'

'You've had one too many sir.'

'I've had plenty too many. Listen to the choir singing. I mean at least take off one of those sweaters you've got on. Pop off into top hole. Here. Fine port. The last of the pipe. Full of nutritiousness. Am doing a bit of shooting tomorrow. Now when a snipe goes rising up from the bog it goes zig and then

274

it goes zag and that's when one goes bang. With one's gun. Before it craps, Mollie.'

'Could I have next month's wages in advance sir.'

'What.'

'I want to take my holidays now.'

'What else do you want to take Mollie.'

'Just my holidays. Starting Friday.'

'When guests are on the way. Good god. Bloody well take your holidays. Goodnight. Take ten years.'

'Am I dismissed. Am I out of my job.'

'No you're not dismissed or out of your job. You've just chosen to take your holidays at the most awkward of times.'

'I am wanting to go to Lourdes.'

'Lourdes. Good god. For a holiday. That bloody place. Where all the left footed crutches are stacked up. And people go crawling to this divine well. Get dumped in or ducked into the water. All that moaning. And catching ruddy unsanitary diseases from relics. The whole thing is a bloody fraud.'

'It is a place of miracles and cures.'

'And what miracle and cure are you looking for Mollie.'

'I am going to pray not to have a baby.'

'Good god. Think I'll have a spot more port.'

A vixen bark and scream out in the night. The smoke of the incense rising high towards the ceiling. Around which there goes the plaster frieze of the egg. Symbol of fertility. And a fox up there too. Watching. Sniffing the air. Choosing which way to run. And from whom. As Mollie stands there, her face illuminated by the fire glow.

> Her freckles
> About to turn
> Into tears
> And
> Fall from her
> Face

17

A horse's hoofs pounding by outside on the front drive. A howl of a wolfhound. And a clatter echoing through the house. In the darkness, Darcy Dancer falling forward over a chair in the front hall. The crash of a vase on the tiles. Mollie, one hand clutching the decanter of port and the other grabbing at the back of Darcy's dinner jacket as he rolls sidewards and plunges to the hall floor.

'Ah god you poor man, we'll wake the dead, the legs have gone from under you.'

'They have Mollie, and on the end of my legs are the feet. And the ruddy feet have gone from under me. And some of the ruddy objets d'art of this house have gone too. Damn horse is loose. But don't for the love of god call me a poor man here on my hands and knees.'

Mollie's giggles and laughter echoing in the hall. A drip of moisture down from the skylight landing on Darcy's brow. Faint moonbeams crossing the floor. Darcy Dancer braying and barking, crawling over tiles.

'Woof woof. Woof woof. Call the hounds Mollie. Call the hounds.'

'It's this late time of night now. And they be securely locked up in the stables.'

'We must let them loose. Chop, chop. Open up the front ruddy door. Call the hounds. Do as I say. I must have my hounds. They are lonely. Lonely. I am lonely. Damn loose horse is out there lonely. But meanwhile the hounds should be loosed too. So that they may venture far and wide to chew up the poachers and trespassers. Ah I am up. Up again. Onward

276

Christian soldiers. Marching as to another ruddy war. I think, if I am not entirely misjudging the situation, that ahead ascends the main stairs of this house. Upon which I shall take upward steps before I keel over again.'

'Let me get holt of you now so as I don't drop the port.'

'Whoops. A slip. Not of the tongue. But of foot Mollie. Get me Mollie. Get me. I've gone down again. Help me up.'

'You're too much of a weight.'

'Take me to Lourdes with you Mollie. I'll require to be cured of an awful hangover. Chuck me in the old ruddy grotto. I need an old pair of those discarded crutches.'

'You need more than a pair of those crutches, you do.'

'Mollie, I'm finished.'

'Ah now you're just that little bit the worse for drink now. You'll be fine. Step up carefully now. You poor man. Ah sorry I did not mean again to call you a poor man.'

'Ah I am a poor man. I am. But we've reached at least the first landing Mollie. Pause for a rest. Now has anyone ever told you Mollie that you are one wonderfully big agricultural girl. Never mind going to Lourdes. Any small farmer would be deliriously delighted to have you as a wife to dig up his spuds in the garden. To milk the cow, make the butter and feed the chickens. Chop, chop.'

'Chop, chop, yourself now. And no small farmer is going to have me as a wife. And I'll surely not be milking a cow or digging any spuds for anybody.'

'That's the spirit Mollie. Ruddy well fuck milking the cow. Fuck the spuds. But the farmers looking for a wife are all over the place after you. Jumping ditches. Tearing their way through the gorse. Climbing walls. Sure they'll be even after you on your way to Lourdes. And be leaping out at you from the grotto when you get there.'

'O god now, no more of that sacrilege. You'll have me cursed. You won't now be driving me out of my job. Sure you won't.'

277

'Of course I won't, Mollie. For I am what is commonly known as a benevolent landlord and kindly squire. Good to those all around me. It's a cold frosty night now. Come to bed with me and be my hot water bottle.'

'I would want to be having a house.'

'A house.'

'Yes, and I would be wanting to have a motor car.'

'A motor car.'

'It doesn't have to be too big a house. A few rooms would do.'

'Ten rooms.'

'Ah I'd not need ten. It doesn't matter so long as there is more than the few bedrooms. And modern conveniences.'

'What brand of motor car do you want Mollie.'

'I don't be knowing all the brands. But me uncle has an Austin Eleven. With an electric starter. I'd have one of those. And there'd be a bit of land.'

'Bit of land, Mollie.'

'For a bit of a garden.'

'Good god, you don't want much for merely being my hot water bottle.'

'My father would beat me within an inch of me life for me to have a baby before I have a husband.'

'Husband. Me. You're not suggesting me Mollie. Good god.'

'Sure, pregnant I would be jumping off the top of the house and kill myself.'

'Heaven forbid Mollie. We are deplenished enough of staff already in this ruddy house.'

'That's all I am to you is it, is staff.'

'No. No. Not staff. Slip of the tongue Mollie.'

'Well you're doing plenty of slipping on these stairs.'

'I am Mollie. Ah but now with your assistance we have crawled up and reached the landing. And see. Out the window. How the moonlight, Mollie, reflects off the boughs and branches of the beech trees in the grove. Like intertwining silvery ghosts. Ah they stand there in great beauty. Doesn't beauty make any impression on you Mollie.'

'Sure trees are trees and moonlight moonlight. But if you'd give me a gorgeous gown, I'd take notice.'

'Ah I do hope we are not being unconscionably obtuse. Complacent. Ah and to be my hot water bottle, all that is required, is a house, a motor car, a bit of a garden. And a gorgeous gown.'

'And a bit of jewellery.'

'Ah and a bit of jewellery as well. Pearls, diamonds. Tiaras. And what about moonbeams. Romantic moonbeams.'

'Hungry they wouldn't do you a bit of good.'

'Touché, Mollie, touché. But we must not remain ignorant even of the beauty of rain. Which a book on climatology in the library tells us is brought by the moist soft winds that, warmed by the Gulf Stream, arrive from that well known ocean the Atlantic. And now that we are on the subject of beauty I shall take out my appreciably expanded cock which is making a nuisance of itself in my trousers. O dear me. I can't get it out. Good god, it really is bloody well stuck, dear me. Mollie stop that laughter. It is not damn funny. My private part is entrenched down my trouser leg like a veritable crowbar locked in a granite crevis. Ruddy well can't shift it out. Ah there now. That's much better. Now Mollie. Stop that laughing. Can you see it in the dark. Ah, how about in this beam of moonlight. Is it glowing. It glows.'

'Sir you'll be glowing red if you don't get to your bed before somebody comes.'

'No one should be worried about coming in this house except me Mollie. Just me. The pasha. I am the only one who should worry about coming.'

'Don't I think I hear someone now. O god put it away. Put it away.'

'I am going to pee.'

'O god save us don't do that now.'

'Of course I shan't. In spite of piss being good for carpets. But if you threaten again to jump off the top of the house to kill yourself I shall. What about we both go to Lourdes, Mollie. Where I can without undue cermony pee into the grotto. What ruddy about that now Mollie. Look at the size of this cock. Come now. Touch it. And get some of the home grown fruit of the juice of Jesus, spit of the horn most high.'

'Stop now. That's blasphemy. We could be struck dead.'

'Don't be a superstitious old girl. God doesn't strike Protestants dead. Only you left footers, who think the almighty is coming down out of the clouds to wreak vengeance upon you, are likely to get a thunderbolt. Now come grab my cock, and show me your tits Mollie.'

'Sir now there's a time and place for everything. And this is no time and this is no place. And it's way past my bedtime. We'll be seen.'

'Not my dear girl in these various stages of darkness. And this is indisputably the time. And why not this the ruddy place. Good god I do think you'd better hold onto me. My dear old Mollie. Some big prosperous farmer with lots of cattle will give you a house and a motor car. And plenty of bedrooms. And you'll ruddy well pop off into top ruddy hole. But meanwhile grab my magnificent cock.'

'Ah it's one great grand size. But I wouldn't be wanting to grab your cock or be popping off into top hole with some old farmer.'

'O dear. Of course you don't Mollie. Of course you don't. I am but an abandoned waif. The ripped out half of my heart gone. Broken by a heart breaker. Leaving me dead but still able to breathe. Should have long ago taken my shotgun and blown out my brains. I suppose I could leave you all carrying on here after I am gone. A little community of your good faithful selves. Hold an occasional little memorial to me in the Whim Room.'

280

Mollie leading Darcy Dancer along the shadowy upstairs corridor of Andromeda Park. Muffled feet on the carpet. Past the portraits of previous pashas. Opening the door to these chambers. Guiding him through the small hall to the bedroom. Darcy lurching and knocking over a side table and plunging forward to land in the swansdown softness of the chaise longue. A screech of a vixen out in the frosty night. The sound of the pounding of hoofs across the hardened turf of the front parkland.

'Jesus, Mary and Joseph, Master Reginald you'll kill yourself.'

'Of course I shall Mollie. Bang. With my shotgun. When the bailiffs come. And when the game is up. Then. Bang. Ah but meanwhile out there Mollie. See it. The night's alive with the ruddy moon. There it is. Spendidly in the cold clear sky. A halo in all the colours of the rainbow around it. The calves out there upon this frosty night, will be tucking up close to their mothers. Glad of warm milk in their bellies. Now let's see in this moonlight those wondrous tits of yours. And come into bed with me.'

'You've not said a word about giving me a house and a motor car.'

'Good god. I say. One thing at a time. You mean you're not going to give the pasha a treat. And why not a nice little cottage and a bicycle. I will have the thatcher come put a new thatch on that empty cottage over beyond by the babbling brook in Thormondstown. Could be tarted up a treat. Bit of a garden too. And down in the barns there are several bicycles. What. What about that Mollie. Daily will come milk, butter and eggs. Come back. Where are you going Mollie.'

'I'll not stay here. Sure the likes of that Lady Lois has no trouble to get furs and what she likes out of you.'

'Good god, Lady Lois is a deserving, great and impecunious artist. You mustn't believe gossip in the household. And if you go, I'll jump out the window Mollie.'

'You wouldn't jump.'

'I most certainly will.'

'I'm waiting then.'

'What. You mean you would let me jump.'

'I would. If it isn't to get me in bed, you've no time for me. I could run this house. Put a stop to everyone stealing you blind.'

'What.'

'Yes. And them just waiting every second till your back is turned or you're up in Dublin to put their hands on something that you wouldn't notice that it might be gone when you'd be returning.'

'Good heavens Mollie. Nonsense. Loyalty and honesty pervades this household. And one has you dear Mollie much always on one's mind. You are a Venus. Come now. Let me see your wonderful tits. Nothing like them even in the Hollywood films. Display them for me. We'll see about a cottage. Roses around the door. Or will you after your trip to Lourdes go back to Galway, Mollie. Those lovely wild lonely uplands and outcrops of granite. Shimmering ponds and lakes. Glowing purple skies. Across which the curlew flies and sounds his mournful whistle.'

'Get rid of me is it.'

'I'm not trying to get rid of you. Just expressing the beauty of Galway. But you're always giving your notice Mollie.'

'It is Crooks who is saying he's giving his notice if you don't get rid of me.'

'Entirely fictitious, Mollie. You mustn't let your imagination run away with you.'

'It wouldn't be my imagination I'd be feeling in my stomach after getting into the bed with you to be your hot water bottle. What's going to happen to me Master Reginald.'

'I hate that name Reginald. And if you must persist in addressing me as Master, when I am far beyond the age for so doing, either just Master will do as in fox hunting or call me Master Darcy.'

282

'They'd be putting the tongue on me.'

'Who'd be putting the tongue on you Mollie.'

'Well known we are as a family all over the county. They'll put the tongue on me.'

'Never mind the tongues Mollie. And pass me the port.'

'No. I won't.'

'Good god. I do verily believe you are refusing to pass the port.'

'You've had enough.'

'Come now me old girl. No nonsense. Port. Decent port that is, is jolly rejuvenating on a cold frosty night such as this. Pass me that decanter. Chop. Chop.'

'Don't you chop, chop me.'

'Of course I'll chop, chop you. If there is to be no riding in bed. If I am not about to be treated to the sight of your beautiful tits. Light a candle. I'm heartily sick and tired of all this shirtiness. And I think for the time being we have had rather enough of this highly insalubrious insubordinate strike business in this household. Mollie. Why are you crying. What for heaven's sake is the matter. Do please stop crying. I order you, stop.'

'It's not me who has been shirty.'

'Come come Mollie. Of course you haven't been shirty. Here, you have some port. There take a good swig. This is a night for a gallop cross country by frosty moonlight. O dear we are sad. Here. Watch me. As Master of Foxhounds I shall divest of dinner apparel and be a bit of a toff.'

Darcy Dancer taking off his dinner jacket, silk shirt, black tie, removing emerald braces and dropping his trousers. Kicking off his evening slippers. Pulling on his cavalry twill breeches.

'Equip in a thrice in my hunting gear. In which my portrait has jolly nicely recently been painted. I shall go riding tonight. If you don't give me a treat Mollie I shall give myself a ruddy treat. Hand me the other boot.'

'You'll get kilt with your death of cold.'

'Never mind my getting kilt Mollie. Ah but what a marvellous relief it is to be drunk. And be full of delightful if foolish dreams. Had you let me have a glance at your tits, I would have in return awarded you your hunt buttons as a sign of my appreciation. But at least before I venture out now and get kilt, strip off so that I may, as a parting sight, wax lyrical over your bosoms. Whoops. O dear here I am yanking on a boot and stumbling backwards crashing to the floor before I am even up on my horse. But then there is no nicer way to die than charging forward upon meadows in the moonlight. Around my neck goes my stock tie. It is by tying these together that Masters make a noose to hang themselves by. Takes a lot of silk you know. Stop one from breaking one's neck. My whip's down in the front hall. Pop on my cap. Light the candle. Regardez moi. O dear. Damn coat is lopsided and which has just returned with alterations from the tailor. But you see Mollie just let down this front flap. With just four buttons marvellously convenient for letting one's expanded cock loose. But then it does not so easily go back in. Ah a smile. At last. You can see I am an imperialist by the way it rigidly stands to attention. God save the King. We must preserve Ireland from its awful fate of falling into the hands of its religiously superstitious population. Which will be its downfall.'

'You're an awful blasphemer.'

'And I shall as a blasphemer take another swig of port.'

'You're lovely dressed up like that.'

'How awfully awfully nice of you to say Mollie. And flattery will get you somewhere. Come now into bed.'

'Hasn't Kitty already put in a hot water bottle.'

'Never mind Kitty. Never mind previous hot water bottles. It is you I want for a hot water bottle. Chuck the other ruddy one out the window.'

'Will you give me a motor car.'

'O dear we're back on to that are we. I can't just give you a

284

motor car Mollie. But perhaps there is the old baby Austin out in the garage which if repaired might suffice to give you a spin.'

'I have a mind to have a smart new one I would own.'

'Good god, Mollie. Motor cars don't grow on trees. Besides even if I were able to afford it there are no smart new motors to be had. Not even up in Dublin. What about a nice donkey, fleet of foot, pulling the old governess's cart. Trot you along nicely. Up and down to the front gates.'

'Good night to you sir. I am giving you my notice. And I will be to a solicitor to get me wages.'

'Ruddy hell. Don't go Mollie. Especially not to a bloody solicitor.'

Darcy Dancer plopping down on the side of the bed. Outside the wind taken up. Vines rattling and scraping against the window pane. Dark clouds crossing under the moon. Cattle moo. Another scream of the vixen. O dear. The door slams after Mollie. The world really does, doesn't it, disappoint. No wonderful big soft tits to pillow my head against. Musky smells to inebriate me more. I do now feel utterly too tired to move. Tomorrow comes. The ball. The heiresses. Rashers. What hope is there left now. If any. And how dreadfully disgraceful, Mollie will fuck only for gain. No wonder small farmers are driven to putting it up their heifers and sheep, when a whole retinue of new cars is needed to prang the likes of Mollie. When dear me I demand obedience. And ere long there could be another bastard running around this house. Good liars. Bad liars. And I lie. Look facts in the face. Except for one dear one I once loved and still love, I would marry for gain. So that I might fill my stables with good horses. Prize cattle in the meadows. Put electricity back coursing through this house. Build hopes up, new walls from the ones tumbling down. To whom can one ever tell the truth. My fists clenched in outrage. Wretched bloody hell. No one takes pride in service any more. All feathering their own self important little nests. One does not want to freeze one's balls off cantering across the miles of frost bitten countryside, but it would soon blow the port wine out of one's brain. O dear. So painfully wretchedly randy. Good old Felicity Durrow-Mountmellton. A social call. Why not. It's not much past midnight. She'd be long enough recovered from her injuries for a romp. Wouldn't have to buy her a motor car or a twenty or thirty five bedroom house. Teaming up with her one could, bang, bang, dine off game each night. Chew the hell out of all the pheasants running all over her lands. Tramp her boglands and bang, bang, suck the brains out of her snipe, washed down with her burgundies. Although gossip has it that while her motor car was being mended, a garage mechanic had freely at her and enjoying a little rough play and in a steamy embrace, they both fell backwards into a six foot deep pit of discarded motor oil. Good sport that she is, old Durrow-Mountmellton vaulted herself up and out, dripping gobbits of greasy black lubricant while laughing like a drain, but left behind the poor bugger mechanic who could hardly swim, shouting for help. And, scratching at the slippery walls, he fell back in, again and again. Old D.M. must by now be dying to be pissed on. Amazing how one's moral standards drop in the face of hoping to get a fuck. Galloping over there to her tonight would at least knock my coat back into shape, which my tailor's ruddy well botched. And exactly at a time in my life when I should look my most resplendent for the American ladies arriving with bags of chewing gum and chocolate. But imagine. The insufferable cheek. A servant declining one's invitation to bed. My attentions fobbed off. The distinction of my mightily tumesced tool ignored. Denied even to finding one's hand on a bare soft smooth patch of her wonderfully freckled anatomy to linger and rub there and especially in the golden orange hair of her crotch. O dear. I am rather myself getting into a tizzy. Suppose that she thinks she's the Queen of Sheba with the prick of every peasant in the parish pointing

286

at her and every gormless gorp panting after her. Even Luke out in the stables loudly enough remarked of Mollie that she'd put a horn on you that would knock the cover off your coffin and bring you awake up out of your grave and although you'd have been long dead, you'd wake up fucking alive. Of course it would be great if she woke some of them up off their arses, sitting around in the tack room, smoking their cigarettes. All a damn sorry mess trying to find women. And not that many years ago one would have had one's wide choice of housemaids, nursery maids, scullery maids, parlour maids, kitchen maids, to prang as did that curmudgeonly bugger supposedly my father. Dear me. Guests due on the morrow. What pranging might there be had. I'd better not then go break my neck out on the frosty hard ground tonight. And be found dead with one's features set in a permanence of melancholic disappointment. But who can tell if Rashers hasn't already pranged both of them silly up in the Shelbourne. O lord I am as weary as the walls that go tumbling down. Undress. Put my lopsided hunting coat over the chair. Put my head on the pillow and into the softness of swansdown. So important that one's bed provides just the right amount of cuddliness which then avoids nightmares. Mollie somewhere used a highly discomforting expression. Modern conveniences. What a horrid combination of words. Can you imagine. Old ruddy Mollie. Silly creature is absolutely imagining she is having a baby in that marvellous belly of hers. Phantom pregnancies are galore all over the midlands. A ten bedroom house. Or was it five. Or seven. Whatever it was, Mollie must think she can go the way of all Leilas and become a marchioness. And then be mouthing her Galway vowels around to servants like herself in a stately house. But by god, servant or no servant, the way things are going here, I could do worse than to tie up with a big agricultural girl. With the powerful twin pistons of an arse on her. That with her backside bouncing could drive down fence-posts like a sledge. Could go out counting cattle, pull out

287

calves or fork hay into the barns and dig out tree stumps. Whose figure, flaming curly and tumbling tresses and bright green eyes would, with those gorgeously flowing tits, be quite dramatic. Although a trifle thick around wrists and ankles, she'd be decently grand enough in a ballgown. Meet Mollie of the manor. She is modernly convenient for a fuck. In her furs and bright new motor car. Sweeping in the gates of her great estate. Horsemen outriders with lances waving emblazoned pennants of her Galway family crest, which is bound to be a blacksmith's hammer and a couple of horseshoes. O god. That thumping. My heart. Will they ever get me. Dispossess me. Drag me out. Out my gate. Beyond my walls. As they did in those gloomy moments when they sent me away to school. As I clung to my home. Where bailiffs now can come with the bull castrator to squeeze and crush my balls. That do not like and abhor to be maimed. Draw and quarter me. Whips to flail me if I am unfortunate enough to have a hard on. Blue eyed Uncle Willie once said when they attempted upon an abysmal occasion to lay siege to his property and take away all his race horses, his house, his lands, that at such times you stand firm. Uncle Willie gone now from my life to the other side of the world to Australia. His words somehow have locked themselves in my brain as I grew up in those sad years following my mother's death. To keep alive my life in debt. Ah you'd stand firm Darcy. Stand firm. And if they want to take possession let them drag you out with a rope. Stay always, me boyo, where you are. In your domain. Even if it means you yourself end up dangling on the end of that rope. Remember through a winter of frosty pastures there'll always be rich grass again in the spring. And to see your cattle packing flesh on their backs, grazing the growing green bursting blazing from the ground, would put great heart into you. Sure six good big slates still on a roof over your head would keep you dry. And a couple of old turnips would keep you from going hungry. And sure now and again in the more gloomy days you'd have a moment of weakness. And why wouldn't you. That you'd want to lie down and die. Or that you'd put your head in your hands and just sit there doing nothing. But even doing nothing has its advantages. Sure it would always make people think you might do something. Like bite them in the hand when they reached to feel to see if you were still alive.

Darcy Dancer peeking out and tugging up the counterpane on the bed. A noise somewhere. Sit up in one's woozy daze. Tip top branches of the great spruce tree out the window. Pools of silvery fog on the low lying land. Moonlight still bright across the meadows and fields. And cutting shadows through the woods where the slates on the meat curing shed glisten and shine. I do believe one was on the verge of a nightmare. O my god who's the enemy in one's life. They are everywhere. Servants in one's household. Neighbouring farmers. The marauder. The Land Leaguers. Trying to take my land for themselves. The shopkeepers inflating my bills. Cattle gone missing. Claims in court. Another threatening letter from my beetle browed agent who was panting after Mollie. Good heavens. What was that crash. Water spilling. Crockery breaking. A creak of floorboards. Bloody hell. The bailiff. Would he dare enter this house. The ruddy fucker is here already.

'Who's that.'

'It's me. I ran into the table.'

'Who's me.'

'Just me. Mollie.'

'Dingbats. I mean Mollie.'

'What was that you said.'

'Sorry Mollie. I was asleep. In a dream. I think I thought you were Crooks.'

'Ah don't confuse me with that eegit waltzing around in women's frocks. Sure I'm back and I'll be your hot water bottle and you don't have to give me a house and motor car. Won't you say something now. So you don't want me back.'

'Mollie a moment please. I've just wakened. I don't know

289

yet what I want. Except for another glass of port. Lock the door.'

'I have it locked. And now I'm going to give you a good look at me.'

'Are you.'

'I am.'

'By jove.'

'Now here I am.'

'My word. Chopity chop. But by god Mollie, you've really got a gorgeous body. Turn there now. Slowly. In the moonlight, closer to the window. Shake your bosoms.'

'Is it like that you want.'

'Yes, like that. My god.'

'Isn't it great we've got skin to cover us up and keep us together without our insides falling out, so you wouldn't be seeing what's inside us like some of those medical books down in the library show.'

'Now you've said it Mollie. Now you've said it. It is indeed and without question, great.'

'Sure I'd guess I'd have a chance, would I not to be going into the pictures as an actress.'

'Yes Mollie. Yes. Undoubtedly you would.'

'I've always been that little bit of an exhibitionist showing myself off. You could be sending me up to Dublin for acting lessons. Would you. To be trained. By that Ria Mooney, Crooks's niece is on about. And fire that niece of his out of here.'

'Mollie, one thing at a time.'

'Aren't them artists up there as well desperately looking for models I've heard tell from Lord Ronald.'

'Well I should imagine that's entirely possible. Although Lord Ronald does tend to exaggerate a mite.'

'I'll turn around now nice and slowly in the moonlight for you. My nipples have gone as hard as acorns.'

'What a grand arse there is on you Mollie.'

'Sure I'd look even better wearing a hat. It wasn't bold of me now to have tried on some great hats of your mother's. Sure it wasn't bold of me.'

'It was of course bold of you Mollie. But in view of the number of liberties taken already by a number of people frequenting this house I regard your trying on of my mother's hats as inconsequential, I assure you. And with or without a hat, Mollie, christ you really are bloody beautiful.'

'Marry me.'

'What.'

'Marry me. Sure I'd make you a good wife. I'd be up and doing early of a morning. I am not always as bad a person as I seem now and again.'

'Of course you're not Mollie. Sometimes you seem as marvellous as you are now.'

'Don't I know how to run a house. I'd make you proud of me. So much that you could love me. Two of me uncles are high up in the Garda. And I could be putting on as many grand airs and graces like that one Leila, who no better than the scullery maid here married the Mental Marquis of Farranistic.'

A scrabbling in the ceiling. Chimes of the hall clock echoing in the house. Low growl and roar of the great black bull out somewhere. Looking for a heifer or a cow or two to screw in the fog. How can life close in upon you all at once. And send tremors and shivers up one's arse. It can. It does. It has. With only the relief of good port wine in one's brain to soothe one across some of the more desperate hours. O god. And Mollie. In addition to this incredibly exciting body has an altogether disarming charm. She first saw my periscope of a cock first peeping up at her from my bath water and dropped a tray on her big toe. We've nearly come to enough grips already over the years. Says I don't have to buy her a house and a motor car. Instead just make her mistress of a great estate. Into which would fit a dozen houses and motor cars. Crooks calls

her a lazy old bitch. And looking out upon her body, it's hard
to believe my eyes. In which tears now flood. As she said
she'd make me proud of her. So much that you could love me.
Pain of such words in the heart. The pain. But Jesus, Mary
and Joseph, and all the left footed saints save us. Mollie, the
Chatelaine of Andromeda Park. The ruddy neighbours across
the counties would have something to whisper and gossip
about. Perhaps the eccentric inhabitants of the great Castle
might enjoy the unnovel fact of yet another of their number
stooping to temptation and socially descending the way of all
flesh. But my sisters Lavinia and Christabel would be full of
nothing but scathing ridicule. Crooks would hang himself.
Everyone on the hunt would be outraged. Hunt servants
already shirty enough would become even shirtier. But by
god. I should, should ever such disaster befall, tell them all to
fuck off.

'Freezing I am.'

'Get in here to bed Mollie.'

Darcy Dancer throwing back the counterpane. Mollie, her
face hidden by her long locks of orangy hair, climbing into
bed. A groan of ancient springs. Sound of the train somewhere
far out across the countryside. Its whistle. Good heavens that
will be turning a lot of gatekeepers out of bed in the freezing
night. Or more likely won't. And as lately happened the train
went all the way to Galway, crashing through the barriers.
And I feel and hear something. In bed beside me. Naked
flesh. Soft and silkily warm. Musky. Dingbats. You've come
back. With a pair of the most frozen feet. Didn't go to
Lourdes or your solicitor. Your hand on my cock. What a
quick tent it made of the bedclothes. I shall bite you. Have a
ration of passion. And I shall be bitten. Feel you. Juices alive
between your orangy thighs. Prefer, that this cost me only
motor cars and houses. Instead of a whole estate. In order that
my fingers sink in your buttery softness. Bosoms. O god.
What bosoms you do be having me old Dingbats. And the

acorns on the tips of your tits. Sweetest softest pillow you are.
Come to me in comfort just as Uncle Willie was relating
advice in life. Never walk by a tumbled wall that you wouldn't
bend to lift up even one stone to put back. Sure you'll come
that way again and lift up another. And it wouldn't be that
many months before you'd notice you had a bit of a wall
again. Stand firm me boyo, he said. Me dearest little Darcy.
The honest and decent don't have to die young. Stand firm. O
god. Dingbats. It stands firm. Pressing between your wonderful curving thighs that every farmer in Ireland would sell
plenty of cattle to climb and lunge and plunge between. And
explode. The good can live. And Uncle Willie loved my
mother so. He'd call her Nettie. He'd pat me on the back.
He'd tell me. Sure you'd have been most of your life like a calf
looking for its mother. Seeing her not, you'd be calling up
from the brow of the hill. To that dearest of all dear women.
My Antoinette Delia Darcy Darcy Thormond. She did die
too soon. In the midst and beauty and prime of her life. In the
gaiety and joy and gardens of Andromeda Park. Across the
ballroom she'd waltz. Servants worshipping. Men adoring.
And calf that you were. Without your mother. Struggling on
small legs to find your way in the deep grass. Had she heard
your voice. She'd have come charging across the meadows.
Consternation across her brow to find you. For lost you were.
Lost. Little boy.

    In
    All those empty
    Young years
    Of your life

18

Upon this morn and somewhere as if it were sounding in my sleep was the whistle of the train. And over the distant foggy fields, the calling moan of a cow. A swarm of jackdaws crying out in the beech grove tree tops. The whine of swan's wings through the mist. The faint footfalls going and coming somewhere in the house. Had a dream I was up in court, bankrupted by the ball. Smyths of the Green had long sent their bill I could not pay. Then wakened by snoring beside me in bed. Dingbats. No sign of her face under her tumbling tresses of glowing orange hair. She said that I could have brought the whole house running to see what was amiss when I nearly woke the dead screaming in passion. And dear me someone is now knocking at the door.

'Who is it.'

'Kitty sir. With breakfast sir.'

Darcy Dancer crawling from bed. Pulling up and covering Dingbats's head under the counterpane, out of sight. O my god I am brain hammering bleary eyed, hung over and still half asleep. Why must port be so good at night and then be next day so bad. Breakfast already come. Tripping over my riding boots and donning my hunting coat to unlock and unlatch the door. I'll be killed yet. But thank god it's dark.

'Put the tray on top of the dresser Kitty.'

'Shall I light the fire and tidy up the little bit here sir.'

Kitty sniffing suspiciously at the table tipped over on its side. Darcy Dancer behind the dressing screen. Kitty wiping her hands on the white apron of her uniform. Means honey, butter, grease or worse is adrift on cutlery and dishes.

294

'No Kitty. It's all all right. Later will do. Jackdaw got in the room last night down the chimney, had to try and catch it.'

'Will there be anything else sir.'

'No thank you Kitty.'

Good god. The hall chimes. The stable clock has clearly conked out. It's late. Never mind breakfast. Got to commit ablutions. Clear my ruddy head. At least freezing cold water is not in short supply. Make sure Luke's gone as instructed to the train station to meet them. But I'm sure I dreamt the whistle of the train. Even if they are taking the early morning train at nine, and providing for the usual derailment and the running out of turf for the boilers, they at least won't be here until noon. And then, if they don't find enough willing passengers to go in search of turf and help push the carriages, it could take them till four or five o'clock. O god. What on earth do I do now with Dingbats. After finding out the ruddy girl's a sex bomb. And I did all the exploding. With no wonder everyone with a prick in the parish is after her. She said to talk Protestant dirty to her. And I couldn't think of a thing. Except getting my Church of Ireland organ to play in her. Good heavens. Anyway it's Catholics who have the dirtiest and filthiest minds. Which was soon evident as she whispered enough nearly disgusting filth in my ear to make the devil blush. And then did something to me I'd never had done before. Which good heavens could have been out of a volume of deviant behaviour down in the library. Written by some German baron neuropsychiatrist on ruddy sexual psychopathology. And now, deviant or not, I'm already wanting to have it done again. Just as she's already showing distinct signs of being shirty. Groaning. And the poking out at me with her elbow when I'm gentlemanly trying to bloody well wake her up.

'Leave me alone, I don't feel like moving. And I'm not going to move.'

295

Standing over the bed Darcy Dancer in his hunting coat. Bare legs shivering in the cold. Reaching to lift up the warming cover over breakfast. The grease already turned white and hard on my bacon and sausages. O god. What have I wrought in my inebriation. As many freckles on her back as stars in the sky. Bloody hell. Her pale green eyes like those of a snake's, hypnotizing me. O god. More servant insolence. This is going to be worse than any strike. Refusing to get out of bed and be about her duties. Which, when she is, could mean that without warning she could dump a bowl of hot buttery cabbage on a guest's head. She's bound to have taken all this too seriously. When all she reads are the penny romantic love stories strewn all over her room. Knights with invisible pricks up on their white chargers. With pikes and staves. The women beautiful, their hair windblown on mountain tops and swept off their feet by tall handsome men like me, and carried away to castles. And god here she is in the ruddy case of reality so disgustingly and pleasantly filthy minded and already in bed with a Master of Foxhounds in a mansion as big as any castle. And speaking of servant insolence I do believe she's just let off one highly fulsomely reasty fart. The surest bloody sign she's feeling entirely at home and had last night a damn good dinner. And now what's that. Wheels. On the ruddy drive.

Darcy Dancer crossing the creaking floorboards to the window. The shiny black bonnet of the Daimler motor car emerging from the rhododendrons. And followed by a second motor passing to the front of the house. Good grief. I don't believe it. They're here. Ruddy well here. Must have caught an earlier train or else didn't get derailed. Or they could have had a lot of farmers aboard who'd make short work of finding turf to stuff in the engine boilers. Or could push like the devil if they had to. And now I do believe I perceive a voice on the front steps attempting to sound very grand and important. Open the window a mite to listen. Ah at least Crooks is on the job, greeting them. O god, have I been seen, draw the ruddy curtains. Someone bollocks naked at a window of a mansion always makes one automatically think there's someone amiss in the head inside. Or has just finished wanking. But I just know something awful is going to happen. I just know it. Dingbats. Is utterly, utterly snoringly asleep again. Lock her in. And she may end up kicking, banging and screaming to get out. She could be off to solicitors, accusing me of promiscuous bloody carnal knowledge. Which one must admit I got enough of last night to fill full to the brim the shelves of Trinity College library. And in court it could be intoned. Did you verily Squire of Andromeda Park put your what for up the meant for of this poor working girl, thereby taking heinous advantage of her. O god it's all quite terrible to grow up into life. And then have what's left of one's minuscule innocence utterly swept away. One's most cherished dream as a little boy was merely that I always wished and imagined that an aeroplane would come flying in over the tree tops of the front parkland with its engine spluttering out of fuel and then would softly glide in to land along a flat piece of meadow. And the grateful aviator in his helmet and goggles would climb down out of his cockpit and smilingly hold out his hand to me as I ran to him. And we would say hello. As the pretty aeroplane sat there unharmed on the green field. O dear I did love that dream so.

Darcy Dancer tearing clothes from the closet cupboard and rapidly dressing. Locking the door behind, and rushing from his apartments. Adjusting his tie passing the landing mirror. Animated voices ahead down in the hall. Stacks of luggage. Damian and Luke hauling more in. Crooks rubbing his hands in front of Rashers.

'The Master's above, and will be informed of your welcome presence milord. It is so good to see and have you again at Andromeda Park. And ladies I do hope one may make your stay memorable and comfortable. Ah, I do believe I hear the Master coming.'

My god. Crooks is laying it on rather a bit thick. But heavens the ladies do look awfully glamorous. And astonishingly good looking from what I can see. Rashers smiling from ear to ear like the cat having got the cream. And also, the ruddy cheek, lecturing on the architectural and behaving as if he owns the place. And god. Could be these ladies by their appearance could certainly afford to buy and sell me. The clothing. So stylishly cut. That one is already feeling tattier and more patched and poor than one already is. My word. We are undoubtedly on to something here.

'This ladies is one of the largest front halls in Ireland. And the dome is a replica of the Pantheon in Rome.'

Rashers's voice echoing, the girls staring up at the skylight. O my god. What utter rubbish he's spouting. The hall dome has nothing whatever to do with the Pantheon in Rome. Or any other bloody dome in Europe for that matter. Pause a second. Hold tight to the banister. I do feel any awful moment I am about to retch. Crooks is really doing his nut. Dear me he's nearly dancing. And a plethora of puke will skid him directly upon his arse. Send his monocle popping out of his crossed eye. And about time someone stepped on it. Every upstart fucker in the county is beginning to sport one. Goodness the deepness of his bows in deference to Rashers. Whose own monocle is flashing all over the place. And the cheek of him. Growling and snapping orders at Damian. Who I must admit is jumping to it. Bloody shifty eyed boy, and at least rushing back and forth to the car, is doing work for a change. Descend I must. These ancient old black stone steps. Still groggy, faint headed and woozy. With this astonishment waking one up. Both ladies nearly as tall as Rashers himself. And both attired in awfully proper and appropriate country tweeds. In spite of which, one is not disabused of thinking that they may be possessed of curvaceous and voluptuous figures. Both so bright eyed. Each with long brown tresses. Each with such splendid legs. They are in fact indubitably

298

gorgeous. Utterly gorgeous. Makes one swallow one's soured breath. And nothing may come out when one attempts to open one's mouth. O god I really am speechless. Not a murmur of greeting is coming out. Not a sound. Even Rashers is at an utter loss for words. Nearly.

'Dear boy, dear me. You're frightfully white. Are you all right. Florida and Virginia may I present to you my very oldest and my very dearest friend, Darcy. Who is of course the very same Sir Reginald Darcy Thormond Dancer Kildare, Baronet, Master of Foxhounds, and member in good standing of the Legion of Decency. And of whom I have related so much. One does, in the fullness that this introduction I think deserves, give him without omission his complete cognomen as it were. Now no gasping at his very good looks ladies. Stand well back, introductions one at a time. Darcy, this is Florida and this is Virginia. The ladies named after those two eminent states in which both their great grandfathers were substantial landowners.'

'How do you do. I do hope your journey has not been too much of an ordeal. And I apologize.'

'O no. Please don't apologize. His grace here has taken care of everything for us.'

Rashers frowning, his eyebrows going up and down, his head nodding towards something amiss. O my god I know what it is. My fly is open. Calm. What a dreadful inconvenience. And if I bow it will only open further. I knew something awful was going to happen. No wonder my voice seemed to remain somewhere deep down in my throat. Rashers already has elevated himself to being a duke. And here all I'm ready to do is apologize. Apologize for everything that I'd ever not believed from Rashers. Apologize for his running up a vast bill at the Shelbourne. Yes. I do. Apologize. To you ladies. For my pot holes. For my mansion falling down. And apologize for what Rashers is doing, has done and will do in order that we can get your millions of dollars into our empty bank accounts. And I am about to sit or fall down on the floor in front of all of you in abject contrition. But my god if girls like you actually also have money. How golden and how marvellous life could be. Back in our respective suites at the Shelbourne. Racing each day. Dining at Jammet's each night. Imagine. Beauty and money. Even your rather whining voices one might come in time to find tolerable. O god. By the fumes out of my fly. Can they smell the musk of Dingbats still clinging to me. I certainly can. As I can do nothing but stand oaflike before them. Black under my fingernails. My breath stinking of alcohol. Grass sprouting out of my ears. And being nothing but a potato digging bog trotter.

'Good god Darcy. Of course you apologize. You damn devil. Not believing me of course. That I should be in the company of such wondrous ladies. Ladies that's why he doth apologize. And seem nonplussed and slightly shattered speechless before you. Never expecting such lovely ladies as your good selves to deign come from that new glamorous world across the seas to this humble but well intentioned old world you find here. And your splendid handsomeness grace these boglands.'

'You see, Florida and I, we thought everyone who lived in Ireland was Irish.'

'Well my name Darcy is rather more British than Irish. But I am Irish. Please do, come in. O of course sorry, you are already in aren't you. Crooks please close the door from the draft. Do ladies come get warm for a moment by the fire. Crooks will show you up to your rooms. For a wash and brush up. Chop, chop. Sorry. Didn't mean that. A little phrase I've been in the habit of using lately. I do believe it is Chinese for hurry up. Which we so often have to be reminded to do out here in the isolated countryside. Where one can so easily sink straight down into one's grave from sheer inertia. And neither of you needs a wash and brush up. You both indeed already seem perfectly washed and brushed up. Sorry that doesn't at all sound right. I don't believe I meant that either.'

300

Rashers slowly ceasing to rub his hands. Alarm creeping across the usually happy smiling features of his face. Good god. It is so easy in one's nervousness to act like a complete nut. Except that it is all too easy to stay that way. Mumbling up and down the halls of Andromeda Park as the household beats a swift scurrying retreat out of one's way. And it might simply be better to remain in that lopsided condition. Even Crooks's mouth is hanging open. And Damian is back. And has now for the ruddy third time, while noisily examining everything, scurried out to the car to lug in sports gear in the ruddy form of golf clubs, a bag over each shoulder. And then back again with tennis rackets. They must think this is a ruddy sports spa. And good grief. Here he comes again. Two pairs of skis. O my god.

'Dear boy you'll be so pleased to hear that Florie and Virgie are extremely athletic ladies. Veritable champions in fact. Isn't that wonderful.'

'Yes. Indeed.'

'And they are also enamoured dear boy of the splendour of your coniferous and ericaceous plantings along the drive and the grace and splendour of this, this Adam interior. Of course worthy of an Irish chieftain. The Kildare, Prince of Andromeda.'

A fit of retching seizing Darcy Dancer dead centre of the front hall. The sound echoing. A spew of vomit erupting from Darcy's mouth and cascading through his fingers and splashing down over the black and white tiles. The monocle dropping out of Rashers's eye. Crooks blessing himself. Two wrens flying overhead. As the girls' mouths go agape.

'O dear, excuse me. I'm terribly sorry. I believe I may have recently eaten something disagreeable.'

Darcy Dancer retreating hurriedly back to the hall stairs. Stopping. Doubling over. Retching again. And spewing another great gobbit of vomit across the bottom step. Wiping his mouth with a handkerchief and bowing back to the guests and proceeding upwards, holding his stomach. Hall clock chiming exactly twelve o'clock. O dear. Crooks must bid the guests have lunch without me. While I repair in ignominy indefinitely to my apartments. Could merely say that one has absent mindedly ingested a tiny fraction of deadly nightshade. O my god, the door locked. From the inside. Bloody Dingbats. Now having to knock to get into my own bloody room.

'Who is it.'

'It's me Mollie. Let me in.'

Mollie stark naked inside the door and locking it behind Darcy and walking ahead back to bed. Wagging her soft white magnificent arse. Which as one follows is no more than a hand's reach away. And even feeling nauseous is giving me a hard on that would shift a hippopotamus out of the ruddy Grand Canyon I once saw in a travel film in the Grafton Street cinema up in Dublin. And also. Good god. Not that I have even the vaguest trace of an appetite, she's ruddy well polished off every particle of food that was on my breakfast tray. And here she is now as I'm trying to shift out of my tweeds, convulsed out of her mind laughing. As my prick has popped out of my open fly. Back she goes on her back on the bed. Two ruddy legs stuck out like wings and wagging an invitation. Into her bifurcation. Got to turn her over. Dog style. That way in my next retch I'll at least be disgorging only across the freckles of her back. If last night I screamed loud enough to loosen roof beams, today I'm surely not able to squeak like a mouse without puking again. And I'm not sure she wasn't locked so painfully around my prick like a vice that I wasn't yelping to get loose. While she said this is how I've got you now, and sure I could keep you here.

'Ah god now you're one boyo. To be at me from behind.'

'Mollie, I am as a matter of fact just that slightly little bit indisposed.'

'Ah you poor man you. Sure I thought you were white as a ghost. When finished there we'll get into bed. And you'll get a rest in me arms.'

302

Sure you'll be
Marrying me now
Won't you
And be getting me
A brand new
Motor car

19

Darcy Dancer asleep. And waking as three o'clock struck ten minutes early as it occasionally did on the hall chimes. Dingbats gone. Dreamt I was standing atop Nelson's Pillar up in Dublin. Guards rushing up the steps to arrest me as I was pissing down on an assemblage of the city's better citizens. Mr Arland among them requesting I stop and come down. Must get up. Ring for Crooks. Bathe. Dress. Get out. And dare face the world. Following missing lunch, at least I may make amends where needed just before tea. O god. They're going to think me for certain a potato digging bog trotter for my unavoidably shocking behaviour. Before I vomited all over the place I could see Rashers could hardly contain himself and wanted to drag me by the arm into somewhere to rejoice and freeze. As he usually favours the arctic front east parlour.

'You rang sir.'

'Yes Crooks. To inquire after the guests.'

'Not to worry sir. Not a bother on them. Gone out for a bit of a walk.'

'Good lord did someone warn them about the loose stallion and the bull.'

'I haven't a clue sir. But if they get back alive and you're able for it sir they will join you for tea in the drawing room. I hope you're feeling better sir. You took a turn. And don't the same things happen at the same time. Didn't Edna Annie take a fall as well down in the laundry room.'

'O dear. Is she all right.'

'She's all right and resting and the doctor's been and he

says she's as hearty as they make them and she has every intention of obeying your invitation to the ball and have a waltz with you. Ah now you'd be needing more rest than she takes at the age of ninety two. If she's not ironing she's at her soap making. Will you be dining sir with the guests tonight.'

'I will be attempting to do so Crooks.'

'Will it be black or white tie sir.'

'Black.'

'Very good sir, I shall so inform the guests. The ladies Christabel and Lavinia have arrived and have been shown to their old rooms. But a bit of a sore point there sir as they wanted the larger rooms in the front of the house with the bathrooms. And may I mention in confidential privacy to you a household matter sir.'

'If you must Crooks. If you must.'

'Well now like it's a matter at the limit. That Mollie sir was the whole night away out of her room. And snoring she was still asleep at this hour of the afternoon above in bed not ten minutes ago. And there was a bit of an ado, upon waking her sir. The language. You never heard such language. Sent my ears red. F this and F that all over the place. Said she would soon be in the Hollywood films. Flung a picture of the Sacred Heart of Jesus at me. Threatened me with a hammer. And telling me I was the one to get the sack.'

'O dear Crooks we're absolutely overwhelmed are we not. No one's getting the sack. Let's see if we might for the time being just carry on.'

'Well sometimes sir the hostility gets so great in this house that you'd be glad to feel the great sense of relief I felt the other day out for a walk when a stranger passing in his cart on the road gave me a friendly wave. And I'd hate for the newly arrived guests sir to hear the language of that one Mollie echoing up and down the halls as she went flying through the reception rooms.'

'Well they can always put their fingers in their ears if they are seriously aggrieved Crooks. How is the ballroom coming.'

305

'Without a bother sir. Sexton and Luke sir have it overflowing with flowers like it was the Garden of Eden.'

'Well let's hope that unlike the Garden of Eden no one takes a wrongful bite of the apple.'

'We had sir but to get some extra candles from the Catholic chapel and the priest said he hoped you wouldn't mind a Catholic flame glowing in a Protestant house.'

'No Crooks. Provided the house isn't burned down.'

'Ah sir, your mother and all before her here were dearly loved all over this parish and no harm would ever be planned to come your way.'

'O, well at least that's a relief to hear. In any event please tell Lord Ronald that I'll join him presently in the north east parlour. Where I would appreciate if you would light the fire.'

'Certainly, as you wish Master Reginald. But there is just a small other matter sir that I didn't want to intrude upon you. But as well as that one Mollie, that devil Damian should be let go and another got to replace him. Sure he's as well raised a fist to me. Shook it in me face. I took him to task after he was heard boasting down the kitchens to Catherine that he plans to make free with the guests at the ball. Wasn't he caught as well as that one Mollie sitting back in your library chair with your glass in one hand sipping down the remains of your champagne, and smoked salmon in the other as if he were to the ingredients and manner born. I kicked him out of that in a hurry I can tell you. Getting above himself he is with tastes for high living.'

'Have him come to see me in the Rent Room tomorrow morning at eleven Crooks.'

'Very good sir.'

'And what is for dinner.'

'Ah now and if I may say so sir that's a question that would indicate that you are returning to better form. Rabbit stew sir. And judging by the ravenous appetites of the guests we'll be needing every bit of the six nice big ones you shot beyond the

306

other day. I have the wines airing. And for an aperitif haven't I uncovered from down back of the cellars several of the very best bottles of old Charles Heidsieck champagne. The people from Smyths on the Green sir are at this moment finishing up with the organizing in the ballroom and the beer, wines and spirits.'

'Champion, Crooks. Champion.'

'The ball sir is the talk of the parish for miles around. Ah it's great now to have things going a bit like the old days when your mother was alive sir.'

'Well I hope so Crooks. I sincerely hope so.'

'And chop, chop, sir.'

'I beg your pardon Crooks.'

'Ah it is sir as you said, hurry up in Chinese, sir. Chop, chop.'

'Of course Crooks. Yes. Chop, chop. Champion. And I think I shall wear a cummerbund tonight.'

Crooks with a nod of the head bowing and raising at the same time his finger as if to remind that he never needed to be reminded. Murmuring repeatedly, very good sir, under his breath as he leaves. My god visitors do at least put them on their mettle. And with the exception of Sexton and Edna Annie they do then pretend to rush around like a bunch of loyal, honest and dedicatedly faithful servants. Certainly helps heaps having a dozen or so extra eyes watching upon their slothful, disloyal and deceitful ways. And they all do take much excited anticipatory notice when a big festivity is afoot. For which the whole reason and the entire why and wherefore is ever being to fulfil my only dream. That she, Leila, would come back. Merely then to know how much and how deeply I shall always miss her. That the news of the ball at Andromeda Park would tell her that there I was and still would be. Waiting. Hoping. Come back. So that I might even see you, however briefly, once more. So that you could see from my eyes that I cherish you. And will always.

Darcy Dancer descending the main stairs. The soft comfort of a silk shirt under his hound's tooth tweeds and moss green velvet waistcoat. Darkness falling. The flames from the hall fire flickering light up on the walls. Hammering in the ballroom. Crying moan of a cow out somewhere. At least to a cow you can always say shut up or I'll sell you for beef. Resoluteness must be my motto now. Cross to the front east parlour. Open the door. Rashers's smile certainly lighting up this room and much of the porcelain in the late afternoon gloom. And one did find the ladies were easily given to amusement evidenced by their continued laughter one heard coming from the gardens. Giving one a paranoid twinge of course, thinking it might be at one's expense. And Rashers has made a distinct recent visit to the haberdashers. And god, he does look so confidently smug, giving me the deepest bow of greeting I think I may have ever witnessed his doing.

'Darcy. Dear darling boy. O how wonderfully good it is to see you upright ambulatory again. I would have examined you but one easily diagnosed it was a clear case of mere mild temporary biliousness.'

'It wasn't biliousness. It was a bloody pathologically bad hangover.'

'Then I do hope for god's sake you're not out of your bed for my sake when you could with such lowered resistance be sickening for a wretched old bout of flu or something. I mean you still do look white as a sheet. Here. I took the liberty of asking Crooks for a small spot of brandy. Pour you some.'

'No thank you. My indisposition, caused by too much port last night, is passing, thank you. And I hope the ladies do forgive me.'

'Of course they do dear boy. Of course they do. But my, you're truly marvellous at vomiting. Very good facility to have at one's disposal. But now out with it. No. Not to puke dear boy. I refer rather to the ladies. I know you're dying to disclose your true and absolutely honest opinion. Do we not both have a lovely reason to rejoice. Over their sallow but wonderful silkily smooth skin. Their tumbling, gleaming brown tresses. Their astonishingly beautiful legs. On both of them. Perfect in the pasterns. Splendid calf muscles. Ruddy health of them glows.'

'I'll admit I am more than slightly surprised.'

'And what good sports they both are. Of course they are both rather used to very grand things. And will take a little time to recover from the shock of barefoot children in Dublin and being out here in the bogs as it were. But then we are rather in the end going to be popping off into the top hole of Newport society. The plan so long in fermentation is jolly well and truly about to be afoot and the nectar tasted. What. Of course I mean always providing a little thing might go wrong here and there. Like your nearly vomiting all over us. Didn't mean that dear boy. Please forgive me. Slipped out. But the unexpected can happen. And did. And has. I've rather more than burned my bridges. Can't go back. My betrothed actually caught me at the Shelbourne. It was appallingly embarrassing. And sad. Slapped my face. Then burst into tears in the lobby. And told me to fuck off. Now please. In sympathy, say nothing. I deserve it. But it can't be said that I didn't more than occasionally give her a wonderful time. Even though it was merely a matter of being extravagant with her money. But always with a true and good purpose. To provide the necessary optimism and setting one occasionally needs in life. Never will she now see the innards of the Kildare Street Club. That does make me sad. And Darcy I did so often imagine that therein I sat with the chaps, my aperitif and cigar, waiting for her to mount the steps to the ladies' entrance and join me for dinner. Darcy if I do go down to doom, at least I shall know that my stay with you here now is to be precisely one of those splendid occasions one shall never forget and always cherish. And of course dear boy my bringing these massively rich ladies into your midst does save

309

your immediate travelling to London and hanging desultory about Claridge's and other London watering places. Which these days anyway are not so chock a block any more with your better aristocracy. Saved too you are, as the most eligible of eligible bachelors, from having to sift through invitations to various balls upon which one might attend in the hope to pick out a lady suitably rich. And avoid all those wretched crowned heads of Europe recently down on their luck and having to become interior decorators or motor car salesmen. And unable to be as we are here, on the brink of stupendous things. And my god not to even mention the marvellous bosoms on both of these Newport and Park Avenue ladies.'

'And of course too Rashers. I am on the brink of having to sell more cattle to pay that big bloody bill at the Shelbourne.'

'O dear, I was coming to that dear boy.'

'Well before you do, and I assure I am not meaning to pry. But I should of course like to know which one, if not both, of the ladies you have already set your cap for and fucked.'

'Low low blow dear boy. O dear. Very low. Don't like that aspersion one bit. Nae. Must have another spot of brandy. Hope you don't mind.'

'No I don't mind.'

'O dear. You have been brooding. Out here so cut off and isolated. But my dear, dear Darcy, I have. I really have tried my damnedest Darcy. Honestly I have. To keep my dying to touch hands off them. Unless someone jumped on top of them at Gander airport stop over, the girls are, as far as I'm concerned, virgo intacta.'

'Well upon such denial I do apologize and withdraw the remark.'

'Frail as I am in curbing my appetites, I don't deny of course having fully, completely and wholeheartedly, a constant hard on. Damn it, I have one now. In hysterical anticipation I suppose. But one has before pranging to considerably prime these dear girls. And for you leisurely to make your selection.

I mean we are after all, following an ancient and well tried tradition. Tying up with those in the new world who made a bit of the old moolah, and who are without title, without the right ancestors, or background and have no real social distinction to speak of and have not been to the manner born. But dear me, from the Americans one has met it's no wonder it takes more than a little lolly to elevate them up and above that appallingly large common mass of humanity. And you must be ready to sympathetically tolerate their total lack of culture, dear boy. But by joining up forces, as it were, with the likes of us, they achieve a sense of real worth about themselves. But most importantly, they are then able to thumb their noses at fellow listees in the *Social Register*.'

'O god. I am finding all this rather more than depressing.'

'Nonsense, dear boy. You're just suffering a little post hangover melancholy. All shall go smoothly. The girls have brought with them the latest American hit gramophone records to play tomorrow at the ball. Foxtrots and sambas. And a ruddy delightful thing called "Brazil". And another being quite sentimentally pleasant called "I'll Never Smile Again".'

'Very appropriate title, if I may say so Rashers.'

'Dear me, you are down.'

'Bloody hell Rashers, haven't we been through this selfsame conversation many times before. While my precarious financial situation grows ever more rapidly precarious. The money I need cannot rest on some whimsical distant hope in the future.'

'But dear boy. That's what I'm saying. Our prospects are about to be realized actually now.'

'Actually now had better be now. The ball alone has cost me four of my heaviest bullocks which were sent to market. And the very last of my mother's jewels I have to bring up to Dublin to sell next week.'

'Dear boy. I know, I know. Is there anyone in this world to whom your words could sound more poignant than they do

to me. We both desperately need mucho moolah, mucho
soono. But this matter we pursue must be so delicately finessed
that even a smile curling wrongly on the wrong side of one's
face could make a shambles of our efforts. Good god, do go
see if there is anyone listening at the keyhole Darcy.'

'No I shall not. To do so, one would simply turn oneself
into the worst sort of gymnastic paranoid, simply because
there is always someone at a keyhole in this house. But they
hear so damn much they don't remember half of what one was
talking about. And what they do remember, they get entirely
wrong.'

'O dear, Darcy I wonder how one might conspire to better
speed things along.'

'I should prefer to dismantle this idea of there being a
conspiracy immediately Rashers.'

'Very well. Then at an early but entirely appropriate time I
shall with your blessing put propositions to the ladies. But we
shall, in giving any sign of haste, be weakening one's bargaining position. In any event, as I have so sadly been in the past,
I'm sure we're going to be referred rather immediately to the
scrutiny of a lot of lawyers. Who are refereeing the making of
a mutual exchange of advantageous circumstances by which
both parties benefit. And if I am examined piece by piece and
too closely, I shall be ignobly fucked. As there are, ensnared
in my title, matters which are commonly referred to as flaws.
And what if such lady assuming such title should then find
herself abjectly unhappy with such circumstance. And instead
of being Lady Ronald, be referred to as Lady bloody fraud.'

'Well then it would Rashers have to be assumed that the
time had arrived to tell her to piss off. But by then I suppose a
social climbing lady, not totally satisfied with having moved
up a few more rungs and to have put neighbours' noses on
adjoining acres a little out of joint, has at least been put into a
better position to further social climb.'

'Yes. I quite agree. But at least one thing one does know

312

about most ladies, is that they might want to get rid of the husband but never his title. Ah but it is so nice to now be able at long last to contemplate that much better days are coming. Imagine damn chaps sacking me after I had rung up more sanitary towel sales than they had in years. Results are what matter dear boy. But they couldn't stand the fact of the unsubstantiated rumour of my operating by telephone over breakfast from my comfortable bed in the Shelbourne and soliciting these considerably massive orders from every chemist shop from Mullingar to Skibbereen. I mean damn it I nearly had a mind to drive them out of business. I mean what are they selling but a few bits and pieces of old wadding fashioned to fit between the legs. But of course one did get a marvellous taste of revenge. Just when it was all over Dublin that I was in bed and breakfast accommodation the wrong end of Talbot Street, who should I see just the other evening inappropriately entering into the Shelbourne Rooms, but the Managing Director and Head of Sales. Both astonished out their petty middle class minds to see me there ensconced enjoying a bottle of champagne with my two American beauties. Of course my Ardagh Chalice was also conspicuous on the wicker glass table. One implacably ignored them to the extent of my joyous laughter and merriment driving them away without them finishing their drinks.'

'Ah Rashers, at least nothing ever seems to keep you down. And for that at least I am pleased.'

'Ah Darcy if a fault you have, it is that you are at times overly solicitous of the feelings of others. And I suspect even when they in turn may not give a tinker's damn about you and your feelings. And speaking of tinkers, I did see a little family of them around a little fire outside your gates. And you know, apropos of our mutual present situations, there is something to be distinctly said in favour of becoming a vagabond and wanderer without possessions. Always used to feel that, especially in London when one was ever passing upon the evening

313

street and was able to see into people's flats with their polished mahogany and silverware on display, and one could sense that within, all were so disagreeably smug and so damn full of themselves. I sometimes think the English are an argument in favour of the shabbiness and innumerable ineptitudes of the Irish way of life.'

'Dear me Rashers, what has brought about this distinct change of heart.'

'Ah Darcy, I know I have often represented myself otherwise. But you know, while up in Dublin as one looked across the Shelbourne Rooms and surveying the very British and ultra Anglo types, one found oneself saying you priggish hypocritical bombasts, you dreadful, pointless people, you. O dear, you do look shocked. But I suppose sometimes I do take it a little hard that I am being searched for high and low as a deserter from my regiment and the British way of life. But this Darcy is for me the very last chance. Having been disowned, disinherited. And I do believe not even mentioned in my father's will. But I wasn't meaning for this to become a requiem dear boy.'

'But why are you not to be mentioned in your father's will.'

'Dear boy an awful old story. Of which you must never ever mention a word. But made quite brief, I attempted to flog several of my father's better medals.'

'Good god.'

'Do you mind if I have another nip of brandy. It was of course done in a moment made extreme by my prolonged desperation and the need for a little temporary emolument to keep up appearances. It was, through an accident of geography, miserably abortive. When contrary to my instructions the medals were displayed prior to auction in a most conspicuous window of a conspicuous London auctioneer which happens to be right round the corner from one of my father's better but less used clubs. Wouldn't you know some bloody passing colonel member of his club recognized a medal as

314

belonging to my father. And asked him what on earth he was doing selling it.'

'Rashers, honestly, I simply can't believe this. Even I know such things as the Victoria Cross have attached to them a life and death reverence. And are utterly venerated.'

'Well it wasn't the Victoria Cross. In fact the damn medals weren't at all that important and had been locked away useless for years. And the old boy has nearly every decoration there is. And no one would have noticed except for one which I must confess was a little more important, and which the Colonel identified as my father's. Unfortunately it was rather of very elaborate decoration and called something like the Grand Order Renaissance from Oman. Conspicuously green, orange, red and with diamonds. And with a gold chain, rubies, emeralds, small rubies and emeralds and diamonds of course. But how was one to get a good price otherwise. But please dear boy, please. Let's get away to positive subjects instanto. Don't you think it's time for a snifter of fresh outdoors and then to join the ladies and set our sights fair for the future.'

Completely clashing with the colour scheme, both the American ladies were bare armed and goose pimpled in red frocks in the drawing room. Florida and Virginia leafing through a magazine and shivering in front of the fire as Rashers and I joined them after checking the stables and taking a stroll in the deer park. With Kitty bringing up the rear with hot water, Crooks and Damian serving tea. The latter nervy little fucker was pretending to dust and clean about the hearth while brazenly staring directly at the ladies' tits and sizing up their legs. And especially as Virginia was practising golf swings with a golf club on the carpet and showing off a quite marvellous and differently shaped arse than one had ever seen before. And presumably the new world developed the globe of their buttocks that way. But one was more than somewhat alarmed at the liberty being taken with this athletic demonstration especially of such an un-aristocratic game as golf. And such ruddy cheek depressed one immensely. Although worn and a little shabby, this floor covering was both rare and of some considerable value. And good god, imagine she might take divots up out of the carpet. However, Crooks's look of utter shock and surprise did make the lady stop mid swing. And in so doing put her number five iron right through the pink silk shade of an old, albeit disused, table lamp. Then plonked the club next to her chair as she sat to take tea.

'O gee gosh, I'm sorry I hit that old lamp.'

Everything was gosh this gosh that. Or else O gee that's really interesting. Or hey gee that must be really old. Of course all this was the first intimation of disaster to be revealed at tea in the drawing room. Where everyone was freezing and attempting to politely get as close as possible to the fire. The Yanks both standing planting their arses blocking the glow and behaving as if not taught such manners as allowed others to enjoy the radiant warmth. Lavinia and Christabel who were already changing furniture round were also giving orders to everyone in the household to dance attendance upon them. And were now immediately after introduction sniffing down their noses and throwing back their manes of hair over their shoulders as they sniped at the American ladies with snobbish and snide remarks concerning fabrics, nylon stockings and architecture. Achieving pregnant pauses before dropping hints as to the important balls and parties of the socially high and mighty they were invited to and had recently attended in London and of which of course the pair of Yanks had never even remotely heard. Town houses and stately homes of lord and lady this, and earl and countess that which were still standing and had not been bombed to smithereens in the war. My god one did rather squirm and want, if not to puke, then to at least unbutton one's fly and piss all over them. And then just at the moment Rashers and I were attempting to introduce

316

a little mild democracy to make our guests feel welcome, Lavinia point blank dared to ask Virginia.

'And who invited you here.'

Poor girl did turn to look to Rashers, who was of course already busy in a distant corner of the room estimating the value of a Meissen figurine. Then Virginia glanced at Florida. And then at the door for some means of escape. And I'm sure she did not look at me for an answer in case I vomited again. Thank god Crooks was back with hot scones upon which there was an immediate descent. And all were busy sipping at their tea cups and hungrily munching. And Rashers smilingly rejoicing over his handiwork. But then before I could interject some polite subject, such as Ireland's influence on Georgian architecture, Christabel made an inquiry.

'And where are you from in America.'

'We're from Bronxville.'

'I see. We were under the impression you were from Newport in the state of Rhode Island. The Bronx. Isn't that like that awful place Brooklyn one has heard about where some people we understand are born and actually live.'

Rashers choked, coughing explosively right in the middle of his scone, sending buttery crumbs, clotted cream and blackberry preserve splattering in all directions. And with a gasp upsetting his rather scalding tea into his lap and jumping up out of his chair, clutching his privates, a great dark stain in his cavalry twill trousers and more than warming whatever erection he was sporting at the time as he hopped from one foot to another in the manner of a fast gavotte.

'O dear, O dear, O dear, milordship.'

Crooks exactly at the moment delivering a refill of hot water. Rushing to offer his towel. And wouldn't you know tripping promptly on the carpet and crashing headlong into the tea table, crushing scones, putting an elbow in the butter and his face directly into the clotted cream. Crooks's monocle dislodging nearly at the same time as Rashers's own monocle fell out of his eye. At least one could look upon the débâcle as some sort of unison. The poor pair of Yanks were aghast. And Christabel and Lavinia exploding with uncontrollable laughter. Rashers of course did have one terribly obvious hard on. Which, dabbing at it in its soaked and twitching condition, made it even more conspicuous. And, having executed a further double shuffle mazurka and pas de deux, Rashers was stammeringly making an announcement.

'I hope ladies you will please excuse me while I go change.'

With a slightly strained smile Rashers bowing deeply as he exited the room past Crooks, who was wiping from his person the larger smears of butter and cream. Which seemed to convulse my sisters further. At least for the moment it had got us off the socially embarrassing question of various seemingly taboo geographical locations in America. Until, would you believe it, Christabel, undeterred by Rashers's clearly scorched penis and poor old Crooks hobbling away, took up further interrogation.

'Well do please enlighten us, girls, about the Bronx. We are you know so interested in America. Forgiving of course your lacking in an ancient culture such as ours. But you did help us a little to win the recent war.'

'Bronxville is not the Bronx.'

'Well goodness what is it.'

'It's a small village.'

'How nice to be in the countryside.'

'No there is no real countryside to speak of.'

'Well then, how on earth is it a village. And with such an awful name.'

'Well it was once surrounded by farms I imagine.'

Florida looked at Virginia and Virginia finally looked at me. Actual fear on her face. Good god. It was awful. Since I was sure I was showing apoplectic alarm myself over the portent of what had been revealed, whacking one across the back of the head like the great bough of a tree. The poor American

318

girls completely nonplussed, obviously trapped in snobberies totally strange to them. But clearly if they did not come from Newport they had to come from somewhere. And that imponderable was now shaking me down to my utter socks. And in order to keep down and calm the jam and cream coated scones that had comfortably entered my stomach, I announced my own departure on the pretext that one had to check the stables to see the horses had their water and hay. Which indeed one had to do anyway in order to see if they were groomed for tomorrow's hunt. But instead of another disgorgement one was feeling the most awful dull pain at the base of the spine which then seemed to reach like a great clutching hand of doom up one's arse. And something, perhaps the unaccustomed draught, made me cross the front hall to the north east parlour and to push open the door which was just ajar. And there in the darkness and by the glow of the fire was Rashers on the sofa, holding his head in his hands. One stopped not wanting to intrude, knowing that Rashers was well and truly hurt. But at a groan of the floorboard, as my weight lifted from it, he looked up.

'No. Don't go Darcy. Please. Come in. I'm just sitting here. Figuring out how best to explain to you.'

'Then you knew, Rashers.'

'Dear boy, in a manner of speaking, perhaps. But in fact, and in absolute truth, I rather more suspected than actually knew. If you gather what I mean. I know you must be heartily tired of my excuses offered to cover what you must regard as just another sham. But there is you see a perfectly justified rational reason behind everything. Virginia is actually related to this very rich aunt who lives in, and is a doyenne of, Newport society and through whose good offices all of this was arranged. Indeed she is a distant aunt of an aunt of mine. And who assured me of their bona fides. And dear boy please believe me when I say, I am myself thunderstruck by the revelation made in the sanctity of your drawing room. You see, over recent years, you know, some people have, due to the lack of proper servants, removed from their large mansions in Newport. But you see, it's not as bad as you think. From what I understand Bronxville is not as bad as your actual Bronx. Actually I am informed on good authority that more than some of the people there are not only quite rich but are socially registered.'

'Damn this social bloody register Rashers, how did you manage to get it all wrong.'

'But dear boy I haven't. The aunt living in Newport assures me both these ladies are from appropriately good families.'

'I did not realize we were looking for good families Rashers. I would have imagined that that was sine qua non. I was under the impression we were looking for rich ones.'

'Of course we were dear boy and that's why one referred to Newport.'

'But bloody hell not to places called the Bronx.'

'Yes I admit not to places called the Bronx. And the only possible hint one had that anything was amiss was when it was quite definitely and inescapably made known that I was to pay the Shelbourne Hotel bill. But you know how rich people so enjoy to sponge on others if they can.'

'Which means Rashers that we are really, aren't we, barking up the wrong tree. Those girls don't even know Regency furniture from Empire. Or for the matter of that, as you distinctly heard yourself, an Adam chimneypiece from a ruddy hole in the wall.'

'But their bodies dear boy, their bodies. And their innocent gaiety. You admit they're beautiful.'

'But I am not marrying a bloody body Rashers. And were one looking for innocent gaiety I should think that might be found in some abundance up in the suburban drawing rooms of Dublin.'

'O dear boy. I am sure there is some misunderstanding here

320

which one can put right in a trice. I mean Virginia's father is in the oil business. Florida's family are prominent in the milk business.'

'Good god, milk. I'm in milk. And have cows. Dozens and dozens of cows. Half of whom have mastitis. And I'm nearly destitute.'

'But Darcy don't you agree, both being such marvellous physical specimens, does make up for this temporary conundrum.'

'I would rather it were referred to as a terrible, dreadful mistake Rashers. And I may as well tell you that it is only because you are invited as guests to the ball and one is still assuming oneself to be, at least for the next twenty four hours, a gentleman, that I don't send you all packing.'

'O god Darcy, I have, haven't I, dearest friend, once more failed you. O dear. I fear I have deeply offended you. I have, haven't I.'

'You may assume in the matter what you will Rashers. But I'm not just some Dublin chancer that you have been in the habit of dealing with.'

Rashers's head hanging down further. The fire flame glowing in the colours of his hair. The moan of a beast out in the wintry dark. The draught of wind up the chimney. And strange how silence grows intense. Made deeper by the tiny sounds one always hears.

'Darcy, my nanny who taught me manners was the biggest and most profound influence in my life. And she always said to me. That while keeping firm to your principles one should do nothing unforgivably cruel. And I have, if nothing else in my life, always tried to adhere to that. She said too, always go where you might be expected to go and do what you are expected to do because you are thoughtful and kind. And never, never let a friend down. Or let the deceit of the outside world intrude upon one's own honesty. And Darcy, one does you know occasionally make sacrifices in this world. And then, I fear, because as you know it is not done to boast or brag, to suffer to keep one's compassion to oneself.'

'But good god, Rashers you're forgiven, forgiven. One is not to let the possible dearth of wealth in one's future to cause you this sort of anguish.'

There in the gentle glow of firelight. The window panes which looked out upon the front parklands were shiny black against the darkness through which one suddenly heard the hoofs of the wild stallion pound. Rashers's lungs seemed to take in a great breath of air and his shoulders abruptly shook with an awful heart rending sob. One knew that nothing now I could say could console. And that it was a moment best left to his privacy. But the sight and sound of his sadness came with me as I went lugging a Tilley lamp out to the stables. And as always, such excursions brought one quick back to the irritations of reality. As you might know there were still left the glowing embers of a fire in the tack room and the audience of empty seats around it. Finding all too soon that although Petunia was readied for hunting the rest of the horses were without hay or water and their stalls in a filthy condition.

'Bloody god damn hell.'

My shout I'm sure was heard across the parish. Having then to go get my boots and with a pitch fork to shake out and put down clean straw, fill buckets and throw hay down from the lofts. I was myself now in an unkempt condition. Flecks of muck in my hair and pieces of old rotten hay down my back. And with Petunia shivering without food, one had to stand on a stool to rub the chill out of the poor mare's ears which she found highly irritating as she munched her hay. All the while as one did this one was thinking of nudging the silkily smooth softness of Durrow-Mountmellton's tit against my face. And wondering at the same time if the American girls' tits would be equally soft. Or as beautifully bountiful as Mollie's.

With the Tilley lamp gently hissing, Darcy Dancer crossing the slippery cobbles of the yard and returning by the servants' side door into the house. Removing boots and progressing down the servants' corridor and past the servants' dining room and the voices inside. And feeling one was being watched. A new terrible anxiety beginning to overcome one. For some reason passing the Gun Room one took the hidden key hanging behind the old barometer and unlocked the door. And sure enough the glass gun cabinet was open and one of my pair of Purdeys gone.

Darcy Dancer rapidly relocking the Gun Room door. Mounting back up the servants' stairs. And stopping to look into the school room, where, with its old blackboard and maps of the world Mr Arland and I spent so many hours together. And now all that is left is a damp musky smell and lonely memory of that dear man who tried to drill erudition into my head. Then along the hall, candles flickering. Look again into the north east parlour. Rashers gone. Rush across the front hall to the main stairs. A distant screech of a donkey braying. Outside the wind rising and rain falling. Will drown the scent tomorrow. Why does it take only two seconds to get hysterical in the calmness of the countryside. And feel an awful doom as if proceeding to a guillotine. As one moves quickly down the ill lit hall past bedroom doors and turns the corner to go along the corridor where Rashers said he always preferred to stay in what was known as the Blue Room. One knocks. And waits. And knocks again. And no reply as one calls his name. Push open the door. Look around the corner of his dressing screen. His sparse luggage. Three candles alight. Embers of his turf fire glowing. And one's heart quickens. With a terrible premonition. That something awful has, or is about to happen. But much more awful than the awful thing that had already happened. And one found oneself repeating, he couldn't, he wouldn't, and running back, out again into the hall. Standing here not knowing which way to go. As Kitty goes by with a groaning tray. And who at least has the good manners to genuflect with a little curtsy as she passes.

323

'Good evening sir.'

'Good evening.'

'It's a sad sort of old evening now isn't it sir.'

'Yes indeed it is Kitty. Indeed it is.'

One then turns to the sound of a window opening. Which seems to come from the rarely used pink bedroom just up and across the hall. And confirmed by the whistle and breeze of a draught emerging from under the door. Turn the ebony handle. And the pearl in the centre, which as a boy I was able to reach to polish its smoothness with my finger. And the door opening. A single candle alight in a candelabrum on the bedroom dressing table casting a large shadow across the wall. And casting light down on the grey slate roof of my mother's doll's house with all its elaborate little furnishings still as they always were inside its tiny windows. As this was her bedroom as she grew up. And as if holding hands with each other, three of her dolls sitting together on a chair and propped near by a writing slate with a poem written to my mother, by her mother.

> I adore worship
> And love you so
> My little girl
> And as you play
> May tranquillity
> Always be with you
> In your solitude
> My little my lovely
> My lonely my only
> Little girl

And there he was. Rashers in his silk shirt or rather my silk shirt and gold cuff links and extremely bright emerald braces. Seated on the sill at the open window. And leaning out. My shotgun held to his head.

'For god's sake Rashers. For god's sake.'

'I was in fact going to disappear far into the distant wood, to avoid distress to your household. Or else use the room where your butlers hang themselves. But I couldn't find it. And now please don't try to stop me. In all honour I must. And just as, while one lives, one must do anything Darcy that makes it seem to others that one is still alive, one must also when the time comes, equally make sure that it is well known that one is dead. For once more I have let you sadly down. And it is only now for me to end it all. And blast the blood and gore of my skull out the window. And deposit my brains in the rose garden below. And which need only to be dug in well and will in the spring bring added colour to the blooms. And by the way I do admire this splendid Purdey.'

Of course all of this rhetoric was slightly more gloomy than glad but was so theatrically dramatic and so typical of Rashers that I found difficulty in suppressing my laughter. Or to maintain a sense of urgency in one's voice. Wondering how long he might keep up this ridiculous charade, especially as I could see he was absolutely freezing his balls off. And something made me think that suddenly Rashers would break into song and sing one of his enchanting ballads, just to put me off the scent of what he was really up to, which was to get my Purdeys to the pawn shop.

'Damn it Rashers, do come to your senses and get a grip on yourself. And stop all this.'

'Darcy. Please Darcy don't come any closer. Or you'll be in the way of the blast. I know you know that the high moral standards the English were credited with before the war have taken a terrible knock. And they and such as me may now rather grubbily behave in an occasional spivvy manner. But contrary to what you may have ever thought of me, or which may have ever seemed to be the case, believe me when I say I have never deliberately done the dirty on you nor been any kind of your serious materialist. Nor, at what I am about to

325

further say, do I want you to think I am a sentimentalist. There on the dressing table you'll find a message addressed to you, sealed in an envelope. Alongside it lies my wallet. Not much in it. But do please see that the contents are given to my beloved up in Dublin. There is you'll find a small photograph of me as a little boy that I should like the dear girl to have. Never should I have abandoned her. And I ask now only one supreme favour of you. That you do one day take my dearest to dine at the Kildare Street Club. So that she may mount the steps and enter the ladies' entrance. You know she did have her comforts. One did sink into her as one does into a pleasantly overstuffed but familiar mattress. And for all her girth in the wrong places she did still look so attractive telling me to fuck off in the lobby of the Shelbourne. She was wearing one of her awfully large hats she wore to the races, blocking people's view from behind her. But she did always love pretty frocks and girlish adornments. At times a little overdressed one might say.'

'Well for god's sake go back to her Rashers instead of killing yourself.'

'I would if I could dear boy, but I fear there is truth in the gossip that she has taken up with that awful old queer who has an electrical appliance shop close enough to Grafton Street to make him presume he's catering to the carriage trade. But one never worries about old disasters my staunch friend because there are always soon newer and bigger ones to take their place. Bye bye my dear boy.'

Although Rashers had on more than one occasion previously threatened to take his life, indeed nearly made a habit of it, one realized that he could just as easily be deadly serious. And one felt slightly ashamed at the thought that went through my brain of my Purdey or Purdeys soon going on their way up to Dublin to be delivered by Rashers to the pawn broker. And bargaining with his English vowels superseding those Irish where it mattered most. But it seemed clear now that he was

326

as surprised as I was over the American girls and was finding it difficult to rebuild his burnt bridges on the way back to his betrothed. And one took the opportunity in our seemingly calm conversation to come still closer to him across the bedroom floor. If rushed, he would of course fall out the window and still get killed breaking his skull unless one used sufficient force to send him flying out past the hard flagstones which straight below paved the ground outside the basement windows, where on clement summer days old Edna Annie sat darning socks. But even if he catapulted far enough to reach the soft ground of the rose beds, he could still break his neck. In any event there was no doubt whatever of one's sensory organs tingling with the dreadful anticipation. As there is nothing quite like the nervousness one feels in grappling over a shotgun which might be loaded.

'Rashers, none of this marrying for money matters a bloody damn, put the gun down.'

'Dear boy, it does matter. I had so hoped to help make certain that your illustrious name and all that you have here at Andromeda Park might endure. Nor, for myself, can I countenance the remainder of my life being spent further suffering the evils one's impoverishment seems to incite so signally in others. And too. And more especially. It's when you can't feel sorrow or sadness any more that you know that you are weary of the world. And lastly now I merely ask that you leave me privately to my fate.'

Darcy jumping towards Rashers. Grappling. Rashers raising the gun out of reach with a deafening roar. A shotgun barrel blasting out two panes of the window. And as the next barrel goes off, a hole appearing in the shutter. And the two of us on the floor before the open window. I could tell it was my silk shirt and gold cuff links Rashers was wearing. His front teeth and the gap between them, which gave him his once ever ready smiling face, now left a visage wreathed in seriousness. And as one struggled up, outside down below one

327

heard the bleat of sheep, loose out of their paddock and clearly wreaking their way through the gardens around the house.

'Good god Rashers. The bloody gun was loaded, the safety off. You meant it.'

'Of course I meant it dear boy. But would you mind, you're standing on my ankle.'

'Sorry.'

'And I'm sorry dear boy about the awful damage I've done.'

'Not to worry Rashers. I'll have the men put it right post-haste. Just a few old anciently pink irreplaceable panes of glass and a bit of shutter missing. Which has taken with it my mother's initials she scratched there as a little girl.'

'O god Darcy. I swear honestly. I'm so mortally sorry. I've clearly long outstayed my welcome in your life. I'm a fraud, a ponce, a chancer and fortune hunter, but I should rather die than ever hurt you again. And at least one's death will then be sudden and not after a long and painful illness bravely born.'

> And while yet I live
> Should it be ever
> Within my power
> I would nae
> Let
> Ill luck ever
> Befall thee
> As it has
> Befallen
> Me

20

Dressed to hunt this day before the ball, one stood staring into the future as one put more turf on the Rent Room fire to make a blaze. Last night Dingbats, whisperingly asking for admission, was knocking on my locked door. And already nightmarishly worried by her getting pregnant, if she were not already, I pretended to be asleep. Then by the time my desperate randiness got me out of bed to let her in, she was gone, leaving me with a hard on to keep me awake. And one was not about to go stumbling in the dark up to her room and perhaps meet Crooks in a similar indelicate state of dress and lecherous intent.

Before my own breakfast came, one could hear the constant thumping feet along halls bringing other breakfasts up to guest bedrooms. When Kitty arrived with my tray, my sausages were cold and congealed and my toast soggy and my soft boiled eggs hard as rocks. She'd also forgotten the butter. So much for service to the Master. And here at my fingertips on the Rent Room table a foot thick stack of bills under my mother's paperweight. Dinner last night was a litany of débâcles. Everything burned or overcooked, with the kitchen stove throbbing red to keep hot the water filling the baths in the house. Neither Yank would touch the rabbit stew and they were suspicious of even the potatoes. And to everything the American girls said in their attempts to be friendly, there was an archly sarcastic tone of reply from my sisters.

'O gee aren't these little cabbages cute.'

'They are actually called Brussels sprouts.'

'You mean they come from Brussels.'

No one seemed to know where they came from but just as one might have imagined might happen, Dingbats did flood gravy over the vegetables and took the opportunity of letting drops from the sauce boat drip down the American ladies' cleavages. Over which Damian was also hovering to get a look, while neglecting to provide a serving spoon for the sprouts. The Yanks too were obviously shocked at Count MacBuzuranti's risqué conversation. Reflecting back on his international days as a ballet star, he kept elaborating on the special support he required to have tailored for his large private parts when he danced Swan Lake in Milano. Then Rashers, who seemed so shortly after his attempted suicide to have regained his usual verve, made an equally embarrassing reference heard up the whole length of the table.

'And speaking of the beauty of private parts, I trust your famed, exquisite old tits Lois are still hanging these days in the Louvre.'

'Yes. Just as I am sure your leathery old dried up foreskin should hang tacked up somewhere as a reminder to all, of your unattractive rudeness.'

And now five bloody minutes past eleven o'clock before Damian arrives in the Rent Room. He of course, all through dinner last night while passing in and out of the pantry and thinking he was out of my earshot, referred to the American ladies by their Christian names. There also could be discerned a smell of whiskey off his breath as he served. Then came from the pantry the sound of a resounding slap delivered by Mollie, the imprint of whose hand was left across his jaw for the trouble he took to goose her. And now the little upstart walks in without knocking and slouches with his hands in his pockets. A ruddy smirk on his face and utterly indifferent to having kept one waiting. Making one tempted to announce that as Master of Foxhounds, one's rank exceeded that of the local curate in the town. And that his insolent behaviour could result in being locked a week in the cellars where he ought to be anyway.

'You're late.'

'I am late sir as I was busy taking up turf to the bedrooms. With Mr Crooks giving me the dirty jobs to do.'

Darcy Dancer staring across the Rent Room table. Under scrutiny Damian shifting from one foot to another. His hands slowly removing from his sides to behind his back. As one could see they were comparatively clean and that he was miles from any turf. But one was not tempted to trap him in his deception, knowing it would lead only to prolonging the interview with even bigger and more blatant lies. Plus one could always be sure that this particular very left footed Catholic would still deny his deceitful deed even when caught red handed.

'In this house and at all times, all guests are to be addressed by their proper surnames and titles. Do you understand. And in the case of ladies, as her milady or as miss, madam or ma'am. Nor are they to be stared at. And chairs in the library are not for you to occupy. And when you are given an order by Crooks, you are to undertake to obey immediately and without question. Am I understood.'

'Well it isn't right I should be obeying a stupid eegit prevert like him who thinks he's god almighty working here for thirty years. Sure he could hardly get himself anything better.'

'What's that.'

'Well begging your pardon Mr Kildare sir. He is a prevert.'

'The word is pervert.'

'Well the man is not the same man after dark as he is during daylight. Wasn't I invited up for more than devilment to his room.'

'How dare you. Attempt to slander Crooks, how dare you. Stand to attention and take that sneer off your face or you'll be sent on your arse out the door on the end of my boot. Let there be no more nonsense out of you.'

One could see Damian's hands brought from behind his

331

back, tightening into fists. And one would have loved to have had the excuse to let fly at him. But the accusation concerning Crooks was probably the only truthful comment Damian had uttered in his lifetime. But best to take a strong bloody line on the matter. In any event Crooks, sporting frilly knickers and issuing invitations, keeps more and bigger troubles from arising. Of course old Count MacBuzuranti didn't help one bit by tweaking Damian on the cheek in the front hall and asking.

'And what my dear lovely boy is your nice name.'

The door closing after Damian. The feel of a cold breeze. The sound of an aeroplane passing somewhere in the sky. From Rineanna to Dublin or Dublin to Rineanna. And one always rushes to the window to see. Catching sight of the two engined passenger plane disappearing into some low clouds. O god how does one live surrounded by all this falsehood. They'd even come running at you shouting that the sun was dancing in the sky. And as exaggeration costs nothing why not make use of it liberally. But they're best at covering their tracks. And tell you straight to your face didn't a fox come and take the missing turkey and goose and the two hens and the three dozen eggs. Sure any decent fox worthy of the name would make a selection to suit his appetite. And one goes on with one's attempts at discipline. Making oneself as conspicuous as possible with one's footfalls echoing along the lengths of the halls. And heels on the cobbles out across the stable yard where one could see the turf smoke from the chimney. And then hear, as the guilty shifty eyed bunch of them heard me coming, the slothful gang of them knocking over buckets and chairs as they jumped up from around the fire in the tack room. Up on their feet and pretending they were on the job. Of course the stupid arses never troubled to realize that all one has to do is examine the tarnished working parts of any implement to know that they, lazy sods, were doing fuck all. But yesterday in the darkness of late afternoon, as they all grabbed tools on my approach and bolted for the tack room door, Luke was not to be seen. And one assumed he at least was at work. But when I then got the lantern to go see how Petunia was getting on in her stall, wasn't Luke there. And by the sound if not the smell of it, putting plenty of effort into what he was doing. For with his trousers down and puffing away on two cigarettes, one in each corner of his mouth, he was busy taking a shit in a shiny new milk bucket under the warmth of the mare's belly.

'Begging your pardon sir, me trousers slipped down from me burst buttons and I be trying to see as to what might be amiss up under Petunia's belly.'

The tiresomeness of it all being so extreme, one did not bother to play pop with Luke over his foolish fib and efforts to provide comforts for himself. But one strongly bloody well objected to the use of a new milk bucket and the dreadful stench emanating from same and which, with two cigarettes puffing away, was clearly assailing Petunia's outraged dilating nostrils. My god, nearly three thousand acres available to take a shit in, and lots of fresh green laurel and rhododendron leaves with which to wipe your arse and here this unconscionable fucker has the witless gall to affront my standards of sanitation and insult the dignity of my mare. Never mind the fact that Petunia detests cigarette smoke.

'When you find out what is amiss up under Petunia's belly, muck out this stable.'

'She does now, Mr Kildare sir, betimes be getting an itch up under here sir that I do be scratching sir.'

'Well do be mucking out when you're finished scratching and Petunia's finished scratching and get rid of that bit of mouldy hay there, and give her a bit of oats. And put the straw high up around the walls.'

'Right you are Mr Kildare sir. Right you are sir.'

One then, before setting off to hunt, had inspected the ballroom festooned with flowers. Despite the odd dilapidation of peeling paint and odd bits of crumbling plaster showing through the walls, everything was looking reasonably smart. There being just enough embellishment to distract. The gilt mirrors shone. And the gold drapes kept for the occasion of a ball were hung. The family portraits dusted down. Not wanting to crow about it, but one did feel a certain awe for one's existence while looking at one's lineage so displayed. And at least one room at Andromeda Park was an optimistically cheerful sight, polished and gleaming, with Sexton suddenly dancing in the door. His secateurs biting like a fish as he smiled from ear to ear. Happier looking than I think I had ever seen him, and with whom one had not these past few days had a chance to chat.

'Ah Master Darcy won't we be all tossing away our crown of thorns. The ball's to be a great treat. Sine dubio. We'll be well ready with every beauty in the book to knock out the eye. Just leaving the one left like the one still intact in my own old head.'

And just outside the half open ballroom door one then did hear the familiar voice of one's former dancing teacher Count MacBuzuranti. Presumably pausing to view my portrait hanging there. His arrival with Lois at Andromeda Park was bizarre enough. Italian ruddy flags waving out the windows of two limousines loaded with his friends and with both his chauffeurs sounding their horns all the way up the drive.

'Ah Lois my dear you are so wonderful, how you paint. Equally as magnificent as the portrait you have done of me. Such marvellous definition and light you give to this side of the face of the so handsome young Kildare. Especially I like so much the eyes. They are like the great Giovanni Boldini painted eyes. And mine god such eyes he painted. Ah but speaking of the devil. Who should be right here but the lovely handsome Darcy Dancer himself, and all in such marvellous pink, to make him so beautiful, n'est-ce-pas. Ah but how good to be among you all again. The wickedly moral and the respectfully immoral. I should too perhaps ride the horse after the fox and sit then for my portrait in my pink.'

334

The Count Brutus Blandus MacBuzuranti O'Biottus sporting an extraordinary exaggeratedly horsy cavalry twill suit. Cut so rakishly that one might think he was already atop a steeplechaser running at Aintree in the Grand National. Lois done up for warmth as usual and giving not a single hint as to her quite marvellous body beneath about fifty Aran Island sweaters, thick tweed skirt and heavy grey wool stockings. Never mind her sensuous feet disguised in stout walking shoes. And yet so astonishing that upon seeing her I should get an immediate tingling in the groin.

'Lois you look lovely.'

'You flatterer Darcy. No wonder I do so like tweaking that cock of yours with which you are so well endowed.'

As one had to hunt, one had to rather rush on one's way. Bedrooms not already full were certainly filling with MacBuzuranti's friends. Some of whom now coming into the ballroom hallway positively minced and sounded twice as queer as the Count. And from an original seven for dinner there were now fourteen. Plus a note one did not want to look at waiting for me on the rent table in the Rent Room, that four of the very fattest turkeys had disappeared from the old hen run in the night.

'Ah sir the sooner you're after killing that fox that did it the better before he'd be back after more.'

Of course the fox that did it was walking around on two feet. And it could have been anyone one was now seeing among all the old familiar faces preening about here at the pub at the crossroads. And the hunt before we even started to move off was eventful enough. Several of the locals arriving early had already drunk themselves into unconsciousness on the road. And upon one of whom the Mad Major's horse stepped. Leading instantly to a whip fight with Amnesia Murphy the farmer slashing the Mad Major across the face with his whip while referring to some ancient previous insult. Then pulling each other off their mounts and wrestling down

335

into the deep mud of a ditch where they embroiled so that you could not tell one from the other. Of course Ryecrisp Brillianton rode up to complain.

'I say Master, that's rather a rum situation there.'

I gave the signal to move off to the first covert and not giving a damn since there would be at least another half dozen fights before the day was over. We found two foxes and had one good chase of at least four miles before the fox went to ground and had our first casualty. One is often said to be blood thirsty hunting and I must confess I was parched watching Baptista Consuelo arrived all the way from Manchester without her husband. And didn't she get one of her still wonderfully fulsome buttocks deeply impaled on an upright sharp prong of an iron gate. Nervy girl went on hunting, a great bloody patch left on her breeches. I must say stretched as they are on her immensely ample arse, one, for the next couple of miles, found it enticingly inspirational to imagine having it off with her from behind. And god didn't she give me a dozen or so splendidly filthy looks to do that very thing.

'You must, you really must Darcy, come over and see me in Manchester sometime.'

The muddy Mad Major, randy old bugger, came on the immediate scene, grass and cow flop pasted to the side of his face and clearly wanting as soon as possible to grab Baptista by the ears and prang her, even if it meant doing it right in the middle of our conversation together.

'Hope you don't mind Master my barging in like this.'

'Yes I do fucking well mind.'

A miracle also occurred when the already bloody nosed and sludge encrusted Amnesia Murphy the farmer got thrown on top of a stone wall, losing his cap and landing on his head. And awake now he forgot all that he'd remembered since first getting amnesia but that he could now recall all before that back down the years including up to five minutes before he was born when he was taking his first peek at the world out of his mother's womb.

Then who should cut right in front of me as if it were his prerogative but Buster Lawerlton Ryecrisp Brillianton. This ruddy previous Master, not only with his three girl grooms but over from London with his English valet and intending to hunt the whole season. And arrived in an Armstrong Siddeley motor car pulling a brand new horsebox. Behaving like some matinée idol with, in the back of his motor, a dressing table and vanity box. With his three constantly smiling hefty thighed grooms dancing attendance. One of whom was acting as a bartender, serving drinks including champagne from a great wicker hamper while he made uncalled for remarks concerning the condition of the hounds, which were admittedly a ruddy mess looking more than a little bit scruffy. But I thought his pompous behaviour and his bloody presumption that his horse was faster than mine a bit much. With his awfully English accent saying I say Master do pardon me, you are being a bit slow you know. Of course as we waited for another fox to be found he was three times full of bonhomie concerning the ball.

'I say there Kildare I hear you've got some very interesting guests staying. And damn decent of you to have me and all my grooms over to your jolly mafficking. Damn well jolly good to give this part of the world a well needed social boost.'

Of course Brillianton kitted out impeccably did lend a measure of glamour to the hunt. And made everyone of the local yokels think their social stations had risen about two octaves when he spoke to them. But I did think this prissy English fucker needed an occasional good boot up the arse. Which as it happened came soon enough a mile or so later when the fox we roused and had already chased five miles in a great circle went through a small farmer's paddock. Brillianton, again trying to upstage me, having taken a short cut, had ridden straight across the farmer's cabbage patch, with the farmer rushing shouting to irately close and lock a gate and trap Brillianton in his yard. Where as it happened the biggest and most vicious boar I had ever seen was loose. And which had in as many seconds killed three hounds.

'I say there you, lock up that damn beast.'

Ryecrisp, a good horseman and his mount dancing around on hind legs, trying to control his steed. Its kicks flying out in all directions as the boar tried to rip open its belly. Ryecrisp finally and mercifully getting catapulted backwards into the air to land feet first, sinking down into a semi liquid manure heap. And then as he tried to move, pitched forward on his face flat as a pancake. And crawling like some prehistoric lizard as he struggled up, spitting out cow dung. So damn funny I nearly fell laughing off my own horse the other safe side of the wall. Then by jove didn't he have the bloody nerve left to strut right back out across the yard, but fortunately just as his mare's hind hoof nearly removed half the boar's head. The farmer, then jumping back into his cottage, came out with his shotgun. One had to admit anyone else would have run for their lives. But to give him his due ruddy Ryecrisp, dripping moist cow flop, stood his ground.

'My good man, if I can't sock you on your jaw faster than you can pull that trigger, then I shall be quite prepared to propose to compensate you generously and buy the boar from you. Plus pay for the damage to any of your cabbages. Now there's a good chap, put down your silly gun.'

Of course one did not want to count the pounds one had already spent oneself indemnifying farmers for broken gates and fences and livestock heart attacks. But at least it prevented there being more shotguns blasting at one. And did make one feel one had a proprietary interest in the land at large. In any event the stragglers in the field had caught up and we were soon off again. But drew blank at the next two coverts. As we stood about nearly invisible in our horse steam, the hounds then found a splendidly coloured big fox that one could spot at a distance misleading the hounds as it stole its way, nipping in and out along the hedgerows and ended us up four miles

338

away after a very racy chase over a wild country of ditches, drains and boggy fields. The wind watering one's eyes and cutting sharp across one's cheeks, with the squalls of rain stinging one's face. Leaving only a handful of us in on the kill. The huntsmen and Baptista, and a young blonde girl on her first outing. Then there was Amnesia Murphy, and the whipper in and my mother's old friend the elegant Father Damian who one had not noticed in his very discreet manner of staying back with the stragglers and the faint of heart to whom he made himself available for succour as they lay injured or to administer the last rites as they lay dying. Ryecrisp Brillianton in his pompous attempts to lead the way and take short cuts had simply disappeared with both my sisters.

Blowing the horn for home as darkness finally fell, it now seemed miles from any sign of a road or even habitation. Even in the faint light I couldn't help noticing Baptista licking her lips and her eyes glistening as the hounds tore the fox to pieces. And then as one was viewing the remaining steam left of the fox on the blood stained grass, Baptista seemed strangely ethereal and beautiful in the vapours rising from her horse. And as we moved off she sidled up to one.

'What an awfully good run Master, don't you rather think.'
'Yes.'

By Baptista's tone of voice there was a clear change in her behaviour from moments before following the kill when I awarded the tail to the young blonde girl and Baptista seemed more than a little bit miffed. Bloody hell what a nuisance trying to keep people happy. And one did want to rapidly now get out of these bogs and driving rain and home into a steamingly hot bath. Baptista not far behind me as we rode on alone looking for a landmark, when suddenly she let out a yelp and I turned to see her dismount, clutching her leg.

'What is the difficulty Baptista.'
'Master I have a cramp. In the back of my thigh.'

339

'O dear.'

There was nothing for it but to dismount myself. And as Baptista leaned against her horse in the pelting rain, one attempted to assist the already injured and now seemingly incapacitated lady.

'Where does it hurt.'

'Here Master right here.'

'Here.'

'Yes Master right there.'

It happened just like the explosion of fangs that had ripped the fox into thin air. Her mouth open and her hand reaching round the back of my head and pulling my face down on top of hers. Raindrops crushed between our cheeks. The visor of my cap colliding with, and knocking off, her bowler. Revealing hair tied with a snood and cut in a style that I believe old Durrow-Mountmellton referred to as a débutante bob. Baptista's same still pretty long lashes fluttering over her large blue eyes. And suddenly the vision one first had of her on her back on a previous hunt as the hairy arsed Mental bloody Marquis pumped away between her legs and I had, on my horse, to jump over the pair of them as they lay aisle centre down an overgrown avenue of lime trees and uninterruptedly fucking. And how my poor tutor Mr Arland from a distance was so besotted in love with her. And here now, my god she is in my arms like a powder keg exploding with randiness. With one stiff prong of a gate already rammed up her backside this day. The inside of her mouth quite deliciously warm. Her writhing tongue seeming that it had not already counted all one's teeth and done a rumba with my own tongue but was now seeking to take a bite of my Adam's apple far down inside my throat. No wonder one's hard on is tearing to be free out of one's breeches. Especially as one recalls her in another vision deliciously naked, whipping the besaddled nude Mental Marquis across a Royal Hibernian bedroom floor. In the comfort of which hotel one would not mind this moment being out of this cold and drenching rain.

340

'I've come all the way from Manchester darling Darcy not only for your ball but for a good hunt and fuck.'

Out in this wild shelterless hinterland, our two horses neighing, kicking, snorting and screaming up a storm, ensnared in their reins. Baptista was out on a stallion which fact soon made itself more apparent as the great seventeen and a half hand brute, with his massive shaft, like a bolt of lightning striking, went for my sixteen and a half hand mare Petunia, their hoofs sending sparks off the stones in the road. And not wanting to get kicked in the ruddy head, one shooed away the horses. Then we fell to the wet but hard ground and one realized one was on an old road where there was only minimal shelter from biting wind and none from the rain. But aside from bumpy stones pressing up into one's arse, wouldn't Baptista have to land upon a small but prickly gorse bush. And as she tried to yell ouch and as our mouths were glued together, her teeth clamped up on my tongue which was just on its way eagerly heading down her throat in the direction of her own invisible Adam's apple.

'Ouch.'

'Sorry Darcy. I bit you.'

'Quite all right. Just a little blood.'

Strange and perhaps not so strange how, as old Baptista and I juxtaposed into a decently comfortable position, one began to feel rather mechanical with having had it so recently pounding up Mollie. That women were just inclined to use one at their whim. And Sexton's words came to mind in reference to cutting hedgerows. Not unremarkable I suppose considering present circumstances. Ah Master Darcy no matter what way you reach, pull or cut with your slash hook you'd get the rip of a briar across your face or a spike of a blackthorn stuck deep in your thumb or arm. Until after a while you'd feel like poor Jesus did himself torn to bits by his sad crown of thorns.

'O Darcy, Master. Come into me.'

Even with frozen stiff hands, amazing the renewed energies

one resurrected to tear down both our breeches. And now at least my prick, sinking silkily in, found a nice warm cosy place to go. Then somehow this body one held became slenderer and darker and sadder and more lonely like the one which one had never touched and yet had been the one body one so longed to touch. Leila. Whose dark eyes anointed me. Whose vertebrae I wanted to kiss from the top to the bottom of her spine. Who said once that all she wanted was someone of her own to long for and want her. Here now in the inclement night. Here now on this stone hard ground. I remember. Another strange vision not that long ago on a late January cold winter's day. The sky clear and a heavy mist falling with evening. I went to examine a tumbled wall and to check the progress of the hedge cutting over its last few days. Climbing over a broken rail fence into a boggy field. Crossing to where the spring is, its marvellous sweet cool water bubbling from the ground. And then walking along the stream, watching down upon the mirror darkness of its surface and further to where it passes along by the bog adjoining the lake. And suddenly to stop. To look up and see veiled in the mist, only slightly more than a stone's throw away, the back of a figure standing facing towards the lake. And through the great old beech trees, their shadows and stumps, I could not be sure it was not an apparition as I watched, waiting for it to move. I could see what seemed to be a woman's head in a black babushka. And if it were a person trespassing, the figure stood so still I somehow could not get myself to disturb their tranquillity. I walked away further along the stream. And then stopped again. Suddenly sure I'd seen, out of the vague corner of my eye, a movement. When I turned fully around to look, the figure seemed to be gone. Then, when I walked still further away and crossed the stream so I would not impinge upon the silence, I again saw the figure, a dark shadow on the foggy boggy landscape. I could make out what looked like a man's overcoat and wellington boots but I somehow was

342

certain it was a woman. I was making for the edge of the lake and, as I looked back, the figure remained a solitary darkness against the winter faded rushes. Then I had the uncomfortable haunted feeling I was being watched. But in about another few yards and jumping a ditch, and turning to look back again, the figure had now utterly vanished. I went into the old boat house. Sat in the white wicker chair, nearly convinced I had been seeing things. Later, with darkness falling and returning to the house through the front parkland, I stopped and shivered. Again feeling I was being watched. I looked back. There the figure was again, silhouetted against the grey pink sky on top of the hill overlooking the lake. And I suddenly knew whomever it was trespassing Andromeda Park, knew this land. And now in curiosity I circumvented the hill out of sight to accost the figure. But as I came round and out into the clearing to where I calculated the figure to be, again it vanished as if it had never been there. And in the only direction in which the figure could disappear, I could find no trace across any part of the field of footsteps in the wet grass. And ever since. And even now as I plough into Baptista. Her body that I hold and all the bodies I have ever held. Always become that of Leila. Just as I imagined she was that figure on that late January cold winter's day.

Baptista rolling Darcy over. Shoving her whip into his hand. And climbing up on top, her wound and bare buttocks spattered by rain and cooled in the gale. Whispers and pulses of one's blood in the ear.

'Whip me Master, whip me. On my right side. Just this last furlong to go. Lash me harder, harder across me arse.'

In an astonishing corkscrew motion, Baptista and buttocks furiously pumping down on top of me. And I did think that I was already smacking her right cheek of arse quite hard enough as one squeamishly feared she might shout out in pain if the stinging tip of the riding crop landed any harder. So

343

much for cruelty. For now I thought I was already hearing a further and strange vibration coming up through my back on the ground. And now one hears a voice nearly thinking that its one's own. Speaking out in the night. And saying to the gorse bushes near by some daft thing such as, dear girl swatting your insatiable arse is making my wrist awfully tired. Then, as one continued to bring the riding crop down as searingly as was seemly on the ample curvature of her rump, a light beam came shining down into one's eyes over Baptista's shoulder and illuminated and enumerated the new red welts appearing across her nether chastised cheek.

'I say, what is the difficulty here. I say there. Stop. Stop that thrashing at once, whomever you are. Can't you see you have drawn blood.'

One of course couldn't see the blood but did recognize at once behind the glare of the torch beam, the voice of Ryecrisp Brillianton and the hoofs of more than one horse with him on the old road. But with Baptista's continued and increasing frantic gyrations and her moans and groans, one did think she deserved her paroxysms. And amazing how one in this unwelcome spotlight had the nerve to administer at least half a dozen more resounding wet whacks. But one suspected Brillianton's attention to be more drawn to the up and down oscillatory motion of Baptista's backside than the identity of my surprised face.

'I say. To you down there. Enough's enough.'

But good lord you'd think old Brillianton had had enough for one day. Already landing himself in the shit without now wandering lost across the ruddy bleak black countryside trying to prohibit ranking gentry indulging in a little healthy erotic outdoor deportment. And the prissy prurient bugger, can you imagine now feasting his torchlight on Baptista's arse, while sporting the intonations of the outraged Englishman condescendingly calling to book a bog trotting farmer out for a day's hunt. And now even though I did stop raining blows of

344

her whip down upon Baptista's bottom, she, however, did not stop thrusting down her bifurcation upon mine and even seemed to be incited to a new rapidity one always hoped one would find in the action of the pistons of the Dublin train heading out to the midlands, when that train had its boilers bulging with glowing turf and was making up time, chugging as fast as it could upon the straight across the Bog of Allen. But in this darkness upon this ground, the rain cutting through the beam of light upon her, Baptista rode me as one did ride out one's troubles on a good horse. And then my god I was coming. Just as Baptista was surely coming. And just as the worst of all embarrassments to come, came. With my sister Christabel's voice. Ringing out loud and clear.

'I say Lavinia, it's our brother Darcy. Who is in some spot of bother.'

> Ah dear sisters
> Not entirely so
> For
> Our horses were
> Fucking and now
> So
> Are we

21

One was beginning to worry that one would be late for one's own ball this night, as it seemed an endless time stumbling across the deeply poached ground and slopping through the water logged bog before Baptista and I found our horses, to then hack back more than six miles via dubious short cuts scratched and soaked to Andromeda Park. Which was not the worst of matters as one had to listen to a mournful recital from a panicked Baptista.

'Gossip of this will be all over Manchester I promise you. Brillianton hunts with the Quorn. And two of my close friends do as well.'

Of course as one might have known by the straight faces suppressing their smiling smirks, word had reached the stable yard before reaching Baptista's husband back in Manchester. In any event pranging the old girl or the old girl pranging me left one's loins still glowing even as one was straining all leg muscles to pull off one's boots. Finally catching a heel in the fire fender and stumbling into my dressing table and putting a sizeable bump on my previously unscathed head. The rest of my soggy hunting kit, with one's coat weighing a ton, cast away in a heap. Making post haste to one's ablutions. Kitty delegated by Crooks to draw my bath. With my bathroom fire only smouldering, one did hesitate a moment at the somewhat glacial appearance of the water with not a molecule of steam rising. But such was the chill of one's frozen hands and feet and with the rest of the naked me quickly cooling, one immersed rather than stepped into the bath.

346

'Ahhaaaaa.'

In my howl of agony followed by much louder howls of rage I must have sounded like some jungle animal. The bloody water absolutely ice cold. And one knew with one's tug that one had lengthened to breaking point the wire down through the house to the wall outside the kitchen in the servants' hall where the servants' bell to my apartments rang and must have jumped off the console as it did. Even then by god it was an unseemly time before anyone arrived. And as I stood shivering in a towel, it had of course to be Mollie.

'The guests your honour have used up all the hot water.'

'I'm frozen Mollie.'

'Ah now your honour, I'll unfreeze you. Soon as you get it to stand up.'

Mollie grabbing and ripping away Darcy's towel as he grabbed for it back. Mollie fleeing to the bedroom. Darcy in pursuit. Candles fluttering.

'Just a cuddle your honour.'

'No Mollie, and please don't call me your honour. We must have a mind for my having to attend to matters. Chop, chop as it were. And don't wear that hangdog face, your suggestion is appreciated entirely.'

'Fine for you, chop, chop now isn't it. We is it. We must mind is it. To have enough of me is it. With now all your worshipful ladies about in abundance.'

'Mollie I haven't had enough of you. I mean I want more. But at this exact time I need and must have a hot bath.'

'Well you can go to purgatory and scorch yourself before I'll bring you a thimbleful of lukewarm water.'

One waited for a slate to slip from the roof with the concussion of Mollie slamming my door. Then one sat shivering out the lengthy delay during the relay of every available kettle and pot ferried directly from the kitchen stove. Recalling Rashers describing his military night manoeuvres and route marches as he led his company of men in a training exercise

347

on Dartmoor mid December in the wet cold and freezing conditions, fording ice cold rivers with all his gear. And now in the door he suddenly arrives to borrow evening kit he was minus for the ball. Seating himself on my bed in one of my borrowed dressing gowns as one huddled, trying to get some warmth from one's feeble bedroom fire.

'My dear boy, you are aren't you quite well set up. Never seen you in a state of undress before. Now then. Heard you had a few spots of bother out hunting. But this is rather a night isn't it.'

'Gee gosh you bet.'

'O dear you still do chastise me don't you over these Americans.'

'I do Rashers yes.'

'Dear boy you must reconsider the prospects there. Now I've just learned Virginia has an uncle who hunts with the Grafton in Massachusetts. I honestly know for a fact we could be on to a good thing here and mustn't abandon.'

'Good god Rashers one is way beyond all that now. I have nothing against these perfectly pleasant girls. But on top of their obvious lesbianism they do have a rather pushy nature. And also, what I find is so peculiar, everything it seems must be described in monetary terms. Imagine saying of my hunting pink that it made me look like a million dollars. Or that I was wearing fifty dollar boots.'

'Of course Darcy you do you know, look like at least that delightful sum.'

'Well I mean one wouldn't say that looks like a two dollar apple you're eating. One would say it was sweet or juicy. Or sour and disagreeable. And calling everything as they do, cute. Hey gee isn't that cute. And if Florida says once more in her flat nasal vowels, that another thing or person is very interesting, I think I shall simply have to leave the room. How could one possibly live with such a person whose conversation is so aimlessly inane. They keep referring to their boyfriends

348

as he's Yale or he's Harvard or Princeton. What the devil is that supposed to mean, as if that made them blue, black or red. Then when they pretend to be deeply intelligent. Virginia asked if I were actually Irish. And how nice it was to meet Irish who were not servants. Bloody woman was actually boasting about growing up and not being allowed to associate with anyone Irish. Can you imagine.'

'Well dear boy let's face it, the Irish out of their normal native milieu are on the whole a rather unfortunate lot. And here in their normal native milieu are even worse.'

'That may be Rashers but bloody hell at least they don't lack for distinctive character and they occasionally show a perception or two. One feels in the drawing room that any moment the Americans are about to say, hey that is a five hundred dollar mirror, instead of exulting over its being Queen Anne. I'm finding their tending being lesbian the only impressing individualistic quality they have.'

'Dear me Darcy you are in bad humour. But we must you know keep our options open in this business. I mean they could be trained up, educated in our ways. For let me tell you Darcy, there are some of these Americans dear boy who don't wait to be treated as ladies. Their fangs are flashing at one with a hissing warning of poison to be inoculated the moment they're not getting what they want. That's why one has had to be so careful in one's selection. At least these ladies are sportingly gung ho. And of course we in return must address our own questions. Hey honey baby, are you really worth one million dollars of a possibly disagreeably awkward future life that I may be forced to lead if I marry you for your money.'

'Well one thing at least can be said of you Rashers, you are the very best person to turn to for the worst advice.'

The great advantage of being utterly exhausted from hunting, one does not give a tinker's damn about nearly ruddy anything. And taking my now hot bath and soaking out the thorns and splinters from one's epidermis, and while musing on whether the most boring guests come early or late and on the astonishing ability of Baptista to administer a fuck, I fell asleep with my periscope up but the rest of me submerged, nearly drowning. Then waking to hear guests' cars already arriving early on the drive. One would prefer now not to face anything tonight and simply to go to bed. Must be stage fright. Anyway one only imagines that one must be there. For you find no one ever misses one when you're not. Plus having those two great London socialites, my sisters, who will be flaunting their roles as hostesses all over the place, there will be no lack of reception, at least towards anyone titled or important arriving. They've already complained of the smell and sign of sperm in the hall outside their doors. And that someone had been masturbating there. Ho hum just another entirely disgusting problem. The latest from the servants' dining room, however, was that everyone was now spouting off concerning their seniority and their traditional duties and especially the duties which were not theirs to perform. Bloody hell one will soon have to print up badges to be worn. Scullery Maid, Upstairs Maid, Downstairs Maid. Plus stripes on the sleeve attesting to the years of service at Andromeda Park. Making of course some of the staff look like zebras. Those females qualifying as having slept with the master of the house would of course have gold stripes and wear rosettes in the manner of the Legion of Honour.

Darcy Dancer dressing. Rain still pelting the windows. Car doors slamming outside. So hard to suppress one's compassion. And one did really try with these Americans. Meeting just the four of us, for sherry in the library, instead of in the cold chill of the Porcelain Room. The Yanks had never had sherry before and were, bless their little innocent hearts, the previous evening at dinner mystified by finger bowls and were staring at us using a fork in the left hand to lift food to one's mouth. But they did adore the trifle and whipped cream and at least, out following the hunt in the jaunting cart, exhibited the first evidence of their enjoying themselves. Although they missed old Brillianton being catapulted into the shit, they did get hysterical with laughter when witnessing a horse trapped in the deep ditch of a stream and the chaos of people getting drenched falling into the water in their attempts to pull the poor animal out in one piece. That is until a group of local layabouts nearly wrenched a leg off the poor beast not realizing that one most safely tugs a horse by its thickest part, the neck. Although, leaving this done by a stupid enough sod leads then not infrequently to strangulation. Then the Yanks were not far away when there was a complete pile up of straggling riders following one another blindly down into a narrow boreen up which was coming a snorting no nonsense bull. Attempting to reverse direction, and with so much inept horsemanship, my god did that send the ever cautious stragglers who cling together for safety hysterically galloping in all directions. But, as there was only one way to go, it ended up their practically climbing on top of each other. Then, as their ill luck would have it, didn't someone breach a hole in the boreen which led into yet another bog. The bull behind chasing them, all sinking with their horses into the muck. Upon which Brillianton of course had an opinion.

'Wonderful thing about your Irish bogs Kildare, they absorb so much concussion. An utter miracle back there. Only a handful of casualties.'

But as you might know it was reported to me out in the stables that there was a broken leg, two dislocated shoulders, one slightly dislocated eye, a badly lacerated hand, a smashed nose, two collar bones bust and a fractured wrist. And although there was minimal blood it did turn all these confirmed dawdlers involved a shade of your darker brown. And Luke was full of the story.

'Ah but one poor sod sir, a Dublin solicitor, whose head hit a bog tree stump, didn't he go immediately non compos mentis wandering unhorsed further into the bog and before

351

he was noticed was already sinking with only his head still left visible. And wasn't Amnesia Murphy the farmer shouting after him. That sure now you won't serve a writ on anyone out in that direction you eegit.'

Of course the fastidious bull had the intelligence not to venture into the quagmire and as you might know a collection of locals from the safety of roadside high ground were remarking it was the wrath of God descending on Protestant pagans.

Darcy Dancer in white tie, closing and locking the door to his apartments. Slipping the key into a pocket and striding along the corridor hall. Stopping to listen at the top of the flight of stairs. The loud volume of voices already down in the front hall. I must say. Considering the weather and the number of injured ferried away from the hunting field, this is a surprise. Only expected the hardy few. And certainly during this particular day's outing, you never heard such bloody post mortem complaint from the seasoned veterans as was heaped upon my ears concerning novices. Diatribes continued even after one had told one or two to bloody well shut up.

'Master some of these up from Dublin people should be warned off.'

There is no doubt that adorning oneself splendidly does instil in one at least a kernel of optimism which although pretended is better than no optimism at all. But O god, I could be accused. You, you naughty, naughty Master, were fucking. Dare I now plunge down these steps of ancient stairs. To reveal myself to my sisters. But with one's vision far more intent upon surveying to confront the face of one one most wanted to see. Just to be alive once more to her dark wonderful eyes in the frame of that white splendid face and skin. And just to know that she had come. All the way from Paris and from France. Had been here. And had even once thought of me. And now I sneak away down the hall. And by the sound of whomever's voice that is shouting the ball is already catching fire. Literally and figuratively.

'Sir would you come quickly, the flames are raging. The ballroom chimney's on fire.'

At least one already knew that it was only a rook's nest alight and that with luck it would soon burn itself out. But it didn't take long before some arriving guests, seeing flames and sparks shooting from the roof into the sky, refused to enter the front hall. Their loud observation of course leading to more than a moment or two of panic and the knocking of people's drinks out of their hands. Then another crush as it was with a gale now lashing pouring rain with too many trying to get back in again, with a local countess declaiming.

'I'd rather my dear die warm than wet.'

But good gracious me what a mix of people and faces one had never seen before. Nor did one lack for a variety of music for every taste. The men were playing the spoons up the corner of the ballroom. A piper marching the floor and through the house. The lady quartet down from Dublin, fiddling waltzes. All this my god in an effort to instil some permanent hope and solace in one's life. And pay for it with a price I can't afford. But somehow it was refreshing to have such as Lois and MacBuzuranti about. And at least that raging homosexualist does know how to bring someone getting too big for his social boots into permanent ridicule with a few carelessly chosen damaging words.

'Ah and you, you are far too insignificant to be even, how do you say, the pipsqueak.'

Entering the ballroom I could see Florida and Virginia were more bemused than impressed. I must confess I could feel my face flush as Ryecrisp and his girl grooms finally arrived, all still in their hunting clothes. The steam rising from Brillianton as he warmed his backside in front of the fire and covered in cow flop he seemed more than somewhat chastened but not particularly grievously embarrassed by our recent confrontation. In fact the bugger seemed more concerned and aggrieved over the substantial amount of compensation he had agreed to pay the farmer.

353

'Kildare, I should like to bloody well inquire of you what that damn greedy fellow meant when he used the expression that he would send my goolies to kingdom come. What the devil was that damn impertinent peasant talking about Kildare.'

'Your testicles Brillianton.'

'I say, bloody damn impertinent bugger. Well in any event Kildare, with my goolies still intact, I do hope you will excuse one's appearance, haven't been able to change. Coming back we rather took the wrong turning at the old quarry. And my damn bloody valet, running into the wrong company at the pub, is hopelessly drunk. Bloody well was wearing my white tie around his thigh as if he were a member of the Folies Bergère. Now then. Sorry I misjudged thinking a lady was in distress. When quite the bloody opposite was the case, of course. I mean when you see something bumping up and down like that out on a dark night where one least expects bumping up and down, you do tend to investigate.'

'Good of you Brillianton, however, to come to my rescue.'

'Ha, ha, Kildare. But what an awfully nice evening we have here. I wasn't aware of your ballroom. You know we must get to know each other better. Have lunch next time you pop to London. What.'

One had to admit old Ryecrisp was a sporting type, and even a gentleman. And he did rather add a nice sophisticated if not glamorous touch to the proceedings. Of course he made poor old Sexton hop up and down with irritation. And he would be astonished to hear I'd not ever been to London. But one did shudder to see just now as he strutted away, clapping his whip against the side of his boot, and dislodging a crust or two of his spattered hardened cow flop, his boot heels grinding it into one's newly waxed parquet floor. Of course one hears rumours of his enormous wealth. And now clearly upon sight of them he has obviously become or is absolutely about to be besotted goggle eyed over the American girls. Totally now

354

ignoring both my highly jealous sisters. And my god, how dare he manoeuvre and corner curvaceous Virginia within my earshot, commandeering her attention and clearly intending by his opening remarks to hand out a large earful of horse talk, steeped in vainglorious swashbucklery, to which Virginia in her scarlet dress seems to awe inspiredly respond.

'Gosh fox hunting it really is dangerous isn't it.'

'Well yes of course it is dangerous. Pumps up the old adrenalin a bit. But death by fox hunting my dear is of course the death one would choose when that inevitable time comes to die. It is for us country gentlemen the supreme way to enter heaven. Galloping as it were, in one's pink, boots and breeches. And to the cry of the hounds.'

'But gosh that poor little fox. Does he go barking into heaven too.'

Well well, the first sign of a wry something a little more than gee gosh that's interesting, coming from the American. And old Ryecrisp Brillianton was rather twisting his neck about a bit at that one. But I mean my god, not to put too fine a point on it, how fake and pretentiously ruddy elitist posturing can you get. Cantering bloody well into heaven. One did sometimes cringe at the swaggering self importance members of the fox hunting fraternity assumed, especially when got up in their kit and on top of their horses, lording it all over both the townsmen and peasantry. And only that one took rather a certain pleasure in doing the same oneself, one would be firmly against all blood sports. But I suppose one has to take care to present a best front to the world. And Ryecrisp was not short of suggestions, clearly not noticing the care Sexton had taken to cover the tender buds of our rhododendrons with egg shells, and recommending that I demolish my plantations and straighten out one's entrance drive.

'Rip out all that old shrubbery. Give a much better approach sight to your quite stately mansion, Kildare. I mean even by English standards this is quite a considerable house.'

355

Not having ever lived elsewhere, one really wasn't aware that Andromeda Park was anything other than a series of rooms most of which one spent most of one's time avoiding. Especially if within, one suspected lurked a member of the staff. Who were tonight at least clearly adorned in better than usual finery. And I am I must say quite chuffed at the whole scene. The American girls were certainly impressed by the particularly conspicuous recently cleaned great portrait of Christabel and Lavinia adorning the ballroom wall between the chimneypieces. Lavinia standing with her arm around Christabel as she sat under the large chestnut tree on the front lawn, a sunset behind them, and the wolfhounds Kern and Olav resting on the grass at their feet. Looking so demure and bonny in their white dresses. Even the pretty crimson ribbons tied in their hair seemed to say, it's summer, the air is sweet and we two are so happy. But then, educated away in their very proper ladies' school, they became so unlike they were as little girls. Clearly both had in England become gossipy snobs, hob nobbing with grievous snobs like themselves. And now so transformed out of their innocence. Especially having confronted their dear brother on his back on an old bog road whipping someone's wet arse while getting his brains fucked out.

Darcy Dancer turning around from warming his hands at the ballroom's blazing fire. With the familiar voice comes a familiar scent of perfume.

'Ah Mr Kildare I presume.'

Emerging from the woodwork, as it were, were other ladies now. And my heavens me, women to whom one had also made overtures to but not always whipped. Imagine good old Durrow-Mountmellton up out of the greasy oil pit into which she had fallen. And she does manage to still look enticing even sporting a cane. Indeed is looking quite stunning in her form-clinging white ballgown. Her charm and blunt tongue marvellously intact as are her risqué inclinations as she gives me a

356

little nudge with her good knee squarely in the balls, while whispering in my ear.

'And why have we not for some time now had a spanking session, you dear old boy. Or have you, you old debauchee, given yourself to attending upon ladies of the night and rent boys in pursuit of a life of degradation.'

But how Durrow-Mountmellton could look so soon so grand coming so recently out of the depths of the boggy countryside really did surprise me. God, how aspirations in a flash can change. The sudden realization that here right before me stands as good a heifer as any. With no gee gosh isn't that interesting about her. She'd really made an effort. Her golden tresses plaited beneath a tiara. And her strong haunches one had so pleasantly once encountered showing under her ballgown. And upon which one cupped one's hands as one embraced her. Although one abhors such a revolting word, she was entirely stylish. Our estates combined would make for a substantial union. Motoring up to Dublin together we could go. Park at the Royal Automobile Club. Stay at the Shelbourne. Dine at the Kildare Street Club. And next day depart leisurely for the races to watch one of our nags run who had been bred up out of our stable of previous winners. I mean one doesn't want to crow about it. But we would clearly make for an attractive couple.

'Well Darcy, cat got your tongue. When are you coming to fuck me again. Or am I no longer your brand of tea.'

It was certainly a new Rashers who came waltzing into the ballroom, Damian in his wake. Looking extremely grand in white tie. I don't think I had ever seen him quite so pleased. Grinning ear to ear, casting glances about him. Bowing to the ladies and obviously making some very flattering remark judging by the delighted look lighting up their faces. Certainly a far cry from the barrels of a shotgun. And one was reminded that he had given me a present of an elaborately framed picture of his holiness the pope in Rome, which he said all Protestants should keep at hand to remind them of that peril.

357

'Ah Darcy but there you are. This is without question an evening of evenings, a night of nights. Smyth of the Green have done you proud. Such a plethora. O god, I am glad I'm not dead and my spirit left for heaven. And the word O god dear boy does not in that context necessarily mean god, as for instance in the expression god awful. And wonderful to have no cause whatever to use such expression. You know, a splendid dinner. A wee bit of hanky panky followed by a sublime sleep. And with a vibrant appetite awaken to a wondrous breakfast. What is the meaning of life if that is not what it is meant to be. And ridding the mind of all nagging ambition. Except to back a few winners at the races. And to have been the champion salesman of all time for ladies' sanitary apparel. What.'

'Rashers. You clearly have popped off into top hole.'

'Yes I have. And feel just as Mahaffy must have felt when realizing his bons mots would, as Oscar Wilde's did, go down in history.'

'Well Rashers now do tell me, who pray is Mahaffy.'

'My god dear boy do you mean to say you don't know who Mahaffy is. Or was. Deceased of course. He is a monument to Trinity College dear boy. A veritable monument. Why even your good gardener Sexton knows who he is. Mahaffy was an exponent of epigrammatic concinnity dear boy. A quality we must aspire to and achieve. Of course you won't believe this Darcy for one moment but before I embarked upon reading medicine I had seriously thought of taking up holy orders. I would have been your sort of chap who, in those days it was required, would have taken up the defence of Trinity College. That was a moment when the buggers were dispersed in disarray. Can't remember if Mahaffy was in fact in that battle. But hoards of papist Fenians were at the college walls and railings, hungering to assault and run amok upon our exquisitely velvet green Protestant grass. Squalid, simply squalid. Treachery. We must purge and keep purged all such conspiracy from our midst.'

358

It was evident that old Rashers was not only more than quite happy but also more than a little intoxicated. But just as he waltzed off to accost a passing lady behind me, one heard the window lift and a breeze come in. Opening the shutters, a shadow of a figure dropping away. Bloody hell, here they were already, peasants up on ladders trying to spy in as news does spread far and wide whenever a hooley is mentioned to take place up at the big house. And it doesn't be long before rabble are outside clinging to sills, attempting to peer in the ballroom, or, when the inmates are drunk enough, climbing in the windows between the shutters. That is of course if Kern and Olav the hounds have not quick put them to rout with their thunderous barks that could on a still night be heard for miles. But one does have them locked up so that they don't eat the guests.

'I say Kildare, rather a good party.'

Brillianton passing by grinning now nearly as much as Rashers. Crashing his ruddy heels down and jangling his spurs. Amazing how quickly friends the English become if you present them with a little splendour. The man now seems, after swallicking down a few more drinks, to positively like me.

'And you know Kildare. I can't remember when I have ever seen such a splendid display of female beauty, right down to your lady servant over there. Have you hired her in. Or is she staff. Girl like that could be in Hollywood.'

'She is, Brillianton, a member of the staff of my household.'

The ruddy bloody cheek. Is she staff. Damn snoopy fellow. Of course one said in reply more than one should have said. The word yes would have been sufficient. But god, one does get provoked by these damn English buggers always sneakily attempting to size up one's wherewithal. Nothing, even a drab black dress, of course could disguise Mollie's fabulously flowing figure and her bountiful orangy mass of hair surrounding her bountifully freckled face. And never mind all the previous

359

arses and tits one has perpetrated one's delights upon. Mollie tops the ratings. As well as the worst of my tribulations. Coming now in the form of burning resentment. Her face positively smouldering as she in her freshly pressed household uniform walked right by as she passed out refreshments to guests. Of course after a few drinks one cared not a fig. Nice to present her with a demonstration of our different walks of life. And that she will forever be doomed to a ten bedroom house, while I remain in mine of thirty or whatever ruddy number there are. O god. Not true. Not true. Lies. Bloody damn creature has me ruddy bloody damn jealous. Even the damn marauder who pursues her had his caravan lit up with bright lights and I heard is sneering at all the guests entering the gates, perhaps it's about time one tried out a little of the old charm on her.

'Mollie please stop looking so damn miserable. And get me a glass of stout.'

'Don't you talk to me. And get your own stout. I'm busy.'

Whoops. That was short and not so sweet. Of course as the evening wears on one can slip old Mollie a goose up her arse. Or whenever opportunity presents when she is not busy as she is at this bloody moment tipping a drink down the cleavage of poor Florida and soaking her dress. O god. Why do women take each other so seriously when it comes to me. And now she's dancing attendance upon Johnny Gearoid who, as he always does, likes explaining himself and his considerably smelly presence to the assembled guests and is now loudly proclaiming.

'After ye fill me own glass up again me darling lovely Mollie, would you then give the woman in the bed more porter.'

Darcy Dancer surveying this large tall ceilinged ballroom, of candles blazing, chandeliers sparkling. And of nearly as many faces unknown as are known. Lois swirling the floor with MacBuzuranti, batting his eyes at likely gentlemen.

Lois's black gown of very see through Chantilly lace. Making her look marvellously exotic enough to be mistress of Andromeda Park. Her face handsome and regal. Good lord. Who in one's dilemma does one fuck next. And there on the sidelines, Edna Annie. As dignified as any queen seated in an upholstered chair. As if upon her throne. Her white hair plaited across her head. Her black velvet jacket and bow tie over her lacy blouse. Her ancient worn and never idle hands now so gently resting in the folds of her long grey tweed skirt. She must have been a young beautiful woman once. The childish enthusiasm in her face. As her blue eyes asparkle watch the dancers go by. Somehow so cheering to see the lady to whom one owed so much and now one had a chance to show one's appreciation for all her thoughtful kindnesses. Given unstintingly all these many years and those years the most fearful of one's young life. Her ebony silver topped cane one had given her several Christmasses ago leaning against the chair was knocked over as she thought she was seeing things as old Mollie Dingbats went swirling by. Grabbed to go dancing on the floor by Amnesia Murphy the farmer.

Rashers coming, bowing and helping Edna Annie to her feet as she laughed, being slowly waltzed around the floor. And one, I must say, just for those few moments that he did such a thoughtful kind thing, would forgive all the unforgivable that he has ever done. For he was undoubtedly the gallant gentleman when not being the rogue, ponce and chancer. And as Edna Annie became now unsteady on her feet, Rashers cradled her in protective arms to guide her safely back to her chair.

In the flickering lantern light of Andromeda Park's front porch more carriages and cars continuing to arrive. And retreating out of the crush of the ballroom one did go stand on the main stair landing to view the figures entering the front door and to again keep a look out to see if the only face I was waiting for would appear among them The crowd grown considerably. Crooks now monocle glinting, hitching up his trousers following his deep bows in greeting guests. And more than once pitching forward into their midst as if he were already squiffy screwy eyed drunk and then upright back on his heels again announcing.

'Upon my word I do apologize as I do believe I may have inadvertently unsteadied myself by imbibing too much of an intoxicating beverage.'

Luke, for a change, wasn't sitting under a horse on one of one's new buckets, but, with his sleeves of his jacket pulled up past his elbows, was helping dispense stout out to the eager hands, while of course swilling back pints himself. And there was no doubt now that with Kitty and Norah's arms around each other's shoulders and singing 'When the Sun Goes Down on Galway Bay', the entirety of the household were the worse for drink. And along with the eccentrics from the Castle who were having a tête-à-tête with the ruddy tinker, all seemed to have abandoned their social inhibitions.

Sexton in his best Sunday suit looked more like one of the town's undertakers than gardener as he sized up each guest. Some of whom Sexton referred to as suspicious customers who might have come for more than the food and drink. He had locked several doors and the wine cellar and was stationing himself strategically.

'Ah now Master Darcy, I don't mind the locals trying to get a glimpse between the cracks in the shutters, but it's them with ladders up against the wall that you'd be wary of who'd know upon this night that with cupboards open and guests free flowing everywhere that they could rob you blind. I locked up the north east parlour and the porcelain. And I'd advise too to lock up the drawing room and library.'

'Good, Sexton, I must say one does not like the look of one or two people.'

'Ah Master Darcy I'll tell you, not any are going to get out of here tonight with any tell tale bulges under their coats. You

362

can count on me for that. Fill their bellies. But not their pockets is the motto for the evening. And may the sacred heart of our lord jesus be beloved, praised and adored throughout the world on this day.'

Then as one went by the dining room jammed to overflowing and then up the school room back stairs and along the upstairs hall and down the back stairs to the ballroom, there was Ryecrisp Brillianton practically foaming at the mouth and going absolutely gaga over the American girls and behaving as if they were his long lost loves. Dancing first with one and then with the other. Festivities were reaching fever pitch, and one did suddenly feel uplifted. Then the orchestra resting, an American record was put on the gramophone. Something called 'In the Mood'. Bringing forth the more lively hoofers out upon the dance floor. Rashers among them, his feet flying out in all directions. And what now. A commotion in the hall outside the north ballroom door. Sexton adjusting his eye patch as he peers in.

'O god mortifying, nothing less than mortifying Master Darcy, leaving more than a little to be desired in protocol.'

'What is it Sexton.'

'I'm getting a cudgel I have hidden here behind the window drape. It's the gang of them tinkers have been peering in various windows and are now got drunk enough to attempt to gain entrance at the front door. And weren't their lord and ladyship over from the Castle arriving climbing up the front steps and were in the dark knocked back down on to the drive by the tack room staff I'd commandeered for the task of stopping that bunch of travellers come in over the fields. Their lord and ladyship got the bum's rush. They did. And if it weren't for their aristocratic vowels Master Darcy they'd both have had a good hiding in the rhododendrons and there'd be ectoplasm all over the place.'

One did rush out and through the mass of inmates already thronging the front hall. To find Crooks in a tottering manner brushing off the highly absent minded eccentrics from the Castle. Who seemed not to mind being mussed up a bit and their evening clothes covered in moss and dead leaves. The pair finally smilingly indoors and bemusedly awaiting Crooks to complete dancing his elaborate attendance upon them.

'Ah your lord and ladyships are you all right there now. Are you all right.'

'Of course we are all right. But do Crooks look to yourself.'

'O be gob, forgive me your highnesses, it's me braces snapped in the mêlée.'

Crooks's trousers dropped like a stone to his ankles. And revealing his customary pair of long lace trimmed pink knickers. Which wasn't the worst of matters befalling him. For as he reached down to pull them up, he was promptly pushed from behind by the tack room boys dragging past another uninvited tinker to be chucked out the front door. Crooks on his knees in front of both his lord and ladyship as if to be knighted, with the eccentrics from the Castle attempting to lift Crooks up and his trousers falling down again. At such a stage of proceedings one does then tend to opt for quieter pastures. Anyway the eccentrics of the Castle were famed themselves for their own contradictory behaviour. And one did think the time supremely ripe to withdraw and ask old Durrow-Mountmellton back in the ballroom to trip the light fantastic. But it was I who was then next in for an embarrassment. As I waited for a foxtrot to finish, an unkempt individual seen talking conspiratorially to the men playing the spoons and who looked clearly to be sleeping rough came right up to my elbow.

'Ah now aren't you a great man to be found dolled up like a prince in here at your duty. Sure you remember don't you, we had that bit of a chat out there beyond when you were mending the road. Great gas there a moment ago. They thought it was me they was throwing out when they threw out the gentry. Would you get us another fill up of this drink now.

Ah I am your sort of gentlemen here who is short of stature and long on thirst. And now let me tell you. Slip out between the shutters there a few old bottles of the hard stuff to be waiting on the sill and I'd be giving you back a few bob.'

'Ah now there'll be none of that. My job wouldn't be worth a farthing and haven't they got off duty Guards stationed every which way and that to arrest anyone taking even a crumb off the place. Sure there's two creatures already locked up down in the dungeons of this place screaming for freedom.'

'You don't say now.'

'I do.'

'Well would you fill a poor fellow up fast with his drink now and soon I'll be going.'

With enough wine down one's gullet one's brogue seemed to be working well and truly authentic. As your man the tinker gave me a thumbs up sign as one delivered to him his pint of stout, which descended his throat in two gulps, the stout foam dripping from either side of his mouth. And one waited till he skulked off between the guests and out of sight before helping Edna Annie to her feet again amid all her usual protestations. Her gnarled fingers grabbing me by the arm. It was quite astonishing that after her fall she was still quite capable of waltzing and we moved across the floor to the smiles of everyone.

'Ah Master Reginald I'm able for this no more. Soon out there I'll be under the sods.'

'Nonsense.'

'Ah no nonsense. But I suppose betimes I do still be having a joy or two.'

As I led old Edna Annie back and seated her again in her chair, Rashers summoned me to the privacy of the locked library. Where one might have guessed he had waiting one of my very best bottles of vintage champagne. He seemed stricken and somewhat panicked over the attention the Americans were receiving from every pair of legs with a prick hanging between them. And the equally surprising revelations emerging concerning both these American ladies as lawn tennis champions. Of course he did not want to be reminded of their dancing close and embracing cheek to cheek.

'Of course Darcy our big beautiful transatlantic Amazonian heiresses do that more out of amusement than anything else. And you must put all this in its proper perspective. And achieve thereby a balance of things. And all is worth it if they are only modestly rich. And we must above all things, strike while the iron's hot. Now having said that.'

'Which is Rashers saying fuck all. They are showing all the signs of being raving lesbians. And I need someone not modestly rich but monstrously rich.'

'Please dear boy, sip your champagne and cleanse your palate and let me finish. That's precisely what I want to tell you. I have new vital information. Now I'm not saying the girls' fathers own veritable streets of New York City but this Bronxville place actually has millionaires studded all over it. And these girls are not adverse to men. They merely shared a room at college together. You saw them both merrily dancing with that pompous fool still in his hunting kit. I admit of course that it perhaps might be considered that they are at the moment a little overfond of each other. I mean after all. In a foreign culture. And foreign land. And women do admire another woman's beauty. You know the sort of playful thing girls are wont to get up to. Rather just innocently prolonging their kisses on the lips a bit. I speak as a man of medicine and professed in ladies' sanitary appurtenances.'

'They are bloody well kissing in the French manner, if I may be so bold as to suggest.'

'Well yes of course. But ladies too, when they do do that, tend then to want to put their tongues down each other's throats, which if I may say so follows quite naturally. Histologically speaking, epithelial tissue is quite erogenous, and,

366

as my professor of anatomy said, can feel awfully exciting. Ah just as does this wine as it pleasures its way down into my belly.'

'Good god Rashers, the simple fact of the matter is that you have haven't you, among everything else, produced a pair of not only raving lesbians but fanatic tennis and golf playing ones who also ski.'

'Dear boy please. All's not lost. And please may I say one further thing. And Darcy our friendship knows no divide in this. Just because two girls knock tennis and golf balls about and are enamoured of each other's magnetically alluring beauty, one puts down to youthful animal spirits. You must be patient. So much work has already gone into the plan. That we must not abandon now.'

'You Rashers were, if I hadn't intervened, already about to abandon.'

'I know dear boy, I know. And in that context, let me play this record I have here on your gramophone called "I'll Never Smile Again". And may I ask of you one very last favour which I wish to have engrossed in my last will and testament. If I am ever found demised and not too very far away, will you bury me here at Andromeda Park. Please.'

'Of course Rashers, if that's what you choose and your next of kin allow. And such shall be written in my will.'

'We shall drink to it, then, the last of this wine. But now I am so ecstatically happy tonight. What a wonderful wonderful evening it is. The music. Don't you like these American ballads. The splendid laden tables. Dancing. The beauty of ladies all about us. My god, even old splendid tits Lois. She can and so often does look like an old nanny goat. But have you ever seen anything so ruddy elegant tonight. I mean why has that woman wasted her ruddy life attempting to be an artist. And my god, that Mollie. Aren't you tempted to prang her. I couldn't bear to have that one about without my prick constantly up her.'

'Well Rashers you are in a good mood.'

'Darcy you see, some utterly bleak black clouds do come and which one does not think will ever pass. And then one does in such precipitously extreme moments consider to blow one's brains out. But you know as one stiffens one's finger just prior to fully pulling the trigger there is already that fractional moment of regret. I mean when people jump from suicidal heights it is well known that on the way down they do then wish they hadn't. And even as I raised that cold pair of beautifully engraved barrels to my head I was recalling many happier times. Such as our very first meeting in the Royal Hibernian Hotel.'

'When if I recall correctly Rashers you tried to touch me for a fiver.'

'Yes I did didn't I, when of course you were relieving the Mental Marquis of his fiver. And then my god imagine that sadistic bugger then making off with that exquisite creature out of your household here. My dear boy have I said something wrong. Dear me I have, haven't I. You suddenly seem to have a sadness instead of the pleasure my words seemed to be bringing your face. And honestly, believe me, we can yet save this day.'

'Rashers, there is no day to save.'

'But dear boy there is, there is. Still subject of course to the respective choice of ladies, and conferring upon them our little bit of ennoblement in return for at least some amplitude of dollars to smarten up the old mansion and perk up the old park here and about. There is much yet to save. It may just be done a little more modestly than we have heretofore thought.'

'Rashers, nothing less than a veritable fortune will do that. And god what would I do with a raving lesbian around this place.'

'They make perfectly adequate companions dear boy. In fact marvellous ones. Although on second thoughts I suppose they might make attempts on others of your female staff. But then they learn and perfect superlative tongue caresses. By the way this champagne is in awfully fit condition if I may say so. What. Come come, what harm should there be in two very beautiful women finding it suddenly impossible not to taste a little of each other's beauty. We should not mind. Kisses and cuddles are of no great harm. The ladies still have their what for there for us still to prang.'

'But what about their falling down and writhing over one another.'

'Well were it done without garments, I suppose it might then merit greater concern. I'd be the first to admit that after a few bouts of that kind of caper one would have to look a little more deeply serious into the matter. But one should not sit about twiddling one's own willie worrying about it or waiting to catch them flagrante delicto.'

Darcy Dancer and Rashers, arms around each other's shoulders and waltzing in step back along the darkened hall to the ballroom. A Highland reel in progress. All the spoons and fiddles and bagpipes playing. The noise deafening. Rashers off to dance with Lois. MacBuzuranti spinning Amnesia Murphy around the floor. And Brillianton sidling over.

'I do like your mix of friends Kildare. And I say, especially those two splendidly delightful creatures. Hope you don't mind but they did ask me to tell you that they'd like to come attend a shoot at my place in Scotland, do a bit of stalking and that sort of thing.'

After the shudder of terror that can go through one, amazing how angry one can get and yet suppress one's hand reaching out and one's fingers going around someone's throat. Ryecrisp this sanctimonious humbug carried away by his own eloquence, and his ruddy smile so sickly sweet as he said these words that I also was sorely tempted to unleash a fist to smash his face as I once did with one of my sister's porcelain headed dolls on a piece of granite, when she refused to let me touch or play with it. Of course afterwards I wept and wept as one

369

might over death, not knowing the poor sweet doll's head would break like an egg shell. And not knowing the exquisite little eyes and face would smash to pieces. But here was another face I would most welcomely smash and would not weep over the pieces. And the son of a bitch was looking over my shoulder to others in the room as if I were not now standing there at all. And then as if he'd suddenly seen a ghost.

'I say Kildare. I have been looking for that person. In the monocle. Out on the floor. Dancing. And damn well appearing to enjoy himself. You do know him.'

'Yes. He is Lord Ronald Ronald.'

'Ah. Ah. The one and very same. Just as I thought. Knew I recognized him. Never forget a face. Father is General Ronald Ronald. I shall go immediately and ask him to admit, if you don't mind.'

'Admit what.'

'To his identity. And that he is, ruddy chap, behaving as an arrant impostor and a con man. Lost the keys to Windsor Castle. And is a deserter from my former regiment.'

'You'll do no such thing Brillianton. Who on earth do you think you are. Lord Ronald Ronald happens to be a guest in my house.'

'Now look here Kildare. This is a damn serious matter. Encouraging a con man. And you are aiding and abetting in the harbouring of a deserter who in the ordinary course of events is subject to being court martialled and summarily shot.'

'That may be, but may I remind you Brillianton, this is Ireland. Irish soil. And you are speaking to an Irishman.'

'Well of course it may be that I am.'

'It's not Brillianton that you may be speaking to an Irishman, you are. And we are all to one degree or another con men.'

'I'll surely second that. But certainly Kildare you don't intend keeping a deserter as your guest and allowing him to consort with your other guests. Not the sort of thing one should allow to happen to Florida and Virginia. Who I understand under entirely false pretences were inveigled by him to come here.'

'I beg your pardon.'

'They were Kildare. Your abode here was glowingly described to them as one of the largest and most romantic castles in Europe, with indoor tennis court in your great hall and surrounded by your own private golf course. And not only had you a private airport but that you had snow capped hills where they could go skiing. And there is not a tee, a green or fairway or a slope of piste anywhere. Never mind playing tennis in your hall. Dastardly misrepresentation. And I shall go over to him and speak the facts to his face. And of course alert the proper authority to his whereabouts.'

A dance just ended. And before one could stop him Brillianton goes pushing rudely past Johnny Gearoid who, still in his greasy mackintosh and wearing his cap and with another foamy pint of stout, was planting himself in front of me. And raising up his glass to remind me as he has already done a thousand times previously of his antecedents who anciently occupied their lands which distantly bordered those of Andromeda Park and which he had inherited from his father.

'Well before your time Master. Well well before your time and before the time of any who came before you we had our little bit of a farm. And drank it away I did over the recent years down in the pub. Only a couple of acres left. Sure what does man need more than a bit of dry straw under a bit of a shed to sleep the night away. Didn't the saints themselves live on bread and water in holes in the ground and were better for it. Ah but I am now not a bit like the father. Sure didn't he believe the earth was flat till I came home from school one day to tell him it was round. And he beat the bejesus out of me. And he still said it was flat. Well he never found out it was round. Didn't he go instead quenching his thirst on a hot summer's day and help himself to some liquid in an old soda bottle left out on a shelf in the shed and draining every drop of it, wasn't he standing there smacking his lips with the satisfaction of his refreshment. And then not a minute later, didn't he keel over dead from the lethal contents. And here I am now meself not a bother on me after ten pints of stout.'

'I'm not sure Johnny that your previous pint was not your tenth and this is your eleventh.'

'Ah well I was never great with me accuracy in counting. But I'll tell you one thing. I have a horn between my legs breaking me fly buttons at the sight of the wonderful women. Ah bejesus the sap is still rising. And after what we're seeing here in the beauty of the flesh you wouldn't want to be having to go home and have to jump up on some old dragon of a wife.'

Knowing somehow that something awful was going to happen, one tried to keep sight of Brillianton amid the heads as he was following Rashers across the ballroom floor. The music makers taking another breather and the gramophone again beginning to play another foxtrot brought by the Americans and something referring to 'That Old Black Magic'. Brillianton retreating now to the sidelines and waiting as Rashers sweeps out on the ballroom floor with the local countess. Swirling her about in a grand motion and then ending their dance dipping backwards and nearly tipping the Countess off her feet as she laughs with delight. Brillianton stepping forward to tap Rashers on the shoulder. O that stupid ass Brillianton, who, it would signally appear, is not someone notable for letting sleeping dogs lie. And one only now waits and hopes that there will be no barking and biting. Rashers turning. Their two faces, facing. Words passing between them. For this moment at least. But clearly not for the next. Rashers's fist suddenly coming out of nowhere and crashing on Brillianton's jaw. Sending him flying out across the parquet on his back. At least this time polishing it with his hunting coat instead of grinding his heels in. Shouts arising from all quarters.

'Hit him in the haggis.'

'Kick him in the balls.'

'Up the Republic.'

The American girls running for cover. The lady instrumentalists playing on unconcernedly. The tack room boys rushing in. Where any moment now, dear god, any guest with a mind to his safety will fear to tread. Amid the screams and mayhem. Old Ryecrisp Brillianton, one hand on the piano, struggling up to his feet. And good lord, damn brave chap. Taking off his hunting coat, throwing it aside. Standing in his braces. His fists held up high in a classically pugilistic manner. Squaring off in front of an indulgently smiling Rashers. The adversaries circling on the dance floor. Rashers feinting and stamping his foot.

'Boo.'

'I say you impostor put up your fists.'

Wham. Out of nowhere Rashers's arm extending like a piston exploding like a bolt of lightning smack on Brillianton's nose. Blood pouring forth. Even above the din of shouts and screams the sickening sound of bone crushing. As down Brillianton goes again.

'Put in the boot. Put in the boot.'

One might have known from whom the unsportsmanlike shouts were coming. And, that given a little contretemps, the bloody tinkers would get back in. Brillianton now up on his hands and knees, wagging his head as if in his senseless state it would help discover a direction in which he might safely crawl. As one made to proceed to interfere, Sexton swaying unsteadily, stopping me by the arm.

'Let them at it Master Darcy. Sure life is a matter of the survival of the fittest. The mighty keeping the less mighty in their place where according to the laws of evolution they belong. Let them get it over and done with. Anyway isn't it time someone's epitaph was written. On me own gravestone I want it spelled out that although I speak no more, my words have already been said, and may they entertain you on your way here, where you like I shall lie dead. What about that now Master Darcy as an epitaph. But I am troubled whether it should be I lie dead or like me lie dead.'

'Good god Sexton. I ought really to go and stop this fight. As for your epitaph Sexton I don't suppose it makes that much difference does it. Whether you say me or I. Certainly the gist of the matter is clear but I do take your point. But perhaps it is better said, here you, like me, shall lie dead. Of course our Mr Arland, whom I have invited but don't see, would have an opinion on it.'

'Ah I did have my differences with Mr Arland but I'd agree with you there. By god but doesn't that Lord Ronald have a mighty swipe on him.'

At one end of the ballroom the party and dancing proceeding, and now at the other Brillianton clearly dazed and on his hands and knees presently crawling in the direction of a seated lady. And his head, as if to hide, pushing in under her gown and up between her legs. Dear me. He would have to choose a formidable past lady Master of Foxhounds, and well known for her no nonsense outspokenness. As she imperiously regards the intrusion with a lifted eyebrow and an adjustment of her monocle, announcing to Brillianton.

'My dear man, although I am old enough to be your mother, if you do wish to do something to me up under my frock I should appreciate it if your attempt was made while I was not otherwise conspicuously seated comfortably and engaged in enjoying myself in good conversation. So be a good chap now and fuck off.'

The tack room boys at the rescue. Standing Brillianton up again on his own two mystified legs and leading him to be seated on a chair along the wall. A bloody handkerchief held to his face. Of course this former lady Master could have

374

given Brillianton her own good account concerning compensating farmers. For in her heyday and together with another grand dame they circulated the countryside and were most adept at flaunting their female assets to soothe the outcry of those small farmers whose fences had been trampled, sheep shocked to death and cattle gone wild breaking out of fields. And as Luke was fond of relating to his avid listeners out in the tack room.

'Ah their ladyships knew how to keep the countryside open to hunting. Sure the compensation they gave to more than an occasional bachelor farmer was to open their legs to him out in a copse somewhere. Now I'm not naming names but you wouldn't have to, for over half the parish the news would spread when the ladies were in the district and every Sean and Seamus not busy milking his cow would come watching from any surrounding shrubbery. But didn't one of her ladyships get cured for a bit in one such instance when she got the fright of her life. Now I'm only naming names for you'd know who it was anyway knowing it was him who just installed his full set of false new teeth. Wasn't your man McGinty the farmer enticed out back over the hill, never mind that he was starved to jump on top of her, instead of as he'd been doing getting up on his ewes and heifers. Well he rushed at the job and then when he was in the very act of sowing his oats, wasn't he in such a state that didn't his full set of false teeth leap out of his mouth and onto her ladyship's face and the teeth by themselves grab hold of her nose. By god the aurora borealis was nothing compared to the lights your man must have seen when she gave him back a belt in his kisser.'

The calming sound of a Viennese waltz striking up. My sisters, apparently with their own party now arrived over from London without any reference to me, all sitting aloof at their private table, demanding Crooks's attention and imbibing bottles of champagne from Andromeda Park cellars. I suppose one's own snobbery and efforts at gentlemanly behaviour did get the better of one's Irishness, and one did go over to old Brillianton so as he might not think us completely boorish. With everyone trying to get their hands on the American girls to hear their accents and asking them to pronounce words over and over again. They had rather deserted Brillianton as he sat there on an upright chair on the fringe, still in his braces and with a large silk handkerchief wiping blood and sweat from his face. But amazingly uncontrite and, to give him his due, quite sporting.

'Packs a wallop.'

'I did warn you Brillianton.'

'Yes, I shall know better next time.'

'Are you all right.'

'Yes thank you, nothing worse than one might receive out on a good day's hunting. I suppose that Rashers chap might have good reason to desert the army. Heard rumours his father would force him on route marches through bogs as a child when he was only five years old.'

One now finding new old faces erupting on every side. Striding into the ballroom in a rather flashily cut suit far too light blue and far too shiny, a prosperous looking Foxy Slattery. Who with me got up to every conceivable childhood trick imaginable. How time, once so slow, suddenly streaks past in one's life. Here he is now with a pretty creature smiling amiably at his side.

'Ah how are you getting on now boss. The old place is holding up. Looking great. Remember the great times we had. Now boss I've got a great car to sell you. This is Sheona. Trying to make an honest man of me. Are you in the market.'

One nearly said yes, for a bicycle, as Sexton, his black eye patch only half covering his missing eye, came now reporting from the battle front. Clearly relishing handing out discipline and punishment where needed. Rubbing his massive hands together which I once refused to shake as a little boy because I said they were dirty.

376

'Ah now we're manning the battle stations now Master Darcy. And if you were at the race course, you'd say the conditions were good to yielding. For drunk, inebriated, intoxicated, fluthered they are, everybody. And out there in the front hall a minute ago, not able to believe my eyes, didn't I see the face of the marauder in from his caravan he's got set in the field across from the front gates. Wasn't he heard saying that he'd own this place one day. The bloody nerve of him daring to make an entrance into this very house. Now with your permission I'll go do for him Master Darcy, the upstart guttersnipe. It's a wonder he hasn't brought his sheep with him. Pick him up by the seat of the pants and boot him sailing out over the rhododendrons and beyond where he can then go on about building his petrol stations.'

Of course outside more gate crashers had arrived, pretending with their glowing smiles to make you think you know them. One could overlook the presumption but then coming right up to one's face to blatantly proffer their ready friendship was really the limit. And strange how one felt one had more in common with the four more itinerants who came galloping up the drive, two astride on each of their piebald ponies. Who, however, met by the tack room boys, didn't succeed in getting in the front door. Cudgels and most of my best walking sticks whistling through the air. The blood spilled from that battle was making it even more slippery on the wet front steps. Rendering it just perfect for chaos. And now with the lanterns kicked over by the tinkers and the resulting darkness, it led to another imbroglio. For there came the arrival of a spinster lady farmer, a long time friend of my mother, who took up to present herself in male attire and with her man chauffeur with whom she was rumoured to have a long understanding, was relying upon a peaceful entrance. And wham bam the tack room team went about their business of bouncing out the unwanted uninvited and thinking in the dark it was a further assault of the tinkers on yet more piebald ponies. And

377

safely now back in the lighted hall the tack room boys were grinning with delight at their handiwork which had dislocated the poor lady's jaw and sent her man servant in a heap to rest among the rhododendrons. I don't know how many writs would be served upon me for assault and maim but I found myself retreating at once to where out of sight I could listen, and, from a vantage point of safety, peek out from the Rent Room spy hole. And what did I see but poor old sod Crooks taking coats and still trying to keep up his trousers and not fall flat on his face.

'O dear, do please forgive me your lord and ladyships and your graces my braces have snapped. And forgive me as I must just bend a little this way so that I do not fall completely that way.'

'Of course with the Rashers fight with Brillianton over, one wrongly tended to assume that one need no longer worry about the awful feeling one has imagining it is merely the calm before the storm, assuming that enough hurricanes, and tornadoes had already happened. But with the tack room boys of Slattery, Luke, Henry and Thomas in action, one at least had a barrier of sorts and did not have to retreat behind the locked door of the library at every violent crisis and there to sit in order to soothe one's nerves in the silence and solitary peace of the turf fire. With the nagging worry of this whole expensively wasteful night turning into a form of nightmare. For as each person came close, requiring one to be polite, one's toes went digging through one's socks into the soles of one's shoes. With the various violence become a relief of sorts. And summoned to the pantry, one was already sighing with further relief. But not for long. Damian, recently nicknamed the Demon Desperate, was stretched out unconscious amid broken glass and splashed wine on the floor, his eye nearly knocked out by a cork exploding out of a champagne bottle pilfered from the cellar, and his prick sticking out of his fly. And Crooks's niece, whom one had not seen much in evidence

378

since she'd witnessed Lois taking my own cock in her mouth, was leaning back against the pantry cupboard, holding a cold compress to her head and pointing to a bent piece of Andromeda Park's best silverware in Damian's fist.

'He tried sir to plunge it into my Uncle Crooks's chest. Pure and simple attempted murder sir. And then tried with his big thing out and coming at me, to rape me. I gave him a belt of the wine decanter behind the ear.'

Damian the Demon Desperate finally moaned into life again, not only opening his eyes but with his prick erecting. Clearly drunk, he tried to get up and then fell down. One treated the gash in his head and ordered him to go to bed. Leaving Crooks's niece to her own theatrical devices, shouting at me that she would lay charges of attempted interference. And sneaking one's way back to the ballroom, one wondered what it was about big houses that made people in them behave so badly. As another instance was about to reveal itself. All happening in an absolute flash and with the reverberation of a thunderclap. For there, swirling past under the rainbow sparkling chandelier and totally utterly oblivious to my presence or anyone else's, were Durrow-Mountmellton and Rashers, wearing smiles on their faces and gazing dreamily into each other's eyes. And the way she held her hand on Rashers's shoulder said everything that could be said. Her mansion, her lands, her barns, her horses, her sheep and cattle. It were as if they were all marching in a massive parade across the meadows, old Durrow-Mountmellton in front, hand in hand with Rashers and leading the whole kit and caboodle straight out of my life. Smitten and shattered, one somehow shrunk within oneself. And feeling a distinct desire to get away, one retreated to the library to solitarily regard the fire flame. Taking along a plate of sausages and a bottle of wine. Until a knock on the door. And my overwhelming sensible feeling not to answer it. But as tragedy seems to befall one in more than one onslaught, one thought it better to get up from one's chair to open the door. Who knows it might be a late night messenger telling me I had won the sweep stakes. But it was Rashers. There grinning ear to ear. A pint of stout in his hand.

'Dear boy, save for a bloody nose or two, it's such a wonderful, wonderful party. I have been looking for you high and low everywhere.'

'Well you've found me, I'm here. Making sure I get at least a tiny bit of my own wine and something to eat.'

'My dear chap what on earth's the matter. You do sound as if you've taken something distinctly amiss. I've come, not to say rushed, to tell you some very good, good news.'

'I know your news Rashers.'

'You don't do you.'

'Yes. You intend to become betrothed as soon as it is at all humanly possible to Durrow-Mountmellton.'

'Now steady on dear boy, steady on. All I am trying to do and as you see me now, is to maintain my resolve to crawl back up out of the cauldron of my numerously accumulated misunderstandings not to say disasters. I know we first met under inauspicious circumstances and that I have since committed more than a dreadful faux pas or two but we must not let that overshadow our enduring long enjoyed relationship. Now I hope it isn't because I popped that old Ryecrisp Brillianton fellow one on the old snooter.'

'No it's not Rashers.'

'Damn chap wanted me to give myself up and be probably shot. When I can, should I so wish, do it myself.'

'He did say that it was known in every Guards regiment you lost the keys to Windsor Castle.'

'Dear boy that was an embarrassment but hardly a capital offence. And dear boy I have something to convey to you. I have now decided that the well established principle of the aristocracy intermarrying with contemporary power and money should rather be amended somewhat. And you as a large landowner, to find a suitable wife, should instead of

380

footling about with these Americans, acquaint yourself immediately with more high ranking members of the local aristocracy. I mean damn it, if not a marchioness then indeed the marvellously lithe Countess, perhaps a few years your senior, with whom I was dancing would do you no damn harm at all. What.'

'You are completely getting off the subject Rashers.'

'O sorry, am I. But believe me, I am quite prepared to have it all out in the limelight dear boy. While meanwhile one's swift intelligence and restless mind and darting energy and roving disposition lead one to declare quite openly that l should earnestly like to help myself to that very last sausage lying there so innocently on your nice Meissen onion pattern dish.'

Rapid raps on the library door. One now having become accustomed to the speed of the knock inevitably indicating the degree of disagreeable news requiring to be delivered to one's ears. Rashers rising to investigate. Crooks in both an inebriated and agitated state, sticking his head in.

'Forgive me sir for disturbing you. And forgiving your presence milord Ronald. But a riot is on. Out in the front hall. It's that one again. Mollie. Making lewd enticements. I told her to be out of that sacrilegious frock she's in.'

'What frock Crooks.'

'Your dear mother's sir. Antoinette Delia Darcy Darcy Thormond's ballgown. Changed out of her uniform into it, she has drink taken and now she has gone berserk. Screaming language that would make the devil blush. Knew we should have got rid of her long ago. Up on the first landing of the main staircase she is flailing your hunting whip and laying out lashes in every blessed direction at the lot of us trying to get up there and get holt of her. And dealing with her didn't that gang of gypsy tinkers we threw out come back in off the road. The king of them enticed he was by her. Made a grab for her. And the family of them are now attacking guests and letting

381

fly with fists and boots. And isn't that bad type who's hanging around at the front gates in this very house and panting after her as well. For safety of the other guests and to separate those who want peace from those who want war, we've locked the ballroom door. Could you come quick.'

'Of course we shall Crooks, as I do believe it does sound as if we may have a difficulty afoot.'

Darcy and Rashers leaving and locking the library and rushing past the closed ballroom doors and along the hall. In the gloomy candlelight up on the landing of the main stairs was Mollie. Dressed in a ballgown that I'd not ever seen before. Magenta in colour and form fitting around the waist and somehow making her, with the flood of orange hair on her shoulders, look astonishingly even more ravishing. Her one hand outstretched anchored on the banister and the other clutching one's hunting whip. And with brilliant skill laying it out with a loud crack over the ducking heads of the advancing tack room boys.

'No one's to put a hand to me. Get back all the fucking lot of ye peasants or I'll take yer fucking heads off your fucking necks you bunch of overgrown eegits.'

Darcy Dancer making his way through the pack of people. And most of them already engaged in their own personal fun. Sounding the horn and galloping on each other's backs, hooting and hollering up and down the Rent Room hall. Out which is coming someone on a bicycle, belting a polo ball with a polo mallet. God but Mollie looks quite marvellous in her fiery fierceness. If only one could give her elocution lessons, a smattering of Latin and French, eliminate her thick Galway accent and quieten down her violent instincts. And presently, so as not to be thought a peasant, I am about to sound as awfully English as one can.

'I say there Mollie. Look here. Steady on. Put the whip down.'

'You too get back or you'll feel a crack of this.'

382

Even as the whip was raised to strike, there was absolutely nothing for it but to continue to be insanely brave and advance up the flight of stairs. Each step trying not to wince in anticipation of the long thong lashing across one's head. What new matters are wrought now in Andromeda Park. The pasha himself to be whipped by a servant. And here one is, ready to offer Mollie one's arm. Holding it up to her.

'Come Mollie. Let me lead you down. I should like if you would have this next dance with me.'

Amazing what kindness and politeness can do. And as one leads her down, a burst of applause from all. With Mollie now breaking forth into a flood of tears. Her arms up around my neck. Her breasts heaving against my chest. Crooks's monocle falling out of his eye and his mouth opening nearly all the way down to his boots. As his trousers yet once again fell. And one simply had to ignore the distinct apoplexy evident everywhere among the staff over my highly familiar behaviour with Mollie. And announce in one's best matter of fact manner.

'My lords, ladies and gentlemen, do please carry on.'

In the ballroom the gramophone playing a rumba called 'Brazil'. Allowing one to mercifully disappear into the dancing throng. Everyone going wild over these recent musical importations from America. As if that place had some miraculous quality to be emulated by we lesser Irish. But good god it had to be admitted, that even dressed, feeling Mollie's undulating hips to the rumba rhythm through my mother's satiny silk ballgown, which was only a mite tight and a mite too long, she was an absolutely devastating armful. Bathing as she did recently more frequently, her usual muskiness suffused now with bath oils and the intoxicating smell of her sweat. Making for a wonderful strange perfume rising from her freckled skin. And she took every opportunity to press against and upon my hard on getting more conspicuous by the second. But then in the middle of our dance came her words whispered in my ear slightly more loudly than one wanted to hear.

383

'I'm no longer to be a servant in this house. And nobody is ever going to call me Dingbats again. If you don't marry me, I'll soon be marrying. I've been proposed to.'

'Good god, not that you shouldn't be, but by whom Mollie.'

'The man John Kelly Kelly in the caravan beyond the front gates. That's by whom. And don't be smiling. That's a real double barrelled name. And I'll not wait around this place forever. He has over five hundred sheep and twenty rams putting them in lamb. And he will build me a fifteen bedroom house. And what's more, unless I hear something to my advantage, I'll be gone out of here in the morning. Are you going to marry me. Or has the cat now got your tongue.'

The cat had got my tongue. And something else, like mute apoplexy, deflated my erection. And bloody damn hell didn't I turn around to look for somewhere to sit to hold my head in my hands and didn't one then see over Mollie's freckled shoulder, Ryecrisp Brillianton disappearing out the north ballroom door with both American girls in tow and stopping and shaking hands as if to say goodbye to the lithe local Countess. But then a miraculous welcome resurgence of some cheer in one's life. Coming in the same door Brillianton went out, one saw someone I thought would not come. In his naval great coat, approaching across the ballroom floor. Mr Arland. Whose august Christian names were Napoleon Patrick. His sad, sad loves, even sadder than mine. His same melancholic serious face underneath whose expression there always lurked a wry smile. I am on the verge of weeping. This nice man has come who had taught me so much. And set always such a marvellous unassuming example. And tears come to my eyes when I recall his Trinity College rooms where he gave his first party for which he had saved for years to celebrate on getting his final exams. And sat away the whole night when no one came. And he comes tonight. One hears all his words again so often spoken upon my recalcitrant ear in the school

384

room. Always be noble Kildare in the best sense of what that word means. Take life's blows standing up. Speak softly when others shout. Keep your own counsel. Blithely ignore sneers. Educate your mind so that you can always privately live and enjoy life in a world of your own. And here he is with a lady friend. As one moves now towards him. Mollie, for the time being at least, one takes in tow, with her mind still full of great big houses and plenty of bedrooms. To greet at last the most friendly of all friendly faces whose voice as it speaks, and just speaking could so often be softly amusing, and put one's fears of the world at rest.

'Do not be nugatory and translate the following Kildare. Bonis nocet quisquis pepercerit malis et bonis quod bene fit haud perit.'

'Whoever spares the bad, injuries the good, and whatever is done for good men, is never done in vain.'

'Ah Kildare. Perfectly brilliant and excellent. Not, shall we make a great scholar of you, we obviously have already. And we are so sorry to be late. Two flat tyres saw to that. And never being a man who's wanted to get up to one's elbows in axle grease, it was four hours in a pub waiting for them to be fixed. The habitués of which all seemed to be highly amusingly insane. One repeatedly scratching his privates and saying over and over again he'd had enough. Clara, I should like to present to you my former pupil I've spoken to you so much about. All grown up now as you can see. Reginald Darcy Thormond Dancer Kildare.'

Clara Macventworth with long flowing blonde radiant tresses and a face full of excitement and mascara. And wearing under a black coat a long tartan skirt. And whom one knew to be an American and another of this loud voiced optimistic strange breed descended from outer space. And all seeming to require carrying with them a tennis racket, an overly big hat or wads of chewing gum. But with Mr Arland's arrival it seemed as if a certain civilization had returned to Andromeda

385

Park. Along with much laughing reminiscences. Even Sexton, upon seeing him, rushed across the ballroom to exchange a few phrases of Latin. On Sexton's part woefully ungrammatical but left kindly uncorrected by Mr Arland. And I warmed to listening. Until of course I felt a sharp poke of a powerful elbow in the kidney.

'Am I not to be introduced.'

'O my god, I am sorry Mollie. This is Mollie. You know Mr Arland. And this is Clara Macventworth.'

One saw a flicker of disbelief in Mr Arland's eyes as he then instantly came to attention, bowed and clicked his heels and leaned to kiss Mollie's proffered hand. O my god, being a gentleman can save the day sometimes. Just as it can perhaps more frequently at other times get you into a god awful mess. But I am sure that from the original look on Mr Arland's face it were somehow as if the main king post in the attic had cracked and sent a few ceilings plunging down within our midst. And a solemn deep voice announcing.

PREPARE TO MEET
THY MAKER YOU ANGLO IRISH
WHO DOTH DECLINE
AND FALL

But one had in this ballroom tonight, bohemians. And I now have them to thank for something. Especially and luckily at this moment when all four of us suddenly had nothing absolutely to say. For the next distracting embarrassment afoot this time was welcome. Lois had lowered the upper half of her ballgown to display her magnificently splendid tits. That any farmer would adore to see on his every heifer or cow. Lois wagging them in every last bit of candlelight as she did a rumba up and down the ballroom floor. Her castanets clacking madly above her head. Sound of glass breaking. Talk about riots we thought were over. One of the greatest was clearly

386

just beginning. MacBuzuranti joining her. Everyone standing back as the pair danced parallel. The Count seeming to be encouraged by his acolytes to make the most rude of rude gestures. And especially when taking to divest of his own garments, flinging them to be caught by onlookers. As he now streaked through and executed a repertoire of extravagant balletic manoeuvres, announcing.

'Now, all my dears. To improve your Irish minds. You must all stop and shut up your mouths for le grand battement. Pay now attention. I start with glissade assemblé. Then I do the lively jolt of the allegro soubresaut and the few sautes for this moment when I shall do for you the greatest jeté to be seen in the classical ballet.'

Sexton of course arrived, rushing over to my side to give me a piece of his moral mind. Ignoring Mollie, who stepped aside as I listened. And the farmer Amnesia Murphy, wasting no time and salivating at the mouth, swept Mollie away. Sexton's eyebrows jumping up and down in indignation.

'Ah no one wants to be an old fuss pot, but I would object Master Darcy. Pure nudity. Pure unadulterated nudity. Offending most who are here. Two men of the cloth. I would object to them being subjected. And wild horses now couldn't keep the uninvited away from climbing and fighting their way back and trying to get space on the window sills to peek in at the goings on. And by god. What happened to that one Mollie. Like a guest. In a frock. I don't like casting aspersions. And there may be no truth at all in it. But that one Mollie has never shut up lying. And with the thousands of words in the language the lies get bigger all the time. Sure she has it rumoured all over the place your marauder out beyond the front gates is going to marry her. Next she'll be telling us the grass is blue.'

'Well Sexton. One really can't add much news to yours. But as one's old dearly trusted nanny used to say. Things may be dreadful but then you thank your luck stars that they haven't become appallingly dreadful.'

'Touché. Master Darcy. Touché.'

Save for my sisters, the gathering seemingly enjoying the dance exhibition given by Lois and the Count. And with the departure every which way and that of potential bed partners, one's attention turned to the lady Dresden china doll one had exchanged glances with out hunting and who was engaged in dance after dance, her diminutive slender form gracefully gliding and her well turned ankle seen as she waltzed. And it was only at a moment when she returned in the door from a presumed visit to the lavatory that she appeared available. There was nothing about her of the hefty wench, rather one might think her light as an angel, a bundle of curly brown hair atop her head. And that with her white delicate wings she could flutter down upon one's thighs. Land there and do something awfully pleasurable. And then just as we stepped out on the floor to foxtrot together, and just as one was regaining one's confidence and a new interest, one's assumed unruffled imperturbability was soon ruffled and perturbed by the sight of Crooks urgently signalling me to the sidelines.

'Sir forgive me for disturbing you. By god it's turned terribly wintry. Instead of rain it's fierce snow. And there is a heifer out beyond by the old stream calving and she do be in difficulties. Thomas and Luke are gone to her. But the vet we can't yet find a'tall.'

One did have more than a passing thought that with the current delicate morsel one might have a future together. Her mere silence and gentle acquiescence to my more clumsy movements made me realize that one danced with a consummate seductress. And flattered by the sweet look of disappointment on her face, one took one's leave with some reluctance. Down the back school room stairs, tripping over two bodies entwined. Kicking off one's dancing slippers, tucking together my trouser legs, and plunging one's black silk socks into one's

388

cold damp wellington boots. Pulling on an oilskin over one's evening clothes. With the snow thickly falling and gusts of sleet, at least with some faint moonlight above the clouds one could still see one's hand in front of one's face. Crossing the stable yard between the remaining guests' parked cars, ponies and traps. Into the total darkness of the tunnel, feeling one's way along the walls and coming up out into the fields. To think all this was built to keep workmen and servants out of sight. God, one's antecedents did know a thing or two. And my grandfather had the gardeners and grooms go out in early morning with towels to soak the dew up from the grass along the rose walk so the shoes on his feet would not get wet when he went for his constitutional before breakfast.

On a hill top in the driving snow and sleet Darcy Dancer stopping and looking back. Candle glow of light in the windows of Andromeda Park. And the faint sound of music. Premonitions gripping one. As if there it was, my mansion tilting over. Its great shadow to go down between the dark hills and disappear under the waves. The ballroom merrymakers within singing 'Abide with Me'. As they did on that great ship the Titanic. Icebergs gliding by and heaving up out of the night. Always reminding one of the story of the dress worn by my mother and which made every woman turn and regard her in envy. Of exquisite black Chantilly lace which she had inherited from her mother, my grandmother. Made in Paris for an ambassador's daughter on her way to America. And her trunk was delayed reaching the ship before it sailed and was left behind, as she and her father went to the bottom of that cold cold ocean. Just as I now, making way over the muddy soft ground, leave life and the living behind me. My boot steps cracking through the frost hardened crust over the ground. God, will I be able to find them. They must be near where the ghost of that figure was that day. And not far from the phantom girl swathed in white who was several times seen on the little ruined bridge. If I do, and if I am ever sinking down below the waves, as debt judges me, I must choose a spot where I can put the shotgun barrel to my head. Shoot away my brains. Take away my worry. Spread the white specks of it on all the dead dark oak leaves.

Beyond the shadows of the trees, the snow descending in larger flakes. Licking them from one's lips. The struggling figures under an ancient sycamore tree. The poor groaning and moaning beast. Charging this way and that. Trying to pull away from the men with a rope tied to a calf's hoof sticking out from the back of the heifer. Which one sees now is one of my best in the herd. As the gusts of snow and sleet streak down, Luke, his sleeve rolled up to his elbow and his arm buried down deep in the heifer's backside.

'Sir I can't get the other calf leg to be coming out. It's in here somewhere bent up. And where I'm reaching and it's stuck. Tugging, we've already pulled off a bit of the calf's hoof.'

Luke sinking his arm in again nearly up to the shoulder and digging into the heifer's bloody rear. Sweat on his brow sparkling in the lantern light. The calf's head at last emerging, coming halfway out. And then stuck. The film of the embryonic sack pulled back on its head. The heifer roaring in pain, swelling out its belly pushing. All digging in their heels tugging on the rope tied to the calf's leg. Tying new knots onto the calf's hoof, the rope cutting into the flesh. Heels of the men ploughing deeper into the turf as the heifer struggles forward into the darkness. Slipping to our knees and sinking through the frozen crust of ground and down into the soft mud.

'Hold on lads. Hold on.'

The big heifer pulling us behind her across the deepening snow. Hours gone. And here I am out in this inclemency this night of the ball. Planned all these many weeks. Thought of all these many months. And dreamed of since the day one last saw Lelia. And now, all of this has happened before. These

390

dumb idiots. Ignoring that the stream is only a few feet away. And here we go. A splash. The heifer is now down all four legs stuck in the deep mud of the stream. Poor animal roaring, trying to keep its head up out of the water. And now with another rope around its neck. More tugging. With Thomas slipping down the side of the bank and sinks splashing chin deep in the icy water. Two of us tugging at him to get him out.

'I can't swim. I'm sinking. I'm sinking. Say me act of contrition. Take care of me old mother. Ah begob I'm a gonner.'

One's hands painfully red raw from the rope. And now an additional tug of war. With matters taking on elements of a highly theatrical event. Making it difficult to suppress one's laughter. And awful how one suddenly thinks, if Thomas did drown it would be one less wage to pay. But here he is prostrate in the mud but at least, along with the heifer, dragged back up on the shore. Strange how one knew before anything had happened that the air of the night told one, only miraculous luck could leave the heifer alive. It being whispered to me that the Mad Vet had been located in the house but would not be promptly summoned from one of the bedrooms in which Baptista Consuelo appeared to be granting him favours. And which her big backside allowed her to grant to so many. Seemed that that poor girl was spending her lifetime in compensating for her origins in the town. And how as a child she'd been once turned away from these very doors of Andromeda Park by my snobbish sisters. To whom she was bringing her present of a silver spoon and was disdainfully pointed away down the front steps and told she had not been invited. And not far from here tonight she was found prostrate on the edge of the bog. No pain was ever bigger she said, no hurt deeper or greater.

A lantern light coming now down over the hill through the flurry of snow. The Mad Vet at last with his bag of tricks.

Already putting on his white coat. He might have to treat Thomas first. But touches the calf's eye for life. And now after all our long struggle it's dead. While it's still in its mother, the vet cutting off its head. Pushing back the remains into the heifer and digging in his blood coated arm, searching for the missing leg. Then finally finding it, pulling it out and attaching ropes and all of us pulling the headless calf's remains out on the frosty ground. The whiteness of snow falling on the dark smooth red brown hair still shiny wet in its mother's waters. Its warmth growing cold with death. This small creature opening its eyes which saw out into the world. Its tongue tasting the chill mist. Its mouth breathing its air. Its whole life lived before it was born.

One's jacket tails resting on the ground as one knelt and Thomas, dripping water from his soaked clothes, stepping on one's socially sacred cloth in his mud caked boot. A knife now lost in the grass. That's all one needs to spear oneself with next. But it would hardly matter, covered as we all are in blood. As one turns to trudge through the falling snow, now turned to rain, back home. Carrying the dispirit one feels with another calf dead. Returning to the party. And just as one had thought, the American girls decamped with Ryecrisp Brillianton and his girl grooms. The Dresden china girl gone too. Off with some gombeen business man one did not even know who'd been up from Dublin for the day's hunting. Rashers last seen taking his luggage with him out to Durrow-Mountmellton's pony and trap, and the pair of them, according to Sexton, galloping away, whiplashing down the front drive. Lois too, who had created a battle royal over her favours, with tables knocked over and drapes pulled down from the windows, also vanished. And most saddest of all one had missed saying goodbye to Mr Arland. Even Sexton sensing my disappointment.

'He had he said Master Darcy to be up giving a lecture at Trinity College in the morning. Ah but there remain plenty of revellers left.'

392

A flushed faced nearly exhausted MacBuzuranti was nothing if not persistent and, with astonishing gasps from onlookers, was still soaring over tables in his bare feet. As now two polo playing gents on the bicycles in the ballroom played a chukker, making their way between guests and batting their ball up and down the ballroom, and making goals between pairs of chairs. But making more collisions. One's sister Christabel standing at her table, hands on her hips and distaste on her face, announcing as loud as she could.

'And who are all these people.'

'Ah you're inquiring madam who I am lurching all over the place. I am certainly somebody but can't remember who. But I'll tell you what I am. I am feeling great. This is in all me life the greatest of all great nights and the best bloody god damn bash ever had. Let me tell you that, and no mistake.'

As one had come in the basement hall it seemed as if all the servants' bells were jangling at once. And clearly being ignored. For passing the kitchen and servants' dining room, another party raged. From which produced various onlookers wanting to get up the back servants' stairs of the ballroom hall and have an eyeful of the gentry. And to even venture into the ballroom to view close up. And by god with the nerve of the Irish as Sexton said, didn't the turf stealer and his wife from out of the bogs come who were nearly blasted to smithereens. But you wouldn't be surprised that they were without question the quietest bloody guests of the lot.

'And look at that Master Darcy both of them, isn't it great gas, standing well away from the fireplaces in case they get blown to kingdom come again.'

Johnny Gearoid raising his glass in one hand and holding up the hand of a monstrous gentleman in the other and announcing.

'Here he is the Gorgeous Gael, heavyweight boxing champion. All over the world he's hammered them down. When they tried to get up he hammered them down again. Give the woman in the bed more porter. And give the man getting in beside her a big finger to fuck her the whole night long while the strength of his arm holds out.'

MacBuzuranti taking to centre floor again. Pirouetting in his stockinged feet. And coming to stop as he set eyes on the Gorgeous Gael.

'My is he not nice. Upon whom I bat my eyes. That big pugilist in the doorway. What a pity. What a waste. He is with such a pretty charming woman who is such a good friend of mine. How nice were he to be a big raving giant who like me, like men and would undo his fly and take out his so marvellous big tool to point at me. Ah my dears. I am, am I not the queerest thing you ever saw.'

Music everywhere. To every shout another shout. Damian the Demon Desperate, up and abroad again, tottering between the guests, asking their Christian names. Crooks's niece presently in the arms of Amnesia Murphy. The piper still playing. The spoons still banging. The sleepy eyed lady quartet plucking and bowing their strings. A contest in the corner as to who might drink a pint of stout fastest while standing on his head. It seemed as one listened that voices and remarks were coming from all sides. A contingent arrived fresh from the notorious Catacombs of Dublin. And now everyone arriving late was called Desmond. Who had all been at other parties, other balls, other dinners. And travelling from one to the next across the snow swept countryside and to now investigate if this bash were any different. One Desmond saying to the other Desmond.

'Well my dear. Despite the noise and the people hardly any of whom are from the best county families, I must say as a hearty trencherman in such pursuits I declare this a most suitably exciting little party which may come to be a most memorable night to remember.'

And as one, blood and mud spattered stood there viewing the scene, hearing glass break, watching gouges appear in the

394

parquet, the tinker one thought one had scared off was back. A pint glass of stout in his hand he was topping up with whiskey.

'Ah now what did the mean bastards do to be sending you out in this weather. With the blood and mud on you. The gentry is a disgrace. Have they left you now bleeding.'

'Yes. And so will you be too if you don't fuck off in a hurry.'

It seemed that one's subliminal self had undergone enough battering and bruising, and with everyone else having such a good time, one could not feel one had not been the best of hosts. And now one realized I was woefully tired after this long, long day, and just as Mr Arland heard the man saying in the pub, one had had enough. All I will be able to do in what briefly remains this night is to scratch my own privates as clearly it does appear that for the unforeseeable future they will remain uncaressed.

Sexton, his head turning like a lighthouse light to keep his eye upon matters, coming across the floor to Darcy Dancer. MacBuzuranti now leaping high enough to tinkle the chandelier. And one dreading any new news that one might hear. But Sexton seemed intent merely to tell me something. And what does one do at this early hour of the morning but listen.

'Ah Master Darcy, there now will you look at that eegit with the two big lamb chops in his fists. Professing to be a poet. Up from Dublin he is drinking everything in sight and professing communism, socialism and existentialism all over the place. And comes up to me to see where he could for a few months be procuring free food and lodging for creative poets. Well I had to tell him, in that pursuit that if he tried commandeering a bedroom above he'd get a swift creative boot up the back of the arse that would have rhymes ringing in his ears for years.'

The Dublin poet in his bedraggled suit wandering into the ballroom and taking alternate nibbles of the lamb chops held in each hand. Suddenly in the doorway, Kern and Olav. Brought on their leads into the house and ready to come each side of me and smell out enemies, when they loudly growl. First, Kern and Olav snatching the chops from the poet and sending such morsel down their throats in one almighty gulp. Sexton laughing.

'Ah now there's a bit of socialism and communism in action. Share and share alike. And I'd suggest that that's put an appropriate end to things. And I can go back to praying as I do each day in my life for a beautiful death. I'd say now despite the blasphemous nature, bad language and disgusting behaviour on a few people's parts that there's no doubt there was plenty tonight to make the evening a great success.'

'Yes Sexton I do think fair to say, all have had a very good night of it. And that the moment has come to call it a day.'

'Right you are Master Darcy. As Crooks is at this crucial time when he is needed, hors de combat, leave it to me to clear the decks and lock up. And if you don't mind me saying you're looking just that little bit sad. Ah now we'll fight, fight, Master Darcy till the last blood vessel is bust.'

Darcy Dancer walking out into the front hall and turning to proceed down the corridor to the Rent Room. A drunken uninvited guest belligerently inquiring as to who I am. And one was sorely tempted to say that one was certainly someone who did not want to know who he was. But even to the most obnoxious one finds it hard to be rude. And one passes on into a place one has come to dread. Light a candle, sit at the table. Sign all the cheques one has to for tonight. One's right hand wanting to stay my left as it writes. Spending money from the very last of my mother's jewels to be sold. And for what was for me a forlorn evening. Sexton's voice out there bellowing.

'Out now the lot of ye, hoi polloi and gentry included. You've had it. The bash is over. This way or that way now to your coats and hats. And mind the front lawn with your wheels.'

Stepping back out into the darkness of the hall. Broken glass everywhere under foot. Proceed to the library. Close the door. Turn the key. Fall back in this leather chair, in which one has whiled and worried away so many hours. On the dying glow of fire, stack more turf. With the bellows blowing the embers into flame. That reach out to wrap warm arms around you. When there are no other arms. Stretched out mud spattered, scratched, evening clothes wet, and from the knees down, soaked all the way to the toes of one's socks. Alone in this room in a silent house. Except for a few unidentified bodies Sexton counted lying here and there along the shiny paving of the servants' hall. Clap one's hands and call out chop, chop. As morning comes. The cock crowing. The birds cheeringly chirping. Must rise. Must sleep. Must live. Must face more days weathering the storms descending upon one's life. Ascend to the cold bleak damp of my lonely apartments. Where the chill and worry will continue to clutch at one's heart. Those guests staying, retired to their bedrooms. And those not, such as Rashers, gone. Last heard brandishing his exquisitely beautiful voice singing 'O Danny Boy' out over the front meadows. Bound now to have the bloody nerve to ask me to be best man at his wedding. And then be my neighbour for life. Departing off with Durrow-Mountmellton without a single parting word. But then one recalls the tragedy in his life. The tweedy young lady he admired at college and teased and pulled off her wig he did not know she wore. And who then killed herself. Now his departure somehow leaves Andromeda Park like some hollow empty shell. With Mollie too packed and left. Crooks socked by her after a screaming argument to make sure my mother's gown remained behind. Her wonderful musky body gone. Imagine, with the marauder in his caravan. And any second on the horizon I'm going to see the unsightly sight of their fifteen bedroom house. His bloody sheep trespassing my fields. And all was to be saved by the Americans. Florida said she was interested in interesting

397

stimulus, and, as one was trying to prise something original out of her brain, I showed her one of one's best paintings. And she said hey gee that is really kind of cute. And when asked about her dear friend Virginia, she said well we sort of feel kind of mutual about each other. Amazing. Such blunt blandness. Leaving everything hopeless. Yet how desperately one does try. Now Brillianton can take them away forever from the bog and bog trotters and can wine and dine their big lithe bodies at his clubs and smart restaurants all over London. And then perhaps bring them both to bed. Where at least he can wank and watch them kiss each other. O dear. Must not be bitter. Must not be sad. And I suppose old Sexton is right when one hears his variations on the theme, what doth it profit a man to gain the whole world and lose his immortal soul. But what does one do when one knows one's soul rests here in Andromeda Park. And then what does one do when one has lost everything and there is no soul left to lose. And so much already lost in feasting all those ungrateful mouths. Accepting of course that always people come who were there just waiting to grasp even more from one. While I was being splashed in blood and mud out on the edge of the bog. O god. I don't think I should let my paranoia get the better of me toright. But it would have helped a lot had I got an attack much sooner. To prevent some of my very best wines, long laid down, from vanishing from the wine cellar. These many who come and take and will never reciprocate. Not that I would care in most cases to accept their invitations back, if invited. And in having this last grand night, I had no other thought or intention but one. The whole reason. The entire why and wherefore. With all my thoughts being only one dream. Of Leila. That she might just notice on the horizon of her world. My invitation. Written by my love for her. To come back. And all the weeks and many months of my desperate hope that she would. Alone. Or even if need be, even with him. So that I might merely cast a glance upon you

398

just once more. As I did in this very room with all its books and pages and silent words shut between their covers. And perhaps you saw then what can now be seen from my eyes looking at yours. That I love you. And will for the term of one's days. But instead. Tonight all in vain. The curtain falling on what seems the longest chapter in one's life. Over now. You did not come back. You never came. You remain as you have always been after you left. A tiny votive glow of flame inside a window along the desperate slum streets of Dublin. Where once I walked. Shocked in disbelief at the poverty. The only small warmth to be seen through the cold fog, put there to burn in front of a sacred heart. And your heart to which I call. Upon which I would press my lips to kiss. Or lie my head to feel its beat. Gone. As no other word can say. Gone. For always and forever. But never. Never from my soul and brain.

> For in my
> Spirit she
> Doth always
> Dwell

22

Looking out on the front parkland from the Whim Room, the ball seemed long gone past, and as if it had never happened. One spent one's days exercising horses and attending upon the hunt. Mostly noticing how the hounds seem to prefer one's own dead cattle to wolf down. And one went two days up to Dublin. To sell a silver necklace of Victorian diamonds. Holding them in one's pocket on the train as if not to let them go. An hour haggling over their value. The jeweller every five minutes going backstage to consult his father, who, when I said I would go elsewhere, finally agreed to nearly give me my price.

Running chores pillar to post, I then ordered various iron-mongery from Dockrell's and seeds from Drummond's in Dawson Street. Stared out the window of one's room at the top of the Kildare Street Club, looking down over the high rhododendron hedge and across the green velvet grass of the playing fields of Trinity College. And beyond past the geology building to New Square where Mr Arland could be perhaps on his way to the common room to take sherry before lunch. One thought of calling upon Miss von B in Switzers but somehow at the very last moment one decided to avoid women and instead take one's sherry in Jammet's back bar for men only. Of course one was served by a delightful lass, who immediately reinflamed one's interest in women.

Dining alone at the Kildare Street Club abysmally empty of members with whom one might have assured oneself of some sedentary camaraderie while reading the newspapers. And except for an old grey headed gent constantly clearing his throat and calling for more coffee and then spilling it as he coughed, I was the only member taking breakfast. One would of course get one's standard joke going and coming from the hall porter.

'Ah sir did you see now the cow that jumped over the moon.'

'No.'

'Well that's because with its bad back leg it can't jump that high.'

Returning to Andromeda Park, I was not ready for what rapidly happened. As my eyes nearly fell out of my face. The longest gleamingest two tone vehicle with a convertible roof, skidding several feet to a halt, drew up in front of the front steps of the house.

'My dear Darcy, my dear boy, just thought I'd pop over. Now you must not jump to conclusions. Just a little item we had spiffed up, found buried in the old Major's commodious barns under the hay as a matter of fact. Happens to be an Isotta Fraschini Eight A. Seven point four litre engine.'

Rashers with driving-gloves and in bright tweed plus fours had indeed with a vengeance taken up with Durrow-Mountmellton. And good god, you'd never seen anything like it. A silver topped walking stick. Tassels bobbing from the top of his stockings. And imagine. With my twenty acres along with him. Jumping out on the drive, grinning at me. And bloody hell if a marriage takes place he'll be a bigger landowner than I am.

One sat there on the settee, taking tea in the drawing room. Listening to his plans. Rashers wolfing down five scones with a mountain top on each of whipped cream and blackberry preserve. Managing to get out words between bites concerning pedigree Hereford cattle. Thoroughbred stallions from Newmarket. Likely mares from all over the place. Watching him cross and recross his legs. Get up. Fan his arse in front of the fire and sit down again.

401

'I am dear boy as one might dare to say, as happy as one can reasonably expect to be. The girl's as strong as an ox. Rides both on and off a horse like a dream. But the marriage is not about to take place just exactly yet. But imminently. And when it does I should be so absolutely honoured if you would be my best man.'

At least for the time being Rashers's news meant he wasn't about to blow his head off with a shotgun. Or pawn my silverware. And other news was that from farm to farm and along the road, electricity was now on its way across the fields towards Andromeda Park. One hearing of its advent in various abodes in between. Sexton seemed most enthusiastic out in his potting shed with his usual fever of excitement over growing things. Dancing from one foot to another as he measured out his map for a new garden design for vegetables.

'Ah simple as pie. In this patch the artichokes. Here beetroot, calabrese, carrots. Over here celery, turnips, spinach. If it's a vegetable to be eaten, you name it Master Darcy and sine dubio you'll be seeing it come up sprouting before your very eyes. And I won't be sparing the begonias, asters and marigolds either. Or the big fat healthy hyacinth bulbs here soon to go in the ground. Sure requests are now pouring in to see our plantings. The Slasher sisters themselves, exhibitors at the Royal Dublin Society, have asked could they come. And rejoice I do for any small esteem shown just a common down to earth gardener.'

'You do, I must say, give one heart Sexton.'

'Well Master Darcy, why not, when wattage is on the way and when above soon there'll be light. Sure I'll be able to better incubate the cypripediums now. Think of that. Be a great day now. Just reach to give a flick of a switch on the wall. But if you're thinking of hiring that pair of them eegits been around inquiring to rig up any wires. I'd more than beware. Never mind the fact that this is the country where batteries were invented. I'd send them on their way. Sure didn't they rig up the electricity to your man McGinty's cottage over there. Put electric in the bedroom and electric out even in the barn. But then when the job was done, if you went to put on the light in the bedroom you found you had to go out to do it in the barn. Ah but them geniuses did, informed of the matter, have a ready enough answer. Sure they said you'll have the comfort and convenience on a stormy night to be able with the switch in the bedroom, to turn off the light in the barn. But then they made no mention to your man McGinty that to turn off the light in the bedroom on the same stormy night didn't you have to get drenched going out to the barn to do it.'

Mollie in the marauder's caravan, two instead of one were now sneering as one went out one's front gates. Imagine owning all the land for two miles the other side of the road and this bastard gombeen spiv gobshite thinking he's grand because his father owns a pub and gave him a bit of money to buy land to which he has his thirteen foot wide bloody right of way on which to pass and repass, now thinks he can continue to stand giving me dirty looks. Which as one first ignored them only seemed to give greater encouragement. To make them even dirtier. Till on the day on my way to the station to catch the train to Dublin here he suddenly was trespassing, his tractor tyre tracks leaving behind a foot deep rut in the field. Pulling out in front of me on the drive, blocking me. Cut up chunks of one of my fallen trees on his trailer. His sneer and sickly smile was classic. And infuriating. And I could not control one's anger. Squealing my Daimler to a halt. Jumping out. Shouting.

'Put that bloody timber back. And get that damn vehicle out of my way.'

'I will in a tinker's tit. Make me.'

One was wearing one's black kid skin driving gloves. And at the unhesitating speed of my dismounting from my Daimler, it was a delight to see the first flash of apprehension across

403

his previously implacably sneering aggressive face. Which now had returned to its usual snarling scorn and contempt. As he pretended to leisurely get down from his tractor and swagger to stand facing me in the drive, a long piece of twine tied around his coat blowing in the breeze. Resembling one of those cowboy and Indian films one occasionally saw in the Grafton Street cinema up in Dublin. And my fists had never been more tightly knotted. Or more eager to land concussing on anyone's face. To smash his sneer permanently out the back of his head.

'Where's Mollie's wages. I'll have a writ put on you, you west Brit.'

'Get off this drive with that tractor. And throw off that timber.'

'Try throw it off yourself. It's part payment of Mollie's wages you owe. And more.'

'Get off this bloody drive. I'm not going to tell you again.'

'Well I'll tell you, you la de da planter Protestant on a horse, with your airs up in the big house. You'll soon get a taste of my fist in your phoney aristocratic gob and I'll break you over my knee.'

'You bloody wretched animal peasant. I'd like to see you try.'

The marauder lunging forward, unleashing a round house fist flying just past Darcy Dancer's jaw, as he sways back. The marauder bending his head down and charging, arms flailing left and right. Darcy Dancer sidestepping backwards as the marauder lunges past, turns and lunges back again. Kicking out with a hob nailed boot, catching Darcy on the side of the leg. Marauder charging again, head lowered to butt. Darcy setting himself, bending forward, flexing his knees, cocking his elbow, and tightening his fist as it rises upwards and drives with a crunch of bone smashing into the marauder's face, his head shooting back, his both feet lifting up off the drive, a cascade of blood pouring out of the

404

marauder's nose, as he stumbles backwards and falls landing
arse deep in a puddle of muddy water. Mollie's head appearing
up over the nearby hedgerow, screaming.

'You have him kilt. You have him kilt. Stop.'

The marauder reaching back to prop himself up, blood
covering his face. Darcy Dancer waiting centre of the drive.
The marauder slowly getting to his feet, raising his fists again.
Wiping the dripping blood away from his nose with his
knuckles. Advancing. Four fists raining blows back and forth
from all sides. The marauder swinging out a punch landing on
the side of Darcy's head. Darcy reeling back. Tripping on a
fallen tree branch and landing arse first on the grass verge of
the drive. The marauder jumping to kick his boot into Darcy's
side. Mollie shouting.

'Kill the dirty British bugger.'

The marauder circling, trying to land another kick. Darcy
shielding with his hands. And as a boot comes sailing at him,
grabbing tight hold of the marauder's leg. Pulling him to the
ground. Bodies entwined, rolling into a large moist pat of cow
flop. Marauder's grubby hands tearing into Darcy's face.
Darcy's fist uppercutting under the marauder's jaw. The
marauder's hands clutching up at his mouth, blood oozing
out.

'Me tongue. Me tongue is cut. I'll kill you, you bloody
shoneen.'

Darcy jumping to his feet. Waiting. As the marauder slowly
stands again and suddenly, head down snorting like a bull,
charges forward wildly, swinging his arms. Darcy Dancer
unleashing a fusillade of blows into the marauder's chest and
belly. The marauder's arms dropping. His hands reaching up
to his mouth as bloody vomit spews out, and he turns his back
and reels away. Mollie climbing through a hole in the hedge
to his aid, and holding up the edge of an old dirty green
sweater to wipe blood from the marauder's face. Darcy brushing down this clothes and taking a silk handkerchief to wipe

405

away a smear of cow flop on a sleeve. Climbing back into the Daimler. The marauder turning around at the sound of the revving engine. Holding up his fist.

'I'll show you, you shoneen, who you can push around. I'll show you. You won't push me around. I'll level every tree. I'll have you out of that house. That kip up there. I'll own all this land. And the likes of you won't stop me. You just wait and see.'

'I shall indeed wait and see. But meanwhile you're more likely to get your ruddy arse broken. Now get that tractor and trailer off the road and don't let me catch you on my land or drive again.'

Reaching Dublin after the train ride, one bolstered one's verve with a half bottle of champagne one took tucked away on a deep soft chair in the cosy privacy of the Shelbourne's residents' lounge. And before one returned to Andromeda Park, one went to Leopardstown to back a horse or two. Both doors falling off the taxi on the way. Driver hammering them back on. And locking me in so that one had to climb over his front seat to get out. Leaving one having missed the first two races. But I did then meet Awfully Stupid Kelly who it seemed was a lot less awfully stupid than he had often seemed at school. He'd clearly become some sort of tycoon of the turf, with a runner in every race. Giving me two tips to win.

'Wild Chrysanthemum in the third and our Radiant Lilly in the last. Two rank outsiders Kildare who, with the brakes off, should bomb along. Both at very good odds. And by the way how are you.'

'I am Kelly I suppose like the dog at its father's funeral, neither sad nor glad. But I assure you I shall perk up should your nags prove winners.'

Amazing how one's former schoolmate could take on a commanding appearance, from his previous frightened condition as a small boy. And as both his horses won, I issued him an invitation to come shoot Andromeda Park's bogs. Returning on the train, my pockets padded thickly with five pound notes from winnings. And with the several one hundred Irish punt notes from the sale of my mother's necklace already in the Rent Room safe, one felt one had a small stack of confidence installed. But the sad grey days still going by as a drizzly rain descended across the countryside. Crooks's niece on any pretext delayed mornings, having brought breakfast to my bedroom, striking what appeared to be balletic poses. But relieving one's urges by hand seemed the more prudent of options, albeit one was weakening further by the day. It was as if one's last failed effort had been made to save and preserve Andromeda Park. And one had fallen down into a smothering dust of the past, unable to rise up into life again. But then remembering one's first hunt, the huntsman smearing the killed fox's blood on me as a tribute to my courage as a young rider keeping up with the hounds. And then one grey particularly dreary afternoon, just as one had returned from shooting the bogs and had dressed for tea, Rashers called, making even longer tyre skid marks as he drew to a halt in his Isotta Fraschini. As if to demonstrate by how much his life had improved. And mine disimproved. Sitting in the drawing room, drinking one's rarest Madeira, looking out the drawing room window, one had never seen him exude such totally contented well being.

'Ah how nice it is to motor these few miles to see you dear boy. What I do so much love about being with you here at Andromeda Park, Darcy, are the silent moments one enjoys in front of your fire between tea time and the time it is incumbent upon one to bathe and proceed to dress for dinner. Here where it is still so full of pleasant memories for me and the utter perfection of the setting seems to so peacefully envelop one's soul, as one stares into the flames and listens to the gently hissing log.'

'Turf as it happens Rashers and not hissing.'

'Yes of course turf. And very properly Irish it is too. And of

407

course one does selfishly at such times tend not to give a tinker's damn about the rest of the world. One's mind miles and miles away from being annoyed. And of course getting so gently getting tight on your marvellous bloody grog.'

'Of which there is considerably less since the ball. Which celebration Rashers has produced this thank-you note from the Americans.'

Darcy Dancer taking from his pocket an envelope and notepaper perfumed and ornately engraved with initials. And handing it across to Rashers, who, shifting in his seat and clearing his throat, wipes his monocle on his napkin and pops it into his eye to read.

Dear Sir Darcy Kildare,

Thank you so much for having us at your very interesting home and meeting so many interesting people. And we were so very sorry to have to rush off so soon.

Yours sincerely,
Florida and Virginia

'I know, aren't people awful. Haven't even got your name right. Damn good thing I popped that Brillianton one on the old snoozzola. It is wretched, isn't it, how people are out only for what they can get out of one. Night of the ball saw a wretched type with an armful of bottles under his coat spiriting them out the door. Caught him just in time and commandeered his booty. Promise it back to you dear boy. From where it presently lies safely at Dreamstown Park.'

'And where Rashers, I take it, you are finding it to your satisfaction.'

'Well now I'll tell you Darcy. Much to put right. Can use as a matter of fact a bit of your agricultural advice. Had to play pop with some of the quite disgraceful liberties her household staff and workmen take. Ruddy butler in the dining room at the dining table practically snatching a piece of smoked salmon off my plate just as I was about to eat it. To taste it no less. One's batman would have been court martialled for such an offence. And then caught the ruddy bugger referring to Felicity by her Christian name. And one morning as she was in the warming cupboard, he comes up behind her and says, may I have sexual intercourse with you madam. Felicity takes to thinking that it's all in jolly good fun. That servants always sat around her father in the bathroom as he took his baths. Scullery maid scrubbing his back no less. Bloody hell I tried to make clear one should not encourage the atmosphere of a brothel. Had to put my immediate foot down. Called an eight a.m. muster in the stableyard. And not a ruddy bugger showed up till nine thirty.'

'Dear me Rashers, rather rum situation over there, it sounds.'

'Of course dear boy for the moment maybe. But I intend to apply a bit of spit and polish and shape the place up. Girl's so damn unstintingly generous you know. And I do take utter delight in my apartments. Never known more romantic moments. Candles either side of one's full length mirror. So helps when dressing for dinner. The old Major and all his regimental portraits. And of course all his sexual exploits do inspire me. Sitting as I have taken to doing before the evening fire in the library. Some damn good books you know. And magazines. *The Field. Country Life. Dublin Opinion.* Copies of *Punch*, going back to the beginning of time. Stimulating reading you know, along with a damn good joke or two. Of course if one doesn't find anything funny, the deafening silence then has a way of deepening one's thoughts. Not to be done too prolonged of course as all too soon nothing seems very funny. Such as the gloom one feels as one's name yet again appears, most inopportunely as happens, in *Stubb's Gazette* with a debt of such minuscule amount that invites people to look down their noses at you for owing so little. Then some damn love smitten motor mechanic from the town one had to see off, drunk out on the front lawn, pleading his bloody love to my intended. O dear one does so much want the common people back down where they belong. And the uncommon like our good selves to then be able to from our loftiness to piss down upon them from a great height. Now I am as it happens at this most crucial time Darcy, just a wee bit short of ready cash. Hate, hate to inconvenience you but you couldn't could you, see your way clear at this moment to top me up a modest bit, could you dear boy. And I might too, if I may borrow a little petrol. Ruddy seven point four litre job out there doesn't half burn up the old fuel.'

One did not know why one did it. Except that Rashers's visiting to one at Andromeda Park and hearing his jolly voice again did make me feel a mite better in one's slow but implacably accumulating lonely misery. Especially knowing that at any moment now one on a drunken night was simply going to go and fuck Crooks's niece. Who casting longer and longer lingering glances at me all through dinner every night. And was, unfearful of rape, putting her not inconspicuous breasts on display with little or nothing on beneath her uniform and freezing into the bargain. I found myself waiting to watch her legs each time as she departed to the pantry. All one had to do was now lose control and have an insubordinate Crooks and a dozen of his other relatives all ensconced. At least having Rashers as a visiting neighbour could lend a semblance of formality to one's life. And so, one told oneself, while opening the squealing door of the Rent Room safe and peeling off one hundred pounds in big white English fivers.

'Dear boy. Multo, multo merci, gracias, etcetera. And even though little I have to leave, never, never will you be forgotten in my will.'

'I need that back Rashers long before I inherit it back in your will.'

'Of course dear boy. But you are you know my sole beneficiary. You really are.'

Crooks came with more hot scones and Damian with additional hot water for tea. Then Crooks having words with the little fucker out in the hall. Something about putting his hands somewhere and mention of Crooks's niece. But here in the drawing room one did not know whether it was nervousness at his newfound situation being so much to his liking or my modest contribution to his present circumstances that seemed to bring Rashers to the verge of completely going over the top. One thing was evident, however, he was really dug in and was fully intending to dig even deeper at old Durrow-Mountmellton's.

'Of course Dreamstown Park has much natural beauty dear boy but with an absence of statuary it lacks classical allusion in its pleasure grounds. There exists no small edifice in which one might sit at the end of a vista in a remote part of the gardens within which to contemplate the view and indulge the satisfaction that a long perspective provides to give the eye. We're of the same sort of stuff you know. Military and all that. Despite her father's modest rank.'

'She must then Rashers take a poor view of your having hopped it from your Guard regiment. Not to mention losing the keys to Windsor Castle. Which might mean also misplacing or losing those of Dreamstown Park.'

'Please don't be mean dear boy. That lengthy reflection on brief mishaps in my past is thoroughly uncalled for. It really is. I mean one might think you were regarding the good luck befallen me as not deserved.'

'Rashers believe me. I am desperate at this moment that the whole world be as happy as it can. But I must confess my mood is at this moment, before petrol stations erupt all around me, to sell up. Take the mail boat to Liverpool. The train to London where the Kildare Street Club has reciprocal arrangements with a place called the Traveller's Club. And finally, in following your advice of long ago, thence on to Paris and Monte Carlo.'

'Ah dear boy, you could do worse. You could do much, much worse. And of course I shall then be here to receive you back with open arms. When some of my more ambitious architectural plans will then have been realized. Now that I have envisioned what will really set Dreamstown Park off to perfection. And that is a Sculpture Hall.'

'Good god, Rashers. If you intend at the same time to fill it with decent sculpture. That will cost a fortune. And done without proper imported Italians and engineers you will have pillars and marble plinths falling down all over the place.'

'Ah but your reference now Darcy to selling up. Shall hate to see you go. But even if you don't, I see a few pieces here and about that you seem not to look at much yourself Darcy, do you. I mean the Porcelain Room is chock a block. A piece or two wouldn't be missed. And certainly you'd want to find a good appreciative home for some of your finer masterworks of garden sculpture. Only of course if you sell up here.'

'Thank you Rashers. I'd be delighted to dismantle every-thing from plinths and pedestals and ship them over to you and Felicity as soon as possible.'

'Dear boy, I don't mean it that way. You are you know rather taking up my suggestions in the worst sort of light. And I have noticed you're being awfully pensive recently.'

'Rashers, in the light of our present conversation, is it any wonder. And bloody hell, why Rashers do you bloody well need a bloody Sculpture Hall, at all.'

'O dear I have, haven't I, rather upset you unduly. Please let me put it in proper context. I'm more thinking further down the line. Being photographed for posterity. On one's country estate, that sort of innocent thing. And if one is in one's own Sculpture Hall, posed with one's spouse, say with one or two shy lacy frilled little children there. And if two, one standing before us, and the other seated in her or his mother's lap.'

'Good god Rashers, you have haven't you, for obviously

412

some totally ridiculous reason, gone the way of all flesh. Immortalizing yourself in some gossipy ridiculous social magazine perhaps.'

'Dear boy, steady on now. Steady on. Why suddenly have you taken up against such things as country life. Parklands, pastures and domains.'

'Well because I suppose I've become sick thoroughly to death of attempting to stop others destroying it. And sick of those who make it a pretence to assume airs to which they have no natural inclination. And would rather solitary take by myself a coffee and bun in Bewley's Oriental Café up in Dublin. And not ever see another servant or bloody parkland or ballroom again.'

'O dear. O dear, O dear. May I just help myself to just a spot more tea. This is sad, very sad news Darcy. And my god coming just at the moment when I no longer have to submit myself cap in hand to some rural chemist in some rural chemist's shop hawking ladies' sanitary wear. I am surprised at you Darcy. And I mean honestly to still be of help. To find you a momentously rich wife. I mean honestly. You know we are booked on a liner to New York. I'm up to Newport first thing to conduct a further search and vetting of a prospective mate for you. Sorry if my voice sounds hysterically hoarse. But I am. Going to search like the devil. No mess ups this time. And I am further damn glad to be out of bed and breakfast hostels up and down Dublin's Talbot Street. And you know Darcy, in that context let me immediately say, that thank god many of the best streets in Dublin are still named after aristocratic Protestants where one may still feel at home as a pedestrian. And not to change the subject completely, I did one particularly dreary evening going down Talbot Street, I must confess, ask once of a chap on this a Catholic named thoroughfare. Excuse me, my good man, is this the way to Purgatory. Chap had a sense of humour, said yes, go neither left nor right at the bottom and come back and if you keep going neither left nor right, Purgatory will be straight in front of you, in fact right where you're standing. Ah Darcy, buck up. We have. We really have come a long, long way. And we may yet not ever get where we ultimately want to go. But at least the struggle has, hasn't it, been worth it all. Here out in the country. Where, spring time on its way, will grow primroses and pretty daisies. With thistles, nettles and ragwort not far away in the muddy ditches. Know ye all that we shall upon this very night at least. Having shot, fished and hunted. Then gone to wine and dine. Perhaps even then to make love. And till tomorrow sleep content.'

'Yes, I'm sure you will Rashers.'

But Darcy
It is for you too
Too hold and keep
And proclaim
Your destiny
As a
Gentleman

23

Although one did not wait in vain for a thank you note from the Americans, I then discovered they had signed Andromeda Park's guest book on their departure, in the same manner of royalty as Lois. Taking a full page each, across which they largely appended their Christian names. All suspiciously looking like Rashers had a hand in it.

'Dear boy, why on earth would I have them do a thing like that.'

'Because Rashers, you can be an awfully cynical bastard at times.'

One found oneself now hating letters arriving. Instructing Crooks not to bring them up with breakfast. But then, in seeing them on the front table as one descended after ablutions and sitting there upon the inappropriate salver, I felt their grubby brown envelopes containing their equally grubby bills were all going to jump up and get me around the neck. One awaiting at least a week or two as they stacked up on the Rent Room table. And jolly close enough to the fire to be just chucked in. Even the newspaper was left. As indeed one was already hearing enough bloody news one did not want to hear on the bloody wireless. Arabs fighting Jews. Atomic bombs vaporizing steel towers. The British Empire shrinking. And as far as one's own damn bills were concerned one felt the whole town stayed up late on a Thursday night concocting them. And then didn't waste much time wondering to whom they could be sent in the hope of payment. It was in such a bleak moment of contemplation and accumulated anxiety that one did open one of those brown envelopes which came by registered post and for which Crooks had signed.

'Simply say I'm not here Crooks.'

'Sir it's only that I thought you might be receiving notice of having won the sweep stakes. You never know when a bit of luck like that might erupt from somewhere.'

'Well rest assured Crooks no such luck is about to erupt as I have never bought a ticket and am not likely to.'

Then laying out the sheet of paper with its heading on the Rent Room table, the reading of this noxious document opened before me did send a brief shiver of painful fear up one's arse.

Dear Sir,

We are instructed to act on behalf of our client Mr Kelly Kelly recently settled in this parish, whom you viciously attacked without provocation and to whom you caused grievous bodily harm while he was in pursuit of his legitimate business, and doing with malice aforethought, a battery with violence having struck him a clout, occasioning our client to suffer a fractured nose requiring remedial surgery. In addition our client had two teeth knocked out, one rib cracked and another broken, and certain internal injuries still requiring further medical investigation which were caused by you hammering repeatedly upon our client's stomach with your clenched fists.

In reference to the above such injuries and damage to clothing and to farm equipment, we initially estimate the minimum damages and costs suffered by our client to be in the vicinity of one thousand five hundred pounds and would be glad to receive a cheque on account for same within two weeks of receipt of this letter. Failing to do so, we have been instructed to issue immediate proceedings in the matter. We also require, having regard to events which may happen in the future, an immediate undertaking for you to desist from any further violent attacks upon our client.

416

We are also aware concerning another matter of a former employee of yours who is consulting with her own legal advisers.

Yours faithfully,
Fibs, Orgle & Justin Case, Fluthered

P.S. Although it is well known that your forebears long enjoyed a high regard in this community, serious changes have since intervened and as stated in a previous letter regarding our client J. Quinn Esq., your former agent, to whom you have owed bonuses and land promised, you clearly remain under the assumption that you are a self perpetuating law unto yourself, of which attitude we assure you, you will shortly be disabused.

Crumpling up the letter in one's fist and throwing it across the Rent Room floor, one's increasing irritation turning swiftly to furious implacable anger and an undying resolve to smash and destroy and put paid to all perpetrators of any threats from any source whatsoever. But past lunch, as agricultural matters come consistently and disastrously to one's attention, one did get awfully gloomy. Only relieved by long tramps across the bogs trying to bag a snipe. But not much else helped distract from loneliness which, when one omitted the effort to dress for dinner, then did in a heap abysmally descend upon one. And so one dressed for dinner. And still could not stop one's eyes from imagining what it would be like to plunge it into Crooks's niece as she bent over, seeming always as she seemed ready for me to do, if one but mildly suggested it. I did at least get some minor solace from playing in the library the records the Americans left behind. And did so over and over again. Making one imagine that America might be a jolly place. However, mornings, if one managed to force oneself to get out of bed and brave a visit to the gardens before servants were up, it did help to cause one to be a smidgen more cheerful. Provided of course it was not pissing down rain and one was already in a nightmare concerning

417

leaks in the roof. But at least down any stray hallway, one was never at a loss for household conversation.

'Good day Master Reginald, and top of the morning to you. It's pelting.'

'Is it now.'

'Ah sir a good dry spell is due to come soon.'

'I hope so. I hope so.'

This litany said more times than one could remember. But it was always a relief when the staff repeated themselves, saying to one what they said yesterday and the day before, thereby not making it necessary for one to invent something new to say in response. But a welcome exception was always Sexton. Seeing the puffs of smoke come out from his potting shed chimney. And to know that within would be at least a friendly face. And a fair assurance of conversation one had not heard before. And one could already just hear Sexton as one knocked.

'God of everlasting life save us from the ignominy of death we beseech thee.'

One knocked again. Pain still in one's knuckles having hit them so many times off the marauder. But one did think Sexton was rather stretching god's powers a bit far. And then entering he was quick on another tack.

'Ah Master Darcy come in, come in. Now this Nostradamus, ah he foretold us a few things that would make you think. And thinking I am. But on more practical veins. Like help here in the garden. A contingent from the tack room. There'd be shirkers. The lot of them skulking about in order to shun observation. Sure it would be less work for them to turn their hand to doing something useful than to be idly freezing over there sucking on cigarettes. And with your permission I'll have the lot of them over here tomorrow. To exercise their backs a bit. And put a shine on the working ends of their shovels.'

'And what's this volume Sexton.'

418

'Ah now that's a great little treatise. *Remarks on the Management of Orchidaceous Plants* written by a great local gardener and antiquary. Sure wasn't he even the High Sheriff of the County.'

'And this Sexton.'

'Ah that now is me own little scribbled effort on the cultivation of ornamental gourds. Sure with a poem or two in there maybe I'll not die without trace.'

'Dear me Sexton, not more morbidity.'

'Ah who'll remember me other than the seeds of the flowers I've planted that might come up again springtime.'

'Sexton, if I may say so, you will be entirely unforgettable.'

'Ah now that remark you could take two ways.'

'And how are the matrimonial prospects Sexton.'

'Well Master Darcy if you mean am I any closer to finding a woman who would give a man enough of everything he needs so he wouldn't have to be asking or looking for more, the answer is, the prospects are nil. Ah sure what does it matter, the process of oblivion is at work upon us all. Didn't St Francis of Assisi give up all his worldly goods and suffer the wounds of the Lord Jesus with the stigmata. Even now to think of it brings tears to me good eye.'

'Please you mustn't upset yourself Sexton.'

'Ah death now, not in the too far distant future will come stalking me down that long barren road. Chasing you as you look for places to hide. But your feet soon drag. Your legs tire. And you stumble on your knees and slowly crawl. I leave nothing behind.'

'Sexton you mustn't.'

'I leave nothing behind Master Darcy. But the bit of beauty of my flowers. But gone I will be just like their scent on the breeze. Rumours there are Master Darcy that some old remnants of the Land Leaguers are agitating to get some of Andromeda Park. They'd be sneaking around whispering. They wouldn't face you man to man. Out to get what they can nothing. Sure you've been an honest man. And nothing but a gentleman. One hates to see any dirty cowardly scum attempting to do you down.'

'Sexton, I assure you, they'll have a fight. And you must, must cheer up.'

'Well, in here as I always am, the likes of me shuns the limelight. I'm not ever going to make the earth wobble on its axis. The years ago now when I used to put the flowers in the Porcelain Room. And your dear mother would go in there of a morning to sit alone to smoke a cigarette. May she rest in peace. And I'll tell you a story now. Your mother was adored. No other word for it. One day wasn't she out riding there beyond the wheat fields where they used to be. And our best working man was Seamus, nearly born on the place. And she came riding alone on this summer's day. Seamus thinking it was an old cow lost coming at him. And he sat there on a stone, wiping his brow, taking a few seconds from an afternoon's back breaking work scything. And didn't your mother find him there sitting. Well he was a man of principle you don't find today and wouldn't be found not on the job. He gave his notice on the spot, and was never seen at Andromeda Park again. Nothing your mother could say or do would bring him back. One of the best workers was ever on the place. Sorry now I'm on to subjects should maybe be left.'

Darcy Dancer stepping out and away from the potting shed. In a ray of sunshine proceeding through the leaves blown in heaps outside the garden's gate. Walk on across the mossy bits of grass. Sink so softly in. One had not been ready for Sexton's abrupt change of mood. But sensed he knew more about the Land Leaguer's threat. And about the marauder across from the front gates. Mollie now an enemy. And that all these things could spell one's encroaching doom. I knew too that he'd made yet another attempt to find a wife. Mick out in the tack room reporting.

'By god she was a brute of a woman, a pair of shoulders on

420

her that would overturn an automobile. Didn't she challenge old Sexton to an arm wrestle and then demonstrate how she could tear the legs off his kitchen chair. He had to show her out of the place. Sure Sexton's been hiding since.'

And in the days passing, one almost took to one's own way of hiding. Taking down Lois's portrait of me hanging outside the ballroom and having it put away facing the school room wall. Lois of course had every male member in the hunt who could afford it now wanting to have their portraits painted up in Dublin at her studio. No doubt thinking they were to be treated between brush strokes to her bouncing tits and castanets and her wonderful greedy mouth grabbing their prick. But amazing how in one's nightly sexual fantasies one had her so often on one's own mind. And of perhaps inviting her, old as she was, simply to be one's mistress in residence. I mean one could start taking a small commission on her portrait sittings and paintings sold. But when I mentioned such a plan to Rashers one got his brief reply.

'Dear boy, you are desperate, aren't you. That old sleaze bag. And you could I suppose install old MacBuzuranti as well.'

Christabel and Lavinia had long gone up to Dublin visiting and then briefly came back to Andromeda Park, their departure back to London being accusatory enough. That I'd deliberately attempted to alienate their friends and make them feel unwelcome. Allowing in all the gate crashers and not calling to book rude servants, Mollie having thrown a whole tray across the bedroom at Lavinia when she complained it was late coming for her breakfast.

'There now that will speed it up for you madam.'

They said I should have appreciated their revealing for scrutiny the status of the American girls. And one did think one might even prefer the Yank females to one's own sisters. My male primogeniture and being master and owner of Andromeda Park of course always harbouring in them a burning resentment, if not outright hatred.

421

One remembering those awful times as a little boy, standing shivering and crying as I would do when they said ghosts were coming and that my mother, before she was killed, had gone away forever and would never come back. How they would ridicule me at meals in the nursery. Or hiding behind doors to jump out to frighten me. I was absolutely delighted to finally wave goodbye and see them go away down the drive. And just as Rashers happened to arrive for tea and a spot of neighbourly backgammon, I was these days actually looking forward to seeing him. But instead of a gung ho Rashers robust of spirit, it was a very troubled Rashers one encountered. This time stopping most gently with his Isotta on the drive and making his way in front of me straight into the library where our game and Madeira awaited, ready for our attention.

'Whatever is the matter Rashers, you look white as a ghost.'

'And that Darcy is precisely what I should like to discuss. There's a ruddy one or more at Dreamstown Park. First I thought I was seeing things. Until last night. After midnight behind locked shutters and doors. Darcy one was there in the drawing room. And forgive me for speaking out on this. One was on hands and knees on an array of sheepskins doing it dog style in front of the drawing room fire. Please no facial expressions. We were merely giving it an old go in a more rural way one might say. Now I don't for the life of me know what made me, but I suddenly turned to look about the walls. You know how one does intending to prolong the pleasure by distracting the mind a wee bit. I mean, it dawned on me, all over the bloody drawing room the eyes of every portrait staring at one. Ah I thought how clever of the painter. But then by god a pair of the bloody eyes moved.'

'Rashers. Really.'

'I swear absolutely, I swear. More than once too. I believe you know how there are secret passages, cupboards, corridors and rooms all over the house. Well then I got a real shock.

When bloody hell this fucking apparition, sorry about the language, in a black cowl and in a mask across the eyes is suddenly grinning at us through this ruddy bloody hatchway opening in the wall, secretly disguised as it usually was, as a ruddy normal bookcase.'

'Good heavens. What did D.M. do.'

'That is the real trouble dear boy. She said don't stop. And I discreetly whispered for god's sake my dear, there is someone behind the bookcase looking at us. And she said, O do please shut up and keep on fucking. Those were her very words. Spoken far more loudly than I thought necessary. As if she knew and it were planned for us to be watched.'

'Does sound awfully advanced Rashers, I must say.'

'Advanced. Damn it dear boy. You've heard of that awful word impotent. Well I almost nearly couldn't continue on the job. I find it more than just a little bit spooky. Didn't half put me off my canter. When in privacy of the next morning, which was this morning, I got up on a chair to examine the paintings. There around the eyes is to be discerned the minutest of lines cut in the canvas. For real eyes dear boy. And the wall hanging the painting as one knocked on it, sounding hollow. Then the bloody chair fell to pieces beneath me and I pulled an entire cabinet off the wall trying to break my fall. Wedgwood in pieces all over the place. Inferior stuff, but all the same, still in bits. And I do hope you don't think I'm trying to unload a whole lot of old rubbishy nonsense on you.'

'Honestly Rashers considering other contentments, surely you're not going to let a little domestic voyeurism spoil life for you at Dreamstown Park. Old Durrow-Mountmellton you know likes to sport about a bit. Rumour is of naked bareback riding. That innocently enjoyable sort of thing all girls like to get up to, and which by all accounts excites them immensely. Take it as just part of old fashioned country life. I mean soon won't you be safe on your transatlantic liner and the thin bulkheads won't allow for a gang of servant onlookers. Even in first class. In which class I trust you and your beloved will be travelling.'

'All right dear boy. All right. I can see you are rather highly amused. And I'm absolutely sure it's not because you think I've rather intruded upon your own vague intentions concerning Felicity.'

'Really Rashers. Your coast is absolutely clear to pursue as you wish.'

'Well I suppose you're quite right dear boy, to be amused. And for me a continued burdened state of mystification if not indignation is not advisable at this time. Sort of thing could land one in a nervous breakdown up out of which one might be slow to ascend. But you know I think the root of everything is that all did not go well with me and my father. As a little chap I would frequently get car sick and once when my father had put me in the back while he sat up front with his military chauffeur driving him, I promptly stood up and vomited over the front seat and down the back of his uniform. As he was on his way to a military parade, my white gobbits of upchuck over the back of his dress tunic did not enthuse him. In fact he positively got hysterical, stopped the motor, kicked the tyres and thereby besmirched the shine some batman had spent the previous night putting there and needed not only a replacement jacket, but shoes as well. Ah but I can remember it now, the secret joy of the occasion, in spite of the fact that one knew one was soon, out of sight of his military subordinates, to be mercilessly castigated. I am my dear boy presently reviewing all of these things, which make up what one commonly refers to as water under the bridge. My previous intended gone. However, she did distract me in trying to overcome a certain frigidity from which she suffered. Said once that in imagining I was after her money and tobacconist's shops she found it awfully difficult to lubricate. O dear that does sound rather awfully medical doesn't it.'

'Rashers, dare one suggest that with your bedside manner, you would make a marvellous doctor.'

424

'I'm afraid the further study of medicine would more than sometimes bore me dear boy. Seems all so fruitless, people destined to die are bloody well going to die. Imagine one having to all day to prod about people's bloody fistulas, sticking fingers up people's arses, down people's throats. With young comely women patients few and far between and from whose orifices one does not recoil. Of course medical degrees following one's name does allow for the running up of credit all over Dublin. And such convenience one did aspire to. As a matter of fact, in Felicity's library at the moment I am reading Haughton's *Principles of Animal Mechanics* from whence was derived the modern art of hanging. Instead of slow strangulation by dangling, presto we now have the wondrous method of practically instant execution by dislocation of the spinal vertebrae. I am but an erstwhile medical student at Trinit'tas Universit'tas, pursuing knowledge of pathology down dank Dublin hospital cellars. The son of an army general. A devout race goer. An imbiber of fine whiskey and a convinced Christian. And above all, your true and everlasting friend, Darcy. And although my present lack of income prevents my calling myself a gentleman in terms of exacting standards of truth, I am possessed of reliability, and do have intact a sense of honour. Although I did purloin writing paper and envelopes from the college Historical Society. Ah but let's get down to our backgammon. Are you on for a tenner. And you know my dear boy you simply must cheer up with all this paradise still about you.'

> And always
> Remember
> That to a nice man
> Like you
> Nothing ever really bad
> Is ever
> Going to happen

425

24

Rashers's absence for over a fortnight made me contemplate getting in the Daimler and driving over. But instead a cable arriving. And poor Crooks rather in a dilemma as to whether it should be given to me, as I sat in the Rent Room with a wretchedly smouldering fire, calculating wages and putting aside those bills that could still wait a month or two before a writ was served. And as one tore open the faded moss green envelope with a finger instead of one's silver opener, one at first took it as another of Rashers's elaborate ruses staring one in the face from the pastel lines across this cablegram of little block capitals forming words.

RMS QUEEN ELIZABETH
AT SEA

MY DEAR BOY I AM NESTLED UP ON THIS
CUSHIONED DECK CHAIR ON THIS EIGHTY TWO
THOUSAND TONS OF SPLENDOUR CUTTING
THROUGH THE ATLANTIC WAVES   STOP   WE
OCCUPY SUITE SIXTY NINE APPROPRIATELY ON A
DECK   STOP   THE WONDER OF THIS OCEAN
TRAVEL IS QUITE BREATHTAKING   STOP   WILL
WRITE FROM NEW YORK   STOP   THIS CABLE
AWFULLY EXPENSIVE TO SEND   STOP   BOTH
FELICITY AND I SEND OUR LOVE

　　　RASHERS

Three whole days passed. Of no one now to speak one's

mind to or hear someone else's revealed. With badly bruised ribs from hunting, one was early to rise and to breakfast for a change in the dining room, following my ablutions. And I suddenly found myself standing in the front hall, hardly knowing why I was there or where I intended going. The post upon this rainy, chill spring morning had come and had been left with the day old papers in the hall and not brought to the Rent Room. Clearly old Crooks was not yet on the job this morning. And one already knew what one would hear from him later in the day.

'Master Reginald it is the rheumatics as has me incapacitated of these damp old mornings, hitting me in both hips, I can hardly get out of me bed.'

Crooks of course I'd recently caught in the ballroom, the gramophone blaring out a Viennese polka and him waltzing on his ruddy incapacitated hips all over the place. At that exact moment I felt awfully like having a quaff or two of champagne in the Porcelain Room. But then I knew it was useless ringing for Crooks to fetch it. And decided instead it was time to soberly grab a walking stick and walk vigorously to and back from the front gates. But something made me remain there in the hall and stare at the small stack of envelopes, a certain strange trepidation growing in every vestige of my being. Even when I did approach the mail in the Rent Room, one would first quickly with a finger push the disagreeable envelopes apart and it was quite amazing how one could separate out the unfriendly bills and demands for payment, threats, solicitors' menaces, and more than a few of these were chucked straight into the Rent Room fire. A certain satisfaction to watch the white paper curl in the flames and briefly glow red, then turn black and finally disintegrate in grey ash.

'Now Master Reginald what would you desire me to do to these bold intruders at the door raising their voices and deserving of a boot up the backside.'

427

Of course now there were summonses and writs delivered by hand to the door which were also, upon my instruction to Crooks, refused delivery. And to give him his due, Crooks did send most off with a flea in their ear. But now one kept looking and looking at these letters still on the salver in the hall. Under the usual brown envelopes, the corner of one, a faded yellow, sticking out. My heels echoing across the tiles, and unable to stop myself, I went to the table. I pulled out and lifted up to read the vellum envelope and saw a French stamp and my name written in that indelible hand I could never forget that I first saw inscribed on a little card placed on the dresser in my bedroom. My heart beginning to utterly pound. The envelope postmarked Paris. My breath short in my lungs as I look the letter, holding it in both hands and walked with it to the library. Only to stop outside the door and then proceed further to the ballroom. But then back I had to go again to the library for a letter opener. And then returned to the ballroom. Looking up and down the hall, making sure to avoid anyone in the household. I closed and turned the key in the door, to lock it. And as I sat on the throne chair, the letter resting in my lap, I felt a strange reluctance to open it. And my hand was trembling. The morning dark outside with squalls of rain sweeping in from the west. The ballroom shiveringly cold. The great portrait of my mother in her riding habit, standing flanked by her two favourite wolfhounds, looking down at me. And now I slit open this faded yellow envelope and unfold the neatly folded lined sheets of paper.

                              Hôtel des Beaux-Arts,
                              Rue de Seine,
                              Paris VI

My dearest Darcy,

I do not know if this will ever reach you and if it does I know you

428

will be surprised to hear from me. But I write to you now from Paris, from a little room looking down into the crowded narrow and noisy market street. And I suppose it is something of interest to see when two cars collide head on as they seem to do every morning at dawn on the corner and the drivers get out and shout at each other and wake everyone up. And when a little chaos such as this happens I sometimes also wonder who it is these days at Andromeda Park who might be serving cracked plates and leaving grease and sticky honey on your tray as I know it used to terribly annoy you.

I have left my husband and have been here by myself, alone, speaking to no one for nearly a month and just thinking. I know that beautiful dreams are not supposed to happen and nightmares always do. Well my beautiful dream happened, which was then followed by a nightmare. I know it has been, at least it seems to me, the very longest of times since we were in touch and that I have no right to write to you like this. I know you must now have your own loves and that you are living your own life. But so much has happened to me that I no longer can keep it from you, although I must leave it to be fully told when and if I ever see you again. Except I must tell you I had a little boy child, now snatched from my arms.

Over now what I suppose is such a brief time but sometimes seems to have been years, things have gone from good to tolerable and from tolerable to bad and from bad to worse. But during all of it I have not ever not thought of you and I don't think my love has ever lessened. As I am trying to pull my life together, I miss some of the luxuries, but I know that castles, titles and privileges are no answer to life, although it seems they make people like one much better than they would if one was without them. And I think I felt more important and more ladylike when I was merely a lowly servant in your house. But perhaps I should say too that although it has been no answer to my life, it has taught me a lot, including my now quite fluent French. I know you know well the man I married so I won't say too much more than that. Except that I did not know him enough. I remember when I was a girl wandering the roads with travellers, I had secretly saved money to buy myself a pretty

429

dress and the first hat I ever owned. Dressing myself up with high heels, rouge and lipstick, I wore it to walk off to a nearby village to go to the pictures and some other travelling women saw me and remarked in their sneering manner, 'Is her ladyship going somewhere nice.' And strange to recall such things as this, when I was once standing in the lobby of the Crillion, a very ornately grand hotel the other side of the river here in Paris, and being an actual ladyship in beautiful haute couture clothes and lovely hat, with flunkies tripping all over themselves running all around me and I was waiting for one of them to say to me, is her ladyship going anywhere nice. And I was. I was on my way to the races at Chantilly. And I was wearing the biggest and most beautiful hat in Paris. And I was so pleased when the concierge turned to me to say, 'Ah. C'est Madame la contesse. Qui est aussi belle que son chapeau.'

Dearest Darcy I do so hope you won't misunderstand this letter and all these disjointed and I fear childish things, I seem to be saying. I have already torn up a dozen letters I couldn't continue to write. But I know you won't misunderstand. And a tear as you can see has just plopped down on this page as I pen these words and as the thought came that you might not want to hear from me. And maybe that's all that's happened to me, I have gone somewhere nice in my life and found only too soon that when the gloss, glamour and grandeur wore off that underneath there is nothing to find but suffering.

Now it is Friday. And although my courage to do so is fading, I am going to make myself continue this letter. But as my money runs out, god forbid what will happen then. I am as you know not religious, but I walk each day to spend a little time in a church called Saint-Sulpice, where beggars lurk in the shadows at the back. And I suppose I could beg like them. I was when I was with the travelling people very good at it. I could wear a little sign to say I was a dispossessed marchioness. Forgive me for writing at this length to you. I have recalled so many times that hour spent with you in the boat house by the lake that beautiful day when we told each other what was in our hearts. I shall treasure it always. And

430

now you seem the only one left in whom I can confide. Sometimes the days down this little narrow street go so painfully slowly as I wash my grapes in the basin and eat them one by one. Yesterday walking down the Île de la Cité by the Seine, I saw the clochards in their dirty rags lying on the ground in the dust, swallowing back their wine and I felt closer to them than I ever did to my husband. On a few very bad days I don't know how I resisted throwing myself in the water. Maybe it was lunch time and I know the French so hate to be disturbed while eating, especially to fish someone soaking out of the river and when they themselves hardly ever catch anything. But I suppose it was when I was closest to jumping into the Seine that I decided to use some of the courage it would take to write to you. I don't know how many more days I'll be here, but I hope when and if this letter ever reaches you, you will find time to answer, but if you don't I'll understand and always remain your friend.

I fell asleep after writing the above and now it is Saturday and I take up my courage and pen again. I did try in beginning this letter to be amusing. And reading some of it I see I've failed miserably. It has not been easy for me to say what I've said but now I've said it I have no regret. You probably know by now that I have already twice come back and stood there waiting out on the land of Andromeda Park, hoping you would see me and come to me. But I suppose if anyone saw me they must have thought me a ghost if not a trespasser. But I want you to know that it is not just now that I turn to you or think of you. My husband never wanted me to see you again and hated for me to mention your name. And I realize now and perhaps too late, that jealousy can become a form of insanity. Now that it is Saturday morning the markets are extra busy and the sun beams down, I suppose I ought to go out and buy some food. And now as I sign this goodbye another two cars have nearly crashed head on and also knocked over an entire barrow of tomatoes, leaving a terribly red mess in the street. A lot of noise and the barrow owner has just crushed a tomato into the face of one of the motorists, shouting, 'Take this you pig, avec mes salutations chaleureuses.' And now I

431

must at long last finish this letter. But in doing so let me say with all the love that is still in my heart that upon one day when you most suspect me, I will come at the end of the long lawn there at Andromeda Park where the roses grow out in the orchard garden and under the blossoms pink and blue of the old cherry tree I will be there waiting for you. And should you still want me I shall be lying on the grass in just the coolness of my skin and my body and soul will be yours forever to keep.

Leila

And
Forever to
Trust

25

My own tears of happiness fell upon the page. The letter for all its sadness did not prevent sheer ecstasy and pleasure overcoming one. For the first time in many weeks, instead of desultorily lurking, one eagerly sought to be out of doors. Leila's pages in my pocket, which I took again and again to read. Out of sight of the house, running, leaping and jumping. Waltzing along down the old walk to the lake. Once even falling over a log and face first into a boggy stream. But never was such an irritating catastrophe so welcome. As one stood up again, laughing. Delighted that in holding the letter up in my hands that hardly a single drop besmirched it. Reading it yet again up in the boat house. And then suddenly realizing there was no time to waste. Returning running the entire way back up the lake path. Between the spruce, birch and sycamore trees. Past the little white aprons of snowdrops everywhere poking up from the grass. As if the whole world were being born. Crying out as I was to be alive. And to go on living. Long. Long into the future.

Darcy Dancer in bright hound's tooth tweeds rushing down the front steps. Luke wiping a last gleam to shine on the Daimler's front hood. To sit back in the leather upholstery. Set square my cap on one's head. Pull on my driving gloves. Press the black starting button. Release the clutch. The wheels spitting up pebbles behind as one roars now past the thick green darkness of one's rhododendron plantations, over the pot holes to the front gates. The marauder across the road leaning over the fence. And not a sneer on his bandaged, busted up face. Or an effort made to shake a fist, as one goes s eeding by and swiftly out of sight. And on the road to Dublin. So as not to have the nosy ones, which would be everyone in the town, telling everyone else for miles around what I have sent in my cable to Paris.

The Daimler's speedometer touching a steady seventy five miles per hour on the road. Up and down over the mild hills. Past the bogs and along by the canal. Slowing to navigate around donkey carts and between herds of cattle. Fog in Dublin. The sweet smell of turf smoke. Mist hovering over the streets. The barefoot gangs of children, noses streaming phlegm. People clustered in the coffee houses and in front of fires. And once this was called Sackville Street. And no cable ever sent from the main post office was ever written and rewritten so many times. And for the umpteenth time again rewritten on the counter in front of an increasingly impatient clerk.

THE MARCHIONESS OF FARRANISTIC,
HOTEL DES BEAUX-ARTS,
RUE DE SEINE,
PARIS VI,
FRANCE

I LOVE WORSHIP AND ADORE YOU AND WILL ALWAYS AND ASK ONLY THAT YOU QUICKLY COME BACK TO IRELAND AND TO ME IN YOUR BIG BEAUTIFUL HAT.

        YOUR EVER FAITHFUL SERVANT
        DARCY

The clerk arguing that one could not use the word chapeau in case it was misunderstood in Paris. But a minor inconvenience and so one spelled hat, hat.

Parking one's Daimler at the Royal Automobile Club, one's feet stepped lightly along Dublin's wet granite pavements. At the bar of Jammet's having stout, and oysters. A thick steak and beaujolais at the Dolphin Hotel. And staying overnight at the Kildare Street Club, where one was always greeted by the porters as a long lost friend, even though one had just stepped out and back in again. I found oneself actually saying hello to all the elderly diehard, killjoy members who usually frowned if one walked too quickly or conspicuously past them. And to one younger baronet whom one knew from an upper form at school, and who'd always affected a princely attitude of superiority. And to whom, following dinner and a vintage port, I actually found my astonished self listening, especially as I heard the words chop, chop and phrases one thought one had previously heard mouthed by Rashers.

'Of course my life has been only moderately interesting Kildare. As an aristocrat I have always done as I chose. And always chose to do as I have done, if you follow my meaning. It's why one cannot associate happily with one's inferiors. Back in one's background there was much chop, chop. Heads removed from the body of course. Being lopped off if they hadn't been hanged. Lands sequestered. Titles acquired. Estates coming by marriage to heiresses. As a result I have had the good fortune to find myself modestly well off. Understand Kildare you're rather a large landowner yourself. But it doesn't, does it, prevent one from being intensely irritated at times. Now where's that damn chap gone who was bringing me more port. Of course Kildare, being an aristocrat does not make you useless, it only, subject to proof to the contrary, implies that you are. Which of course is the whole point in being one. Don't you think. That's why aristocrats get so frightfully jealous of those who do actually do things. Now where is that damn waiter. Would you mind ringing the button again. And you know about clubs Kildare, the better the club, the worse the service and marmalade.'

After a night's surprisingly deep sleep and dreams of wild horses pounding through a wood, and one riding bareback among them, one woke. Out the window, the sun beaming

435

down across Trinity College's playing fields. Making it seem as if the green velvet grass this morning would rise to come and gently make itself felt softly on the skin of one's face. Which reminded of my appointment soon to the barber's just up the street. Where, after a sumptuous, sausagy, leisurely breakfast and in the most amazingly day dreaming manner and nearly falling asleep, one got shaved, trimmed, shampooed, manicured, powdered and finally massaged by the great rotary brushes brought down from the spindles across the ceiling. But one did not venture to the lady chiropodist again who had turned our lonely little toenail cutting session into a most memorably indiscreet treatment. Over which one has often fantasized since.

Stepping out into Kildare Street to stretch one's legs. Down past Buswell's Hotel. Where it was rumoured the whole government often conferred in its tinkling Georgian interior. Along Molesworth Street. The Protestant Orphan Society. And the Masonic Hall across the road. Inside a doorway visible up high on a wall, out of which it was said stepped Masons wanting to feel what it felt like to drop like a stone. Even dirty Dublin, with all the furtive downcast eyes passing and semi imbeciles in the street directing traffic, did not subdue one's blithesomeness and gladness. And I sauntered up Dawson Street, turned right at the top and before one finally pointed the nose of one's Daimler to streak back west, I put in an order at Smyth of the Green.

'Good heavens sir, where on earth have you been. I trust all went well at the ball. We were expecting we would be of service to you again long before now. But of course now is not too late. What can we do for you. Ah, along with telegraph poles from Finland, grape, wine and brandy cargoes from Spain and Portugal have just arrived in the Liffey, with many another exotic on board. And we have from the Caspian, caviare. My little pad is here all ready to record your order. Ha, ha. Put you down for a pound, shall I, of the caviare.'

'Yes as a matter of fact, do.'

In the sun blinding one through the windscreen, one drove home again. Awake, asleep or galloping miles across Andromeda Park on Petunia, nothing was on my mind but the hours passing and waiting and wondering. Total despair one moment that she would not come. Elation the next, that she would. And if she didn't, it didn't matter because I would be dead. Somewhere out deep in the woods from a gunshot wound. My corpse getting sodden in the downpours of rain. But to keep hope alive each day now, going out to Sexton in his potting shed. And to him, the only one to whom I divulged the news. And now three full days of silence. Utter and complete. I walked to the garden and opened his door, even forgetting to knock.

'Ah Master Darcy. I wondered what was suddenly at my back. Sure you've left a wind coming in that would blow a child away from its mother. And I've been thinking now, isn't that wonderful to hear. About that great lovely girl.'

'But Sexton I haven't heard back. My cable may have never reached. And she may not come.'

'Ah I feel it in my bones, she'll come. And we'll have ready for her flowers in abundance, the very task I'm at this very moment. And by god Master Darcy from what I remember she'd surely be that bit more beautiful than my best bloom. And certainly a more wonderful beauty than ever came to my door.'

> To bring
> Happiness instead
> Of hardship
> To a poor old
> Gardener
> Like me

26

The misery of now three full days' suspense. The uncertainty and doubt seeming like centuries. And then just at the moment one was plunging into the black abyss of a permanent melancholia, and with a red sun sinking and the evening settling over the countryside, it ended. I was stepping down from Petunia in the stable courtyard and heard the unmistakably rickety post office van on a special visit pulling away to go in its acrid cloud of exhaust back to the front gates. My awkward riding boots constraining on my legs as I ran up the cobbles to the front of the house and in the door.

'I was just about to summon you sir, a cable has arrived.'

Crooks standing there scratching his privates, but with the small green envelope already on the silver salver and ready to hand to me with an opener as if somehow Crooks knew by reading my face and in the speed with which one came bouncing up the steps, that it contained the most fateful of all fateful news. And that it might even be good instead of bad. Tearing the envelope open with one's fingers there in front of Crooks in the hall. To see the only words one only ever wanted to see. And for which one desperately waited, delayed as they were a whole further day reaching me.

WAIT FOR ME ON YOUR DOORSTEP LEAVE PARIS
TONIGHT AND VIA DIEPPE NEWHAVEN LONDON
HOLYHEAD DUN LAOGHAIRE DUBLIN AND ACROSS
THE BOGS OF ALLEN I WILL BE WITH YOU

LEILA

438

'By jove sir is it the sweep stakes, we've won.'

'Yes Crooks. And more. Much, much more.'

'By golly sir I knew in my boots to put the cablegram on the salver for you. Will you be having some champagne. And there's the caviare keeping cool down in the dairy.'

'Yes. I hope later. When the evening train gets in.'

'Very good sir, that will be shortly as I just heard the train passing on now to Galway. There's now a nice bottle or two I had long stored away for an occasion.'

Not enough time to change from one's boots, breeches and hacking jacket, as one stood in the Whim Room, looking out across the trees. The moon rising over the oak forest on the distant hill. Blue strips of sky between bleak clouds. The shadows of cattle grazing the front parkland. When one saw far off in the direction of the front gates the slowly approaching flashing of headlights across the tree tops. Holding my breath as the beam of light shone its way between the rhododendrons and the wheels sounded on the drive. The evening train from Dublin was for the first time in recent history, early. And one rushed down the main stairs two at a time to be on one's doorstep. The front door already open. As one just stood there in the moonlight splashing brightness on these black and white tiles. Where once it so pained me to see her kneel, cleaning out the grate. And is she here. And has she come. Taxi door slamming shut. The sound echoing back from the fields. A breeze of cool air. And earlier this day one heard newborn lambs bleating. And now with the wind rising, a clearing sky and moonlight, and an untimely crow of a rooster from the stable yard.

Darcy Dancer stopping halfway across the front hall. The chimes of the clock tolling seven. In a long flowing coat, a dark head and figure ascending the steps. The moonlit sky silhouetting this graceful form in the doorway. Coming nearer. And gently and gracefully trips on a tile. Hold my uncertain hand ready to offer to shake hers. Her absence from my life requires me to be formal. To bow. To the wan smile of her beautiful teeth. The glow of gladness in her eyes. As she comes straight at my. Her hat in her hand. Arms reaching out. And up around my shoulders. To enfold me in the soft sweetness of her smell. The darksome silken hair of her head laid gently against my breast. No more wonder as to what part of the sky she might be under. At this end of day. Come home. Never leave this domain. Walk as once we were. Across the dewy meadow grass. Under the rainbow colours reaching over the lake that day from shore to shore. With the squall of passing rain. And when the gleaming white wings of the pair of swans came. Faithful for life you said. Sweeping down to land through the green. The blue. And the yellow mist. That was purple too. Like the ribbon you always wore in your hair. And your lips. Nothing trivial did they ever say. And upon which this moment I kiss.

> For with
> My body now
> You shall always
> Dwell